GIRL, UNEMPLOYED

Desiree Prieto Groft

Book cover and inside skyline design by Macy Jett.

Printed in the United States of America

First edition

For Ava

"Living is like tearing through a museum. Not until later do you really start absorbing what you saw, thinking about it, looking it up in a book and remembering—because you can't take it all in at once." – Audrey Hepburn

ONE

Life is Like a Box of Girl Scout Cookies

It was eighty degrees with sunny March skies, but a dark cloud hovered over our heads as we approached the Girl Scout Center in a large makeshift shed near the U.S. Route 281 Highway and the San Antonio Airport. Beyond the chain-link fence, I caught a glimpse of the green letters "Million Air" along a private hangar near a small Cessna jet likely reserved for an elite few among the blue-collar workforce: George Strait, a Spurs player, or a founder from the city's only successful internet company, MoreSpace. The latter also happened to be one of a few internet companies besides Google that made real money after the dot-com bubble burst. It was obviously a cosmic accident they were headquartered in my hometown.

The Cessna jet featured four windows above a blue stripe and was identical to the one I'd flown in a few months earlier while on my final leg back from a European trip from New York City to Chicago. And yet, here I was. On the other side of the chain-link fence. After a cramped economy flight from Chicago to San Antonio. And now even worse—in a black Ford Fiesta. Being chauffeured around by a twenty-two-year-old. Because God is funny like that.

Missy was girl-next-door pretty with steel-blue eyes, a cute round face, and full, dirty-blond hair. She puckered her lips as she scrutinized herself in the vanity mirror above the steering wheel, smearing some pink lipstick on with one hand while pulling her brush out of her purse with the other. "So, how do I look?"

"Really?" I turned down the radio blaring an Obama recap of the recession, job creation, and economic growth. "Who are you getting ready to see?" I pointed out the window, where women dressed in black and khaki skirt suits hurried up to the facility door. Some carried manila folders stuffed with resumes or the same Samsonite briefcase. Everyone here looked like me, or maybe I looked like them: brown eyes, dark hair, olive skin.

"Hey, I'm just here to get the job," Missy said, applying three coats of mascara before twisting her wand closed. "If there happen to be guys here too, then I'll kill two birds with one stone."

We stepped out of her black Ford Fiesta.

"If you get a boyfriend out of this," I said, "I'm going to wonder what he's doing hanging around the Girl Scout Center."

Missy and I had met at one of the local job fairs we'd both been frequenting. She was originally from a small town in South Texas known for hunting, cacti, and honey, although Missy came from a long line of women who made a living antiquing. My family and I often spent my childhood driving back and forth from San Antonio to Laredo, the border town my parents were from. Seeing the sign to Missy's hometown marked the halfway point.

Missy rolled her eyes, sighed, and turned to chase the job fair's closing entrance. "Hey, can you hold the—" Missy's voice faded as a young woman's ponytail wagged in the distance. "Door."

"See?" I said. "Another door closes before we've even had a chance to get our foot in it."

Missy grabbed the door handle, her pointy black heels clacking against the pavement. "Sometimes the universe is listening."

I dropped my knockoff Samsonite and stared up at the sky. "Hello? Universe? If you're listening right now, can Missy and I trade places? Also, rain. We need some rain."

"Very funny."

It was easier to poke fun. I didn't want to tell Missy that I *did* believe the universe was listening. But sometimes, we can hope, wish, and pray and still find ourselves in the same place or no place at all.

In May, I would turn twenty-nine again. Missy had just turned twenty-two. It felt strange to be so close in age yet in such distinctly different generations. And if she had left to pursue her "dreams," maybe she would have learned that, despite being in the twenty-first century, we were still from an area near the border where time had yet to make a change.

We approached one of the Golden Girls staffing the registration desk. They stood everywhere, each donning one of those green Girl Scout vests with patches and pins. This one's name was, appropriately, Dorothy. "Please sign in," she instructed, pointing to a clipboard with March 31 scrawled at the top.

Dorothy's erect bouffant paired well with her sparkling veneers. She pulled up her pink Old Navy stretch-pant capris. "The non-profits will give you brochures and an introduction to their companies. They have available volunteer positions, internships, and even some paying positions."

Missy and I gave each other a peripheral glance as we picked up the complimentary job fair bags with the event pamphlets and maps.

Golden Girl adjusted her bifocals. "Please take a free bag with brochures—err—Melissa Jennings and Jessica Puente. My, what beautiful names."

"Oh, thank you," I replied.

Golden Girl shuffled through papers scattered on the table. "Please also be sure to fill out a name tag..." Her eyes widened. "My goodness. The English nametags are gone. We have a few bilingual name tags left. Here you are. Good luck, ladies."

Missy and I feigned smiles as we signed our names on the custom-made tags. *"Hola,"* Missy began as she taped the tag to her blazer. *"Me llama, Missy. Yo quiero trabajar."*

"Hola," I mocked the nametag while we walked through the double doors to greet the non-profits. *"No quiero trabajar!"*

"Jess, is that the way to greet your future employer?"

"Missy, how do you think they can call this a job fair if paying jobs do not exist?"

"Oh, they'll put you to work, alright," Missy said, biting her lip. "Whether a paycheck comes regularly is a whole different story."

"No," I said. We rounded the corner to find the nonprofit booths with tablecloths, signage, and décor. "This time's going to be different." The last two booths at the end came completely stocked with kittens, kennels, and puppies. Suddenly, a giant red cross jumped out in front of us. "What the—" I yelped as a costumed human directed us to the booth.

An older lady with an orange mullet sat organizing her brochures. She stood up, tossing her arms behind her back and tugging on the elastic waistband around her khaki shorts that barely moved from all the starch. "Can I help you, ladies?"

"Yes." I smiled, gesturing gracefully with my upturned hand to the bullet points of my resume, like highlighting amenities in a tourism package through Rome. "As you can see, I worked for Applebaum & Kirk, or A&K as you might know them—the grandfathers of luxury travel. I have a wealth of experience in international tourism. Most importantly, my global volunteer work during shoulder season reflects the Red Cross mission." I stepped back and narrowed my eyes, concerned and thoughtful, as the Red Cross representative scanned my resume. "How is Haiti coming along?"

She seemed to be in shock. "My, what a fantastic background and the volunteer work."

"Yes, while I lived in Europe."

"You're a perfect candidate, especially with your experience and familiarization trips. How are you with underdeveloped countries?"

That was an interesting question, considering that even luxurious familiarization trips often transformed into visits dedicated to "hidden gems," a.k.a. underdeveloped areas desperate for tourism dollars.

"I can honestly say that while I've stayed in the finest four, five, and even seven-star hotels, I've also had just as many opposite and unpleasant out-of-body experiences." My last statement reminded me to shine: "I've managed to conduct my business in a hole in the ground, or no hole at all, if you know what I mean."

"Wow, well, that just about sums it up, doesn't it?"

I nodded, trying not to look too pleased with myself.

Missy silently waited for me. I'd caught at least two eye rolls.

"We'd love for you to start as soon as possible. As you know, ninety percent of our workforce is volunteer."

A momentary setback, I told myself. Conceal the frustration on your face, and a real job will come to fruition. "I understand. But there aren't any coordinator positions, or perhaps doing what you're doing as well?"

"Unfortunately, we are fully staffed right now. But we should be able to place you rather quickly into a volunteer position. I'm sure your work ethic will stand out in no time."

Why do I keep going to these things?

We visited a few more representatives from another animal shelter, a food bank, and a humane society. After several blank stares, I knew I should just shut up, take the brochures, and then be on my merry way, thank you very much.

But then I heard it. Loud and clear, a voice from my subconscious: *"No!"*

I was tired of losing. At the very least, we could get some Thin Mints out of this Girl Scout-sponsored job fair. Each non-profit organization had an unopened Girl Scout cookie box with a clever ribbon tied around it on their tables.

"Missy," I hissed, covertly pinching her hip. She was conversing with a non-profit veterinarian about their *One Beady-eyed Beagle at a Time Project*. "Ask her about the cookies."

Missy flipped her hair in exclamation. "I don't think those are for us."

In Missy's world, no meant no. In my world, no meant ask again in a different way.

"*Psst.*" I pinched her hip again. "Why else would they have put a ribbon on the cookies and then put the cookie boxes on each table?"

Every table featured a different cookie box: Samoas, Thin Mints, Trefoils, Tagalongs. One of the Golden Girls managing the event began to approach—her bifocals sliding further down her nostrils with each step. By the time she reached us, her carrot orange Old Navy stretch-pant capris were long out of style.

"Ladies, Girl Scout Cookie time is seasonal. It's almost April, so no more cookies are left for sale right now."

Drats. "Thank you, Blanche."

Golden Girl slowly strolled off into her continued retirement. I wondered whether she could discern that the American Dream had died for my generation. If she knew the truth, she would have insisted on Girl Scout cookie time all the time. Everybody talked about baby boomers and up-and-coming hipster millennials—but somehow my generation got sandwiched into oblivion, attending irrelevant job fairs that had yet to host any real jobs. I was on the cusp of both Generation X and Generation Y. My identity, like my employment prospects, seemed to be forgotten. Passed over. Obsolete.

A woman's voice from the Wish Upon A Star Foundation interrupted my thoughts. Her voice was soft and urgent, like a kind carnival barker. "Hello, ladies, please join us in helping children make their one great wish come true. To help them enjoy life and be in that moment no matter what misfortune befalls them."

I kept walking.

"Jess? What about this booth?"

"I'm good, thanks. Ready to move on to the next job fair." I sensed Missy's apologetic smile while I approached another table. "And how about these Samoas right here? Are we going to be opening these today?"

"Jess, we're here to get a job." Missy smacked my hand away from the Samoas.

I dropped the box as she grabbed my elbow, pulling me away from all the tables. "*Oww*, is it time out already?"

"Jess, birds of a feather flock together, and pretty soon, everyone will know I'm with you."

"Are you crucifying me for participating in this jobless fair?"

"No, I'm simply trying to get you to focus."

We shuffled along, but I inconspicuously grabbed a box of Thin Mints from an unstaffed booth, stashing them inside the job fair bag. "Missy has it occurred to you that the food bank will not be offering their employees a job that will put food on their table and that the humane society has yet to offer a job that does pay—which is very inhumane, by the way."

"Once again, Jess, you don't seem to be a good fit for any of the companies at this fair."

"I'm sorry!" I no longer bothered to keep my voice down. "But back in my day, you only needed 'transferrable skills' to move into a new position laterally. Now, you must have very specific requisites for watching some kittens at a job fair booth where real jobs do not exist? Mind you, the kittens are already locked up. They're clearly not going anywhere."

Missy glanced around like she was hoping nobody had overheard me. "Can you at least pretend to be interested in these jobs?"

"No, I can't." I held up a sheet from the last booth, helping juvenile delinquents. "These specific requisites are meant to distract you from the fact that *there aren't jobs*. Companies don't have the money or resources to hire, train, and pay new employees with decent, livable salaries and benefits. It's all a big joke. Everything's a big joke."

"Jess – you're –"

"I know I'm getting loud!" I was no longer inconspicuous but awfully visible, digging deeper into my bag and tearing open the Thin Mints. I stuffed them into my mouth like the Cookie Monster, crumbs pouring onto the chiffon blue blouse peeking out of my blazer.

"*Yessica?*" A woman's voice with a thick Spanish accent called behind me.

Oh, no.

Oh, God.

"Is that you?"

Please let this be a dream. Please let this be a dream. God, I'm going to close my eyes, and when I open them on the count of three, please let me be back in bed on a sailing yacht docked along the coast of the French Riviera. There's no place like home. There's no place like home. Wait, God. I meant any other place but home, any other place but home.

I turned to find a full-figured woman wearing a bright *folklórico* dress. Conchita.

She fixed her big brunette bun on her head, "Yessica Ann Ventura Puente, Miss Fiesta Pageant Class of 2000?"

I pretty expertly jumped behind Missy. "Save me. I will do anything for you. Anything, you name it."

"Oh, I cannot wait to see this." Missy slowly stepped to her right—with giddiness and hand-clapping—so Conchita was directly in my line of sight.

"My goodness, is that you?" I brushed Thin Mint crumbs away from my blouse and face, attempting to be graceful but realizing I had literally been caught with my hand inside the cookie jar. Then, I prepared to struggle through my Spanish. "Conchita Hortencia Consuela Saldaña, Miss Fiesta Pageant, Class of 2000?"

Conchita quickly turned serious. She flexed her body and arms, preparing for some sort of salute. She threw her right hand over her head and yelled, "*¡Olé! Viva Fiesta! Viva Fiesta de San Antonio!*"

Sounds throughout the Girl Scout Center ceased. Booths stopped interviewing, kittens stopped purring, and puppies stopped pouting, all to watch us.

Missy yelped, then briskly covered her mouth with her hand. "Forget everything I said, Jess. I love going to places with you. We can totally do whatever you want from now on and steal all the cookies while doing it."

"Yessicaaaa?" Conchita said, her right hand still wavering above her head. "Where is your *Viva Fiesta*? You did not say *Viva Fiesta*."

"Yeah, Jess, come on. New Orleans has Mardi Gras, and San Antonio has Fiesta," Missy mocked, quoting the local newspaper.

"Oh, Conchita," I whined. "Do I have to? It's been so long, and we both know you're the real Miss Fiesta winner. I wouldn't want anyone to think I was trying to steal such a coveted crown."

"*Si*, that is true. But you were a finalist. I never forget my finalists. I went on to tour for three years in a row." Conchita gazed at Missy, eyeing her up and down. "And who is this *gringa* you have brought? Does she want to intern for me at the Fiesta Commission?"

Then it was as if Conchita and the whole world zoomed in on the bilingual name tag on my chest, Conchita looking down on me from her ivory tower of *folklórico* dancers. "*Huh*, are you looking for a job, too?"

I didn't think I could loathe Conchita's accent anymore, but that sentence in that accent pretty much summed up how I felt about myself and my life.

"Oh, don't be silly," I shook my head. "Part of what I do is mentoring the new college graduates. I come down south every so often to give back to the community. Have you ever heard of Doctors Without Borders? This is the same thing. Schools Without Borders. Well, Schools Along the Borders."

Conchita continued roasting me while everyone watched. "But you have the pamphlet in your hands. And you are wearing a welcome sticker on your *camiseta* that says, "*Hola, me llama Yessica, yo quiero trabajar.*"

Missy smirked, mumbling something under her breath that sounded suspiciously like, "She's the one publicly crucifying you, Jess—not me."

But if there was anything I learned when I had a real job, it was how to save myself from tricky situations.

I scanned Conchita up and down. "My, Conchita, you look so different now. I must have passed by this booth a million times earlier but didn't even recognize you."

The Girl Scout Center got quieter.

"Well, yes. Maybe I am bigger, but I am over four months pregnant now."

"Oh, wow, over four whole months? I didn't want to assume or anything."

Conchita took a deep breath, brushing a few fallen bangs into her fake *folklórico* bun. "I am pregnant with my fifth child. We are hoping for a boy—they cannot all be Miss Fiesta winners. But we haven't formally announced it yet. I would appreciate it if you kept it to yourself. From one Miss Fiesta to another, well, Miss Fiesta finalist."

"Of course. And I hear this is such a big city now and all, so I bet nobody here has heard us or knows who we are."

"Yes, it is." Conchita's voice rose as she straightened up her back.

"But they probably know who I am. My husband and I helped with the new sign at the airport. We were on the news. You may have seen us, too. I still get stopped at the grocery store."

"Oh, wow." I raised my eyebrows as high as they could go. "Do you mean the new sign that added 'international' to San Antonio Airport?"

"That is right. Many people don't know our airport is international: San Antonio International Airport."

"How about that." I held up a few fingers. "Yep, I heard that we now have three whole nonstop flights to Mexico instead of just the one."

"And Canada." Conchita's high hair bounced back and forth as if to emphasize her point. "With a layover in Atlanta."

"Anyway, how about you? How many do you have?"

"How many do I have, what?"

"*Chiquitos? Pequeños?* Little ones? Kids? You are so tiny, *flaca.* Let me guess. Only two? Three?" Conchita's voice screeched. "You cannot have more than three."

Wow. Did people have *only* two or three? That sounded like so many kids to be living on my unemployment checks. "Oh, umm, thank you? I'm happy to say I'm the proud auntie of a little four-legged blonde mutt named Hazelnut. My brother got full custody in his last breakup and everything, you know? We're all very supportive. She and her family were from Mexico, so a little too—"

Stop while you're ahead. You are back in Mexico now.

"Anyway, sorry, I'm here to help Missy with Schools Along the Borders. We better finish our stops at the rest of the booths."

Conchita looked at Missy's name tag. "What do you do?"

"Yeah, what do you do?" I said.

Missy roused her innocent charm. "I worked for the Tilly Worth store for two years while I went to Texas State University. Many people don't know that San Marcos had the first Tilly Worth store in all of Texas. My dream job is in fashion PR or advertising. Then, maybe one day I'll get enough experience to work for the real Tilly in New York City."

We both stared back at Conchita, who appeared to be fathoming Missy's speech. She squeezed her dark hazel eyes together and said, "Tilly Worth? Is that the skinny *gringa* with the flats?"

"*Umm,* yes?" Missy shot me a sideways glance. "She did become one of the first self-made female billionaires, which many people attribute to her two-hundred-dollar 'ladies who lunch' ballet flats."

"The lady who *whata what* with her lunches?" Conchita pinched her eyes so tight her fake eyelashes seemed to stick together.

"Like the Upper East Side?" Missy perked up her head. "Her ballet flats are inspired by the Upper East Side ladies who lunch?"

"Forget it." I nodded. "Stop while you're ahead."

Conchita pointed to a clothing rack behind her, to some dated pageant dresses overdone in sequins. "We use fashion in the Fiesta Commission. And we sometimes meet for lunch."

I leaned into Missy. "Yes, please. You can tell them to get rid of that gaudy clown crown. Even Queen Elizabeth doesn't have a crown that big."

Conchita opened one of the flamboyant fiesta brochures, holding the mission statement out for us. "Since 1949, Miss Fiesta has been one of the thirteen reigning Queens and Kings of Fiesta. Miss Fiesta's charitable community service is rewarded with a scholarship, and—"

"Oh, how nice," Missy struggled to fake a smile. "Thank you. I'll have to take a brochure to learn more about the Commission. I have an interview coming up that my amazing and worldly mentor, Jess, from Schools Along the Borders, helped me to get. We should get going."

Conchita motioned us to step closer to her booth. "Yes, our brochures, and let me get you my card. Yessica," Conchita pointed her index finger at me. "It looks like you may need some too. Don't forget. Miss Fiesta Commission can always use help from former finalists. *Si, si...*" Conchita paused, sorting through more fiesta brochures and business cards on her table. "Especially from such a talented flutist. Do you still play the flute?"

Missy's eyes darted to mine. "The flute? Oh, Yessica, you must play us your flute. When do I get to hear your flute?"

"Oh, *si, si*, Yessica serenaded us during the talent portion. Did you know that she played in the youth's orchestras of the city and that she was so good with her Russian and French composers that she and the orchestra traveled and played in the Oprah House?"

Conchita always had the best mispronunciations. My eyes darted above her head, and my lips rolled in as I struggled to keep a straight face. "Oh, thank you. Such a good memory. It's actually flautist, and we performed in the Sydney Opera House in Australia."

"Ah, *si*, you should have helped us with the sign at the airport. Now maybe you can fly directly. I hope you remember to pray to St. Christopher, patron saint of travelers."

"Jess, you've been to Sydney too?" Missy looked genuinely surprised. "Still, so much I don't know about you."

"But, you know, Missy, as I said to Yessica back then, her French composer for the talent portion should have been Spanish or Mexican. Maybe she would have won Miss Fiesta or been the first instead of the second finalist."

I flashed Conchita the biggest fake pageant smile she had taught me many years ago. It was best for under pressure and constantly while under the crown. "And as I told you back then, Conchita: Six Flags over Texas is also part of our history. The French flag was one of the six flags that flew over *Tejas,* too. We can appreciate other cultures besides Spanish-speaking ones, especially since we know all about them, being close to the border."

"Okay, fine, Yessica." Conchita held her card out to me with a brochure. "But as always, you were so passionate about every other country and culture than the ones closest to you."

"Thank you, Conchita." I snatched the card and brochure from her. "And, as always, so passionate about the culture closest to you. Remember, you can't think outside the box unless you've actually been outside the box."

Her face darkened with her squinting eyes. "You know what your problem is, Yessica?"

"You. You are my problem, Conchita."

"Your problem is that while you were too busy being a coconut up north...I mean...do you know what a coconut is?"

"Conchita, you didn't invent the trite racial epithet describing that I'm brown on the outside and white on the inside—wait, do you know what an epithet is?"

Conchita nervously fiddled with her bun. "Don't be ridiculous."

"Exactly. If we were 'up north,' as you call it, I'd say that you and your epithets are so pedestrian. And so is your Fee-esta Comeeshion."

"Well, we are down south, Yessica, and nobody cares about your crosswalk around here."

I laughed aloud. "Okay, I didn't mean pedestrian as in crosswalk."

Missy grabbed my arm, attempting to drag me away. I waved goodbye to Conchita. We meandered toward the exit, weaving again through all the nonprofit booth accessories, signage, décor, kittens, and puppies. Missy whispered over my shoulder, "Jess, of all the things I would have thought you had done in the world, a beauty pageant? Seriousl—"

"Watch yourself. Think first before you say it."

"Not that you aren't a beauty, because you definitely are—"

"True. Keep going."

"But I wouldn't have thought that was your style."

"Thank you, Captain Obvious." I pulled another Thin Mint out of the box in my bag. "I can assure you that of all the things I have done in the world, I would have hoped never to have to remark on that one. However—" I took a bite of the Thin Mint and continued while chewing. "We all have a past we may not be proud of, and, if you must know, a scholarship was involved."

Missy laughed. "Oh, that's what they all say, Jess. Sure, you were in it for the scholarships."

"Missy, I'm telling you, the winner got a thousand dollars. Do you know how much money that was back then? Italy was still switching currency from the Lira to the Euro. I could get a roundtrip ticket to Rome from Nowhere, Texas, for around five hundred bucks. That was before the taxes and fees on a flight to Europe were almost the whole cost of the flight itself."

"Let me get this straight, Jess. You wanted to be the Queen of Fiesta, an event that celebrates all things San Antonio and its rich history so that you could dump the city for a better city?"

I stopped our walk in the middle of the thought, placing an astute finger above my chin. "I had never thought about it like that, but I guess when you put it that way—"

Missy laughed. "You're such a piece of work. I'm going to need to start taking notes."

We arrived back where we started, at the end of another fruitless job search, past the last Golden Girl in another pair of Old Navy stretch-pant capris, this time in lime green. "Thank you for the lovely afternoon, Rose."

Missy and I donned our oversized sunglasses to leave behind the Girl Scout Center. I caught her staring at my Thin Mints as we settled into her car. "Missy, you think I don't know that I no longer have access to A&K work lunches and dinners at Michelin-starred restaurants? Yes, I'd rather eat *risotto* in its *Piemontese* birthplace, like on my last trip to Italy, or polenta that has been perfectly stirred all day without the inconsistency of even one second of a spoon's delay."

"Boo-hoo," Missy mocked. "Life is so hard. You probably only have money for some chains like Mama Margie's or Denny's. But don't worry. They might have their version of Italian food on the kid's menu."

I sighed. Missy's words stung. What a cruel juxtaposition to go from the thrill of accomplishment to some watered-down version of life without any foreseeable progress or change. To finally live out my dreams, only to have them torn away. And yet, what choice did I have other than to keep going? "I suppose it's not *Taverna Trilussa* in *Roma propio, Trastevere*, where on a good day I might sit next to Mel Gibson or a Coppola director, but rather a chain sitting off a great big highway next to a strip club. Nevertheless, I'm sure they'll have something for me and this temporary low budget."

Missy removed her sunglasses, instantly turning serious. Her big, bleached smile vanished. "Temporary? Do you think you'll leave and—" We waited for a loud plane to depart from the private hangar along the airport, the whistling engine crescendoing as we heard the final sound of the wheels against the ground before it turned up.

My eyes followed the wings ascending through the sky. Looking out the window, I considered how my 2009 end-of-year holiday vacation had extended into a layover well into the new year. "You know what I always loved about our airport that was different from other airports around the world?"

"What?"

"Its location. Practically in the city center." A tear bled down along the other side of my face. The tarmac was so close, yet it felt so far away. "The planes always pointed straight up into the sky as soon as we departed. I asked a flight attendant once about their noise abatement procedure: why the sudden exertion straight into the sky?" Other planes at other airports gradually made their way up and through the clouds, perhaps turning left or right before finally reaching thirty-five thousand feet of cruising altitude.

"Why?" Missy turned her key in the ignition and checked her rearview mirror.

"Because our plane was too loud for the city—all the nearby houses and businesses." I couldn't even look at her. Instead, I kept my runny eyes on the Cessna, but the departing wings and increasing decibels only managed to rub the past in my face. "I guess it was best to get out of sight and sound as soon as possible."

Missy strapped her seatbelt and started reversing before slamming back on the brakes. "Are you going to answer my question? Do you think you'll go back to the life you had before?"

"Who knows." I wiped my tears. "I don't know how to answer that question." Removing my sunglasses, I finally turned to Missy while straining to produce a sliver of that pageant smile. "What if life really is like a box of Girl Scout Cookies?"

"Oh no." Missy shifted gears to Drive and accelerated. "What do you mean now? I was trying to ask you a serious question for once."

"And I'm trying to answer you seriously. Think about it," I paused. We hit the stop sign and waited for all the other traffic to pass us. I took a deep breath. "What if, like a tasty little seasonal cookie, the best part of our lives and career was oh so good, but over all too quickly? What if our successes are short-lived? What if they're meant to be seasonal? Does anything good last?"

TWO

A couple of weeks later, I landed an interview at Harrison Publishing. It lay in the northeast part of the city on a street named from a Native American tribe's word for arrowhead: Bulverde. The thin, sinuous, freshly paved asphalt sparkled black beneath a bright spring sun. The road ran between two wide open spaces of flat and undeveloped ranchland surrounded by barbed wire, caliche, and sparse cacti. Bluebonnets began to flourish through a few new green fields. Texas heat often created ripples on the horizon, and I hoped that those weren't just mirages in the distance but that a new job would lie ahead.

An assistant escorted me up through an elevator and out a set of back doors. The outdoor walkway was covered and connected the two vastly different buildings. I was escorted from the first building, with its decorative limestone bordering and old-fashioned estate furniture, to the second building, which appeared to be a nondescript concrete block. Inside, I was led through a maze of cubicles crammed together, the tops of heads barely visible over their walls, until we finally reached a small office without a window.

"Hello, I'm Carlos," said the hiring manager. He unbuttoned his blazer to stand up from his chair beneath an analog clock that read eight o'clock.

I put my hand inside his. "Hello, I'm Jessica. It's such a pleasure to meet you."

"Please." Carlos motioned to the chair across from his. "Have a seat."

I couldn't help but notice the one little frameless picture hung on the wall above a single particle wood desk with three tall sides. It reminded me of high school detention. I suddenly missed real offices with windows overlooking skyscrapers and water and artwork that spread the length of a wall. To think, just last year, I'd visited Bilbao's acclaimed Frank Gehry-designed Guggenheim Museum, its titanium and glass half-shells flanking the Nervión River and the Pyrenees foothills.

"Shall we get started?"

"Footprints," I said. "In the sand. Along the shore on the beach. My parents had a picture like that in our home growing up."

"Sorry?"

"The picture." I sat down, pointing above the detention center.

Carlos vacantly stared at me. Of course. He missed the cheesy Christian trends. How about everybody everywhere just be younger than me now?

Carlos scratched his chin and bowed his head. "Ah, sorry. This room isn't my office. We don't really have an office. It's, you know, more to meet or have a conversation. Kind of like what we're doing now."

I nodded and decided to shut up until Carlos invited me to speak.

"So, Jessica. I have your resume right here. Very pleased. It looks like, aha, yep, that's what I thought. You've got some editing experience."

"Yes," I jumped in, possibly a little too eagerly. "I wrote a lot of travel proposals and itineraries, destination descriptions, brochures, and websites with SEO—search engine optimization. We were going digital, especially during the end of my time with the company."

A nod and a glance up, then back down at my resume. "Sounds very interesting. We won't need you to do much of that while you're here."

"I understand. I'm certainly open to new responsibilities. I'm sure you'll note that I have a lot of transferrable skills."

"The position that we had in mind for you is Scorer—someone who scores tests."

I blinked. "Tests?"

Carlos threw my resume on the desk and inhaled. "Harrison publishes many textbooks, education, and higher education materials."

"And also owns one of the largest publishing companies in the world, Pelican Books." I attempted to steer the conversation back to my strengths. "Not to mention its renowned travel books, Hoofprints."

"Pelican is more in London and New York. We don't have anything to do with that here."

"You don't?" I held my smile tight, dismissing my big dreams of publishing a solo travel book. Sometimes, it felt like my hometown competitively vied for all the jobs people in other cities did not want.

"We do a lot of test scoring."

Test scoring? All day? In those cubicles without any windows? "Excellent," I said without missing a beat. "I do have an eye for detail."

"That's the spirit," he said, smiling for the first time since the interview started. "Yep. Test scoring K-12 subjects. Science, Mathematics, English." Carlos leaned back in his chair, crossing one of his legs. He placed both hands behind his head. "You know, Harrison's education-slash-assessment department is headquartered right here in San Antonio. We have a lot of people from all over the country—all over the world—knocking down our doors."

"Oh, I bet." I tried hard to play along in a convincing sing-song tone. "What a wonderful opportunity." For people looking to be in the education-slash-assessment industry.

"We did see you were inquiring about a copy editor position, but there aren't openings. Maybe one day, though, since Harrison does promote from within."

"Of course." I shifted my skirt and grasped my folder tighter. "I'll have to keep that in mind."

Carlos leaned into the desk and read from what sounded like a script. "We have reviewed your application and would like to extend a conditional job offer to work as a scorer on the Washington English Language Proficiency 2010 grades nine through twelve Writing project."

"Oh, wow." What were the grades nine through twelve Writing projects?

Carlos grinned. "Yes, ma'am. You heard that right. Washington."

I forced another smile.

"Most new hires don't get to start out scoring high school tests. Scoring high school is the crème of the crop as far as test scoring goes. But with your experience, we're confident you'll do great in this role."

I nodded again, feeling like one of those bobblehead dolls. "Absolutely."

Carlos continued his script. "This project extends from Wednesday, April 14, 2010, through approximately Wednesday, April 21, 2010."

My stomach fell. That was less than two work weeks. All this build-up—the driving out here to be told in person, rather than an email or over the phone, where I was better at lying about my excitement?

"Now." Carlos put his arms back down, then crossed them over his chest. "That's once you show us your degree. Human Resources requires me to tell you the offer is contingent upon providing proof of a degree and completing hiring paperwork within the timeframe requested."

His eyes twitched to my resume to clarify that I had a college degree.

"I have my degree. I think it's in storage. You know, with the move and all. I have official transcripts, though. Would that work?"

"We'll accept that." Carlos uncrossed his arms as if I had unlocked the door to almighty Harrison, the kingdom of the education-slash-assessment industry—where people from around the world competitively vied to make their dreams come true.

My mind drifted to a thought that would often come and go: what's in a dream anymore, anyway?

"I bet you're wondering..." Carlos paused. "About the pay."

"Oh no, not at all. Places like this . . . I know the jobs are always commensurate with experience."

"The compensation is as follows." Carlos leaned into the desk beside him again to read from his script. "Training: Training will be paid at ten dollars per hour plus milestones. Scoring: Once qualification and training have been completed successfully, scorers will score on the live item. Scorers will receive thirty cents per response scored. Rates are based on the average scorer earning twelve dollars per hour. Notes: Note that your pay will be totaled each week to ensure you are earning a minimum of ten dollars an hour for all work completed."

"Oh, I see." A college degree to make ten dollars an hour, and maybe one day a whole twelve dollars an hour?

"Positions may fill quickly for this project. If we do not receive notice of acceptance soon, the position could be offered to another candidate by this Friday."

"Oh," I said in a high pitch, taken aback. My favorite part about the generous job offer was the kind threat at the end. "Thank you so much. I know you're busy, and I'd hate to take up much more of your time."

"It's not a problem at all. We like to give our best candidates, the high school scorers, as much time as they need to ask any questions."

"Oh, no, you've been so thorough."

"I bet you didn't expect to leave here with a job."

"Nope." I shook my head. "Nope. Definitely not."

"Very well. I can escort you to the door and show you toward Human Resources so you may take your official transcripts there by the end of the week."

"Right, right, of course."

***

The last of my unemployment checks coincided with the day I was born, the first day of May. Happy thirtieth birthday to me. I spent the rest of the afternoon in front of my laptop, applying for jobs in my parents' cramped kitchen. It was the only place I could go for peace, as the remainder of the house was typically littered with extra furniture from the several lives each of my three older brothers previously held themselves. A red drum set, guitars, oversized couches, and an array of coffee tables harkened to a time when each had briefly decided to be an adult. They'd eventually rebounded into the real world so I could have the empire to myself.

Well, not entirely to myself.

Hazelnut was my brother's puppy from a relationship gone wrong, a spoiled little mixed-golden retriever left behind for my parents in lieu of grandchildren. Although she was more of a blanched Hazelnut, her golden fur seemed almost white.

As I poured some coffee, I noticed an old, creased photograph of my mother and me on the refrigerator. Taken on my fifth, maybe sixth, birthday. My hair was still baby-fine and straight. The length skimmed my waist, but my bangs hung short and crooked over my small forehead; I had tried to cut them myself. I wore a blue jean jumpsuit, and a blindfold covered my eyes while I tightly held a thin wooden stick, impatiently waiting to bust my Rainbow Bright piñata into pieces. My mother's skinny arms clung to my shoulders as she knelt above my head, the photograph profiling the Aztec bone at the top of her nose as her cheeks and lips stretched into a long, square smile. Suddenly, I could see my younger mother turning me around and around in circles below the piñata. I could hear her voice counting. "Eight, nine, ten…"

Even back then, and every year since, my mother would say to me on my birthday, "You were born in the afternoon at twelve-fifteen. And I always wanted a little girl. But I got three boys. And then you were born. I had always had natural deliveries without drugs, but for you, they put me to sleep—stupid doctor, his wife was an anesthesiologist—and when I awoke, I was all alone, and you were gone. It was the scariest feeling I have ever had in my life. I put my hands on my stomach, and you were no longer there. But I saw lots of pink balloons, strings, and ribbons. The nurse came in and told me I had had a girl. And I said, 'no, I do not believe you.' When they brought you to me, I said, 'take her diaper off—I have to see for myself.'"

I had forgotten about that photograph. And about Mercy Hospital, the first hospital along the American side of the border. But that photograph made me remember what I wanted to be when I grew up. "A dancer," I would say. "And an astronaut. I will be the first ballerina to dance in outer space."

Smiling at the memory, I pulled the picture out from under its refrigerator magnet and peered at it even closer. Since the first time I returned to Texas, that picture made me feel like maybe I *had* been a dancer in outer space; that's what my life had felt like sometimes. I was so happy; it felt like I was floating.

I paused with the picture in hand, thinking about everywhere I'd flown. As my plane often flew east over rippling oceans, every other passenger's closed eyes trembled up and down, back and forth, during the richest, most vivid, deepest parts of their sleep. But I knew I was already dreaming. So instead of sleeping, I gazed out the window and watched the dark sky gently and silently pivot around the sun. I stared, mesmerized, as the dark indigo sky slowly churned out new colors, from blood orange to apricot to peach, finally to the pale blue of a new day. As night diminished, I discerned skid marks in the sky, trails of clouds, that all the planes that came before had already made. Yet, with each mile our wing flew across a new continent, it was as if we were the ones who carried the light with us, dusting each shoreline and city with a new morning. On my twenty-eighth birthday, I looked down as the light followed the capstones crowning the peaks of Egyptian pyramids. I remembered my mother's story. Except her story was finally different than I had remembered it before. "Twenty-eight," I said aloud, stirring a sleeping passenger beside me. By the time my mother was twenty-eight, she had already had four kids.

A loud noise pierced through the clouds and my thoughts. I hung the photograph back where it belonged on the refrigerator as I heard my mother's house slippers sliding down the kitchen steps.

"Poopies, Poopies, come here, Poopies."

"Mom, quit calling her that. She has a name." I returned to the kitchen table where my new life awaited, my laptop having fallen back to sleep.

"Yeah, but she still likes to poop everywhere—she hasn't learned how to go outside yet, and when she does go outside, she wants to spend her time playing with all the other doggies." My mother searched desperately for Hazelnut under the kitchen table. Her curly raven hair was a frizzball from years of waiting on the men in my family.

"Mother, please get her fixed before it's too late." I typed my new password on my laptop: #anywherebuthere30. But my thoughts were cut short as an odd scent of ammonia mixed with my brother's dirty socks arose. "Gross. What's that smell, Mom? I already picked up her mess in the kitchen and took her out this morning."

She shrugged. "It's time to remove the carpet in the dining room anyway." My parents' 1970s home was built in an open style with uneven levels throughout, as if Frank Lloyd Wright's falling water architecture had finally reached their neighborhood thirty or forty years after his famous breakthrough. Running back over to the kitchen sink in her old pink house dress, my mother grabbed a sponge, a tattered rag, and the bathroom cleaner she kept in the kitchen for such occasions. She ran up the steps to the dining room, avoiding the loose Saltillo tile that everybody in the house knew about, a tile that wasn't really a loose tile but a completely torn-off tile regularly placed back on the spot where it initially stuck.

The dining room I had long ago nicknamed "The Time Machine" was covered in mint green and yellow wallpaper that complemented the 70s wood paneling. It also seemed to complement the adjoining yellow kitchen or maybe the yellow*ing* kitchen; I couldn't remember if the room had always been that color.

"Mom, bathroom cleaner is not the same as carpet cleaner," I pointed out. "And you're going to get it in your hair."

"Poopies. Poopies, no! Why does she love the dining room and the office so much?" My mother kneeled on all fours in her pink housedress as Poopies—I mean, Hazelnut—seemed to move on from peeing to jumping and humping her back. Hazelnut was at that age where she was starting to hump things.

"Hmmm, let me guess…" I tapped a blue pen against my chin. "Your son, her owner—although who would in a million years guess that—plays internet chess in the office when he visits and practices his guitar in the dining room. Maybe she's following his scent."

My mother looked up mid-scrub to yell. "Happy birthday, Jessi! Have you found a job yet?"

"Thank you. And yes. Kind of." I clicked on another job board called Monster.com. "For two weeks, and maybe longer. But I'm thinking of going back to school or something."

My mother lifted her head again. "There are jobs down here if you have a hard hat. And sales jobs, *mijita.* You always said Chicago was a capital for advertising."

"So, about that. I'm not sure why salespeople are referred to as advertising account executives down here, even if they've never done an ad campaign, product launch, copywriting, market research, and other things the job description advertising entails. I mean, it's perfectly fine to sell ad space to the strip club on a billboard off the highway, Mom. I just think the job description should be called something else like, I don't know, billboard sales. Somehow, the job is reflected on the job description and resume in a much haughtier way, like 'Advertising Account Executive, Clear Channel Communications, Outdoor Advertising Branch.'"

My mother kept scrubbing, her haphazard ponytail wagging along. "What about UCAA? Their headquarters is down here."

The United Car Association of America was the Chrysler to my hometown, so throughout high school and college, everybody repeated the mantra, "You about to graduate? Maybe I can get you in at UCAA." It had become more competitive over the years, and working for the company meant you had made it in life because it had great benefits and pay. But my heart sank when anybody recommended applying there because it signified my life was over.

"Mom, did anybody ever think, 'one day, when I grow up, I want to sell auto insurance to the military?'"

"Maybe. It's a reliable job." My mother kept up with her lecture from the carpet. "You never know—they're saying the recession didn't reach Texas. Keep sending out your resume. There are some good white-collar jobs here, but you must be born into them or have a few family members working there. Otherwise, the big, white-collared companies like to bring business executives from their corporate headquarters up north."

Things were finally making sense.

The phrase "up north" was a frequent colloquial expression I heard at home. It often came out of someone else's mouth, sounding like Big Brother, another planet, or this great big world that wasn't accessible by a two-hour plane ride. "Are you working up north?" an old friend from high school once asked when I was visiting from Italy. I suspected that "down here," the phrase "up north" was synonymous with progress.

"You know, I was talking to Elsa today," my mother said, as if Hazelnut wasn't all over her, crouched along the carpet. "And Elsa said my kids are boomerangs. Have you heard of this? Boomerangs?" My mother huffed with each scrub her hand made against the carpet. "We called it late bloomers in my day, but it makes sense. Elsa says, 'Like a boomerang, Ariana. You throw a boomerang out in the air, and it comes right back.'"

"Thanks, Mom. Lots of insight on my birthday and super helpful. It motivates me to get off the couch, I mean, out of your kitchen, like all the women who came before you. Oh, look at that. I come home to find you still in the kitchen."

My mother ignored me, as she usually did when I got all feministy. She stopped mid-scrub like she had a premonition, glaring off into the distance. "Elsa says, your home is a revolving door, Ariana, a revolving door. I know you love your kids, but you should make them pay some rent."

"Mom! Who has Elsa been hanging around with in her Sharpie eyebrows? I'm paying for utilities and groceries, as agreed. Plus gas, insurance, and a new lease on a car so Missy can stop driving me everywhere. How much do you think I get for unemployment?"

"I know. Can you believe that? I said to Elsa, 'Elsa, where did you get this from?' She said, 'the other ladies that work with me at the new Southwest Airlines Call Center.'"

"I see San Antonio is still vying for those competitive, blue-collared call center jobs. Wait, will you tell her I'm looking for a temp job and that I have travel experience?"

"It's a bilingual call center job, so you must speak fluent Spanish."

"Your fault, Mom," I said in a tongue-in-cheek tone.

When my parents were growing up on the border, society taught their generation that they and their children would never prosper in the U.S. if they spoke Spanish. Being white had equaled economic prosperity, power, and wealth in the U.S. As a punishment, the nuns at my parents' school would charge them up to a quarter for every Spanish word they accidentally spoke in class. So, when my parents grew up and started their family, they raised my brothers and me to speak only English, even though Spanish was their first language. But enter the 1990s with Selena, J. Lo., and Ricky Martin. Big corporations like McDonald's, Proctor & Gamble, and Liz Claiborne began to see the Hispanic market as an untapped resource. They started spending their advertising dollars in markets like Telemundo and Univision. We became re-branded as "Latino." That word made me feel like I needed big J. Lo Hoop earrings, dark purple lipstick, and those trending Homies T-shirts with a picture of a big, souped-up hooptie.

"So basically, Mom, I spent the first half of my life shamed not to speak Spanish, and now I'm going to spend the rest of my life shamed by both Hispanics and non-Hispanics—sorry, Latinos— because I don't speak Spanish? Why aren't 'Anglos' shamed for not speaking Gaelic, Finnish, or whatever language that is consistent with their ancestry? Because it's about money, Mother, just so you know. I promise you, the world doesn't suddenly care about Hispanics or Latinos, but money does."

"That's right." My mother finished scrubbing the defecation made by our family mascot and stood up. "You want the job? I can start speaking to you only in Spanish now. Do you want me to? Like we practiced when you were in high school? Come on. If you can learn Italian…"

I shook my head at her. It was like she was already anticipating me living back home forever. "Just think, Mom, how my life could have ended up so differently…" I trailed off, mumbling to myself while opening another job board on my laptop. "Not that it's so different now. I'm back at home, going to the same events as Miss Fies—"

"Did you say Miss Fiesta?!" My mother began waving the old and now soiled rag over her head. "¡*Olé*! *Viva Fiesta de San Antonio! Sí, mijita*. If only you could've eaten those *gorditas*. We were cheering you on in the audience. But you gave up so quickly. Conchita has a real passion for the gorditas. Even after they rang the bell, she sure kept going. But you could've won."

"You're right, Mom." It was hilarious that everybody seemed to have their version of why I didn't win. "If only I had played a song written by a Spanish or Mexican composer on my flute. And maybe if only I'd been able to eat three more gorditas, I could've caught the attention of a local guy from the army base. And then he would've swept me off my feet to live in exotic places like Killeen, Texas, while he did army drills all day."

"Then you would have had health insurance." My mother nodded her head. "I bet Conchita got health insurance."

"That's what I was going to say next. And then we could've had four kids—almost five—because I had health insurance."

"And you would have had your very own kitchen right now to be on the laptops." Even though my mother's Spanish accent had faded over the years, she often added the letter "S" to everything as if giving a Sesame Street demonstration on the letter "S." Walmart was "Walmarts." She also added the letter "G" to a sandwich, pronouncing it "sangwich."

"Yep, you're right," I said. "And then I could've had my very own kitchen, where I could be cleaning up my very own son's dog's pee. And after my husband retired from the military, he could work at UCAA."

My mother tuned me out as she headed back down the steps and toward the sink, always back toward the sink.

I kept going regardless. "And then I could go to nonprofit job fairs where I recruit young women to ensure that we lift them up and mentor and prepare them for a life of procreating. Forget Betty Friedan or Simone de Beauvoir."

I heard my mother turn on the sink and listened to the water running down the drain with a few delays, her hands washing and unknotting, washing, and unknotting.

Gosh, what was I thinking when I got that apartment in Rome, just steps from the Sistine Chapel and Michelangelo's ceiling? "What more could I want?"

The faucet abruptly stopped. For a moment, it was quiet.

"You always wanted to be the farthest away from here. That is what you always wanted. Like you used to say, you never wanted to be the one big fish in the sea."

I closed my laptop and looked up at her. "No, Mom, I think you meant I didn't want to be a big fish in a small pond. I wanted to be a small fish in a big pond."

"There you go again."

"There I go again, what?"

"It's the reason you didn't become Miss Fiesta. Always wanting to hide behind everyone else. Never wanting the attention. Never wanting to be responsible. Well, my daughter is a big fish. A big worldly fish now with a lot of experience and know-how."

"Mom, nobody says know-how anymore. You're starting to sound like Little Grandma."

My mother turned to me and stepped toward the kitchen table, waving her old wet rag around again. "And I would like her to be the big fish in this pond. It is your turn. Be the big fish."

I didn't like where the analogy was going. "I am a big fish. It's just not easy. Stop waving that bacteria-infested thing at me!" I reached across the table and took the rag from her. "Big fish have bigger problems and larger appetites—and—sometimes the water just gets too warm."

I trailed off, not knowing where I was going with my analogy, life, and pretty much everything. Being back home made me feel like a little girl again. It was as though my mother and I picked things right back up from where we left them. And as if to put an exclamation point on that sentiment and drive that thought home, Hazelnut chimed in with a bark that sounded more like a yip.

"Mom, she's peeing again—over there." Hazelnut had squatted against the retro china cabinet. The little dog concentrated on me, pointing at her, like a ballerina focusing on a fixed point to finish off her pirouettes—nice and proud, performing for an audience the opening night. It occurred to me that dogs, like humans, could also smile and communicate with the middle finger without physically doing either. My mother grabbed a newspaper hanging off the corner of the kitchen table and headed back up the steps to start shooing Hazelnut.

"NO. NO. NO, POOPIES, NO!"

"Mom—no, not that newspaper." When I took a break from scouring the internet job boards, I liked to job hunt the old-fashioned way—with the newspaper classifieds and a pencil behind my ear. "Mom, I'm going to kill the both of you. Where is your son? Your son, Mom?" I pointed at Hazelnut. "Where is he?

Poopies is *his* dog, *his ex-fiance's* dog. I'm going to kill all four of you!"

I ran up the steps and slipped on the loose Saltillo tile. I screamed, trying to lunge far beyond myself so that I could fall on the carpet instead. "Nooo!" I caught my balance as my knees hit the floor, clinging to a downward dog position. Hazelnut calmly finished her pee, stared at my face, licked my nose, wagged her tail, and sauntered off. For all those foreign memories of flying east, it was like flying southwest had sent me back in time. Now I was fighting with my mother and brother again—my brother who wasn't even there but left us with the responsibility of raising his baby. It was like no time had transpired at all.

"Look, I'll tear this part off, okay?" My mother opened the newspaper and ripped off the top of a page. "See? The stuff you circled is still dry."

I gave up and fell to the floor, laying down on my back next to the pee, next to the paper, and next to the stress.

"Come on." She stood over me, waving toward the kitchen. "I'll make you a birthday breakfast, and we can go through these classifieds together. I can make you one of those vegan omelets you like."

"Thank you," I mumbled from the floor.

My mother walked back to the kitchen, sparking on the gas stove. I had a feeling that the gas stove was no longer up to the carbon monoxide codes. She shouted, "You got another job interview lined up though?"

I tried to breathe, staring at the popcorn ceiling where watermarks peeked through.

My mother glanced at me from the kitchen. "Oh, by the way, what is News School? Do they write about the news?"

Sometimes, my mother heard about savvy things on the "TVs," as she called it.

I gazed back down toward the kitchen. "Mother? It's pronounced 'New School,' and it just happens to be one of the most important institutions of our time, founded by philosophers, doctors, and the brightest minds of Europe—intelligentsia in exile, in fact—minds who were forced to flee their homes."

"Oh, okay. News School."

"No. New School. And they don't write about the news. Have you been watching another one of your Tom Brokaw specials again?"

My mother grabbed a pan above the stove and waved a spatula around with her next breath. "Oh no. It was on the envelope that came in the mail earlier with your name. Don't worry, I put it over here so Poopies won't get to it." She pointed to a kitchen counter. "What do you think they want?"

I jumped up and walked back down the steps and into the kitchen to grab the letter. "Probably to tell me my life is over. Another rejection." Most grad schools sent out acceptance letters for the fall by March 1 at the very latest.

"You never know." My mother handed it to me. I opened the envelope and took another deep breath of the stove's carbon monoxide, preparing for the millionth automated response—*We regret to inform you.* I had often considered that perhaps I'd already peaked like one of those Al Bundy high school football captains turned shoe salesmen. But, like Al Bundy, I would continue going through the motions, opening all my rejection letters one by one:

Dear Jessica Ann Puente,

It is our pleasure to offer you a spot in our two-year Master of Fine Arts Program. Congratulations, Class of 2012!

Silent, thick pools of tears began to flood my eyes. I knew that I did not deserve that acceptance letter. I thought that truly, just enough wealthy kids chose Princeton or Columbia instead and that my name automatically got bumped up the waitlist. Perhaps the whole automated acceptance letter was even printed, mailed, and stamped without one official university board member noticing. But I did not care. It took me three-quarters of a half second to decide to take it anyway. I would be honored to be the next great thing News Schools never even knew they had.

"Adding it to the others?" my mother asked.

For some reason, another move away made me think about my late Little Grandma. She had died two years before, on Mother's Day. When she'd died, I'd selfishly thought that at least she got to see me become a fully formed human being. I thought I had finally become the person I was meant to be. But one of the last things my grandmother said to me before she died was so uncanny it scared me:

"Ayyyee, *mijita*, I love you." She crooned over the phone in a hospital bed while I was lying in another bed two thousand miles away from the border in Chicago. It was three o'clock in the morning when my brother called from the hospital, handing the phone to Little Grandma for the last time.

"Don't worry about anything right now," I told her, half asleep. "Just worry about getting better, okay? I'll see you soon. I have a flight out in the morning."

But as usual, and even when she was dying, my grandmother was still thinking about me procreating. The last thing I remember her saying was, "*mijita*, please get married and have some babies."

"Jessi?" My mother continued from the kitchen. "Adding it to the others, I said?"

"No, not this time." My voice cracked from crying, but I couldn't help but start laughing. "Little Grandma would be pleased but disappointed about me leaving."

"What? What do you mean?" Her face fell, the frown lines suddenly visible. "You just got here. Okay, I can talk to Elsa today. Maybe there's something."

"I'm not getting married, and I'm not having babies. But I am leaving again, going up north. Unfortunately, Poopies will have to be enough for you right now."

THREE

A tall, thin man with sparse hair around his chin called out to me in a heavy New York accent. "Are you a model? I'm yow agent." He stepped out from a crowd of lanky men loitering and lighting their Camel cigarettes. "How 'bout I be yow agent, sugar?"

"Oh, hello, gentlemen," I snidely remarked, pulling along my two pink pin-striped suitcases and hauling them up the last subway steps. "No need to help me with my luggage," I struggled to say. "I'm sure we've all had a daunting week at work."

Kit's apartment lay in Crown Heights, a few blocks east of Brooklyn's Botanical Gardens, where the A and C train ran back and forth through the East River so often I never knew if the train had initially come from Brooklyn or Manhattan. The diverse, up-and-coming neighborhood reflected the tradition of my final Uptown Chicago neighborhood. However, there wasn't a homeless man cooking a can of beans below a tree by the front door of Kit and Sam's six-story brick building. Nor was there a defunct, boarded-up psychiatric ward down the street, where an assortment of half-dressed citizens gathered in groups smoking cigarettes at specific times throughout the day. And I did not see a dodgy ethnic market where all the cab drivers met during breaks. Yet a cluster of men stood under the trees in front of the building.

Kit had been leaning against the rod-iron fence casing her building. She ran toward my suitcases, her short, wavy strawberry blonde locks fanning away from her face.

"You made it," she called, grabbing one of my suitcases. "Shirley, you didn't tell me you were looking for a new agent. Your first day here, and you already got a job as a model."

I shot back at Kit, recalling the little nickname game we used to play in our old office. "Hello, Laverne. Wait, give me a hug first. You're the bestest friend a girl, unemployed, could ever have, thank you! And I'm going to make you some *carne guisada* for dinner. I brought you homemade tortillas because I cannot wait to be your live-in *Chef de Cuisine*."

Kit and I were often the last two misfits working late in our Chicago department at Applebaum & Kirk. When budgets began to dwindle, when profits plunged, and when annual raises were rescinded, we reckoned that our cushy life of luxury began to resemble that of a factory reminiscent of Laverne and Shirley. Customized tours were no longer customized but featured the same Rail Europe tickets, and titles of once exclusive tours changed from "private" to "semi-private."

"Isn't that just a wonderful way of saying that we're selling group tours now, like some Family Disney?" Kit had said shortly before she'd been laid off. It was a few months before my grand and tragic exit. Toward the end, when our former boss at A&K was on sabbatical—our term for her long and hot yoga lunches— we would open a bottle of Barolo sent from an Italian supplier or the dry sherry from a bodega in Andalucía's *Jerez de La Frontera*. I never fully understood why they aged the brandy and white grapes in American oak barrels, but I insisted it tasted better as we made our own maps of the world. "I think you can tell everything you need to know about a country from how the men greet you when you arrive," I'd say to Kit, and she'd start charting out sayings like '*Ciao Bella, aye,*' above Italy.

Staring at Kit's new building in Brooklyn, I pulled away from our reuniting hug. "And here I was, Laverne, expecting some whistles and catcalls as I cruised into my new life. *Pssshhh*, Chicago, such rookies. I'm a model now. New *Yaaawk*. Even the tawdry pickup lines are clever."

The sun began to set, and the crowd of men dispersed around us while we made a trail through them. "A'ight, you let me know, I be yow agent. Small cut, I'll only take a small cut, sweetheart."

"They're so funny," I told Kit as we threw the suitcases up the short steps leading to her entrance. "I missed my sexist big city cat callers and construction workers. Plus, it's good to know I have some options out here on the street, provided that my new job does not work out."

Kit halted her suitcase rolling and brushed her strawberry blonde bangs from her face. "How is that new gig coming along, and what are you doing exactly?"

Uh oh, not again, I thought, while avoiding direct eye contact. The worst thing you could ask an unemployed person was questions pertaining to their non-jobs. Crafting a reply felt as much about convincing myself as it was about convincing everybody else. I pushed my suitcase and rallied a response. "So far, so good. My contract got extended. I'm a top scorer for one of the world's most important and leading education scoring companies. They'll be sending me some remote work, too. I'll be on one of the first live remote teams," I paused. "Live international remote teams."

Kit opened her lobby door and tried to tightly fold in her lips. "Live international remote teams? As opposed to dead national remote teams? Nailed it." Her laugh clapped across the vaulted ceiling. "Look at you and your resume inflation. You don't need me. Although my friend's mom is hiring..." Kit's voice softened. "Anyway, you're going to do just fine and get along well with all the other New York City resume inflators." She continued her suitcase rolling. "God, Sam and I were at another event last night with this guy who kept talking about his IMDb page."

I smiled back with some relief. It felt good to have a friend who got it. "Thanks. I think it's starting to sound like I might have a plan. And graduate school sounds responsible to employers."

"Employers haven't gotten the memo that graduate school is just the latest hideout from the crappy job market?"

"Nope, apparently not. Also," I continued to mumble as my uneven suitcase wheels scratched against the tiles. "I saved my last unemployment check to settle in New York this summer."

Kit picked up the suitcase and dragged it through the lobby while I followed. "I have some bad news. I'll go ahead and tell you the *not*-so-bad news first."

"Hold on. Kit, where's your doorman?"

"Crown Heights is, well, there's no doorman. Unfortunately, in real life, Sam and I have discovered that even when two people work for a living, they do not end up in a place like Charlotte in *Sex and the City*. Who, by the way, did not really work for a living."

I stiffened. "But Kit, your neighborhood is titled 'Crown Heights.' That's false advertising." I glanced up at the paint chipping from the ceiling.

"Jess, we do not have a doorman. Crown Heights is up-and-coming, but maybe it'll finally be here in a decade. Possibly by the year 2020 or 2025. Also, we live on the seventh floor."

"We have the penthouse suite, then? Is that what you're telling me right now?"

"Yeah, I'm just going to start ignoring you now. We're on the seventh floor, and in New York, that's called a seventh-floor walk-up because, as you probably already know, we have to walk up all the flights of stairs to get to our unit."

I wrinkled my nose at her. "What about the elevator? A building this high should have an elevator."

"We certainly do have an elevator, but the thing about the elevator is that—" Kit glanced at her watch. "It's getting kind of late. So, right about now, it starts to smell like urine."

"Wait, what? You're joking, right?"

"I wish I was."

"It smells like urine because the men's restroom's next door?"

"No. It starts to smell like urine because, for some folks, it pretty much *is* the restroom next door."

"I'm confused."

"We are, too."

I followed Kit up the stairs. "Glad I didn't pack everything then." I struggled between deep breaths. "At least I gave you the light suitcase. I bet it feels light as a feather compared to my 49.9 pounds."

Kit, too, struggled between breaths. "How many pounds did this one weigh in at the airport?"

"49.1 pounds."

"Yep." Kit rounded the second floor. "Light, *eeeh*. As, *eeeh*. A Feather."

"God, remember when we could check as many heavy suitcases at the airport as we wanted to without paying for any of them? It seems like only a couple of years ago, I could pack my whole closet."

"That was only a couple of years ago, Jess. And I'm sure the airlines changed the rules thanks to you and your baggage."

"How is the seventh-floor walkup the *not*-so-bad news first?"

"Oh, right. Sam got a grant to finish his dissertation upstate this summer. So, we'll be in and out."

I froze mid-step with my foot hanging in the air. "No! I thought you were going to show me the ropes."

Kit stopped to look back at me between floors. "Jess, you got this. You've been to New York City how many times?"

"Duh, but that was to Manhattan for work and never as a local." I dropped my suitcase between the floors. "Are we there yet?"

"Not even close."

"I'm not going to see you guys much? Is that what you're telling me?"

"Yep, and we need a pet sitter."

I wavered to grab the railing and level my vertigo. Kit couldn't have meant me. "Okay, no problem at all. So, you just need me to leave a key out for the pet sitter, then?"

"Yes, we'll leave you a key, Pet Sitter."

"*Hahaha*, that's a good one."

Kit did not laugh back.

"Wait, what??" That was not what I expected her to say. It was beginning to feel like I was competing with pets for a place to live.

I took another step, sensing my arms turn numb. "You want *me* to be the pet sitter? But you have such a variety of pets, and I'm not a vet."

"Shirley, come on. Pet hotels are expensive in New York City. And it'll be like old times—us doing each other favors at work." Kit peeked down at me from the stairwell above while momentarily stopping. "Ya know? Like when one of us changed our flights to stay two extra nights in Monaco with an Arab Prince or *Sheik*, or whatever they call it, so we had to cover for her?"

I looked up. "It was the French Riviera. And we started in Monaco and ended in Nice. Anyway, let's be real. As long as you have *some* money in Saudi, they call you a prince. It's not that big a deal."

Kit threw her head back to emphasize her statement. "Oh, sorry," she mocked the sound of my voice. "I didn't realize they were referring to twenty-million-dollar yachts as just 'some money in Saudi.'"

I loved how Kit could make my life seem more impressive than it was because I was single and could go to more events. Yes, a handful of times, I met interesting people like the All Blacks from New Zealand, Andrea Bocelli, or a "prince" from Saudi. But the reality and lack of sleep were more or less the same: meetings, tradeshows, hotel inspections, all of which became more predictable with the same bottles of wine from Montepulciano or Champagne. Same, same, same. Europe would always stay the same. But my purpose for more would not. Toward the end, I wanted more, more, more. But what kind of more? Before I could answer that question, the rug was pulled out from underneath me. I felt punished for my lack of gratefulness because instead of more, I was suddenly cursed with less. I shot a pleading look up at Kit between floors five and six. "So, what's your point? That I went from twenty-million-dollar boats back to basically the border, with

Mommy and Daddy, and now to be your assistant, even worse, your pet's assistant? Noted. God has a sense of humor. My life does not have the same cachet that it once did."

Kit tsk-tsked her head left to right. "Jess, you're going to have the place mostly to yourself off the A and C train—q*uid pro quo.* You'll tend to the pets and check the mail. Sometimes, we get notices for packages." Kit got quieter, almost like a whisper. "You'll need to pick them up from the post office a mile down the street."

"*Umm,* are the packages big?" I flung my suitcase wide around the stairwell corner. "I feel like when you get in trouble in prison, they make you carry a bunch of packages and 49.9-pound suitcases up the stairs."

"*Your* suitcases, Jess. Focus. Free apartment mostly to yourself for the rest of the summer."

"Right. Focus. That's what Missy used to tell me."

"And…" Kit finished pulling the suitcase up the last flight in front of me, dropping the suitcase to the ground. "We're here!"

I reached the top of the stairwell, dropping my suitcase and my entire body across it. "Did you give me all the bad news? Please tell me there isn't more bad news?"

"That's it. For now." Kit pulled her keys out of her pocket to open her door. "Welcome to New York. The bad news comes in waves. Just when you think you couldn't get any higher than a kite living in this magnificent city—" Kit pretended to fly a kite in the air with her keys. "*Voila,* the kite abruptly takes a precipitous dive. There it goes—making its quick descent." She motioned her keys down, facing the ground. "Maybe the kite will make a soft landing into the Hudson or the East River."

I lit up. "Oh, yes, the Hudson River. I've always thought of myself as a West Side Highway kind of a girl, although I wouldn't mind the FDR too much. Both options have helicopter pads. As long as my beautiful apartment overlooks the water."

"Nope. Lands head first, smacking straight into the concrete."

"No! Why, why? The water was so close."

"Nope, not close enough. Too far away. Just far away enough for you." Kit pulled my luggage into the entryway as I followed.

"But we're thirty! I thought life was supposed to get better," I pleaded, trailing in the apartment behind Kit. "Everybody said life gets better after thirty. They said thirty is the best decade when you're old enough to be knowledgeable about the world but young enough to still have a great time navigating its ups and downs."

Kit closed the door. "And lastly, I'll need some help cleaning around the place, especially with the kitty litter."

My face turned to stone. I was grateful for the accommodations but resented the assumption that I was the maid. We made our way to the living room, stopping in front of the cats and turtle.

"The cats, as you know, love to jump on the aquarium." Kit brushed her hair back, putting her hands on her hips. "I cannot say this enough. Do not let the cats jump on the aquarium." Her hazel eyes grew big as if to preemptively reprimand me and the cats simultaneously. "The cats try to poke their claws through the hole at the top to get at Turtle."

The turtle's name was just "Turtle," which reminded me of Holly Golightly's cat named "Cat" in Truman Capote's *Breakfast at Tiffany's*. Although I did not have furniture to keep selling at that point, nor did I have fifty dollars for the powder room, fortunately, I'd acquired good friends throughout the years and cities I'd lived in.

"Hey." I peered through the tank. "What happened to Other Turtle? The smaller, slower one I used to talk to?"

When I'd visited New York City for fashion week a year before, Kit and Sam had just bought the two tiny turtles. They swam across from me and lulled me to sleep. I stared at them in bemusement as they swam in their temporary fishbowl. For some reason, the way the turtles swam fascinated me. While they appeared to enjoy wading through the water, that never stopped them from swimming vertically toward the surface and outside of their bowl.

"Other Turtle died," Kit said ominously. "Other Turtle died shortly after you left. You were the last guest to see him alive. He had pneumonia and was probably already sick when we got him, but then Turtle became dominant and ate all the food."

"*Huh*, are you talking about the one percent right now? Turtle, did I come to New York City just to work for you?" I glanced back at Turtle, who was delightfully swimming in circles—backstroking—through all his square footage of water. And I knew it was stupid, but as I stared at his arrogant splish-splash, something inside me felt genuinely sad for Other Turtle. I remembered his beady little eyes and that frightened look when I held him for the first time, too shy to come out of his shell: retreating, returning, retreating, returning.

"Earth to Jess," Kit snapped. "Are you still with me?"

"I'm sorry. I'm just tired from the travel day. I wish you had told me. I would have sent flowers."

"It's okay." Kit opened the aquarium lid and shook a little yellow can of Turtle's food in. "Turtles are probably fine together if, when you buy them from a pet store, they're older and they've been together for a bit. Those first two years are touch-and-go. Also, the more turtles you have, the more space you need. A forty-gallon feeder tank minimum, and a fancy filter because turtles are messy, two turtles even messier," she added, slamming the lid shut. "Now remember. Do not feed Turtle too much food. Otherwise, he'll keep eating and die."

"I hope you aren't foreshadowing, Kit. Anything else?"

***

Black and white cat hair covered Kit and Sam's couch at the start of the cool summer, and within a few weeks, the sofa became covered in my dark hair, too. Warm, large, and comfortable, Kit and Sam's old brown couch sunk in, often taking parts of me with it. My body fell between the crevices of each cushion, discovering new territory every time: a zipper clinging at my side, imprinting my skin; crumbs trickling in the cracks of my toes; cold quarters or pennies sticking to my feet. This scenario is acceptable if you're twenty years old—not thirty. I'd awake to the scratching noise of the cats—Ender and Zelda—thrusting pebbles at me with their hind legs from the kitty litter box beneath my feet. And in the middle of the night, on my way to pee, I'd also step into theirs.

"It's either you or me," Ender's yellow eyes and black tail balked at me first thing in the morning. The sun barely glared through the two living room windows across from me, but Ender managed to lie out on my arm, his dark mane soaking in the rays. I don't remember when, but eventually, he graduated to sitting on my head while I slept.

It was cruel, and I knew he knew what he was doing. Cats cannot talk, but they can communicate, like Hazelnut, especially when the four of us—the three of them and I—shared the one-bedroom Brooklyn flat with a couple that happened to leave for the weekends, leaving me responsible.

Each time I fed Turtle and the cats, I monitored the amount while wondering aloud, "Maybe I should measure it exactly with a tablespoon or something. What if Kit and Sam return and Turtle is dead? Cats are much easier. But my track record with turtles wasn't great, as Other Turtle had died after I was the last one to speak to him. How could I feed and take care of Turtle if I could barely manage to feed and take care of myself?"

I thought it was possible—perhaps time to accept—that I was behind schedule. My big city thirty-something friends were married with jobs, money, apartments, and pets. Me? I was starting a new job, going back to college, and crashing on couches. I wondered if I would ever hit the socially mandated milestones again and if it would be possible to catch up to those milestones after setback, after setback.

FOUR

Background noise vibrated through the phone receiver: *Tink. Tink. Tink.* It was the sound kernels of dry dog food make as they hit tin bowls. First slow, then fast. *Tink. Tink. Tink-tink-tink-tink-tink.* But it sounded like the kernels of dry dog food were hitting several tin bowls.

"I want to hear all about your summer," my flustered mother said over the phone. "But right now, I'm entertaining."

"Who are you entertaining on a Monday morning?" I placed my hand against the phone to order a cup of strong coffee for my morning commute. "Black, no room, please."

"It turns out we have had our hands full this summer too." My mother's voice faded as she addressed my father in the background. "Pour him a little more—honey—pour him a little more."

I paid the cashier and sipped the first grounds of caffeine that morning. "Mom?"

"Sorry. I was talking to your father. And, well, we didn't want to tell you."

"Didn't want to tell me what?"

"It's about Hazelnut."

My breath hitched. "Please tell me she didn't get run over."

"No, she did not."

"Please tell me she has her collar and tags." When I moved to Rome ten years before, our dog Rufus had snuck out of the house and never returned. If only they had put Rufus's collar back on after they had bathed him. He was a little black mutt, but my brothers had dyed the tops of his head an orange mohawk while the rest of his mane maintained a mangy black color.

"Hazelnut had her collar and tags." My mother audibly swallowed. "It was something else. It had happened before you left. That's why she kept, you know, going to the ladies' room in the house."

"What happened?" I pushed through the business suits on Lexington Avenue, wondering if the dog had a UTI or something. Did dogs even get UTIs? I wasn't sure.

"Hazelnut, she, she…" my mother trailed off to clear her throat. "She got knocked up."

Silence.

"Jess?"

Silence.

"Jessi? Are you there? Hello?"

Police sirens rang through my thoughts. "Mother, of course, she got knocked up. What did I tell you when I was back home?"

"I know, I know, you said to get her fixed, but I don't like stuff like that."

"Mother, getting spayed isn't like having an abortion!" I yelled while remaining stuck at the crosswalk between everyone else. "How many times do I have to tell you? It's for prevention."

"I know, but I don't like stuff like that." My mother sighed. "It happened, and she has delivered her puppies."

"What? She already had the babies?"

"Yes. Dogs are pregnant for a much shorter time, you know."

"I didn't know. But now that I seem to be learning everything about pets—" Horns honked at me as I became locked amid bikers and taxis. "Hey—I'm walkin' here!"

My mother kept going. "And the neighbors can't believe it because Lenny Kravitz lives in the wilderness with the coyotes, and they see him in the creek and on the street from time to time."

"Thank you!" I yelled, putting away my middle finger and returning to my mother. "Sorry, Lenny Kravitz moved to South Texas?"

"Oh, no. Lenny Kravitz is Hazelnut's, umm…" I could hear my mother muffle the receiver while talking to my father. "Honey, *come se dice?* What did Delores's grandkids call Lenny Kravitz? Baby's daddy?" I heard my father mumbling. Then, the kernels of dry dog food hit the tin bowls again. My mother unmuffled the phone. "Lenny Kravitz is Hazelnut's baby daddy."

I choked up my coffee at the corner of Lexington Avenue and Seventy-Second Street.

"He is part boxer, part bulldog."

"Okay, Mother. So, the dog's name is Lenny Kravitz? That's kind of funny but mostly wildly inappropriate."

"Yes!" My mother said with zest. I could see her sultry shoulders leaning in for effect. "He is black, and wild, and handsome, and everybody loves him, and he moves to the beat of his own drum. At first, he was infamous. We all thought he was Big Foot because he would show himself privately to different neighbors at different times throughout the night and day."

"Umm, he would show himself privately, Mom? You may want to re-phrase that story before you tell it again."

"But he would never show himself to everyone together publicly. At the neighborhood association meeting, we all decided that maybe if we were all nice to him and started offering him food, he would come out more so we could catch him."

"Your plan did not come to fruition in time for Hazelnut's sake."

"And so he did come out even more, but he's still wild and sleeps by the creek by the train tracks with the coyotes and the deer. But now we've grown fond of him, so we don't want the pound to take him anymore."

"Okay, Mom. I think I get the gist of it. All this to say that you're entertaining the runaway bandit that lives alongside coyotes from the wrong side of the tracks right now?"

"Yes. Since the puppies are starting to grow bigger—Hazelnut had six—we'll leave the backyard gate open for Lenny Kravitz, and he comes in to play and chase his children. Some of them are still breastfeeding, but some of them are already eating dry food."

"Is he paying child support?"

My mother laughed. "Silly girl."

"Poor Hazelnut." I sipped my coffee. "No job, and the single mother in this contingent workforce, showing up to the unemployment line with a litter of six babies."

"They are all different shades—*mulatto*," my mother described. "Some are dark brown, light brown, huh, and one is ebony..."

"Are we sure there isn't more than one baby daddy? That might help her unemployment case. Although, I'm not sure what the canine currency is for bones."

Finally arriving at my office building, I stepped aside, sipping the last of my coffee and resting my back against the red brick entrance. I finished the conversation as the rush hour crowds divided throughout the city. "I guess we're all taking turns living off your and Dad's baby boomer retirement."

"Huh, that's right. How has your other job been? You never even told me what you've been doing all summer."

I took a deep breath and prepared for my sales pitch. "Kit's friend's mom offered me another unique business opportunity. I'm working as a social media coordinator for a company called Last Chance. It's a luxury consignment boutique that sells gently used luxury fashions like Gucci and Louis Vuitton handbags, Hermès scarves, and Cartier jewelry. It's on the Upper East Side. I got on and off the Six, like J. Lo—"

"*Mijita*," my mother interrupted. "This whole time, you've been working at a pawn shop?"

"No, Mom—"

"I didn't even know they would have a pawn shop in such a nice place like Manhattans, with all the high risers."

I couldn't figure out which stung more: Calling home for support and never getting it because I was doomed to be upstaged by everybody else's four-legged pets turned precious grandbabies and now great-grandbabies. Or the fact that my mother could reduce my life even further from something I already thought could never be redeemed. "Mom, it's not like that. And they're called high-rises. You make them sound like bleachers at the high school gym. Missy says there's a lot of money in reselling expensive items on the internet now. It's not about the brick-and-mortar anymore. I'm writing and posting blogs on the company's Facebook and Twitter."

A couple of low barks in the background furthered my mother's statements. "But did you tell them that you have your degree?"

My mother and the degree.

I could write a three-hundred-page thesis on, "did you tell them that you have your degree?"

During the baby boomer generation, you simply had to get a degree. The degree could be from McDonald's University, but as long as you had a college degree, you could work at the plant, take care of your spouse and children's benefits, and retire after thirty years with a fat monthly check. You could become a wealthy real estate mogul, an actress, or the president. The "degree" that my mother was referring to was eventually equivalent to not even a high school diploma but a high school GED. A bachelor's degree was pretty much only worth anything during the recession if it said something like Yale, Oxford, or Princeton. That's probably why so many of us were going to grad school.

"Mom, they know I received my degree almost a decade ago, and I'm getting another one at 'News Schools,' okay? But it doesn't work like that anymore. Everybody has their degree now. Getting a bachelor's degree today is like graduating from middle school, except you get a piece of paper that imprisons you and your next of kin to a life of debt. Anyway, I'm going to be late." I looked at my watch and tapped my foot.

My mother exhaled a loud and sad sigh this time. "How much are they paying you? Are they paying you well, at least?"

"Of course," I said quickly. "I negotiated twenty-five dollars an hour." For only three days a week of work—information I did not feel necessary to volunteer. Last Chance had never hired a social media coordinator before, so they wanted to try it out on a part-time basis. My job did not come with a salary or benefits. It was a part-time hourly position—a gig, in other words.

"*Pos,* that's not bad. You can come visit us for the holidays then."

The last of the crowds thinned out. A sidewalk sweeper pushed me aside. "Mom, I just got to work. I'll have to call you back. Have fun with baby's daddy." I put my hand on the door of Last Chance.

"*Mijita,* wait."

"Yes?" I gripped the handle, pausing before making an entrance.

"Your father and I…we love you very much. And no matter what, we want you to know we are very proud of you. We have always been very proud of you."

My fingers fell from the door. My mother's sudden words struck me, and I could feel the distance of twenty states compress between us. A chill crawled up my spine, and goosebumps spread across my skin. I stared through the glass door of Last Chance. The morning sun shone through, blinding my view. But I could still make out the steep staircase and the top of the second-floor landing. It was another uncanny feeling. There are other currencies of wealth than money. My tight-knit circle of family and friends always surrounded me no matter where I went.

"I love you guys, too," I choked out. "And no matter what, I am proud of you all."

"And so is Hazelnut. She is very proud of you and loves you very much. Right, Hazelnut?" Hazelnut barked, "Woof, woof."

And, as if on cue, all the other puppies and Lenny Kravitz barked back too. "Woof, woof, woof, woof!"

"Aww, thank you. I cannot wait to meet all your new illegitimate grandchildren one day and Hazelnut's sancho. Anyway, I'm at work, so I must let you go."

"Okay, Jessi, one last thing, I promise. Conchita was on the news again. Did you know they're making her head of the Mayor's Global Council?"

"They're *WHAT*?! And who are they??" I huffed incredulously, in an octave higher than even my flute could play, as if I knew what the Mayor's Global Council was. I *didn't* know what it was. But I was pretty sure it was yet another tactic, some other city-wide initiative that aimed to identify my hometown as something else other than obese, like the Mayor's Fitness Council.

My mother didn't respond to my rather pointed question but instead responded in a way that suggested our conversation had shifted toward gossip. "*Fíjate*, can you believe it? I guess that's why she was trying to help with the sign at the airport."

My jealousy got the best of me. "So, because Conchita went to Mexico a couple of times to visit her grandparents before they died, she gets picked for a Global Council? Mom, *I am* the Global Council." I slammed my hand against my chest for effect, as if she could even see me. "I'm the one who has been around the globe, which I would think would be an obvious requisite for someone on the board of a Mayor's Global Council."

I tried inhaling slowly and gently, then counting backward from five.

My mother started eating what sounded like cereal. The thin cornflakes crunched between each adjoining phrase. "Maybe you should reach out to her, *crunch, crunch*. I'm sure they'll need global travel writers like you who are, *crunch crunch*..." My mother trailed off as she tried to understand and explain my life, which I could not yet do myself. "Travel writers like you who are...writing about jobs? *Crunch, crunch*. "Is your travel book going to be about all the jobs you've had in every city?"

I squeezed my eyes shut and rubbed my temples with my free hand. It's hilarious and tragic how your parents can sometimes put your life into perspective in a way you never can. After Kit had lost her job and kept going to grad school, her dad had said, "And at what point do you think you can simply learn by doing?"

At what point was my life going to make sense?

***

Old Money. My father's family was from it once upon a time, so I thought I could pretend to belong on the Upper East Side. That's all Old Money was anyway—pretending it was still coming in, while behind the scenes, you were a magician juggling a dozen deals with the bank, a cattle rancher, and some hunters to lease the ranch. Perhaps negotiating with a realtor to sell the last property. Then there's the fighting about debatably existent oil and mineral rights. And what about the new toll road leading into Mexico, shaving ninety acres off the ranch? How much will we get for that? Anything to swindle more money out of old, dying land assets that were never really yours but instead bequeathed by a Spanish King when that was still a thing.

"Misho?! Where are the shoes, the blue Manolos?" Lenore, a heavier-set woman I called Cruella, yelled as she did every other day when I arrived at Last Chance.

I could hear her screeching as I walked up the steep internal stairwell that stood between a Mexican Restaurant named Gringos and a pet shop named Pooch Patrol UES. Last Chance was located above both Gringos and Pooch Patrol UES, so foreign scents—both good and bad—whiffed their way up through the vents.

Neon pink wallpaper flooded the second floor of the boutique's interior while matching awnings surrounded the exterior. Both areas featured signs with a young cartoon brunette wearing black oversized Burberry sunglasses. The cartoon character's skinny arm held an oversized black classic Gucci handbag. Accessories always had to be bigger than the people who shopped at Last Chance because when you're rich, it's like you're poor again—you can't eat anything. Clearly, I started to fit in.

My antique desk stood in the middle of all the clothing racks. Hanging jackets and purses towered up alongside me. Sometimes, I would scare the customers as I suddenly emerged from between Goyard trunks and piles of hanging clothes. "Bwaaaaah!" a customer once yelled when they saw my elbow. "I thought I was here alone."

"Misho?! Where are they?" Mid-sixties, Cruella yelled in the cold as I arrived that morning. She purposely kept the temperature low. If you asked her about it, she'd rattle off some gobbledygook about lambskin leather and vintage attire. Preservation. Sure. But I knew it was really so she could don tattered old white fur coats. Her shoulder-length locks burned a glossy orange-red, a trend copied from her college-aged daughters.

But you can't buy class.

"I said, where are the shoes, Misho?"

"I almost done." Pink tape measure in hand, Misho, a nineteen-year-old Georgian immigrant, worked behind the display window mannequins. He was always there, arriving early and staying until after I left. "Double-check." Misho wrapped paper over the top of a pair of cerulean blue shoes. Finally, the lid. "Here, here are shoes." His hands trembled as he passed the familiar pair of satin stilettos with a crystal-encrusted square crowning each toe.

Misho's and my job was to measure each 'gently used' luxury item. Then, we'd add the dimensions, color, cut, designer, price, and other assorted details to eBay. Usually, Cruella needed us to namedrop in the description below the item as well: *Worn by Kate Winslet while filming Titanic. The actress has since said it was her favorite item on any film set; Sarah Jessica Parker and her mother tried it on while in the boutique last week. Unfortunately, it did not fit, but she said it was her favorite item. 'If only it had fit.'* I also had to teach myself Photoshop and HTML coding, while sitting on Kit and Sam's couch late at night. It angered Cruella that I didn't come fully equipped with such skills. Finally, I had to quadruple the store's website traffic, Twitter followers, and in-store purchases.

Cruella threw off a fur to throw on a vintage woolen Chanel jacket in charcoal with gold buttons from the Cruise Resort Collection. I should have known more about the Cruise Collection in luxury travel, the rich embarking on vacations to take a break from their winter; how sad the rest of us had to suffer. But we looked down on cruises at A&K because the consensus was that cruises were for lazy people. Our rich people were active, adventurous, and wanted to fully experience the destinations to which they traveled. "I still remember when we lost fifty-thousand dollars on Bill Gates' one-hundred-thousand-dollar safari to Africa," my old boss had griped about her heyday, before things like recession and digitization. "When you had to book a flight at a brick-and-mortar."

Cruella half-grimaced in my direction, checking the pockets of the vintage jacket. "Nice of you to join us. It's ten o'clock."

"Sorry?" I looked back and forth between Cruella and Misho. "My schedule says I start at ten o'clock every Monday, Wednesday, and Friday morning."

"Didn't my daughter tell you? In addition to your eBay and social media duties, you will also assist guests with trying on shoes and unlocking the dressing rooms at the cash register. Whatever they need."

"Okay, so I'll be working more hours then?"

Cruella's loud and evil laugh vibrated against the glass cases and unfinished wooden floors. "No, you will not be working more hours then."

And now, apparently, I was supposed to be working in retail because, despite what the president said, the recession wasn't over. Providing salary and benefits to employees while paying for two weeks of training and providing a technical support department was so late 90s. Now, companies hired you to be an Al Bundy shoe salesman, the social media coordinator, the web and graphic designer, the tech support department, and work the cash register while you were there for only THREE DAYS A WEEK.

I nodded quickly, swallowing the ball in my throat. "But uploading all the daily incoming merchandise on eBay is taking longer than anticipated, and now we're starting the website so customers can purchase directly from there, too."

"You are to use social media between customers. Got it?" She paused behind the glass counter containing gold Pearls, Chanel Camelia brooches, and Cartier bracelets. She removed her Prada bifocals for emphasis. "They…"

She paused again like she always did when it was super important. Except everything was super important. "They cannot catch you sitting down typing away and measuring while they are shopping. Understand?"

My life was feeling like déjà vu. Every situation I was in was still the opposite of what I expected. "Thank you. In between customers."

Cruella revisited the box of cerulean blue satin shoes with crystals again. Obviously, she needed to make sure they were still there.

I reconvened with Misho, stepping into his makeshift office behind the mannequins and display window overlooking Lexington Avenue. "Any new merchandise in particular?"

He tied a Hermès scarf around one of the mannequin's necks, responding in his deep Georgian accent. "I come in this morning, and she handing me those *Sex and City* shoes. She say, 'we have *Sex and City* shoes. We have *Sex and City* shoes.' Then she say, Misho, please add following description, 'worn by real Carrie Bradshaw, Sarah Jessica Parker. On *Sex and City* film."

Was her favorite item from *Sex and City* film," I continued mockingly. "Was her favorite item from any film set." I looked back at Cruella, opening, closing, opening the shoebox again. She picked up a rag, polished the shoes, caressed them, and polished them again. "Misho, those shoes have been duplicated so many times. What makes her think those are the original ones?"

Misho broke his concentration from his scarf knot. "Do not let her hear you say that."

"Okay, you're right. Those shoes were Sarah Jessica Parker's favorite item while filming on the set. They were her favorite item out of all the sets and films she 'as ever been on in dee 'ole wide world."

"No funny. Here, hold this." Misho handed me the pink Last Chance tape measure. He pulled the tape out and lined an emerald green Marchesa cocktail dress in neoprene fabric. "How many? How many?"

"Thirty inches. I hope it fits."

"Eh?"

"The mannequin? I hope the Marchesa dress fits the mannequin?"

Misho attended to the broken furnace lining the windowsill. A slab of plywood covered the top of the furnace, which had been repurposed for his desk. It sat littered with pens, pencils, a Kleenex box, and one of the store's two laptops. Dinosaurs, the laptops were the cardinal editions Steve Jobs ever made at his first Apple job. Neither we nor our computers knew how to do the things we needed to do, like write code and Photoshop.

"So that's it, then?" As he typed in the measurements, I threw the Marchesa cocktail dress over the mannequin.

"No. She also angry because we receive more returns yesterday."

"Customers are returning used items? Isn't that a bit redundant? I thought all sales were final."

"They complain clothes delivered from internet smell like restaurant and pets."

"*Ahh*, so they didn't order a side of *chimichanga* with Cruise Collection Chanel?"

The doorbell downstairs chimed.

"Never mind. I must start hustling."

An older woman with short golden hair slowly ascended the steps. She wore a navy pantsuit and carried the new Hermès Crocodile Birkin in rose.

"Hello, and welcome to Last Chance." I nervously straightened the wrinkles in my black blazer. "We have some beautiful fall finds. I'm happy to say we're one of the first stores in Manhattan with Chanel's vintage Cruise Resort Collection. You know…in case you're already booking…in case your assistant is already booking those New Year's plans."

She nodded at me without making much eye contact and wandered over to the jewelry cases. I felt like one of those annoying salespeople. I *was* one of those annoying salespeople.

Did this count for in-between customers?

Yes.

Finally, sitting at the antique desk on the other side of the store, I pulled up the new Twitter account. But here came Cruella, marching toward me as a thin woman with long dark hair and a Welsh accent began to speak behind her.

"Mother, the Goyards are on this side," the woman explained to the older woman carrying another Hermès Crocodile Birkin.

Cruella silently snapped at me in front of her body, barking urgent orders while trying to conceal her frustration from the customer. How inconvenient for her that she had to hide her natural behavior in front of others. She kept mouthing her red lips at me till finally I deciphered her miming and pointing: "Keys. Ladder. Now."

"My apologies to keep you waiting," Cruella explained. "We've been meaning to move the Goyards to the other side of the store. But we have so much wonderful merchandise always coming in, especially with the changing seasons. Please don't leave before seeing our vintage Chanels in black quilted lambskin and gold-plated hardware."

Grabbing the rickety orange ladder from the storage closet behind another mannequin, I followed Cruella toward a back shelf as she persisted, discreetly pointing out my path. The ladder creaked and shrieked as it opened. I held my breath, bracing for the first step.

"There they are." The woman pointed to the bags on a high shelf, playing with her Chanel Hollywood sunglasses. Cruella flickered a finger at me, gesturing up the ladder.

'*Which Goyard, which Goyard?*' Three centuries later, the rich were still fawning after luggage that was once for horse carriages. I slowly clutched the top of the leather bag, thinking, what is the name? What is the name of the print? Think, Jess, think. You posted it on the internets with Misho last week. Green? No. That's too obvious. Shamrock? Four Leaf Clover? Start with the designer first, start with the designer first.

"This is the Goyard leather handbag that we call St. Louis. It's the size large." I cocked my back to face Cruella and the guest but froze instead.

Our guest had entirely removed her sunglasses, and suddenly I recognized her, the Welsh accent, and the brown almond-shaped eyes staring at mine.

"Thank you, Jessica," Cruella said. "Handbags aren't T-shirts, darling. The size is large. What else? Never mind. Please forgive her, Ms. Jones; she joined us at the beginning of the summer. Do you prefer to be called Ms. Zeta-Jones or——."

"No problem, either is fine, thank you."

Our special guest held her arms out toward me as I attempted to politely hand off the handbag to her gracefully while stepping down the ladder.

Instead, I missed the last three steps: tripping, falling, and plummeting to the floor. I was nose-diving in slow motion, just like my whole life—everything always in slow motion. I kept plunging down, down, down to the ground. It seemed so far away—rock bottom—ever so far away—finally, a loud smack and a crack.

Instantly jumping back up, I pretended nothing had happened—*just kidding*! —endeavoring to save myself from the worst day of my life, one of the worst days of my life, the next worst day of my life—it was hard to tell at that point, as all the worst days seemed strung together, competing with one another.

"Chevron." I remembered. "This is the Goyard in the chevron pattern, Ms. Jones, Ms. Zeta-Jones. It has a wonderful pattern and fall color, but I'm sure you might find it festive for Christmas and St. Patrick's Day. We also have an emerald green Marchesa dress on the mannequin at the front of the store if you're interested in the greens, sorry, or emeralds, and, like, such as." I handed the chevron bag to Ms. Jones, Ms. Zeta-Jones, Ms. Whatever She Preferred To Call Herself. Attempting to assuage the awkwardness, I changed the subject. "*Zorro* is one of my parents' favorite movies. My father is Spanish, and my mother is Mexican."

Drip, drip, drip. Red. Drip, drip, drip, in every direction, red. Ruby red. Fresh. The color dripped from me like a broken faucet. No. A broken fire hydrant. It tasted like metal. Metallic. Iron. And the smell. Iron, no, copper, zinc, a penny. Drip, drip, drip. Blood poured to the floor, over Ms. Zeta-Jones's fingers, onto the Goyard, and all over Carrie Bradshaw's shoes—the cerulean blue Manolos and their crystals. Wait. When and why did Cruella put on the shoes I thought we were selling?

"Jessica, your nose. My Manolos. Your check, your paycheck. Ms. Jones, on Ms. Zeta-Jones' How could you—"

There it was, yep, her Jersey accent. And Cruella's real character. She finally stopped herself as she heard whom she really was to everyone else.

"Do run to the restroom *dahling*." Now, Cruella was British. Perhaps she thought adding darling elevated her Jersey accent. "To clean up that little knick of yours."

Ms. Zeta-Jones, on the other hand, failed to react. The actress did not act out any emotion at all. She stayed calm and frank, slowly and eloquently pulling a tissue out of her bag and wiping her polished, French-manicured hand. The tissue was conveniently waiting, carefully and strategically placed in the inside top zipper of her Birkin.

"No problem at all." She looked me in the eye, handing off the Goyard to Cruella without even looking at her. Cruella stumbled to grab the bag, bending down to her Manolo while holding out her hand, not knowing if she should wait for Ms. Zeta-Jones to give her a tissue, too.

"We all fall sometimes," Ms. Zeta-Jones continued. "It happens to the best of us. So long as you can still bleed and show signs of wear. Otherwise, I'd worry."

Her tissue. She gave me her tissue that smelled like roses, and perfume, and rainbows, and salvation. And I soiled it with another one of my failures. "Thank you so much," I mumbled. "I am sorry to have inconvenienced you."

***

After work, I stood under the awning of Last Chance, rifling around my purse and finally grabbing my cell phone to check the voicemails. First Missy:

"Hello, Pretty. I may have some news for you soon. I hope to visit you in N-Y-C this fall. Stay tuned and call me when you have some time. Love ya!"

Then Kit:

"Hello to my favorite pet sitter and house sitter in the whole wide world. It sounds like Sam and I missed you again. Sorry, we had hoped to see you more over this summer. But we also hadn't expected to enjoy our quiet time away. And I have some news. I wanted to tell you this in person. But I know you're busy with your jobs and school starting, so you haven't answered the phone. So here it goes. In exactly seven months, Sam and I will go from a family of five to a family of six."

I quickly counted Turtle, Ender, and Zelda, Kit, and Sam, then—

"That's right. We're having a baby."

A baby?

"Yes, a baby." Kit laughed in the recording as though she had heard me. "But okay…" Kit resumed with all the details from the other side of the phone, but what felt like a million miles away. Suddenly, there was a mountain of space between us as she spouted off the details about their lease, moving, a bigger place, and finally, what to do with me.

"I have some good news for you, though. Remember when you put your name on the waitlist for that fun hotel for women in Manhattan on Thirty-Fourth Street? You got an acceptance letter. Congratulations! I hope you didn't mind me opening it, considering that whole federal law thing, but I was so excited for you. Yay, I'm going to visit you in Manhattan! You always said you were a West Side Highway kind of a girl, and I hear they have a view of the Hudson. The letter says that most women stay at The Winifred for an average of three months. That'll give you enough time to find the right place."

It was six-thirty when I stepped out from the store's awning, joining the little Upper East Side world leaving work: guys in white overalls climbing down their ladders after spiderwebbing all the old buildings with scaffolds in preparation for their restoration; a dog walker and a poodle on the sidewalk where canines had adapted to going on the concrete; a middle-aged man in a ball cap dressed in New York Transit Authority blues.

And me.

All the little people behind the scenes pulling strings to turn the pretend world of wealth into reality, a trick unbeknownst to tourists.

The sky had faded into a dark sapphire, and hard raindrops slowly and sporadically settled along the dry earth. I pulled my red hood over my head but decided against it; I wanted to get wet. Passing the pet store, I noticed a few puppies in their cages slept while one in particular, a black fox terrier, ran in circles. It chased its tail and barked along with the lightning that flashed on and off like a light bulb, painting the sky white. Outlines of buildings lingered long after the flashes subsided while the rain continued to trickle. I did not take the train. I walked down the wet path on Lexington, finally going west on Sixty-Fifth Street to Park Avenue, then down to Grand Central Terminal. I took cover under awnings of various storefronts, high rises, and homes as the rain dribbled from rooftops, gutters, drains, and puddles onto my body and feet.

The rain was hard at first, but it felt good to be alone. To be soaked and alone. It felt good to decide to stop fighting. To accept that I was exactly where I was supposed to be. Exactly where I needed to be. I was happy for Kit. But a husband and a baby? Not for me. Not now, anyhow. While the steadiness of success may only come in waves—or never again—I knew I could still take comfort in certainty. The certainty that I was meant to be somewhere in between things. *In media res.* Latin for in the midst of things, in the middle of things. In the middle of *my* things. I didn't know what the future could hold, but if life was a series of hills and valleys, I figured I might as well set up camp in the valley and enjoy the journey, which started with relinquishing my frustration and expectations. I'd already had a brilliant past seeing the world and working in travel. Now, I had a couple of new jobs and was getting another degree in one of the best cities in the world. Maybe I had been looking down when I needed to start looking up.

After all, I suddenly had a new place in Manhattan. And I couldn't think of a better way to end the day than Catherine Zeta-Jones, blood on blue satin, and crystals. Tennessee and Botticino marble as I stepped into Grand Central Terminal. I bent back toward the ceiling like I once had when I arrived in Rome to study abroad. And then I thought of myself ten years before. If someone had shaken me and said that one day, I would trade the High Renaissance of Michelangelo's ceiling for a French Belle Epoque oil painter's ceiling in the West? In this same life? Never.

I stood momentarily, craning my neck farther back as if I could ever truly reach the stars above. Spinning and soaking wet, I soaked up the sky. I marveled at the antique green star atlas and considered the infamous accident: Fashioned in 1913, the plaster mural was initially painted backward, West facing East and East facing West. Even the famous Orion was in the wrong spot at the wrong time. It, too, would fall apart, the plaster chipping away until the masterpiece would finally be made anew in the mid-century.

I dragged my feet forward, hoping my renovations would not take quite as long.

FIVE

I thought my heart would hurt more to leave my last two hundred dollars until payday as a thank-you for Kit and Sam's generosity over the summer. But it felt so good to do. I turned down the lights and said goodbye to Turtle, Ender, and Zelda. I grabbed some blank stationery on the entryway table.

Dear Kit and Sam...

I chewed on the end of the pen. Being a good person and demonstrating thanksgiving was harder than it seemed. A few voices echoed through the hallway, and I pressed the pen back to the paper.

I didn't know what to expect when I arrived in the city, but you two gave me a couch to call home, a place to land back on my feet, and another chance. I'm so grateful for my first gigs in the city, even if they were simply house-sitting and pet-sitting. I hope to repay you one day, but for now, here's a little something for groceries or Baby. Congratulations, by the way! I can't wait to meet her. And who knows? Maybe one day she'll be pissed at you, and I'll have a couch for her to crash on too.

Love,

Jess

***

An acrid smell of several coats of white paint overwhelmed me as I walked into my new 115-square-foot Winifred "guest room." Inside the tight space sat a two-shelf bookcase, a twin bed, a desk, and an odd sink with a mirrored medicine cabinet. But outside my window, the world opened up. Crowded skyscrapers hung above my bed like a living picture frame chronicling the changing days: steel frames against colorful faded bricks, mixed metals, and glass windows. Wooden water towers stood on rooftops, and clouds of white smoke rose from sewers and networks of pipes along the streets and buildings.

The city's newness juxtaposed the antiquity I'd left behind in Italy. If a third of my life had already been lived, I hoped I would eventually become like one of those significant old buildings I'd left behind in Europe comprising grand additions from every era— ancient Greek, Roman, Gothic, Renaissance. Unemployment was one of the many influences that would build the story of my life. Just a step, not even a whole staircase, a floor, or a hallway—but it could help contribute toward a grand building. Without unemployment, my life would not have abruptly stopped, tail-spinning me around in a different and opposite direction. I knew that there had to be a clue somewhere. There just had to be some providential reason my life had turned upside down.

"There was a Mr. Winifred. In fact, there were two," read one of the yellow forms we received during our tour of The Winifred after the hot and sticky summer.

"Follow me, Winifreds," said an older woman with frizzy gray hair and a walkie-talkie around her waist. "As you can see," she pointed to a tag on her breast, "my name is Agnes." She handed out laminated nametags with a pin. "Please find yours, then pass around the rest. You will need these upon every arrival."

A group of ten of us filed in a jumbled line—the mother hen's newest little chickadees. Tick-tock went the antique grandfather clock as we entered a stuffy mahogany library overlooking Thirty-Fourth Street.

Agnes pointed to a portrait of an elderly aristocrat sitting above a fireplace lined in brass finishes. "William B. Winifred—ahem," she coughed to clear her throat. "And his brother were the first cousins of Rowland H. Macy, the senior partner of R.H. Macy and Co., as in Macy's, the famous department store down the street, and Macy's Thanksgiving Day Parades. When William B. Winifred died, he willed his entire fortune to build apartments for women." She pointed to a quote published in a July 1922 article in *The New York Tribune*. "'The apartments shall not be conducted for profit but solely for the purpose of providing unmarried working women with homes and wholesome food at a small cost to them and, in deserving cases, without cost to them.'"

I didn't believe my twelve hundred dollars a month in rent for a 115-square-foot guest room was at a small cost, but whatever.

Agnes fiddled with her beeping walkie-talkie while regurgitating the last of Mr. Winifred's regal magnificence. Escorting us to the front desk, she waved her hands at a wall of 1920s mailboxes with tiny keyholes and peek-a-boo windows. Then she waved at the sign-in desk, where a Caribbean man supervised guest check-ins. "We believe in romance and traditions of the past. True to times of courtship and waiting for the right gentleman caller to arrive, men still aren't allowed past the first floor."

A devious smile accompanied the gentleman's hand wave in an almost perfect illustration of a fox guarding the henhouse. And then I felt a punch in the gut. To go back in time to the starting line meant I was much farther behind Kit than I previously thought.

"But Winifreds," Agnes emphasized her next statement with an index finger triumphantly waving in the air. "Keep in mind that men can join you in the first floor's Greta Garbo and Marlene Dietrich-themed alcoves. They were once used as beau parlors—a place for wooing potential suitors. Also," she paused, us coming to a halt at Greta Garbo's pencil-thin eyebrows. "The ballroom is to the right of this hallway, and the practice room is to the left. While not as famous as The Barbizon, where other names like Rita Hayworth, Grace Kelley, and Joan Crawford lived as rising stars, The Winifred's accommodations are similar to such hotels for women built during the turn of the century…" Agnes suddenly paused again. "Is there a problem, Jessica?" Her breath made it across a few Winifreds until it hit me.

I clutched my backpack tight and froze at her sight, eventually surrendering to my obvious grimace. "Oh, you know—the beau parlors. Just wondering. Is there a curfew, too?"

A few of the Winifreds that seemed Missy's age laughed at the preposterousness of it.

"You have until midnight in the beau parlors," Agnes quipped in a stern tone, turning another knob on her walkie-talkie. "Got it? Men will need to leave by then, too. Anything else?"

Her last words felt like another reprimand.

More Winifreds laughed at each other and whispered about their internships, fashion week, and their late schedules. "Midnight? Dates don't even start until then. This is New York. The city that never sleeps."

"Winifreds, shush!" Agnes snapped her head at us. "Once the tour concludes, you will not get another. Now, let's resume."

Passing the mirrored walls, I marveled at our next stop near two early twentieth-century telephone booths with a blue bell logo and white wings emphasizing 'Long Distance Telephone.'

Agnes cleared her throat again. "A ninety-year-old red brick building with limestone bordering, construction of The Winifred was put on hold during World War I, finally opening its doors in November 1923, three years after women gained the right to vote."

She pointed to framed photographs of women in white floor-length dresses—one or two in polka-dots. I got lost in their distinctive flower pins, which I'd also discovered at Last Chance. The pins recalled the famous Chanel Camelia brooch, a trend duplicated and resurrected for generations. The Winifred was not the only artifact that tied us, the women of the past and the present, together. When I stared at the photographs, I felt like a copycat of a copycat, finally assessing the original.

"Winifreds, it will be tight, but try to keep up." Agnes punched the elevator button. We crammed in shoulder-to-shoulder, the aged elevator dragging us higher as its heavy weight jolted us together. "With thirteen floors and three-hundred-seventy-three single-bed guest rooms, The Winifred's most beautiful asset is its rooftop terrace overlooking Manhattan north, south, east, and west."

The sun's early fall glow emanated across the city like a spotlight, so no matter how broke you were when you checked in, here was your hopeful, million-dollar view. Red, white, and blue luxurious cruise ships slowly trudged through the Hudson River. Inhaling, then exhaling, I smelled a calming aroma of freshwater mixed with saltwater. If I stared at the sky long enough, the ends of the earth appeared to bend into a sphere along with the surrounding towering buildings, their sharp edges fading into the softness of the clouds above. Later, I'd watch the One World Trade Center under construction in the same spot—the southeast corner—where other women no doubt watched the original World Trade towers piling up—and then sadly falling down. The Empire State Building and the iconic New Yorker Hotel's bright red sign were closest on the horizon. I imagined them both lit up for the first time.

The views below differed. I noticed transient, graffitied blocks near a developing area called Hudson Yards. Thirty-Fourth Street appeared to sit between another one of those "up-and-coming" areas between Ninth and Tenth Avenues. Once again, I thought of my own transitional life and how I, too, stood in between things.

I raised my hand. "Are we in Chelsea, Hell's Kitchen, Midtown, or all three?"

Agnes stretched her legs, leaning down to pull up the white stockings that failed to reach above her knees. "The dividing line, the end of Chelsea, is Thirty-Fourth Street. But technically, the heart of Chelsea is the Twenties and Teens. Hell's Kitchen starts at Thirty-Fourth Street but doesn't *really* start until the Forties."

A brief east wind nipped at my naked shoulders. I surveyed my surroundings, noticing an adjacent black building Agnes pointed to where 1930s rowhouses once stood. Below, the traffic and pedestrians were amassed near The Winifred's entrance, where an American flag hung over its doors, a prominent symbol of freedom, equality, and hope.

"Did you see her?" One of the young interns whispered and discreetly pointed while I tried to breathe over her perfume with strong hints of peonies and lily-of-the-valley. "Gloria? In the elevator?"

I followed the intern's pointing finger, where a woman with wrinkly leathered skin, silver hair, and aviator sunglasses sunned on a lawn chair. She wore a black biker jacket with extra zippers and swigged a tall boy in a brown paper bag while balancing a cigarette in the other hand.

"Her family just dropped her off one day, never to return," the intern said. "She once had sex with Mick Jagger. She tells everybody that."

I couldn't wait for the interns to experience setbacks. Feeling a sudden solidarity with this older Gloria, I chimed in. "Everybody once had sex with Mick Jagger. He tells everybody that."

"Winifreds!" Agnes snapped again. Her spit flew through a piece of frizz floating in front of her face, along with the wind. Then, her eyeline followed ours until it got to Gloria. "Ms. Gloria Grace…" Agnes waited, scratching her head. She advanced closer to the corner of the rooftop so that her round, bloated belly was comically aligned with Gloria's head.

Poor Gloria. She seemed so lonely and sad. When life doesn't go as planned, there are detours. When life really doesn't go as planned, there's Gloria. But she was unphased and mechanically took another drag of her cigarette at the speed of a snail while a thick pile of ashes lingered at the end.

"Ms. Grace, I hate to ask again." Agnes widened her stance, her orthopedic shoes sliding against the concrete roof. She lowered her head. "But please abstain from throwing your cigarette butts on passersby below today; The Winifred thanks you." Agnes fanned away the loose frizz still falling on her face. "As you could have guessed, there has been discussion of no longer permitting rooftop cigarettes, so I'm sure your cooperation would go a rather long way."

A few chaotic car horns cried out as an ambulance siren neared. Gloria took another drag as more ashes accumulated at the end of her cigarette. Then, she blew a puff of smoke into Agnes's face.

Rooted in her etiquette or "traditions of the past," Agnes kept her composure. Her eyes remained closed. She held her breath. Until she finally spoke. "Very well, then." Agnes resumed her steps toward us. "That concludes your rooftop tour, Winifreds. Our final stop is down below in the dining hall. Remember, your boarding includes two meals daily: breakfast and dinner. If you prove that work keeps you from dinner, we will pack a lunch bag for you instead. But again, that must count as your second meal of the day. You must make arrangements no later than six in the evening prior."

Gloria, as I would later learn from rooftop jaunts, was loud—nonstop loud. Her voice sounded deep and crackly like someone who'd either spent a great deal of her life smoking or else a great deal of her life yelling over the speakers at concerts. Her presence on my first day's Winifred entrance was a wake-up call: We were all either the lifers or the potential lifers. The sentiment later became punctuated by high-pitched screeching sounds in foreign yelps from another Winifred. After sustaining more screeching yells one day, I finally decided to call the front desk. "Okay," they relented. "We'll send somebody up. You're on the sixth floor, right?" The very calm monotone of the voice indicated that the screams were routine-as-usual. And then I wondered: is this what happens when we don't hurry and partner up with one of those gentleman callers in the beau parlors?

When I first checked in to The Winifred, I thought they "temporarily" housed students interning in the city or graduate students starting classes for the first time, as well as young women from all over America and from around the world who'd moved to New York for work. The Winifred website said that accounted for seventy percent of their occupants. However, after just a few days of occupancy, I discovered that welcome mats and wreaths decorated some guest room doors. I learned some women called The Winifred their home for years—troubled women like Gloria whose families did not want them or did not know what to do with them. And here I was, suddenly one of them.

SIX

I knew I was meant to be in between things, but somehow, everything still felt off—or maybe I was off: my bank account, jobs, housing, and school—especially at my age.

The New School buildings stood on Eleventh and Twelfth Streets in lower Manhattan. I'd read in a guidebook that the building with black brick and steel stripes was designed in the mid-century modern style by renowned Austrian architect Joseph Urban. Such features reflected the tradition of art-deco and the Secession movement of his home country. The inside housed the famous egg-shaped Tishman Auditorium—the supposed inspiration for Radio City Hall. The building was an abstraction of Urban's entire life influence and seemed to borrow from the past and present.

Rows of windowed classrooms faced Eleventh and Twelfth Streets while the two buildings were linked from behind by a walkway above an intimate courtyard. The tall courtyard trees had already started shedding their red and orange leaves. And since many windows were open, you could hear a faint sound like thin foil crunching as the leaves swirled around and off their branches, finally mingling around the concrete below the trees' feet.

Inside, a handwritten sign was tacked to a corkboard by the elevator:

Again, this is a university-wide policy. There is no smoking in the courtyard. Our faculty have offices in the basement, and the smoke is circulating through their vents.

I sat at one of the long rectangular white desks, creating a grand square at the center of the classroom so students could face each other during the workshop. The remaining rush of students trickled in from that courtyard: hipster millennials dressed in throwback attire—90s nose rings and round, iconic John Lennon sunglasses with blue reflective lenses. Butt-length Brady Bunch hair. White shorts with midriff tops. It was an Urban Outfitters commercial. I felt awkward in my black business-casual Banana Republic dress. Still, I had spotted one or two Generation X'ers on the first day of class, which I discerned from forehead wrinkles and their more conservative attire of button-down polos and lighter cashmere sweaters. Perhaps some of us still had jobs, I thought. Perhaps their companies were even paying for their graduate education.

I felt as though I did not belong to either group.

Seated at the head of the class among fifteen students was Professor Cavaliere, a short and stalky Italo-British New York transplant with dark eyes and a bald, shiny head. After several wasted minutes of class discussing attendance and handouts, Professor Cavaliere lectured on Russian short story writer and playwright, Anton Chekhov. The lecture was about being a writerly writer, and if there's a gun in Act I, it will go off at some point. Finally, it was time to discuss our own short stories. We were assigned a writing exercise during which we had to write about 'disparate' parts of a home.

"Lastly, and before we get started," Professor Cavaliere said, scratching his chin. "Please do remember the tenets of the workshop. We respectfully refer to the author but remember that the author should rarely comment on their work during the workshop."

It was my turn to share my story, but I wished it weren't. During our first couple of classes, I'd learned that students at The New School were interested in writing intensely private, personal essays on weighty topics like abuse, sex, and family members who were inappropriately avuncular. But I could only manage to write comedy.

"So," my cohort Allie scowled as I recalled her smoking pot with a small group in the courtyard. She wore a tiny diamond nose ring on her left nostril, and the top half of her wavy mane was stark black, with the bottom a burnt orange. "Some of us were discussing your piece before class, and we, like, noticed that the mother used the word," she stopped to air quote, "'*mulatto.*' And I was deeply offended that you would use that word because I'm like half-black and half-white. People usually overlook my biracial background due to my lighter complexion. But anyway, I, like, couldn't take anything you—sorry, 'the author'—wrote seriously after that because I was so offended."

I wasn't sure what to think. Was Air Quote Allie telling me, one of the few minority women in the class, how to be politically correct when writing about race? "I understand what you're saying," I said, breaking the workshop tenet of speaking on my behalf. "And it wasn't my intent for the character to offend you. Hazelnut is a dog with golden fur who had puppies with a stray dog named Lenny Kravitz in the neighborhood. As a result, the mother referred to their babies as *mulatto*. *Mulatto* is a Spanish word for mixed-race."

"Yeah, about that." John—a tall, pale kid with thin, black-rimmed eyeglasses—chimed in. "You, like, said that Lenny Kravitz sexually assaulted Hazelnut."

Oh no, I thought. Not again.

"Sexual assault has such a strong connotation. What if someone in your audience has been, like…you know…and, like…by a black guy? Are you proposing that all black, excuse me, African-American men are criminals and sexual offenders?"

"I understand your concerns," I continued. "The story's title is *Hazelnut and The Tramp*…it was a play on the original *Lady and the Tramp*…But these things don't always have a happy ending. And Hazelnut is a naughty dog. If only she had a job…I was simply writing a warning. The contrast of black and white in Hazelnut and Lenny Kravitz was simply a semiotic reference to good versus bad…"

I was only digging my hole deeper. Suddenly, I was the racist old white male chauvinist in the room.

"Hold on a second." Air Quote Allie badgered again. "So, it was Hazelnut's fault she got sexually assaulted? Like she was asking for it because she was 'naughty' and snuck out of the house?"

"Thank you for your comments," Professor Cavaliere jumped in. "Let's keep our constructive criticism focused on the writing. With that said, I can see where both sides are coming from, and the author does need to consider their audience." Professor Cavaliere's eyes looked at mine. "Who is the audience, by the way? In what genre are you working?"

"Sorry?" I played dumb. It worked at first. Those crackling leaves in the courtyard grew louder as students stepped over them between classes. I leaned in again like I couldn't hear my professor over those loud crackling leaves.

"Your genre?" Professor Cavaliere repeated. "In what genre did you say you were working?"

"Oh. Right. Sorry. My genre. In what genre am I working?" Repeat the question, so I have time to stall. And make sure the question doesn't end with a preposition. "In what genre am I working? Here. At New School. On this cool fall evening. In late September 2010."

"Right," Professor Cavaliere asserted.

The class looked at me, waiting. I took inventory of all the trendy heads staring at me with piercings and sleeve tattoos—one or two with shaved heads—a guitar player with long crimped hair and a beanie, and finally me. Me. I was the outsider. Why did I have to wear this classic red lipstick, I thought. Why didn't I dye my natural dark wavy locks into that edgy ombre hair with black roots and orange ends? And where was Missy when I needed her? She was good at translating my words and thoughts to these young hipsters. If only I could've returned to my old job where I belonged, with my generation.

"Didn't you say on the first day—" Air Quote Allie said in another accusatory tone, flipping her hair and pointing her pen at me as if she were the prosecutor and I the defense. "That you write travel and nonfiction? So why does this piece read more like chick lit?"

"Yeah." John joined as her co-counsel. "And you know, chick lit is like a dying genre. Also, many publishers and industry experts refuse to use the term anymore."

"Ugh, I know," Air Quote Allie said. "O-M-G."

That was the first time I'd heard anyone use the text message acronym instead of 'Oh my God.' She was literally speaking to me in a text message. Should I communicate back to her in a text message? "I-R-L," I said.

But Air Quote Allie and John kept up with their prosecution instead. "Chick lit is not P.C. It demeans women—we are not chicks, and we desire more than writing about, about…" Allie searched hard for her next words. Then, she used more air quotes. "It inspired that 'classic' politically incorrect series."

"*Sex and the City*," John said enthusiastically. "I know. Umm, hello, feminism? Women are more than chicks, and yet their work is still reduced to men and sex."

"The author needs to seriously consider editing Lenny Kravitz and Hazelnut's characters." Air Quote Allie pointed her pen at my pages, then looked me directly in the eyes. "This is casually racist."

The classroom seized in silence. Heads nodded at me for a response. Casually racist? Was that a new phrase? Maybe my peers were right. If anything, I found comedy in how baby boomers could sometimes boil everything down to a stereotype. Leaving out that nugget of characterization to avoid offense in the present would've been inaccurate, but were we to rewrite history? I had no idea how this conversation led to where it did. I thought I would receive helpful editorial tips on structure and grammar and perhaps ideas on where to pitch the story next. Maybe a publication credit would lead to a job, but I wondered if I would ever work at a real job again or if I would just keep going back to school with these kids.

"Okay, that's enough. Let's get back on track." Thankfully, our judge intervened. "Remember, we want to keep our focus on the writing."

I cleared my throat. "The class is right, sir."

Professor Cavaliere leaned in, one arm resting on another as he scratched his head and cuffed his chin in an oh-dear-what-is-she-about-to-say-next gesture.

I proceeded. "A white supremacist patriarchal society forsook Lenny Kravitz. That is the lesson, the moral of the story, that I was trying to get at but could not articulate as eloquently as my peers. Also, Hazelnut's mulatto babies should respectfully be referred to as mixed-race. And Lenny Kravitz should have visitation rights and not go to prison with all the others—I mean, he should not go to the pound."

"We should go ahead and end it there. I'm afraid we're running out of time. Miss Puente, there's some good writing here, but I think keeping your audience in mind might help. Also, the genre in which you are writing is known as 'commercial women's fiction.'"

"Thank you, sir." I could still feel the sting the moment my cheeks flooded from light pink to dark red.

Then, a low, soft, formal, yet stern voice spoke. "Sir, may I add a conjecture to the lovely Miss Puente's work we have had the pleasure to discuss this evening?"

In unison, the class shared the same look of confusion, as it was pretty much agreed upon that I was an idiot. What more was left to say?

We bent our heads away from our backpacks, the floor, the desk, and to the back of the class. Huh. It was Colette. My literary crush. Her minimalist writing of sophistication and grace spoke to every heart and soul. She was the lone black student and Generation X'er, hailing from Connecticut by way of the Caribbean. She typically sat against the wall outside the workshop square in her preppy Polos, often accentuated by her thick, short dreads crowned with salt and pepper roots.

Professor Cavaliere coughed into his fist. "Colette, it's been a while. We'd love to hear from you. Final remarks, please. The night is getting on."

"Thank you. If I may add my sentiments to Ms. Puente's work…" Colette shuffled through my pages and leaned forward. "There appears to be symbolism and contrast between the lightness and darkness here, a literary detail we often do not enjoy witnessing in present-day comedy. And the semantics of chick lit or commercial women's fiction is irrelevant where money is to be made."

Stunned, everyone froze and did not return to packing up their bags. They listened while all other sounds and smells outside our windows ceased. The trees in the courtyard stopped swaying, and the leaves stopped crackling. The circulating smoke disappeared as if the whole university listened while Colette spoke.

"If I may, Chekhov is a 'writerly writer,' as you say, sir, but everybody got to pay the bills. Commercial is where it is at. There would be no high culture without the low culture, the mass appeal of the latter funding the loftier luxury of the former, sir. And if we are taking the light-hearted humor of Ms. Puente's genre into consideration, then we would not expect this piece or other pieces in the genre to be the answer to the next civil rights movement." Colette flipped another page. "And as far as naming goes, the author can work on that, but Lenny Kravitz sounds realistic. We had a housekeeper from Cuba that my father kept calling Mexican. He said she spoke Mexican too."

The class snickered, including me. I envied Colette's frankness. Did she have a more delicate nature that kept her shielded from accusations of casual racism, or was she simply allowed to say certain things the rest of us weren't?

"That is a good point. Anything else before we depart this evening?"

Colette dropped my pages and pursed her lips. "*Sex and the City* just needs a little more color in it. Otherwise, it is alright."

Everyone laughed, including the professor. The courtyard trees and the freshly sparked joints rustled again as if on fire. Colette was an old soul in the wrong time. Her conservative clothes, distinctive hair, and perfect diction *sans* contractions wore well.

Colette. Colette. Colette, Colette, Colette. My new bestie who gets me. I couldn't wait to get to know her.

***

After returning to Penn Station, I exited out the north side of the building, near the corner of Seventh Avenue. Up, up, up the steep escalator. Finally, cell phone service. Another voicemail: Missy. I couldn't wait to tell her about my new bestie Colette.

"Jess, guess who's on their way to New York City? *Moi*. Without telling you, I put myself on The Winifred waitlist a few months ago. Maybe it was wishful thinking that I'd get a job there and join you. I honestly thought that if I planned for it, you know, that it would happen. That's what you would do. You always told me never to get complacent with the strip clubs and Girl Scout Centers in Nowhere, Texas. Here I come, Big Apple! I'll tell you more later, but basically, someone dropped out of this position at Tilly that started earlier in the month. Okay, I need to go because I'm being summoned at the non-job I have now, which I literally must keep until the day I fly to New York at the end of the month. I heard I get two free meals daily at The Winifred with my rent. Maybe we can meet for dinner or breakfast or something? I heart you and

New York. The Great Recession is over, biatch. Jess and Missy take the town!!! Byeee."

Missy's voicemail was all things good and all things bad in the world. I worried I'd oversold the city. I felt like a big sister who needed to protect my younger sibling. The city wasn't going to be everything for Missy that she needed. But what if it was? Maybe she had finally landed her dream job with Tilly. No matter what, I told myself, I couldn't—wouldn't—let the disaster of my twenties and early thirties tarnish her experience. Keep it positive. Keep it upbeat. I would be a positive and protective big sister: The Winifred is the best, what an incredible opportunity, the city is fantastic, yadda, yadda. I'd tell her that when we met.

SEVEN

Sitting up on my cardboard bed, I rubbed my closed eyes in circles with my fists. The familiar screeching yells in a foreign language called out to me, or was it in my sleep? No. There was something else going on.

Boom. Boom. Boom—the noise had been in the middle of my foggy dream, in which I had learned from a doctor in Czechoslovakia that I had something called Helen's Disease, or some made-up Cronin's Disease, or some other random disease my subconscious had cooked up in my sleep because I had recently developed dizzy spells in my waking life.

I jumped out of bed, pulling a clump of hair from my head that had started falling out from all the stress.

Boom. Boom. Boom. My body involuntarily flinched with the noise as I tried to level my vertigo—the trashcans. The one guy allowed upstairs came to empty the four trash cans on the opposite ends of the hallway every morning. It felt like his real job was to bang the trash cans against the wall over and over and over again. The towel I had placed against the opening along the bottom of the door at night did not help to muffle the sound.

Boom, Boom, Boom.

Looking at my eyes in my little mirror above the sink, I realized that The Winifred was not like it was billed on the internet.

Or maybe New York wasn't like it was billed on the internet.

Or maybe I wasn't like I was billed on the internet.

It had only been a couple of months, but my stay at the temporary women's residence felt permanent.

At least I finally had something to look forward to. It was October 1—the day Missy was taking over a new position from someone who had unexpectedly quit.

I got dressed and took the elevator downstairs to the dining hall, where I ordered breakfast. Like the lifers, I had my usual spot in the dining hall. I sat in a hidden corner in the back of the basement, beneath Dyer Avenue, and unloaded my brown tray with white plates of oatmeal, fruit, and coffee.

Footsteps neared me, and a familiar voice squealed out. "Jess, I made it!" Missy's blue eyes sparkled. Her radiant, girl-next-door grin brought a smile to my face. "You were easy to find. Nobody back here in the corner by the window."

"Missy, I've missed you so much. I cannot believe I'm seeing you. Here. At The Winifred. In the flesh."

Missy threw her red Tilly Worth bag on an empty chair. I opened my arms and hugged her tightly, her black cashmere sweater warming me up. For a moment, I didn't want to let go. I inhaled her fresh Herbal Essence hair, the smell of a little sister I'd never had.

"Sorry. I was supposed to call you when I got in last night, but it was so late." Missy released herself from my suffocating embrace. "Umm, Jess, where are you?"

"What do you mean? I'm right here?"

"No, like, where is your body? You're so skinny. You used to be curvy. No more tortillas? Gosh, even in all those layers, you look so thin." Missy finally let me go while her eyes moved up and down my thighs. She stared at me like she was trying her hardest to withhold judgment. Finally, she said, "anyway, I have to hear all about grad school and your fabulous new job."

"Sure. Right." I scooted my mug toward Missy. "But, umm, aren't you going to get coffee or orange juice?"

"*Ugh*, I don't have enough time. I only have a few minutes to catch up with you, and then I'm off to meet the rest of my life."

Well, I thought I had something to look forward to. Missy's final words rolled off her tongue and stung. By thirty, the rest of her life would look like worthy, tangible, accomplished things: a real job, home, money, and savings. Perhaps her life would even be rounded out with that husband and baby. A wave of anxiety washed—no, crashed—over me. I felt closer to lonely and sad Gloria than when I stood mere steps from her on The Winifred's rooftop with its deceptive hope, promise, and million-dollar views.

Nevertheless, I pushed down that ball in my throat and threw my shoulders straight back. "How exciting, congrats! Are you going to be working directly with Tilly finally? I bet they were impressed to learn how you assistant-managed one of the first Tilly stores in Texas. You must be excited now that all your hard work is finally paying off."

Missy shifted in her seat. "So, yes. Yes and no."

I sipped more coffee. The hot, nutty aroma soothed me. "Where's Tilly's office? Oh my God, Missy, I must know where the—what did *Forbes* call her?—'The second youngest self-made female billionaire' works. Can you please invite me to something? I'll pretend to be your freaking courier with some bagels; I don't care."

"So—" Missy hesitated, her eyes rolling around the morning dew on the patio beneath Dyer Avenue. "Yeah, I'm going to be working in the Flatiron neighborhood. It's off Eighteenth Street, near Madison Square Park."

Missy will have an actual office like an adult while I'm back in college like a kid? "Too good to be true. That's near my school. We could do a happy hour between my work and classes. What job did you say you were doing now?" I gulped more coffee.

Missy began to get a little more shifty, progressing from tapping her foot to biting her cuticles.

"So, yeah, I got a job at Tilly. And we should totally do happy hour. Umm, but like, not the job I'd hoped for."

Missy got to work for not just *her* fashion icon but for apparently one of the world's leading fashion icons, and here she was downplaying it? "Oh. That's understandable, right? This city is competitive. You got your foot in the door, though. Right?"

"Not sure about a whole foot. Maybe a toe, a pinky toe. No, more like a pinky toenail." Silence. Awkwardness. Missy's foot tapping ceased, but her nail-biting resumed, except the biting had made its way to the beds of her nails and skin.

"Missy, you're going to eat your whole hand off." I politely slapped her arm down.

She stole a sip of my coffee. "It's like entry level."

"Stop." I took the first bite of my oatmeal. "What do you mean entry level? Like, coordinator entry level, or like assistant entry level?"

Her voice trembled as she confessed. "Like, umm, like kind of intern entry level?"

I almost gagged up my oatmeal. "Wait, you're an *intern*?" I couldn't help but pronounce intern in a higher octave with my astonishment. While several years younger, Missy had at least a few years of real-world working experience, especially since she worked full-time at the Tilly retail store as an undergrad.

"It's not the most ideal situation, I know. But…"

I squinted my eyes at Missy and felt terrible that a part of me was slightly relieved. Not because I didn't want her to be successful but because I'd wondered if the recession was easy for everybody else but me. Still, Missy had such talent and commitment. Tilly would be so lucky to have her in any position, and I hated that she reduced her aptitude and dreams to an internship. I felt anger and resentment for Missy as if it had been me.

I reached over and put my hand on her arm, but she shrunk more in her seat. Perhaps, like me, she thought that if she stalled long enough, we wouldn't need to discuss the job details. Maybe she thought the ten minutes she had with me that morning would elapse quicker than they did and that by the time we had met again, she'd have figured out a better explanation, a better way to sell her situation.

Finally, Missy began to break down, the blue sparkle in her eyes withering into tears. "Jess, you have no idea what it was like after you left."

I hugged her and began patting her back like a baby. "Whatever it is, you can tell me. *Shh*, there, there. You're here. Whatever it is, it's going to be fine. You get to be in New York City now."

I kept patting Missy's back to calm her screeching wails. Over her shoulder, I could see dirty looks from the geriatric ward of old ladies in lanyards already finishing their breakfasts. You'd think they were used to Winifreds crying in the dining hall and just about every other corner of the building after learning the great truths of life. Or is it the great non-truths of life? There is comfort in being young and believing that one day when we grow up, all of life's uncertainties will be resolved. It's a hard life lesson to learn that most adults simply wing it day by day.

"It wasn't only job fairs at Girl Scout Centers, Jess," Missy assertively pushed me away. "It got worse. It was job fairs at convention centers with strange guys in toupees and those child molester mustaches."

"Ah, the outliers, I remember. Those adult braces and retainers are making a comeback."

She recounted between sniffles. "It was job fairs at hotels, motels, and job fairs at an old, abandoned Air Force base on a sketchy side of town. All the job boards kept listing: Kelly USA, Kelly USA."

"Basically, not Manhattan?"

"No." Missy laughed. "Not Manhattan at all."

"Here, have a tissue." I pulled a Duane Reade Kleenex bag out of my fake chevron purse.

"Thank you." Missy wiped the snot running down her lips. "And I tried to stay positive every time I went to a new job search. I wasn't like you. I wasn't. I didn't complain about the blue-collar jobs, the billboards, or even the strip clubs."

"Or the seventh largest city. Or the international airport with only flights to Mexico and a non-stop flight to Canada with a layover in Atlanta."

"Exactly. I'd put my best foot forward with an even better resume than the last each time, no matter how many times I felt defeated. I'd dress in my best Tilly. But when there were open paying positions available, they were for companies like Bridgestone Tires, or like, maids—"

"You mean, 'housekeeping,' Missy. Don't let anybody, especially my new peers, hear you say maids."

"Right. I meant housekeeping. Housekeeping companies where you drive around in those red Volkswagen Bugs with a wet mop and bucket logo on the door." Missy flipped her hair behind her ears. "I even interviewed with the U.S. Border Patrol."

"Nice. Hey, I bet you'd always have a job there, too. People are getting tired of those gosh darn immigrants taking our jobs."

Missy laughed, and her tears began to stall. She wadded the tissue to brush up the last few drops from her cheeks. "Then I finally got a job, and my parents were like, 'see? The recession never reached Texas. Texas has the best economy in the country.'"

I rested my elbow on the table and put my head in my hand. Of course, I'd heard it all before. "And San Antonio, in particular, has the best economy in four main industries—local tourism, hospitality, education, and the military…"

I trailed off. It wasn't worth fanning the fires by mentioning the slew of other dream jobs at the thriving call centers and concrete plants. But thinking about it again renewed my indignation. I slammed my fist on the table. The silverware clanked together, and a bit of coffee trickled down the side of my cup. "If you don't do any of those things, you get to work at Bridgestone Tires, UCAA, or a restaurant. And let's not forget Harrison, so again, providing education for jobs that do not exist.'"

Missy wiped her eyes and checked her gold Tilly Worth watch with a beveled bezel. "I don't know. Sometimes, I wished I'd just become a teacher. But guess where I ended up getting a job? Sears."

I nodded my head in circles and threw up my hands to illustrate. "Yep. You could conquer the world but must return home for unforeseen circumstances. Then blue-collar ubiquity is like, 'that's amazing. We have something perfect for you. Our auto parts division at Sears is looking for someone great in advertising.'"

Missy stole another sip of coffee. "Exactly. Except it wasn't for their auto parts division. It was for their appliances department."

Some Winifreds across the room scowled at me as my voice escalated. "What did you do?"

Missy lowered her voice almost to a whisper. "At that point, I had to take the job because I had already told my parents, and they were excited for me. My mom was already talking about one of those candy apple red KitchenAid mixers with the powerful motor."

"Those standup mixers got a facelift recently with all the new colors. Missy, why didn't you tell me any of this? You could have called. Hello, we have AT&T in New York City." I'd begun to trail off. "Sometimes we have AT&T in New York City. The cell towers and the system are always overloaded. Sometimes I feel like the last woman standing on a deserted island, and, anyway," I placed my hand on Missy's and toned down my voice to carefully rein it in. "Listen, please tell me next time. We've already been through so much together. No matter what, I think of you as my sister, okay? I want to support you."

"How was I going to tell you, Jess? Especially when you were up here at your fancy grad school, working for cool websites, and meeting Catherine Zeta Jo—"

"Oh, Missy, no." I repeatedly nodded my head. I put one hand on her shoulder. "The emperor has no clothes, okay?"

Missy waved my hand off her. "What, what does that mean? What emperor?"

"It means things aren't always what they seem. There is always a struggle. For example, how much money did Tilly Worth's ex-husband give her to start her company? And how much stock did he sell for her to become the 'second youngest self-made female billionaire?' I don't buy it—no pun intended."

"Okay. Well, I'm here now." Missy searched my eyes for approval. "That's what matters now, right? I made it."

"Yes, you did. And now you're on the inside of Tilly, so you can scour the job boards and apply before anybody else. Introduce yourself to everyone, connect, and attend all the events." Some Winifreds got up from their tables and started snaking through a line to dump their trays. "Do not be one of the forgotten women."

"What? What do you mean?"

"You'll see. No, actually, I sure hope you don't see."

Missy picked up her purse, pulling out an old compact I remembered from the Girl Scout Center. She concealed her puffy undereye circles, painted on more lipstick, and powdered her forehead and chin. "Okay, Jess, stare much?"

"What?"

"Do you like, have a crush on me now? Stop staring at me, creeper."

But I couldn't. It was just so damn good to see her. Sometimes when we're alone for too long, we forget who we are. But like a mirror, all it takes is seeing an old friend to see ourselves again. Now, *I* was the one who wanted to cry.

"Okay," I said, tearing my eyes away before they got embarrassingly misty. "Anyway, I have some pages to finish before work to prepare for another meeting with Colette. We've started meeting weekly."

"Who's Colette?"

I bounced my head back and forth as I repeated her name. "Colette. Colette. Colette, Colette, Colette. She's like my literary luminary teaching me things. Apparently, you can't just write fun books people might actually want to read. You must aspire to save the world through writing and get these NBCC or PEN awards that only people in obscure literary circles care about. Yawn."

Missy slammed her compact shut. "And what about the forgotten wome—"

"Ladies." A Winifred staff member with a high white bun on her head and a chain of keys hooked to her waist assembled a seasonal pumpkin patch near the center of the room. She waved her hand at us. "Breakfast is ending early today. We have our annual board of directors meeting this morning. The sign was posted last week, and a reminder also sent to your mailboxes."

"Yes, Mother Superior." I stood up and gathered my tray. "Whatever you say, Mother Superior." She nodded and walked away as Missy and I giggled like two re-united sisters in the empty room.

EIGHT

We called it the fishbowl because the tiny classroom had one large window for a wall while a crammed bookshelf covered the opposite end. Sarah Clemens taught from the top of our workshop square by the door, often dressed in black with a matching Prada bag. She'd published in every genre and New York City glossy. We needn't discuss the sordid details of her life, as we could digest the most indulgent facets in one of her essays and books—the many tell-alls on sex and alcohol. Four-foot-nine with shoulder-length wispy-thin hair, she'd blown in late from God knows where, someone who'd arrived—or returned to us—from a life of too many stories to tell.

"Now, as I said before we ran out of time at the end of class last week…" Clemens opened her lesson while fumbling through her Prada purse for a pen. "Today, we're going to discuss the shortest story ever written, which has also been considered a novel in six words. It's often attributed to Hemingway. Allie, can you read those six words to us?"

Why did Air Quote Allie have to be in every class I took? This was turning out to be a long semester.

"Yes, ma'am." Allie sat up straight, coming to life from behind what looked like a Venti Starbucks Mocha Frappuccino topped with whipped cream. "For sale: baby shoes, never worn."

"For sale: baby shoes, never worn." Clemens repeated. "Do you see the beginning, the middle, and the end? So final. Isn't it? Especially with careful, calculated punctuation and grammar. We don't know, yet we know exactly that—what?"

A student chimed in. "That somebody's baby has died."

"Exactly. That a baby has died." The words seemed darker coming from Clemens.

"Excellent." Clemens raised her pen.

I still didn't understand the lesson. Obviously, we could all agree that a baby had passed away somehow, but was the lesson—our assignment—to demonstrate the economy of words in storytelling? Punctuation as an illustration, perhaps? A warm-up? Was this going to enable me to write better blogs at work, finish my travel book or my self-help travel job book, as my mother would say?

Clemens smiled at me. "Jessica, would you like to go first?"

I sank into my chair. I'd stopped going first a long time ago. If anything, I wanted to go far away and find a big hole to camp out in. I thought maybe Professor Clemens wouldn't notice me if I went a little lower and sank under the tabl—

"Jessica?"

"Okay. Perhaps I should explain it first because I'm not sure everyone will—"

"We're all in graduate school. Surely, by now, your work can stand for itself, and you can accept constructive criticism. The assignment is simply meant to be an exercise for your work. Anyway, actors audition, writers pitch. There's no way around it."

"Okay, right." I swallowed a lump in the back of my throat. "Banana Republic, The Gap, Old Navy."

"Banana Republic, The Gap, Old Navy?" Clemens repeated.

"Yes, ma'am." More blank stares from the fishbowl. I was sure my novel, novelette, was so typical that everyone would understand. I was wrong.

"It-it-it could be interpreted in many ways," I stuttered. "It's a commentary on capitalism and blind consumerism. There's an allusion to corporate America recycling a concept for the upper, middle, and lower classes, rebranding them as different, yet the same, although we know the upper class doesn't shop at the latter…"

The class remained quiet.

But my nervousness compelled me louder. "First, I had a job but no time to tailor dressy work clothes so I could run into Banana Republic for something fitted. Although sometimes I shopped at White House Black Market." A couple of young students shot me a disapproving look. Crap. Was that racist? My foot tapped nervously. "Then, when I'd lost my job but still had savings and unemployment, I'd shop at The Gap for a few staples that seemed professional for job fairs and interviews. Finally, after depleting my savings and assets—my unemployment checks—I shopped at Old Navy, hence the novel. Or I'd like to think of it as a novella: Banana Republic, The Gap, Old Navy. And…" I continued my magnum opus on unemployment sarcastically. "Like the American Dream, the same parent company owns all three retailers, so all your money is going to the same place—China. And Sri Lanka now, technically…"

I trailed off into oblivion, or maybe I was already in that oblivion. Focus, focus, I told myself. Stop while you're ahead. But the deafening silence from all the students kept me rattling off instead. Even worse, the passersby outside the fishbowl were looking in, stopping, and sitting on a hallway bench, listening to my words echo through a small wedge of the open door. "And by then, I only shopped at Old Navy for the flip-flops in the summer. Old Navy has those twenty-four-hour sales every year. For one full day, flip-flops are a dollar, and the long lines snake out of the store and around the corner. But you must get there first if you want the standard black and gray flip-flop colors." I sounded like a fashion column. Stop saying flip-flops. "Otherwise, you'll get stuck with hot pink or brown or turquoise flip-flops; usually, the only ones left are the colors nobody wants, like Indian orange."

Oh great, was that racist too?

Clemens smiled. "Insightful. Thank you for your novel, Jessica." Then, she moved on. "Would anybody else like to volunteer?"

No more comments from the instructor. And no comments from my peers. I couldn't discern which was worse: too much criticism of one's work or no criticism at all.

"I will go next," Colette said.

Winter was approaching, and while a dark blue peacoat was draped loosely over her back, Colette remained in her signature preppy attire. She always accessorized her black dreads and salt-and-pepper roots with summertime in Connecticut: Sperry shoes, Polos, and pairs of Brooks Brothers shorts featuring monograms of whales, sailboats, and umbrellas. She looked like she'd just stepped off a yacht.

An interested silence fell upon the classroom, as it often did when Colette spoke. Colette was such a poet. Everyone revered her because her words were timeless, semiotic references. The class leaned into the table, staring at Colette as she sat on the opposite far end of Clemens. We held our breath in anticipation.

Colette removed the only other semblance of winter she wore, a gray beret; it was a preface, perhaps, a grand introduction to her novel. "Love wrought an apple in sun."

Exhales in unison.

We could see each other repeating her novel in our heads: "Love wrought an apple in sun."

The silence eventually broke, and eager students chimed in one by one. One with purple hair went first. "The Bible, mythology, and Shakespeare inspire Western literature. Your novel appears to recall the Book of Genesis."

"Thank you. The Bible," Colette stopped to jot a note, "was not taken into consideration when I wrote this passage. But perhaps it should have been." Colette stopped again to scratch her chin. "Now that I think about it, perhaps I was recalling Apologist C.S. Lewis's thoughts on pain. 'The greater the love, the greater the grief.' I have been mulling over the idea that those who came before have already addressed everything we feel in our hearts."

Another student asked, "I suppose you're channeling Harlem Renaissance poet Langston Hughes's canonical poem, 'Harlem?'"

The tone of Colette's next words rose into a question as she removed her peacoat. "Maybe even Lorraine Hansberry's later play, *A Raisin in the Sun*? I could never understand why love was missing from a dream deferred, or maybe it was always implied. Love, or the lack thereof?"

"Yes, you appear to be recalling Adam and Eve and the apple," another eager student in piercings said. "Their love did spoil once the apple had been eaten—"

"But the apple is us," another student said. We are the apple. We are the forbidden fruit. We are a *tabula rasa* when we enter this world. It is not the sun that rots the apple; it is love. We, as human beings, desire love. All of the mistakes, pain, and hurt we acquire are by the nature of our own infliction."

"Brilliant. It is not the sun that rots the apple. It is love," another student sitting beside me whispered. "And the layered symbolism suggested from the homophones—it could be rot with an 'r' or wrought with a 'w.'"

Colette sat calm, quiet, and still, except for her dark eyes bouncing from student to student. I could never discern whether Colette wanted or needed a reaction to her work. And yet, I believed the world needed her work once she finished it. I thought about all this in the few moments between student remarks.

As if on cue, as if what I was thinking was coalescing with my surroundings, a slow tear emerged from Air Quote Allie as she spoke up. Her bronze skin seemed to glow against her short new locks. The tear trickled down her nose, stopping at the left nostril surrounding the miniature diamond piercing. "I am non-binary. Your novel speaks to me." A long pause. Interruptions from student to student ceased. We stared and listened as more tears filled Allie's eyes. "We do what we do because we search for love. The search for love is what wrought us, not the sun."

When I looked at Allie, I felt I had been selfish. I thought I might cry, too. While there were many matters to occupy one's mind, there was typically one central theme, one hurt, one pain at the mind's core.

Mine had been unemployment.

But for these students, these young kids, I understood for the first time that they had been searching for a leader to voice their new concerns in a different world than their parents' world, than my world, in a world where there had not been an established leader.

***

The West Village restaurant, Café Soirée, lay a block northwest of our classrooms. An older, wealthier population patronized the establishment as the drinks were pricier than the neighboring hipster hangouts our cohorts liked to drink at after workshop. I loved that the French restaurant, surrounded by adults who worked at real, full-time jobs for a living, did not have a silly jukebox in the corner. French soundtracks of live jazz recordings blared, and if you arrived earlier for dinner, a piano player on the baby grand sat alongside the bassist strumming next to a slinky dress and a sultry tune. Black and white framed pictures of the past covered the distressed brick walls in white paint: Bob Dylan on a motorcycle, Jackie Kennedy in a white dress, or dusk along the Mediterranean Sea. The framed pictures often hung crookedly in comparison to one another. On the left wall near the entrance, a floating shelf carried little odds and ends from other times and places: a rendition of a Bernini portrait bust, books, a black-and-white of Cole Porter, a pink head of a pig, and two cases of teapots and plates made of blue Portuguese porcelain.

Below lay white table linens set on small round café tables. Above the tables, a narrow wooden bar hovered along fourteen stools. Sometimes, we sat at the stools, hanging our bags on the old gold hooks by our legs, people-watching, taking turns swinging our backs to and from the other patrons, only to find Steve Buscemi's snaggle-toothed smile or Patricia Clarkson's unassuming black velvet hat. I'd once read that her career stalled when she hit thirty. But at least she had a career. I could no longer articulate mine.

"Your novel was six illustrative words. So, you appeared to have mastered the lesson." Colette sipped a freshly bubbling Stella from the bar tap. "But something was missing."

"You think?" I sipped my Côtes du Rhône *sans* dinner. "Maybe, like, a whole novel?"

She smiled, knowing what was really on my mind. "What kind of reactions were you expecting?"

I shrugged because the truth was, I hadn't even allowed myself to worry about what the students in the class would think. If I had, I probably wouldn't have written anything at all. "I guess I was bracing myself for some more of that, you know, constructive criticism. I couldn't decide which was worse. Hearing too much or hearing nothing at all. But considering that our program is geared more toward writing something weighty or magical, I should have kept my mouth shut."

Colette curled one of her hanging dreads between her fingers. Her eyes twitched as she caught sight of her knuckles, and she self-consciously hid them, throwing them under the table. "Greatness and the journey to greatness are not always easy." Colette's metaphors increased when she drank too much, coinciding with her search for meaning and clarity. "It is inevitable that the journey to such a feat comes with a long and daunting trek up a mountain without any sleep. But that is similar to what we might call the hero's journey in literature. Your economic worries might sound simplistic to ears who have never experienced the burden of being on their own, but you are onto something. What if, then, you changed your perspective? What if your cohorts are simply experiencing your early drafts leading to greatness? What if you took their merited criticism and discarded the rest?"

The temperature grew warmer. I could feel my cheeks flush, so I had to look away. "Your words are very kind and encouraging, you know that, Femingway? And insightful too. But sometimes I wish you didn't always have to speak in metaphor. I don't want to be on a hero's journey. I just want a real job."

A coy wrinkle stretched from the corners of Colette's lips. She took another sip of her Stella and finished her speech in a snarky tone. "Perhaps we should be humbled in your presence, as the time to hear early drafts of greatness is limited; once one makes it to the top of the mountain, one needn't continue looking up or down or around to gain a sense of direction."

Colette exposed a brief smile, a laugh, a ray of sunshine that rarely emerged from her dark and mysterious features. She took another sip of beer and resumed her lecture, drowning out a small crowd of tourists arriving for their nightcap. Everybody at the university looked up to Colette, and if you could get that half smile from her, it was a victory. It meant you, or she had made a breakthrough or something. Only I was still trying to patch together what that breakthrough was, exactly. And her hands. What was the deal with her hands? I didn't want to come out and ask.

"When you are training in the armed forces, you must endure an obstacle course. When you are nearing your last mile and begin to think of the glory of the finish line, the finish line becomes farther. Smoke grenades and barbed wire are a few of the obstacles that will keep you from your goal. You will notice the smoke and barbed wire become thicker the closer you get to the finish line. It is the last chance for the obstacle course to prove you cannot cross the finish line. And later, in the real battle, you will be sprayed with bullets. But what will you decide to do?"

"Great, and also, the twelve-year-old students who are throwing the smoke grenades and laying barbed wire and spraying the bullets have never before used a smoke grenade, or laid barbed wire, or sprayed bullets. Maybe they've like interned on it, but let's be real."

"Distractions. Distractions, you see." Colette's pupils seemed to dilate. "The distractions are there to deter you. The distractions do not want you to realize how far along you are, even when you may be one step away from the finish line. You must endure the distractions now. These distractions will always be there waiting for you."

"And then what? Please do finish with your ominousness. I'm on the edge of my seat here." I stubbornly hid my head behind my wine. What was Colette even talking about? Sometimes, I couldn't tell if she was wise or just enjoying messing with me.

"The sun will always rise, Jessica. Where will it find you when it does? What legacy do you wish to leave?"

"No, you're right." I sarcastically begged. "Tell me more, guru."

"Guru?" Colette raised her voice in a thundering clap to mock me. "You will remember this moment in the not-too-distant future, Jessica."

I jabbed back. "Are you reading my tarot cards, too? Is it the fool? Or the guy with all the daggers in his back?"

"Ah," she raised her glass along with that mocking cadence. "I can see that more struggling lies ahead for you. I do not think you are yet prepared to finish your journey."

Now she was starting to piss me off. I shifted in my seat to rub my lower back, which suddenly felt strained from carrying my books across the city from The Winifred to work to class. Colette may have figured it all out, but that didn't warrant her speaking to me in this pretentious, holier-than-thou way. "How enlightened of you, Siddhartha. Anything else?"

"What is more," she continued before I could defend myself, "I believe you may *not* want to finish this journey quite yet. For you know something that many do not."

"That I'm apparently addicted to suffering?"

Colette raised her arms wide and high to gesture. "It is never about the finish line or the top of the mountain."

"It isn't?" I smacked her arms down.

She self-consciously hid her hands again. "No, not for you. For you, it is about the journey. For you, it is about being in the thick of the wilderness."

"Oh, so now I *like* the smoke grenades and the barbed wire?"

"The journey is easier than the real battle. Once you make it to the top of the mountain, others will seek you out. And the task will require you to have compassion. You must have compassion and empathy. But the contradiction is that you cannot always take everyone with you. It will be up to you to decide whom to carry on your shoulders. Whom to allow to walk beside you in the New Kingdom."

"Oracle, can you repeat all this? I feel like I should write this down—all this stuff about the Promised Land, barbed wires, and looking around from the tops of mountains." I couldn't help but get even more agitated with her last sentence. "Are we still talking about my six-word novel? Neo? Is there a red or a blue pill?"

Colette leaned in and got serious, rubbing her hands under the table again as she sharpened her eyes at me. "My point is if I could have done things differently...There are things I wish I could have done differently. There will always be suffering, but we must choose how we respond. It takes a lot of perspective. And that perspective takes practice so that when we are in war, perspective and reaction are automatic."

I pushed my arms off the table to scoot farther away from Colette as if that could bring "perspective." How did I deserve what happened, I wondered? The Federal Reserve said there may not be enough time for my generation to catch up. The lack of well-paying jobs during the recession occurred when I should have put money into appreciating assets like real estate. Instead, my money was going to higher interest on credit cards, deferred student loans, medical bills, and car payments in Texas.

I opened one of the black and white menus with sketches of Old Hollywood actors. My fingers traced the pâté with cornichons and niçoise olives. Then the Blue Point Oysters and skirt steak.

"Let's order some pomme frites." I motioned to our waitress and placed my order. "Colette, why don't we ever talk more about you? It's like you're perfect and have it all figured out. What's this nonsense about wishing you could have done things differently? And anyway, isn't that why we're all here?"

"Me?" Colette fidgeted and tossed her head down to her lap. She aggressively rubbed her hands. "What is there to say?"

"Why are you here? Who were you in your past life? We all have a past life here. I want to know more about yours."

"Please." Colette drew her hand up to say stop. "You already know about mine. I came back to New York because I wanted to serve more. But in a different way. To teach." I knew that Colette emigrated from Jamaica as a child. I knew that she had been a Marine. I knew she had also studied at the London School of Economics and once worked on Wall Street the first time she lived in New York. I knew that she loved a woman. But sometimes I felt I did not know her.

"Your hands. They're purple. They're frequently purple."

Colette placed her beer down to conceal her hands below the table again. "I know, thank you."

"Perhaps you should wear gloves in the winter."

"You know I do not wear gloves." Colette casually turned to open her satchel.

"Did you see the doctor? You said you were going to see the doctor."

Colette pulled out a lighter. A pack of Dunhills followed. "I did."

"And?"

"And she said to stop smoking."

"That's it?" I put my hands on the pack to slide them away from her.

"It would appear smoking is not good for you."

"It would appear cancer sticks are bad for you."

"What can I say? I feel I am still young, but it appears I am not."

"No more packs of Dunhills, okay?"

"Probably not a good idea." She picked up her beer again.

The waitress dropped off our pomme frites. I dipped one in mayonnaise and waved it in Colette's face. "Well, if you want to teach, you already are—in six words, and I would think even fewer."

"I am? How?"

"Today, in workshop."

"You think they may have taken to my little novel?"

Colette's sudden modesty annoyed me. "Oh, I don't know, maybe just a little. Did you have to go right after me?"

"Hey, it was not a competition." Colette grabbed a fry. Her eyes turned on like a light when she chewed. She rushed to grab one more, drowning it in ketchup and salt. "Do not worry. At some point, those kids must be out in the real world without the Bank of Mom and Dad, student loans, and roommates, and then they will realize there is no way to live off nothing, and they will remember the relevance of your six-word novel."

"No, it's not about me. I don't care about me. It's about you. You change people. Somehow, you lead people out of the depths of murkiness—after thoroughly confusing everyone with your mixed metaphors. They will remember you. They will always remember you."

"Murkiness? That is a bit of a trip." Colette brushed her dreads aside while leaning back, her chair shifting from four, three, two, one leg, then tilting, returning, abruptly back down. "You think?"

"You help to eliminate the fog. To bring reason and clarity. Although, I know you cannot always do that for yourself."

Colette tilted back again, grabbing another fry. "Me? Clarity? Who said I needed clarity for myself? I am doing what I came to the city to do."

"I wish I could do that for others. No, God, I wish I could do that for myself."

Colette did not say anything, but I could tell she was thinking. Her eyes lingered over my shoulder, glaring, people-watching out the window.

"The students in class. Allie. You made Allie cry. You almost made me cry. You touch people. You are the people that other people look for. We all want to understand life. And purpose. Our purpose. It hurts sometimes, you know?" I savored the last of my Côtes du Rhône.

"We should not take life too seriously. This time here. It is momentary, and yet you focus on the monetary. Enjoy your time in this city. It is limited. It will change. There will be other seasons with other preoccupations."

"Did you know that life would lead you here next?"

"I knew that the time in life was coming for me to…" Colette trailed off as if she had seen something through the window on Thirteenth Street.

"Coming for you to what?"

She began to answer, but her eyes remained fixed outside. "I knew it was time to be back in New York. For a little while. For the last while. I have some unfinished business."

I wish I had known that my time with Colette would be limited, too. There would come a day when there would be no mountain to climb or obstacle course for her to pursue. There were early warnings—those cold, numb, purple hands against her espresso skin. But sometimes, even the wisest and most perceptive of us cannot see what's right in front of our eyes, even when it's as bright as a clear summer day.

NINE

The downstairs lounge at The Winifred was a little too dark and drafty with its cold hardwood floors, and practice room mirrors on the wall alongside the piano. Outside the window overlooking Dyer Avenue, beams of white headlights exited the Lincoln Tunnel. The glow cut through the misty evening while the screeching cars breaking and honking disrupted our silence.

Missy sat on one of the denim blue couches in her usual leggings and an oversized Texas State sweatshirt. "Jess, where have you been?"

"Where have *I* been?" I pulled my hands out of my black hoodie pockets and sat on the smaller loveseat across from her, parachuting an old Burberry blanket over me. "I keep knocking on your door since neither of us can make it to dinner anymore, but you're always working late in what's become your second master bedroom here."

Missy sat crisscross, one of her legs dangling off the corner of the couch, the stacks of magazines spilling from her lap. She looked back down, flipping through the pages of fashion magazines to dog-ear for Tilly. Part of Tilly's advertising strategy was that she didn't have to pay for advertising because they got mentioned so many times in fashion magazines. It was Missy's job to flip through them painstakingly and scan the mentions into their system.

She took a break from dog-earing the pages. "I loved being back in Texas with my family for Thanksgiving. And, did you check your Winifred mailbox?"

"Sadly, yes. I saw the rent increase." I felt a chill and pulled the blanket tighter. "I can barely pay the rent now, and I finally decided to accept more student loans for living expenses."

Missy let out a long sigh. "How are we going to live here now? Just when I thought I had so much to be thankful for."

"No kidding. All I could think about when I read the letter was, 'Merry Christmas, Winifreds, and Happy New Year!'"

"I know, and why do they always have to call us Winifreds?"

"To demonstrate that we're all in this together. Yay."

Missy flipped another page, stopping to shoot her eyes at me. "Oh, and even worse, can you believe the new rule?"

"You mean not being allowed to stay at The Winifred longer than five years?"

She nodded. "I asked the front desk to clarify because you know women have been here longer than five years, Jess."

I straightened up. "Oh, wait, are some of the women getting kicked out? Is Mick Jagger's ex getting the boot? Well, you know what they say: You can't always get what you want. But if you try sometime, you'll find you get what you need."

"No." Missy kept flipping. "Everybody else who's already been at The Winifred longer than five years get two more—like a grace period." The end of her sentence broke up. I could see her eyes turning cloudy, the tears thickening and bleeding from the corners.

Standing up, I scootched closer and placed my arm around her shoulders. "You still have so much time," I said softly. And I meant it. I may have been a shriveled-up old lady, but Missy still had her twenties left before her. "How amazing that you're only twenty-two and have already made it to Tilly in New York City."

Missy's tears continued. "Oh, yeah, whatever, thanks. What's next? If I work harder, maybe I can get promoted to mail clerk or receptionist." She wiped her cheeks.

"Hey, I'm a thirty-year-old college student living in a dorm. I'm probably not the best person to ask." I squeezed her shoulders tighter. "But seriously, so what if you were only a receptionist or the mail clerk at Tilly in New York City?"

My words must've been inspiring because Missy closed a magazine.

"I'm serious. You're here doing it all on your own to gain more work experience with one of the biggest brands in the fashion industry and the world. I know you miss San Antonio. And despite my harsh criticism, I do too. And for so many reasons: It's a great place to settle down and raise a family. It has the best cost of living. I miss those affordable McMansions compared to our 115-square-foot guest rooms and communal showers that keep clogging. And where else can you get bottomless chips and salsa and fifty-ounce refills on Big Red and Coke for free?"

"Oh, I know, Jess." Missy laughed and wiped some of her tears. "Can you believe they charged me for chips and salsa when I went to pick up lunch for the team at El Camino in Meatpacking?"

"Exactly." I tried to steer the ship back. "But you have your whole life to return to that life in San Antonio. You get to be here now. Doing something for yourself before returning to serving *la familia*."

Missy's crying paused, so I stood above her to dramatically finish my speech. "But guess what? You're doing it all by yourself. You're spending all your hard-earned money to gain more experience and to live in Manhattan, not on a flashy car back home that ironically doesn't take you anywhere."

Missy lifted her head higher. "And what about you, Jess?"

"What do you mean? What about me? I'm just starting a new chapter."

"Really?"

"Yes, *really*. I love being here with you, knowing I've already checked many items off my bucket list."

"You don't miss all the traveling and meeting cool people anymore?"

I didn't dare miss a beat. I didn't dare let Missy hear even an iota of hesitation in my voice because I knew that if I paused for just a second to miss my old life, she would hear a gaping chasm of silence and sadness, and it would justify everything she was afraid of for herself. I couldn't bear to do that to her.

"Absolutely not," I said. "And I'm already sitting with someone cool right now. I'm so over things like first class on Lufthansa Airlines with a Wolfgang Puck menu or meeting Andrew Zimmern while he makes me eat his famous geoduck clams from his *Bizarre Foods* show on the Travel Channel. Okay, maybe that was a little sarcastic."

"The what clams?" She cracked a smile, and I felt my heart melt.

"They're these funny-looking saltwater clams that have a giant penis growing out of them. They're native to the Pacific Northwest but pretty popular in Asia, although they did get banned from China for a while. He was my hero, but I wasn't a fan of the geoduck clams, so I told him food doesn't have a taste at that altitude—anyway, that's not the point. I told my mother the other day about all the hard work you've been doing for Tilly."

Her smile faltered again. "But it feels like life is at a standstill."

Stay strong, I told myself. Missy needed me to, even if it felt like my life wasn't just in something as momentary as a standstill but that it had arrived at a complete and permanent halt. "Unfortunately, you had to graduate from college during a never-ending recession."

Missy returned to a page in one of her magazines. "Feels like a depression." She glanced down at a page featuring a pair of Tilly sterling silver earrings with lime green stones for fifteen hundred dollars. "Tell me about one of your last trips, Jess."

I leaned back against the couch and pulled the blanket back over me. "I did everything, and God was like, you've completed your bucket list, everything on that bucket list, even the penguins."

She perked up. "Huh, tell me more about the penguins." Missy loved to hear anything about God, and especially God and penguins. "They mate for life," she had once said.

And maybe it was Colette, or perhaps it was the penguins that had nothing to do with anything, but I couldn't stop by then. And the more I kept talking, the more my thoughts became a stream of consciousness.

"I reached the end of my little bucket list when I felt such an emptiness. The penguins were all there along the water, soaking in the cooler current as always when I arrived at the Galápagos."

"I love the penguins. They're my favorite. And then what?"

"But then I just thought, '*meh*.'"

"*Meh*? Why *meh*?'"

As much as I wanted to remember that day fondly, I remembered that day forlornly. Maybe I couldn't play survival of the fittest, I'd thought, thinking of Darwin and natural selection. Or perhaps I didn't care about being on top of the world anymore. But I couldn't make sense of it all. "I kept thinking about how much I wanted to be stranded on that island without any options. Staring at dusk in the only place in the world where penguins do not live along the ice, gazing until dawn without ever having to look north again."

"What did you do??"

"I prayed that I could be a penguin one day."

Missy abruptly shut her fashion magazine. "But Jess, you know penguins can't fly. Penguins flap their flipper wings up and down but never fly."

"That was the first thing I thought. Yep, I did not want to get on the next plane. The first plane, the plane after that." I stopped my train of thought as something else came to me. It was like I was in a trance. My gaze aimed like a bow and arrow at a target on the wall. Everybody wants to make their dreams come true, but do the exhaustion, the sacrifices, the debt—and all the other valuable pieces of our lives and selves lost in the process—make it worth it?

"Jess?" Missy leaned in.

I suddenly recalled a lesson on relationships I'd learned in a psychology class when I was young. "When the benefits and rewards outweigh the consequences, the relationship is healthy. But when there are more consequences than benefits and rewards, that relationship ceases to be healthy. I guess I had no idea that could pertain to jobs, too. The relationship I had with my job."

A boisterous voice from the corner vibrated against the walls, interrupting our conversation: "And some of the girls like to watch TV in here." Agnes entered in her khaki staff uniform and a green sweater from the rear doorway. She held a walkie-talkie with a matching green fanny pack around her. A few prospective Winifreds trailed behind her on a tour while she fiddled with the frizzy hair falling from her bun. "You can also reserve the room to practice on the piano. If you need to book the room to practice, we ask that you book it as far enough in advance as possible."

Missy wiped the last of her tears from her face. We gathered our belongings, me folding the Burberry throw and placing it on the lonely loveseat's armrest for someone else. Missy finished stacking her magazines.

"Hey, I'll help you carry those up," I offered. Then, in a conspiratorial whisper, I added, "and next time the warden returns with her tours for future 'working women,'—sorry, 'Winifreds'—I'm gonna tell them that the remote control never works and that if you do get the television to work, the channels come in and out."

"Isn't it a little bit late for tours?" Missy forgot that staff was working overtime due to the demand of women moving in; resources would become even more limited. But I still didn't understand why The Winifred prioritized certain resources over others. As we walked out of the front entrance and through the hallway, we passed Christmas decorations in red, silver, and green. Gold gifts sat under the tree, while candy canes and Hershey's kisses lined walls and end tables.

"And why are they always on the ball about decorations? Halloween, Thanksgiving, and now Christmas? Are there going to be decorations for New Year's? And what about Valentine's Day?" Missy kept adding. "We're all single, nobody has a boyfriend, and if they did, said boyfriend isn't allowed past the first floor—not even to consummate Valentine's Day, Jess."

Ding. The elevator chimed.

"Now that you mention it, Missy, it's like we *are* stuck in the 1920s when this place was originally bu—"

"But by golly, at least we have a freaking Christmas tree even though we can't get much internet or cell service in the room!"

"Missy, wow. Grumpy butt is my job. What happened to your sunny, 'save-the-world-and-dolphins-and-bees-because-my-hopes-and-dreams-have-never-been-dashed' disposition from the Girl Scout Center?"

A crease appeared between Missy's eyebrows. "She grew up."

"Do you want to keep talking about it—"

"No."

"Okay."

The wheels on the heavy elevator doors slowly began to screech. We overheard Agnes as she continued. "You can take a book from the library if you'd like. We just ask that you return it and—"

"I took a book and never returned it. Jhumpa Lahiri's *The Namesake* is a keepsake from The Winifred Library, which sits on my shelf today."

"Yippee," Missy said in a sardonic monotone.

We got one last glimpse of Agnes and the line of following women. They crossed our path before the elevator doors shook with a thunderous clap shut. "Hey, wait a minute." I got a closer look at Agnes's dark hunter-green wool sweater.

"I have a sweater like that...I used to have a sweater like that."

"So glad I made you get rid of it, Jess. Way too big for your shrinking frame. Clothes should be tailored, especially if you want to look your age."

"Thanks, I know, Tilly Worth Ambassador. How odd she had the same sweater I'd only seen at Old Navys in the Southwest. It's very Native American looking with its pink scrolling at the ends of the bell sleeves."

"Not really, Jess. Didn't you put that small box of clothes in the laundry room for the monthly Goodwill donation?"

"Wait a minute. That *is* my sweater."

"I thought so."

It was *Seinfeld* moments like that when I realized everyone there, the staff, the residents, the housekeeping, the cooks, the engineers—all of us needed The Winifred.

The wheels on the elevator door screeched open again in front of us, jerking up and down before finally letting us out. We sluggishly glided down the hall with our glamorous stacks of magazines. At the end of the hallway, Missy threw the magazine stack onto mine so she could pull her key out of her purse to open her door.

"I don't know anymore, Jess."

"What do you mean?"

"I mean, moneywise and jobwise."

"Is that why you're grumpy butt? Phew." I rolled my eyes and head in relief. "I thought I'd created a monster."

Missy flicked her guest room light. "This unpaid PR internship is becoming around-the-clock. If I keep this up, I'll hit a minimum of seven-hundred hours by January. I've been counting."

My eyes scrolled back and forth as I tried to do math in my head. "That's roughly sixty hours a week of work without pay for someone who already has internships, education, and work experience under her belt."

"And as you can see," Missy insinuated by pointing her head at the magazines. "I'm evidently not learning anything." We set the stacks down below the radiator against the window. Missy haphazardly tucked in the corners of her bedspread. "You want to sit for a second?" She hung loose items of clothing that had fallen off the metal garment rack wedged between the wall and the end of her bed. Other Tilly Worth products were hanging galore: white and plum skinny jeans; brown, purple, and black leather handbags with the famous Worth logo ripped off from Morocco. Sighing, she finally said, "I was hoping it would turn into a full-time paying position by the spring. I'm running out of money. I'm thinking of nannying until I find a real job."

"But I thought you were already interviewing for paying jobs at the company these last few months?"

"Yeah, but each time, the people who've interviewed me just drop off the face of the Earth. The last lady I met with said, "Oh, I'm excited to meet you. Thank you so much. We'll definitely be in touch." And then nothing. Not even an email. Not even one of those automated emails: Thank you for your time; however, we regret to inform you."

I leaned in to squeeze Missy's shoulder in sympathy. "Why didn't you tell me?"

"When would I have had the time to tell you, Jess? My relationship with Tilly is turning into a relationship with an ex-boyfriend. After all the sweat and tears, am I getting back with them, or am I not getting back with them? I even applied to work at one of her retail stores again."

Missy continued recounting the gory details about her non-job and how she didn't think she'd ever become a real employee. It was like Missy's whole, entire family and life died a very long, torrid, bloody, excruciating, drawn-out, unsolved, tragic death. And we stayed up past midnight as we tried to solve the mystery clouding the murder. After all, Missy's clothes, shoes, bags, accessories, and sunglasses were all Tilly Worth. When she got paid—at the former retail job, not at her internship—she'd put most of her money back into Tilly Worth products. In fact, Missy's guest room at The Winifred did not look like any other guest room at The Winifred. It looked like a Tilly Worth boutique. Tilly Worth had a boutique, a pop-up store, and a residency at The Winifred: only thirty-some blocks from the Tilly Worth Flagship Store on Madison Avenue, the Tilly Worth Boutique at The Winifred stood as a great halfway point to hit before heading to the Meatpacking Tilly Worth Boutique—especially for last-season finds or gently worn "vintage" items.

Missy lined up more Tilly jewelry and accessories on a board atop the radiator, doubling as a shelf. "I was thinking I might start selling some of it on eBay to keep living in New York." She smiled, longingly grabbing a belt with another gold logo inspired by Morocco.

"If you sell some of your Tilly, we can both keep living in New York."

"Check out my closet."

We barely had closets in our guest rooms at The Winifred, and if you opened Missy's all the way, it extended to almost the other end of the room, almost hitting that odd dysfunctional sink with the medicine cabinet. That didn't matter to Missy. She was resourceful.

"Missy, the floor of your closet is not only covered in Tilly Worth shoes and boots, but look at your door." The inside of her closet door had the hanging shoe rack, on which Missy had every type of Tilly Worth ballet flat doubled, even tripled in each pocket: snakeskin, brown, black ballet flats, ballet flats with the silver logo, ballet flats with the gold logo. Yes, those two-hundred-dollar ballet flats *Forbes* stated were partly responsible for Tilly Worth becoming a billionaire and not paying Missy, who was buying ballet flats with the money she no longer had. If Missy wanted to buy more Tilly Worth ballet flats, she would have had to sell some of her old ballet flats to pay for them and make room for them.

"Missy, for as long as I live, I will never forget your first day at The Winifred." I pointed at her two-shelf bookcase that came in every 115-square-foot guest room. "You did not use yours for storing books."

"Oh, I know. I remember first walking into your guest room and saying, "Oh my God. You have a bookshelf? Why don't I have a bookshelf?""

"You had a bookshelf, but Tilly had already staked its claim for her belts and accessories."

Missy pulled suitcases out from underneath her bed.

"Uh, what the heck is all that?"

She unzipped a dark green suitcase that had been hiding more Tilly Worth loot. "Oh, I forgot to show you. I got some new Tilly at her sample sale." She showed off another pair of purple floral skinny jeans covered in pastel flowers. "And this handbag." Missy did not need another Tilly handbag. They were hanging from the walls and ceilings and her cheap garment racks. They were on her little white chair, the little white dresser, and in suitcases underneath her bed. There was even a cubby hole below the sink. I wanted to help Missy more; I wished I could help Missy more. She'd been all about Tilly, Tilly, Tilly for so long, but what if she could find something more? Surveying the Tilly stash across her room again, I thought that perhaps she wasn't quite ready to hear more.

"You're such a collector, like your antiquing ancestors. Except instead of furniture and lamps, you collect ballet slippers, purses, and pants."

"I know, right?"

Missy was not only drinking the Kool-Aid, but she'd become an addict, and like many of the smooth-talking charismatic addicts that came before her, she exercised her powers of persuasion. Fumbling through her suitcase loot, she finally displayed a black and gray leather clutch in a snakeskin pattern. It had a dangerously long but sexy metallic chain and a leather strap at the top. A giant gunmetal Tilly Worth logo covered the clutch flap. It was the perfect bag.

I sighed and reached my arms out in defeat. "Can I borrow something at least?"

"Oh my God, yes! You can totally borrow whatever you want until I sell it."

I didn't have much money to get out of The Winifred, but I would look fabulous while living there with that bag hanging by my side.

TEN

Thanks to the last of my frequent flyer miles, my plane touched down in Texas before midnight on the twentieth. Little middle-aged Mexican ladies rolled full trashcans and vacuums across the floor. I followed, strolling my carry-on along the small airport through flocked Christmas trees and jingle bell wreaths. Loud scrapes and vibrations against the epoxy echoed against the empty facility. I felt my phone vibrate in my pocket. Mom. She must have been waiting for me outside already. As soon as I answered, she spouted out a monologue listing everything we needed to do and the people we needed to see during my stay.

"Tita? Wait, Mom. Who's Tita again?"

"*Mijita*, Tita." Even over the phone, I could see my mother's head shaking in disappointment at me. "One of Little Grandma Ventura's sister's daughters from Brownsville. Silly girl."

"Hey, how am I supposed to keep track of all our extended family without some sort of a diagram?" I skipped, almost tripped, barely missing two housekeepers who were Windexing glassed portraits of the Alamo, Shamu, and the Tower of the Americas.

"One of her great-granddaughters is having a baby, and I have already sent the RSVP for you and me."

"Wait, one of Tita's great-granddaughters is already having a baby? Mom, isn't Tita your age?" One of the Mexican ladies stopped her Windexing and Shamu-wiping to twitch her disapproving head at me. I lowered my shoulders, talking quieter. "And why does everybody still live in biblical times down here—wedding and procreating so early as if life ends at thirty-three?"

"*Mijita*, don't say any of that when we arrive. I already bought a bunch of those little onesies and jammies, and you and I can split the cost of the Jungle Gymboree."

I stopped dead in my tracks. Someone behind me almost tripped over my carry-on. "Sorry, sir." I rolled on. "A Jungle Gymboree, Mom? That sounds expensive." I arrived at the sliding doors and approached the carousel of cars circling the airport. Opening the Toyota Venza passenger door, I jumped in beside my mother.

"Think of it this way," my mother countered, accelerating past the stopped cars along the curb and toward the outer lane leading to the vacant highway. "One day, it'll be your turn." She lifted her right finger from the steering wheel and pointed toward the dark horizon. "And then they will all come to your baby shower and bring you all your baby gifts."

***

The following morning, we parked alongside a ranch-style house at the start of the hill country on the city's northwest side. Texas succulents, prickly pear cacti with yellow flowers, crushed stone, and red lava rocks covered the lawn while flower beds brushed against the house.

"This is kind of a cute house."

My mother glanced sideways, suggesting what I said was suspect. We walked up the pebbled pathway leading toward the front of the house. Pink balloons and streamers dangled over the porch, announcing, "It's a Girl!"

"Perfect," I snidely remarked to my mother as she rang the bell. "More great-granddaughters to carry on the torch of making more great-great-granddaughters."

"Keep quiet." My mother snapped her fingers at me.

I clutched the Jungle Gymboree wrapped in the gaudiest colorful Mexican paper crowned in big bows and glitter. "Now, Mom, is it redundant to say that I'm carrying a gift wrapped in tacky, bright, and colorful Mexican paper, or can all that already be discerned from the words *Mexican paper?*"

My mother responded to my question with angry eyes that squinted smaller together for effect.

"What?" I shrugged my shoulders. "I'm just editing in real-time here."

The door finally opened.

"Yessica, how good it is to see you again and so soon. I heard you might be coming."

"Oh, no, not soon enough, Conchita." I shot my mother a glance. Why hadn't she told me we were crossing the wire into enemy territory?

Conchita stood barefoot with an infant on her right hip. Pink, red, and turquoise flowers and birds were stitched around the neck of her long white Mexican dress. Underneath the stitching were the words: *los parajitos van chirp, chirp.*"

"Oh, how about that? The little Spanish birdie likes to chirp in English."

The baby spit up into a faded blue burp cloth on Conchita's breast.

"And is this the boy you were hoping for when I saw you last?"

"*Si, si.* My daughters were happy to finally have a brother."

I put my hand on his delicate head, brushing the full head of hair back. "Because they can't all be Miss Fiestas, right?"

"You remembered!" Conchita waved her hand at me. "Come on in. It is good to see you again, Yessica. We are still so happy about him that when I heard you were coming, I decided to let bygones be bygones. No reason for us to keep fighting."

"Wow, that's so big of you. Heavy is the head that wears the crown and all that."

"Excuse me?"

"Nothing. I love the garden with the cacti in the front. Is this your house, Conchita?"

"*Si*. And *mi casa es su casa*."

The inside of Conchita's house was exactly how I would've pictured the inside of Conchita's house had I thought that far ahead. Her antique furniture aesthetic included decadent oversized couches with tassels and a medieval dining room table in walnut finish. Matching chairs with intricate armrests and pointy spires on the backs surrounded the table. Immediately, I envisioned Conchita in her crown, drinking from her chalice and espousing wise fiesta advice passed down from *la familia* over a lit candelabra. Above the furniture were bronze chandeliers. Large portraits of Conchita in sexy white bridalwear hung from walls along the entryway. At the top of the very end of the hallway, a blown-up image of a tan and busty Conchita in a red and blue dress hung down. We looked up at her brunette beehive hair neatly tucked behind the iconic Miss Fiesta crown.

My mother made the obligatory compliments as we walked beneath the queen's feet. She always deferred back to her colloquial tongue when she was among members of our native tribe. "*Que bonita*, Conchita. What beautiful photos you have, and *mira*, what a gorgeous house."

"What a beautiful house," I agreed.

"*Muchas gracias*." Conchita gazed back at us while her son smiled, gurgled, and waved at me.

"I don't know, Conchita. Is there a Mr. Fiesta Pageant down here yet? Because he seems to have perfected his wave already."

Conchita stopped to wipe some of the drool from his face. "He arrived early and is over six months now. He is also ahead of his class, already starting to sit up without my help."

Of course, Conchita's son was an overachiever like her.

"And he must like you, Yessica. He only smiles and waves at people he likes."

I patted his head. "Can he sense evil like dogs do, too?"

"*Mijito*," Conchita bounced him up and down. "This is Mama's runner-up. She was good, but not good enough. And, okay, I will give her a break. She was the youngest to compete. We all had pageant coaches, and it wasn't our first pageant."

"*Si*, my one regret," my mother said. "How was I supposed to know you girls needed pageant coaches to win these things?"

Clearing the end of the hallway, we stood at a precipice overlooking a crowd of loud and happy Hispanic women spanning several generations. Among them were Conchita's accomplishments carefully arranged in frames throughout the house on coffee tables, in alcoves, and above the fireplace: all five of her kids, her husband, some grandparents, a couple of cats and dogs, an associate degree in dance from the community college, and another degree in cosmetology. I sat our Jungle Gymboree near a crying Virgin Mary statue below the gift table. The baby spit up again. Conchita wiped his mouth. My mother caressed the baby's toes while Conchita kept bouncing him up and down. I played with his fingers until he wrapped his fist around my pinky. I brushed my hand along the light brown peach fuzz on his head.

"What's his name?"

"Mortimer. It is French, a family name. My husband always wanted to name his son after his great-grandfather Mortimer." Conchita crouched down to grab a mimosa sitting on the entryway table. "The doctor says I can finally drink this holiday season." She raised her champagne glass and took a sip. "You know I've pumped so much breastmilk that my freezer is stocked." Conchita coughed up some bubbles and fake-clinked her glass at me in the air. She stole a sneaky look at my mother. "How is lonely New York? Is it everything you thought it would be?"

I, too, stole a look at my mother. *Lonely?* What had she told her? Staring down at my pair of second-hand boots Last Chance couldn't sell, I thought of The Winifred, rent increasing, and ballooning student loans.

"I'm living the dream," I said airily. "So many jobs coming my way, so little time. I can't decide where I want to live next."

Conchita's face seemed flushed. It beamed red as she turned her head to someone calling her about the plates. "Please make yourselves at home, ladies."

Conchita wandered off as we meandered toward a lightly flocked Christmas tree near the fireplace. "How about that, Mom? The Christmas tree also appears to be Mexican. Actually, Conchita did that tastefully. I would *not* have been able to pull that off."

The tree matched the wrapping paper, and its neon ornaments screamed, "*¡Feliz Navidad!*" We held our breath and peered at it from the bottom to the top. Several yarned *Ojo de Dios* ornaments swirled diagonally up the tree, interspersed with figurines of smiling Mexican Santas in *sombreros*. Tri-colored sashes matching the national flag were draped across the Santas' chests while some of the Santas strummed guitars, played the trumpet, or, in lieu of an instrument, held a bottle of tequila.

We continued traversing our way through the living room among women in long dresses of pink, blue, yellow, white, red, green, and gold—all the colors of a rainbow. Tita was sitting on a weathered brown leather couch against the floor-to-ceiling windows. She balanced the Christmas-colored paper plate in her lap, loaded with *chori-queso* and tortilla chips. We watched her scoop up the hot, melting cheese. It stretched off her tortilla chip as her lips and mouth quickly closed just in time to catch the cheese before it skimmed her lavender house dress.

"*Aye*, look at me," Tita said in a thick, embarrassed accent. She finished shoveling the last of the *chori-queso* into her mouth.

My mother and I kept stepping through the crowd. Tita bounced her shoulder-length white bob into place with her right hand. Finally, she set her plate on an end table covered in empty champagne and margarita glasses, the rims stained from the pulp of freshly pressed orange juice and margarita salt.

Struggling to stand up, Tita fanned her dress out like an umbrella and, with both hands, washed away the tortilla crumbs left on her stomach. She stepped over more babies and ladies to kiss my mother and me. "*Vien, vien*," Tita called to someone else over our shoulders as several gold bracelets kept jingling from her wrists. "Cecilia," Tita said to her great, great, great—I couldn't remember how many greats anymore—granddaughters across the room. "This is my mother's sister's daughter and my mother's sister's daughter's granddaughter, Mrs. Ariana and Miss Jessica Puente."

The tips of Cecilia's long, dirty-blonde hair touched the top of her red baby belly. She untangled some of the hair wound around her gold hoop earrings. "We are so happy you all could make it." Cecilia looked like a college junior or senior at the most. Twenty-one, if I had to guess.

"I heard you were one of Conchita's friends."

"You could say that, yep. And my mother is related to your Great something-or-other Grandmother Tita."

"Ah, and Conchita is sweet. So, Jessica, how do you like being a mother?"

"I'm sorry?" I froze in disbelief. "Wow, I'm so embarrassed right now. Do I look old enough to be somebody's mother?"

"Oh, no. I'm sorry. I just thought, you know, since you're friends with Conchita, you must have some kids of your own?" Cecilia got nervous and tried to preoccupy herself with the aluminum pull tab at the top of her empty Coke can.

I wasn't insulted. If anything, it felt reassuring that someone thought me mature and adult enough to be a mother. If only they could tell a real employer. "It's okay. I'm trying out this new thing called waiting."

Cecilia's head slowly turned to the right as she tried to comprehend what I was saying. "Waiting?" Suddenly distracted by Conchita crossing the living room, she changed the subject. "We were about to start one of the games. Please help yourself to the food and take a seat." Cecilia pointed behind her. "There are more stools and chairs in the kitchen that you can bring out too."

My mother sat next to Tita while I headed to the kitchen. I made a chicken fajita plate, grabbed a Coke, and sat at a barstool.

"Okay, everyone—" Conchita clapped through the crowd, interrupting the loud gossip and laughter that suddenly turned to whispered gossip and laughter. "Marisa is coming around to give you all your Baby Bingo cards." She clapped again, "*callate, por favor. Mira*, remember that five in a row wins. Marisa, Marisa!" Conchita yelled and waved her arm toward Marisa, whom I could only assume was her Miss Fiesta assistant. "Make sure the ladies back in the kitchen get one. Yessica, you too." The teenager lifted the bottom of her sparkly blue pageant dress as she dropped off the remainder of the bingo cards and a small bag of candy at the bar in front of me. I grabbed one of the Christmas napkins to wipe off the salsa sticking to my fingers.

Tita dangled her small bag of candies from where she sat squished on the couch between my mother and other young Cecilias. "We are getting some Skittles to eat, too?"

"No!" Conchita yelled back as Tita and everyone else struggled to open their bags of candies with sticky fingers. "The Skittles are for the little square spots on your cards. Cover each bingo spot you get. Five in a row wins."

'What does the winner get?' I thought, sticking a fork in the last of my fajitas and staring down at the card's vertical and horizontal rows. 'Another baby?' I laughed at my own joke. If only Kit, Missy, or Colette were here. They wouldn't believe me—or they would yell at me. But my laugh stalled as the small, fuzzy Spanish words in the squares of the fiesta bingo cards began to make sense: three kids, four kids, five kids, six kids. *Six kids?! Why stop at six kids?* I felt borderline nauseous. On the one hand, I had a sneaking suspicion that making so many babies was a way to avoid life because carving out another purpose and career was so competitive and overwhelming. On the other hand, I felt like the bingo card was trying to tell me something I was missing.

"Okay, I'm shaking up the sombrero now, everyone." Conchita stopped momentarily to adjust a new necklace with Christmas lights she'd thrown on to match the festivities. "Okay, are your cards ready? Get ready." She continued shaking the Christmas-themed sombrero adorned in what appeared to be Rudolph's jingle bells.

The ladies hushed together and stared at their cards as if the calamitous jingle bell noise was a signal officiating the bingo playing.

Conchita accidentally pulled two wadded-up papers out of the sombrero, her face scrunching as she apologetically announced, "Oops. I meant to grab one. Okay, I know that's not fair, everyone. I'll put the other piece of paper aside to read that one next—that's only fair." Conchita bent down to put one of the pieces of paper on the floor near the playpen, exciting Mortimer. Mortimer pulled on the playpen fence like he wanted to stand up but couldn't. "Yes, *mijito*. Here, play with your toy for now." Conchita handed him a matching blue and yellow maraca. She stood up and continued as he waved it while lying on his belly. She flashed the wrinkled paper to the crowd. "The first bingo square is 'Newborn.' Those of you who've had a baby in the last year can put a Skittle on the word 'Newborn.'" Mortimer kept shaking his maraca back at his Mama. "Oh, I guess that's me too." Conchita quickly retreated to her hidden card sitting atop the ledge along the fireplace.

"Hey, no fair!" I half-joked, shouting across the living room. "The gameshow host isn't allowed to play, too, Vanna Brown."

"I know what you're thinking, Yessica—first Miss Fiesta, and now this. I beat you at everything! Don't worry; I will not take the prize this time."

Conchita said it playfully, so I didn't snap back. It took willpower, though.

"Okay," Conchita leaned down to open the other wadded-up paper still sitting by Mortimer. "The next one is *Tres Niños.*' If you have three kids, that's another bingo spot for you." Conchita kept shaking the sombrero with the jingle bells and singing out the words listed on the wadded-up pieces of paper: "First Anniversary." Conchita flashed the piece of paper again. "For those of you who've been married for one year."

Whoa, whoa, whoa. The Coca-Cola bubbles oozed from my nose. First an infant, three kids, and *then* married? "That's kind of putting the cart before the horse, isn't it?"

Conchita shook her head in disappointment. "So happy you are always here to lighten the mood, Yessica. Ladies pay no attention to the New Yorker in the back. She is an old friend."

Conchita shook the sombrero and pulled more wadded-up paper from it. "Whoops. I pulled two more again. This one is *'Escuela.'* Okay, for those of you who went to school with the mother-to-be. I think everyone will get that one. And the next one is *'Viente Anos.'* For those of you who've known the mother for twenty years."

"Hold on a second. That must be a mistake." I made sure to keep my last thought to myself. Are we sure the girls here are even twenty years old?

Conchita started losing focus. She began fiddling with the Christmas light necklace flickering around her neck. She bent down again, but this time to grab her mimosa sitting next to her card along the fireplace. "And *'Diez Anos.'*" For those of you who've known the mother for ten years."

"Bingo!" Somebody shouted from the floor near the backyard door.

"Oh, we have a winner!" Conchita shouted, raising her glass.

And then I felt a sudden pang, a jolt in my stomach, or maybe it was my heart. As I stared down at the bingo card, I realized I didn't even remember opening the stupid bag of candy, yet there they were, all the Skittles haphazardly scattered, the rainbow trailing from my bag, surrounding the edges of my bingo card. I guess all this time, I was playing along. And yet, empty spaces, all of them empty. Every. Last. One. All the years chasing success, some semblance of a career, to be left with nothing. To make the sacrifices in which one gives up things that make life worth living: Love. Husband. Home. Baby. Family. And the saddest part of all was that I no longer had the things for which I made all those sacrifices: Bank Account. Independence. A career with benefits—

a fabulous job I thought would save me from my mess of a personal life. The mess I had made. And what was it all for?

Conchita tried to clap for the winner, seemingly feigning excitement as she balanced her mimosa glass and continued fiddling with the Christmas lights around her neck. "*Oww, oww, oww.*" Conchita's eyes turned tight. "This is getting very hot."

Conchita's young assistant, Marisa, stepped out from a room behind the fireplace, parading a pink gift bag stuffed in matching cellophane. All the ladies' heads followed as Marisa picked up her sparkling blue pageant dress again. As she continued making her way to the winner, some of the ladies said "*boo,*" and "*aww,*" but eventually, everyone clapped and yelled, whistled, and said congratulations to the winner.

"*Oww, owww, oww,*" Conchita kept saying through all the commotion. She tried to spin off one, then two lightbulbs strung along her Christmas necklace. "Hot, hot, hot." Mortimer banged his maraca at her louder and faster while tightly holding onto the fence with his other hand. The house commotion grew, and a spark seemed to jump out from Conchita's necklace, from another bulb below her breast she had yet to notice.

"Conchita, Conchita!" I saw a spark and jumped off my stool to rush over to her. "Your necklace, your necklace!"

By then, Conchita seemed confused, but not from all the loud commotion. Was she drunk? Her dark hazel eyes seemed glazed over while looking up at me between sparks. "As usual, Yessica," she said so aggressively that she accidentally spat at me. "Always making fun of everybody else because you can't stand to look at yourself."

"Huh!" I reacted in astonishment. My body felt electric. I marched back a couple of steps in shock and bewilderment. I'd thought the bingo card had said it all, but there it was. Loud and clear. Whereas Colette's direction had been gentler and vague, Conchita's had been merciless and explicit. And then I suddenly thought of Missy. I thought she wasn't ready to hear certain things about Tilly. Did Colette believe I wasn't ready to hear certain things? Was Conchita here to tell me it was finally time I heard certain things?

I involuntarily jolted forward as another spark ignited along Conchita's neck. "How do you take this off? We need to take this off."

"Whaaat?" Conchita stammered out in a lethargic state. She looked at me, then back down, balancing her mimosa glass while I turned the bulbs.

I brushed up her disheveled hair, looking for the hooks. "Your necklace isn't safe, it isn't safe." I tugged at the necklace, which inadvertently pulled on some of Conchita's hair on the other side of her face.

"*Oww!*" Conchita spilled her mimosa down her shirt, sparking another breaking bulb and talking out of character. "Bitch, what are you doing?"

"We have to get this off before it lights you on fire."

The loud crowd of ladies finally settled down. They turned toward us. By then, all you could hear and see were Conchita and me going back and forth and the bulbs sparking up again.

"Conchita, stop fighting with me!" I was trying to keep my voice calm, but an edge of panic crept in.

Conchita kept jerking harder and harder away from me, finally yelling, "*Ouch*, Yessica, Stop!" One of her hands reached back to grab my head, causing her to spill the rest of her mimosa all over her dress and across the Christmas lights. The spill finally triggered one last spark, a small fire, and then a big fire.

"Holy shit!" someone yelled.

There was a chorus of "Conchita! Conchita!" And finally, my mother, "Yessica, Yessica!"

I made one last tug of Conchita's festive necklace. Finally, it popped off, one end of the string clutched in my hand, the other end soaring over my head in a flaming trail as my derriere landed against the hard Saltillo tile.

Without any time to think, I tossed the necklace far behind me right before the fire caught my fists. I rushed to the coffee table, where a water pitcher stood between margaritas and mimosas. I grabbed two more drinks to throw onto Conchita's dress. As the fire on her faded, I took a deep breath of relief only to notice another fire igniting along the Christmas tree, where I had carelessly thrown the necklace. Fortunately, the ladies were jumping up to follow my lead by then. Bingo cards and Skittles were flung across the floor as they ran to the tree with their drinks. Tita and my mother ran to the kitchen to fill more Solo cups with water while the fire alarms rang throughout the house. Smoke spread throughout the rooms, and one of the elder great-grandmothers grabbed Mortimer from his playpen to take him to the backyard. A Young Cecilia followed as she dialed and put her phone up to her ear. She paced the backyard and watched the rest of us through the window.

The fire kept dancing up the tree, as there were so many flammable ornaments to absorb and ignite: the yarn from the various *Ojo de Dios*, the cotton vestiges from the Mexican Santas, the red poinsettia flowers. The flames kept climbing higher. As they ascended, we kept rushing back and forth to and from the kitchen. Someone even found a bucket in the garage, but we couldn't tell if the fire was getting bigger or smaller.

"That's it, that's it!" My mother yelled as the last of the orange and blue fire diminished. We all froze for a few moments, which seemed to run on ever so long as the room dimmed darker without the fire and Christmas lights sparkling up the tree. Even the clouds seemed to eclipse the sun through the picture-frame window over the couch. Clutching our glasses, cups, and buckets, we waited to see if we'd extinguished the fire that seemed like an omen on this baby and Christmas. And then I had a thought: You can't successfully run from your problems when you're the one causing the problems. Because everywhere you go, there you are. When you're running away from the house fire that is your life, you're bringing the arsonist with you. Even when I tried to make things better, I always seemed to make things worse.

The end of the fire was slow as the black-and-white smoke billowed out from different sections of the tree where more pine needles had congregated together. The dissipating smoke seemed to speed up. As it cleared, black charred pieces of pine began to emerge and break off from the tree. And then there was nothing left but silence. While we'd finally extinguished the fire, we could see that it had already climbed most of the tree, during which it had taken out the shining white angel crowning the top.

In the distance, we could hear the first soft and then brazen sounds of a fire engine's sirens. The sound seemed round in my ears as it grew nearer, then farther, nearer, then farther again, turning the streets and corners as it approached. But when it finally drew closer, the sirens faded as we all focused on the loud wails crying beneath us: Conchita had fallen to her knees. She stared up at her tree, weeping and wiping the tears from her face. Young women crowded around her, trying to hug her, but she pushed them away as she inhaled and exhaled loud winds that seemed to contract with the last sounds of the fire engine sirens outside the door. Finally looking up, she turned just in time for her cheeks to turn bright white and red, reflecting the fire truck lights flooding through the windows. Suddenly catching her eyes on mine, I looked away. That feeling of guilt and remorse reminded me that instead of improving people's lives, I had the ability, talent, and voracious appetite to make their lives worse. How could I build anything: jobs, relationships, family—myself—when I clearly had the knack for lighting everything on fire and watching it explode?

***

The winter daylight relented earlier than usual as the forecasted hail would hit soon. Raindrops dove down in fragments: one or two here, five, six, seven there, then one or two here again. The firefighters pushed us out to finish extinguishing the fire while the ladies said their goodbyes and began dividing to their kids, their cars, and finally to their homes. My mother gave me a stern look before running to the car herself. I slowly approached Conchita. She stood in the street along the curb and stared at the smoke that filtered from the chimney and surrounded her home.

"Conchita, I'm so, so sorry."

She blinked at the clouds of smoke that seemed charcoal gray against the black sky.

I pushed on. "I just want you to know I was trying to help. I was worried you were going to catch on fire. Are you okay? You haven't said anything."

"No, I'm not okay, Jessica." Conchita kept her gaze on the smoke spinning out from her chimney. "I'm so tired and drained. It's hard. The family. All the kids. And the events. And the community. And my weight. It's hard. And that tree. That Christmas tree and the ornaments. Handed down from my *abuelitas* and handed down from their *abuelita*s…" She sniffled as she tried to catch her breath. "How will I ever replace it?"

"Conchita," I whispered. "Is that what you're worried about? The tree? The ornaments? That's so… replaceable." Even as I heard the words coming out of my mouth, I knew I sounded insensitive. I barreled on, trying to explain myself. "In this day and age, you can find ornaments that will still honor the original ornaments' sentiment."

"Oh, can I?" Conchita shot back. "What do you know about tradition? What do you know about the work of raising a family?"

"I know I watched it make my mother crazy when we were young. And I know it didn't get any better until she decided to give up."

"Give up? What are you saying to me right now?" Conchita turned to me. I expected to see anger in her eyes, but they seemed to plead with me instead.

"Not give up as in, give up your kids or husband," I rushed to explain. "Maybe you can pick your battles and eliminate some of the work?"

"Oh, I'm sure you'd say that. I'm sure you're glad to see my *Ojo de Dios* go down in flames, along with my heritage." Conchita changed her accent to mimic me. "Can't you hire a nanny? See if you can get a housekeeper or have somebody else throw the baby showers?" Conchita struggled with her last words as she blinked back her tears. She raised her fingers against her chin. A few tiny drops fell from her eyes and skimmed the tips of her dry, cracked lips. "Who are you to be giving me advice?"

I let the silence linger. Then I conceded. "You're right. I'm the last person." I rubbed my eyes, realizing for the first time all afternoon how drained I felt. "I'm starting to see that more. The more I resist, the more the truth finds me instead." Here was Conchita, working hard for everybody else when I seemed to work hard only for myself. Maybe that's why I could never get ahead.

"Yes." Conchita began, but she stared off into the smoke, and I wasn't sure if she was referring to herself or me. "Let someone else host the baby shower next time or announce the baby games while I sit on the sidelines bouncing Mortimer. Try to do one thing at a time instead of ten."

Sensing it was safe, I added, "and maybe you could get some rest? Carve out a little vacation for yourself?"

"You're right, Yessica." Conchita wiped her eyes and sniffled back the last of her tears.

"I am?"

"Absolutely," she said, sarcastically adding, "and you're just the one to help."

I wasn't sure if this was a trick.

"I think I need to come to New York for a few days."

"Sorry?"

"That is what I will do," Conchita said deliberately, clapping her hands like she was hatching a plan.

"Really?" I raised my eyebrows. I still couldn't tell if she was being genuine or if this was another one of her sneaky chess moves.

But then Conchita got that focused look reminiscent of her days performing on the stage—her breaths rising, her pupils dilating. "Delta, well, the city, we recently announced a new nonstop flight from San Antonio to New York. That is exactly what I'll do." Conchita's facial features didn't exactly smile so much as they instead relaxed from all the stress and dismay. "And thanks to you, I already have a place to stay." Conchita made the last declaration without waiting for my confirmation. It was as if it were more of an affirmation.

"Oh, uh…" I wrestled with what to say, but within milliseconds of my delay, I could already see the lines around Conchita's eyes and lips begin to change. I suspected she was waiting for my abrupt "No." We both gazed up where the sky seemed to spread, returning to its natural infinite darkness. It was as if the vastness had cast a net onto the charcoal gray smoke; the remnants of the fire appeared to mysteriously and inconsistently disappear through small holes of darkness. And for a moment, as more clouds moved in and the rain briefly stopped, I thought of how life is kind of a miracle. The way things happen and then don't. And then do. But differently than we had expected.

Drizzle picked up, turning to cold, hard rain again. We felt the first slaps of hail on our backs. I studied Conchita's profile. The light freckles around the bones of her Aztec nose were so similar to my mother's. To my faint surprise, I realized the resentment I'd once held onto so tightly had evaporated into the chill night air.

"First things first," I said. "If you're gonna be a New Yorker, you'll need some walking shoes."

ELEVEN

It was still January, but the overeager Winifred staff decorated the lobby in red, white, and pink for Valentine's Day. Like little working ants, they scattered across our ant pile, carrying full vases of pale carnations and silver bowls overflowing with Sweetheart candy.

After I'd already been waiting for twenty minutes, a lazy Missy moseyed off the elevator. "Ooh, thank you." She stuck out her hands as the ants dropped off one of the silver bowls with candy at the coffee table in front of us. They hung streamers and cut-out hearts along the lobby walls and even stapled a Valentine's Day-themed dining menu to the bulletin board.

Missy read her lavender heart-shaped candy to me. "Will you Be Mine?"

"Only if you promise to 'Call Me,' or 'Kiss Me.'" I showed her the pastel hearts I picked next.

"I thought you'd never ask, Jess." Missy grabbed extra Sweetheart candy, quickly stuffing it into her pocket.

"So, what took you so long?" I asked as we zipped up our jackets. "I thought we wanted an earlier start on the new apartment search."

Missy stared at her feet as she spoke. Something was fishy. "I mean, I was thinking about it, and living here is a great deal. Our rent includes two meals a day, and we live in the middle of

Manhattan." She also twisted the end of her ponytail around the tips of her fingers. "You know, my twin bed isn't so bad now either. Also, I got one of those memory foam bed covers from the Penn Station K-Mart. I also bought some flip-flops for the communal showers—"

I was confused. "Okay, so that takes care of your athlete's foot. But what about how our rent is increasing? And I thought your student loans were increasing from all the unsubsidized interest? And that you could barely afford the rent even before. How will you do it now that the rent is increasing?"

"I, I—"

"Did you finally get hired for real at Tilly? I knew you'd move up soon, but I didn't think it would be that soon. That's great."

"Not exactly."

Suspicious, I sat back on the couch and stared at Missy. "Are you leaving New York? Did you find other roommates? If you're breaking up with me, I can take it. Just promise to write sometime."

"No, it's not that." Missy looked down again, swirling her right foot in a circle across the floor, pulling on the loose threads at the ends of her old Christmas sweater. "The Winifred knocked off some money from my rent."

I crossed my arms over my chest. "They knocked off some money from your rent? Can they do that?"

"They can, but only in extreme circumstances."

"Extreme circumstances? Aren't your parents still helping you out? Didn't they pay for your flight back to Texas for Thanksgiving and Christmas?"

"Umm…"

"How much money did The Winifred knock off your rent? Obviously, it's significant if you're considering staying."

"It's, like, a few hundred dollars."

"How much is a few hundred dollars?"

"Umm…" She hesitated. "Like four hundred."

"Four hundred dollars?!"

A lady working behind the front desk turned her head up at us.

Missy pleaded, throwing her face down and shaking her head. "I shouldn't have said anything. I knew I shouldn't have said anything."

"So, you're only paying two-thirds of what everyone else is? Is that why the rent is increasing? So that some of the girls can take care of the other girls? That's like the blind leading the blind."

Missy finally sat beside me, burrowing her head into her hands. "I know, I'm sorry, I'm sorry."

"No, it's the poor leading the poor. The poor taking care of the other poor. Why can't I get a discount on my rent too?"

"Full-time students can't get subsidized."

"What do you mean full-time students?"

"You have to be working full-time."

Missy's words only rubbed more salt in my wounds.

"You have to be able to show that even while working full-time, you still can't make ends meet, and apparently, my internship counts."

My pulse raced. "But Missy, I couldn't make ends meet. That's why I went back to school. I've only been able to get part-time jobs and gigs. I've still been applying for every full-time job I can, even at the university. I applied to be a teaching assistant, and—"

"Sorry. You can try talking to them. I don't know all the rules. I just——my mom and dad told me to ask them if there was anything they could do for me, and before I knew it, they were handing me the forms and then telling me to sign, and, and—"

"Missy?" I narrowed my eyes in suspicion. "Did you do that thing where you started crying hard, or did you go in there already crying?"

Missy got up. She circled her scarf around her neck. "I'm sorry, I didn't know how to tell you. I was trying to figure out how to tell you. But I absolutely want to search for apartments with you still— I even brought a list, see?" Missy pulled a piece of crumpled paper from her pocket. "I just didn't know what to do. Please don't be mad at me."

I stayed seated. "I'm not mad." I just felt like lighting a fire to the entire Winifred building.

"Then why are you looking at me like that?"

"It's—" I stood up and started pacing too. "You haven't even hit rock bottom. Do you know what rock bottom is?"

"Rock bottom is how I feel right now."

"You better hope things start looking up then. It gets easier, you know."

"What? What gets easier?"

"Taking the handouts. First, it's 'Mom and Dad are simply going to give me a little bit of money to cover part of my credit card and the flight,' then it's 'oh, they won't feel it if they help with one month's rent,' then next month it's 'I need two months,' then—"

"No!" Missy said. "I never asked for a handout. That's not what I asked for. It's not like that."

Sometimes, I forgot how much younger Missy was, and when I remembered, I suddenly felt depressed all over again. Still, I knew that if she kept taking the help, it would get easier to keep taking the help. Her life would have ups and downs, and I thought she needed to figure out how to overcome them independently. "I understand getting help for a bit. Heck, I moved in with my family for a few months. But now that your rent is perpetually locked in four hundred less than the real rate, which was already lower than rent in Manhattan…how are you ever going to…" I cut myself off.

She looked down. Of course, I immediately felt terrible for making her feel bad. "It's fine, Missy. You're starting out. Sometimes I forget you're younger than me. I have to remember that."

Missy looked up. "But let's keep our commitment to search for apartments. Let's not get too comfortable here at The Winifred."

***

Missy and I walked north to Hell's Kitchen to view a few apartments. The second one, a fifth-floor walkup, had three rooms, each accommodating two bunk beds for four people. The rate seemed exorbitant, including the first month's rent, a deposit, and a broker's fee.

"Let me get this straight." I leaned closer to Missy as we walked west on Forty-Sixth Street, trailing farther away from the Restaurant Row awnings and signs flashing on. "The broker wanted us to pay six-thousand-eight hundred dollars each upfront, so we get to sleep in a dirty closet with several other roommates?"

Missy swung her head at me. "And that's just in one of the apartment's closets. Who would pay so much for a place like that?"

"When I saw those bunk beds crammed into one tiny room, I had an eerie flashback to this creepy national news story when I was a teenager."

Missy pulled the directions out of her Tilly Worth crossbody purse—my favorite one with the dark snakeskin and dangerously long but sexy metallic chain and gunmetal logo. "Let's see . . . where was the next place?"

"The news story was about Heaven's Gate, a cult that claimed to be a religious group from California, where almost forty people committed suicide in the middle of the night. Do you remember that?"

Missy briefly stopped, dodging a dog walker, and then pointed to the blocks like she was counting. "Umm, no. I don't. Let me see, we're on Forty-Sixth Street but west of Ninth Avenue…"

"Yep, you were probably five when that happened. Anyway, the same video footage from the story aired on all the television stations when the news broke. Are you ready for this?"

"Oh, it's over here." Missy folded her directions back into her purse and walked faster. "Okay, tell me. I'm ready for it."

"As they prepared for their suicide, members of the cult lay down next to each other in bunk beds wearing all-black clothes with black Nike tennis shoes. They shrouded their bodies with purple blankets. When they showed the TV footage of them lying dead on the bunkbeds, the black tennis shoes and white Nike logos peeked out from the end of their purple blankets."

"Okay, that is a little creepy," Missy said. "Maybe you shouldn't be telling me this story in the evening, as it's getting darker. And while we're alone."

"My point is, I wish I could forget the image, along with that apartment we saw."

We crossed Ninth Avenue and made our way toward Tenth. "Wow, this area is still close to all the restaurants, shops, and transportation while even closer to the water. Are you sure it's a two-bedroom for only twelve hundred a month?"

"That's what the ad said on the internet. Maybe it's rent-controlled. We'll have a roommate, but it's fine."

"One roommate? Not three-hundred-seventy-two roommates? That's such a bargain. I hope you brought your checkbook." We walked another block to glimpse the old Naval ships at the Hudson River. We stopped at a ten-story, pre-war brick building and noticed old air conditioning units hanging outside the windows.

Missy buzzed the unit, and a woman's voice answered. "I'm on the fifth floor, in the north corner."

We scaled three stories, and when we arrived at the fourth floor, I asked Missy, "hey, I thought the ad said this was a third-floor walkup?"

"I know, I was thinking the same thing."

"Okay. It's in the corner if we can figure out which direction is north."

A young, stocky blonde woman with cleavage popping out of a white T-shirt answered the door. Upon introduction, she held an orange American Curl cat in her arms and therapeutically pet it.

"Hello. I'm Helena. Please come in. I'd expected you here earlier, but it's fine."

"Hi, I'm Missy, and this is my friend Jess. Thank you for having us today, and I'm so sorry we're a bit late." Missy continued to placate our grumpy greeter. "I read that you act. How cool. I wish I could act."

I followed Missy, making sure to get some therapeutic cat pets in, too. "What up, Garfield. Got any lasagna? Oh, wait, that's Thursday. It's Monday, you hate Mondays."

"It's *she*," Helena said. "And her name is Queen Elizabeth."

"Oh, sorry, Your Majesty." I politely petted the cat's neck. "What I meant to say was, 'What up, your Royal Highness, Queen of all the Commonwealth.'"

"I've been here for about two years now," Helena said while stroking Queen Elizabeth. Her voice faded into the background of her grim accommodations. Missy and I examined the apartment. Adjacent to the kitchenette was an entire bedroom set—a set that would've been perfect in the master bedroom of a large house but not in such a tight space. A pine sleigh bed, two dressers, a stuffed clothing rack, and other bedroom furniture covered the only ray of light almost shining through a small, squared window off the main living area. The window overlooked a dirty, un-swept courtyard below and the windows of several other apartments. Above us, wet clothes hung from lines spreading from building to building.

I feigned excitement. "I guess there isn't an in-unit washer and dryer in this one either," I yelled back at Missy, pointing to the clothing lines. "But hey, it'll be like you're living in Italy with all the hanging clothes—except not."

"Oh Jess, you're so funny." Missy looked back at Helena while slapping her hand against my shoulder to excuse me from the stranger I knew I'd never see again. "My friend loves to joke. Jess, you know I've always longed to go to Italy with you."

"And look, there's *graffiato* too." I pointed to the building across from us where red spray paint spelled the letter A in a circle, illustrating the anarchist symbol. "Missy, if you add one more circled A to the wall, we'd call that *graffiti*. Can you guess why?"

"Oh, I don't know Jess, ha, ha, funny, as usual."

"Because that's the plural form of *graffiato*: *graffiti*. And we didn't even need to go to Italy or down to Little Italy to get some Italian culture. *Graffiato* means scratching. But with more than one scratching comes drawings, and then we get—"

"Graffiti, Jess! We get it!"

"*Va bene*, Missy, yeesh. Can't take you anywhere." I took one last glance at the anarchist symbol. "We hate you, Government. Bring back the jobs. Sometimes it feels like we're all actresses in this economy waiting for our big break."

"Jess."

"Sorry, that was a joke. I'm sure you'll have luck as an actress." I turned around to face Helena's assets, still spilling out.

"It's act*or*," Helena corrected.

"Ah, I like it. A nod to equality, okay." I winked at her. "Got it." Missy and I crossed the kitchenette that sat along one wall in the living room. In front of it stood a carpeted cat tree tower. It was the most giant cat tower I'd ever seen. I couldn't help but say aloud, "Missy, look—that's Her Royal Highness's Buckingham Palace."

Missy giggled, then politely put her hand over her mouth, remembering she was mad at me. "Jess, can you just stop right now?"

"Oh, sorry, you're right. That's way too modest to be Buckingham Palace. Missy, look—it's Windsor Castle."

"Is this a two-bedroom?" Missy asked, trying to remain calm and professional as her eyes rested too long on the king-size bedroom set engulfing the living room.

"It's a one-bedroom, but you would have the bedroom, and I would take the living room."

We walked toward the bedroom, passing the bathroom that wasn't a full bathroom but rather a toilet right next to a shower drain below a faucet. A dingy yellow curtain loosely hung between the toilet and the faucet knob on the wall. I didn't need to go any farther into the third-world country. Staying by the entryway, I watched Missy politely go through all the motions.

Missy stalled, pivoting across junk that canvassed the entire area. "Oh, I see there's a closet." The bed and floor stood covered in trash, a stained goose-down comforter, and several overflowing Tupperware bins.

Helena finally put down Queen Elizabeth. "What do you think? Do you want to live here, then?"

Missy tried to buy some time to come up with an excuse. "How much did you say it was again?"

"It's only twelve hundred a month."

"Oh. Yeah, it's definitely reasonably priced…"

Missy was really bad at this.

"Thank you, Helena," I said. We had hoped there'd be room for the both of us, but seeing now that the place is made for two instead of three—"

"Yeah." Missy piggybacked on my excuse. "If we don't find a place together, I'll get back to you soon."

"Just email me then."

We would not email her then.

***

The apartment door slammed shut behind us. I waited until we were out of earshot before I snickered. "If you get that apartment, would you be under the reign of the longest-ruling queen in the twentieth and twenty-first centuries?"

Missy didn't respond. She kept rushing down the steps.

I paced faster down the stairwell to catch her. "Like, do you think Helena expects you to be Queen Elizabeth's serf? Ha." I laughed at my own joke. "No, seriously, did the ad say you'd have to change out her kitty litter and fill her bowls with water, food, and all that? I stayed at Kit and Sam's apartment over the summer, and it was becau—"

"Can you just stop talking already, Jess?!"

My throat clenched. I didn't know what to say next. Missy rarely got upset, and what's more, her voice seemed to crack between her words. We silently retraced our steps back toward Ninth Avenue. Our jackets weighed heavier with each passing block. The dark winter days seemed to hang on longer, and persistent intervals of silence between us were amplified by the last of the rush hour car horns, ambulances, traffic, and police sirens. Bright Times Square lights blinked at Missy and me between streets and buildings. The first blizzard of the year would hit soon, and we shielded ourselves from the dropping temperatures with our parka hoods. Or maybe we tried to shield ourselves from one another. I tried to tread lightly. I didn't know what triggered Missy, but her abrupt comment sliced through me, and I knew that I would need to choose my next words carefully.

"Missy?" I tried to say gently. "Do you want to talk about it?"

"No!" She snipped back at me. "No, I don't want to talk about it, and no, I don't want to hear about graffiti, Italy, actors, and Queen Elizabeth, and Hell's Gate."

"Heaven's Gate."

"Whatever!"

A woman at a halal cart turned toward us while we rushed through her and the rest of the line, waiting for their dinner.

I tried to keep it together and act like the helpful, cooler big sister. "So, maybe you *do* want to talk about it?"

"No, I do not." A few tears slid down Missy's face. She fled a few more paces ahead of me. Seeing the construction south of us, she walked east, and I followed her across the street. The crosswalk signal's red hand flashed, and I ran narrowly through Ninth Avenue before the red hand flashed *stop*. Then, Missy abruptly jerked herself around. "You were doing great with your encouraging speeches at The Winifred, and…"

"And what?" My voice squeaked up. I couldn't help it as I started to lose my cool. This was about *me?*

Missy persisted. "And being there for me when I confided in you about Tilly. But you just couldn't help yourself today. Not only can I *not* afford to stay at The Winifred for even four hundred dollars less and meet some stupid 'bar' of yours," Missy made air quotes in her expensive leather monogrammed Tilly gloves. "But I apparently can't afford anything else halfway decent either."

A bus stopped behind the Port Authority Terminal, its muffler emitting black fumes into our conversation. A skinny homeless man with a dingy blanket around his head sat on the concrete, shaking a can of change. While facing the terminal, he talked to his reflection in the window.

Missy's accusations hit a nerve. I, too, was fed up with crap jobs, crap apartments, and crap pay. As the can of change impatiently jingled at me in the freezing temperature, a ripple of heat shimmied up inside me, compelling me to urgently speak. "You know what, Missy? I'm tired of saying I'm sorry to you and to all the little kiddies at school who can't get their feelings hurt because they were raised to get medals for last place, and let's not forget participation trophies, too. But guess what? Life is hard, and it has many more downs than it does ups sometimes. And you're just mad at me because I'm witnessing you experiencing those downs, so you can't simply pretend they don't exist like all your friends do on your social media."

Missy wiped some of the tears from her face. "Oh, tell me how you really felt this whole time, why don't you!"

"The downs aren't my fault, okay? The downs would be here waiting for you like they're waiting for everybody else because life doesn't give you medals and riches simply for breathing on Planet Earth."

Missy cried harder under her parka while she kept yelling. "You're so damn dry and mean sometimes! Why can't you just understand me? Why can't you try and pretend to understand me? They made getting a good job sound so easy in school, okay? Compared to what it is."

"The American Dream, you mean?" My words cracked, and I realized I also struggled to hold back my tears. I wasn't ready to tell Missy that my hours got cut at Last Chance, that I wasn't getting any more remote work at Harrison, or that I still didn't know why I was going to college at thirty—and how would I pay for it?

The homeless man's voice got louder. He kept talking to himself in the window, turning around to shake his can of coins at us. "Penny for your thoughts? A penny for your poem, perhaps? A penny for your fortune?"

"Go to school, do your internship, find your passion." Missy's breath puffed out circles against the frigid air while she spoke. "It was all about finding your passion and your stupid dream." She waved her arms in emphasis. "And how amazing and special you are. I thought I was so amazing and special."

"One penny," the homeless man said again.

"And the truth is," Missy continued, "all of it is garbage. Even that stupid Oprah stuff that my mother loves, 'you can have it all, just not all at once.' That's the thing, you can't have anything at all!'"

"Only one penny," the homeless man said yet again.

The conversation was not ending, so I pulled the last three quarters from my pocket and dumped them into the can.

"Cha-ching, you will be spared. Thank you for paying the pied piper. And now it is time to gander into your future."

"Seriously, Jess?" Missy and I waited to see what would happen next.

The man jumped and twirled in a circle like a ballerina. Then, he pulled down the blanket resting above him. "I must search your eyes first. Yes, the eyes tell us all we need to know about the soul."

Missy and I suddenly jumped up as he yelled, "beauty, ah, beauty! And I can see in your eyes lots of happiness too, yes, lots of happiness. But also very much sorrow. Very much sorrow if you do not meet the world halfway. Sorrow will consume your souls, and it will cloud your judgment."

Missy's tears paused. Rush hour died, busses stopped accelerating, and the dropping temperatures froze, too. One, two, three lonely and lazy snow flurries calmly fell between us.

"See, Jess? Sometimes, the universe *is* really listening." Her eyes swelled with tears, and then she just started running, running back toward The Winifred.

"Thank you, Yoda," I said to the man, my shoulders nudging his as I sprinted. "Stop! I wasn't finished."

The farther we went, the more I could see the snow barreling its way up Hell's Kitchen from Chelsea, slickening the roads with a thin coat. "And you haven't experienced black ice before; slow down!" We both crossed back over the street, leaping beyond a construction site once we made it to Thirty-Ninth Street, and by then, Missy's purse had begun to slide off her left shoulder. "You're going to hurt yourself!" The green tarp covering the chain-link fence on the west side of Ninth Avenue blocked our sight of Thirty-Eighth Street. "Missy, stop. The street ends, stop!"

She turned to yell back at me, too. "Stop following me. Go away, Jess!" Finally, the construction ended, and the road opened up again. "*Ahh!*" Missy started to slip. A yellow cab slammed on the brakes but hydroplaned instead.

"Missy, Missy?" A loud clunk broke through the flurries' silence, and a yellow cabbie tried to slam on the brakes before it was too late.

It all happened so fast. I heard myself shouting Missy's name again before I consciously understood what had happened. "Missy, no!"

A small Indian man jumped out of the cab, but her body was on the other side and beyond our view. I yelled again, "What did you do to her? Jesus, couldn't you see her?" We both ran to the other side of the cab, where Missy lay limp on the ground against the taxi cab. "Missy, Missy, are you okay? Tell me you're okay?"

Missy's hair had swept across her face, and I could see that her long purse strap had caught the rearview mirror and wound itself into a knot with her on the other end. Small pieces of broken Valentine's Day Sweethearts sprinkled around her body and trailed off her jacket and into the street.

"Missy, Missy…" I gently touched her head. "I'm so sorry, I'm so, so sorry." Tears stung my cheeks. "You're right, okay? Open your eyes, and I promise never to make another joke about our hardships ever again. I am so sorry, please open your eyes! Please? I promise, I promise, if you open your eyes, I promise."

I hugged her, and the idiot cab driver said, "no, no suppose to touch, no suppose to touch." He dialed his phone. "No touch."

I was sobbing now, crying so hard I could barely see in front of my face: Crying for everything I once had, crying for all the things I still wanted, crying for the most important things I still seemed to keep losing. "I'm sorry about the jokes." I rocked her back and forth in my arms. "It's something I learned when I was little, okay? When there were too many of us and no food in the fridge. I'm sorry I couldn't help it, but I promise I will help it."

Then coughing. Missy started coughing. Her free right hand slowly began brushing the hair off her face.

"Missy, how many fingers am I holding up?" I looked into her eyes. "No, what's my name? Say my name first."

Missy listlessly opened her mouth and her eyes. A flurry touched the tip of her tongue as she spoke. "Satan? Is that you?"

I cried and laughed, hugging her again. "Yes, yes, it's me, Missy. I'm so sorry."

"*Ouch.*" She pulled back her left arm, tangled in the purse strap.

"Sorry, I'll untangle it." I unknotted the strap from the rearview mirror.

"Satan?" Missy massaged the back of her neck. "Objects," she began to stutter. "Objects in mirror are closer than they appear."

"Okay, so maybe you're not so okay."

"But one thing's for sure," Missy continued. "If only I hadn't been wearing this stupid Tilly purse."

I couldn't tell now whether I was laughing or crying, or if Missy wanted me to joke back. "Damn Tilly."

"That witch."

"I knew those long crossbody bags were foreshadowing your demise."

"I think, maybe, maybe—" Missy stuttered and laughed, looking up at me, her eyes slowly blinking open, then closed. "Yep. Now. Now I am done with Tilly, at this very moment. I have decided. I am breaking up with Tilly."

I stopped laugh-crying and stared at her. "Really, Missy?"

"Yes."

"Okay, don't move. Play dead. I'm going to get pictures of you caught in her purse strap. How much money did you say she has?"

"Billions, billions, and billions of dollars, like McDonald's."

"Like McDonald's."

"And I have to take out the trash."

"Yes, you do. That is one of your job duties."

Missy raised her hand in the air. "For free. I do it for free. Hello, my name is Missy, will work for food. No, will work for free." A cop car's blue flashing lights advanced toward us as the Indian man kept talking on his cell phone. "And the immigrant," Missy kept yelling. "Even the immigrant makes more money than me."

"I don't know if you want to keep shouting that."

"But this is my country." She yelled louder above the police sirens behind us. "But hey, at least I'm an errand girl, dropping off a suit at Christy Turlington's loft in TriBeCa or Novak Djokovic's penthouse."

"Say what now? You didn't tell me you met Tennis Hottie Pants. This changes everything. You can't leave Tilly now."

Missy started laugh-crying more. Her yelps continued in syncopation with the sirens.

I turned my head back. "Missy, you know all those police sirens we hear daily in the city? Well, this time, they're for us."

"Oh no." Missy's eyes darted over my shoulder. Red lights bounced off her steel blue eyes in the dark. "Please tell me that's not a fire truck, too."

I turned my head, then back at Missy. "That is, without a doubt, a fire truck. I'm getting used to them, as they seem to follow me wherever I go. But how else would we meet men since we live at

The Winifred?" I disheveled her hair again. "Quick. Get back to playing dead, damsel in distress."

Missy tugged at her purse and rubbed the wrist that had been stuck around the rear-view mirror. "There are so many men getting out of the fire truck right now, and do I hear another cop car coming? They must be bored tonight."

"Crap. Maybe I should play dead, too." I dropped behind Missy, pitching my back against the cab, and finally disheveled my hair. I threw my head to the side and stuck out my tongue.

Missy laughed as an officer in a tight NYPD jacket outlining his big biceps approached us. "How are you doing this evening, ladies?"

"Officer?" Missy said while she continued to rub her untangled wrist. "While my friend always sounds like she has just been hit by a car, it was actually me."

The officer laughed as he squatted down above us. His dimples flexed in and out as he tried to keep a straight face. A hot firefighter jumped out of his door and walked in our direction with a paramedic kit. The firefighter also bent down, opening the paramedic kit. "Okay, which one of you ladies is—"

The police officer moved to the side to make room for the firefighter, then joined the remainder of his unit, directing traffic around our accident. One firefighter removed Missy's boot.

"She's just trying to get a foot massage, sir. Don't be fooled." He looked up at me, smiling, then back at Missy's foot.

"I try to get hit by cabs regularly, and I use that pick-up line at every bar in town—*ouch*. Sorry, that hurt a bit."

"It's not quite a sprained ankle, but there is some inflammation. I can get you wrapped up for tonight, but you'll want to go see the doctor tomorrow to be on the safe side and maybe take some X-rays. It'll probably be bruised by this weekend." He put down Missy's foot and sorted through the supplies in his kit. "You're lucky. It's starting to come down now. The weatherman says this week we'll see the first blizzard. Finally. I can't believe it's almost February."

"*Oww, oww*," Missy squealed.

"Sorry, a few more rounds," the man said.

"That just about does it then, Miss—."

"Missy. The name is Missy." She blushed while he looked into her eyes and held onto her foot.

And then I saw it: the tan line around his left ring finger.

"My, look at the time." I stepped to my feet, wiping off the wet gravel from the back of my coat while the two kept dazing into each other's eyes. "Come on, Cinderella. I think they need us back at The Winifred before the curfew. You know? In those tiny twin-sized beds that men will never see anyway because they're not allowed past the first floor?" I pretended to lose my balance to nudge Prince Charming off his squat. He fell over, releasing Missy's foot.

"Whoops." The firefighter tried to catch his balance and remain calm. "Ma'am," he said, standing up. "You be real sure to take care of yourself, okay?"

I crossed my eyes and stuck my finger down my throat behind his back.

"Of course." She put on her sock and boot. "Thank you for all your help. My foot is already starting to feel better."

***

The cop car abruptly halted at the American flag hanging over The Winifred's entrance. The faded, weak snowflakes turned into thick, white masses fluttering, then finally flapping, carrying the flag whipping against the sudden gusts of wind.

"*Oww, oww, oww*," Missy said, straightening her leg.

Staring down at her foot, I knew I had been a bad friend. If she hadn't been running from me, she never would have been side-swiped by the cab. As the snow picked up speed, twinkling above us, I thought about Conchita, her home, and her Christmas tree on fire. About how, in both this disastrous scenario with Missy and the disastrous scenario with Conchita, I was the common denominator. But how could I be the person I thought I was or the person I thought I was meant to be if my life felt consistently on pause *in media res*?

Two cops and I walked over to Missy's door. I grabbed her, putting her arm around my neck as she hopped on one foot with me back up the steps of The Winifred entrance. She put her right hand on her chest. She snidely recited: "I pledge allegiance to the flag of the United States of America, and to the Republic, for which it stands, one Nation, under The Winifred, Indivisible, with Liberty, and Justice for all. Indivisible. What does that mean, Jess? Indivisible?"

"Come on, you know what that means." I stopped to reconsider. "I guess we don't use that word much in any other context, do we? But it does mean undivided, no, undividable."

"Like together?"

"Yes. Like we will always be together." And I hoped we would. Déjà vu struck as we peered at the flag valiantly rippling against the high winds. But a good déjà vu. I could see it plainly: I would never have met Missy if I hadn't lost my job. I wouldn't have reconnected with Kit, Conchita, or even my mother. I wouldn't have met Colette with her—okay, sometimes pretentious—dispensations of life advice I was beginning to enjoy puzzling through. Maybe we somehow all needed each other. And maybe I already—no, finally—had all the things I needed. Maybe this was the *more* I had been seeking. Sometimes, the problem with trying to be that strong, independent woman is that you lose all the friends along the way because you're too busy trying to be better than everybody else without asking for help.

"Oh no," Missy frowned. Her low grumble sounded like she was piecing together her own breakthrough. "But do we always have to be together at The Winifred? Will we ever get out of here?"

I couldn't help but smile. We crossed the lobby, the front desk, the mailboxes, the phone booth, and finally, the guest check-in.

Missy leaned against the wall. "What the hell is up with the elevator today?"

"Three-hundred-seventy-three guest rooms."

"Jess? Was that the rock bottom you were telling me about?"

"Well, rock bottom is different for everyone," I said sardonically. "Only you can know your true rock bottom."

"But my rock bottom…" Missy flicked the tip of my nose. "Is so amazing and special and unique. Whose rock bottom includes black ice?"

"Ha." I nodded in agreement. You're lucky an ambulance didn't come. You would have had to pay a thousand dollars, and that would *really* have been rock bottom."

"What?" Missy shrieked. "Why would I have had to pay a thousand dollars?"

I raised my eyebrows. "Because that's about what it costs without health insurance? When the ambulance has to come and pick you up?"

Missy shook her head. "Oh, I have health insurance."

"Sorry, what?"

"Insurance. I have health insurance. I gave the details to the firefighter just in case when you were talking to the police after."

I wouldn't say I liked where this was going. Something was folding over unpleasantly in my mind. "Wait. How does the intern who works for free and makes less than the immigrant have health insurance?"

"Oh, duh, I can be on my parent's insurance until I'm like, I don't know, twenty-six or twenty-seven now, thanks to this new Act thing in the news."

Of course. How could I have forgotten about the new Affordable Care Act? Kids today would get to keep living the dream and living off the Bank of Mommy and Daddy. Being dependents forever. All I managed to say aloud was, "Wow."

"What?"

I struggled to find words that wouldn't make me sound like the resentful old bat I felt inside. "I'm happy for you, Missy, I am. I think it's great. I, I..."

"What?"

"It just feels unfair, is all. Meanwhile, my generation falls farther and farther into the pit of Peter Pan's Lost Boys. We really are the Lost Generation, The Last Generation, whatever, either way, we're lost."

"The Lost Generation? What's unfair?"

"Basically, when I was a young adult—

"Jess, you're still young."

"Thanks, but you could only stay on your parent's health insurance until you were twenty-one *if* you were in college full-time. So, if you decided not to go to college, you were pretty much off the health insurance by age eighteen."

"Eighteeeen?" Missy drew out the number's last syllable in disbelief. "How did they expect you to pay for the dentist, and health insurance, and the ambulance, and school, and rent, and your phone, and car, and gas, and car insurance, and subway, and clothes, and—"

"Ideally, eighteen is the age we're all supposed to be adults and contributing members of society. You know, like when we can vote and join the military?"

"How is that supposed to happen if we're all chasing our dreams and passions and—"

"Competing to be so special and amazing and unique?"

"Yeah." I smiled. Maybe she did get it after all.

We heard voices in the corridor nearby before Missy could fully bask in a newfound appreciation for her health insurance. The Winifred's warden, Agnes, rounded the corner with several young women behind her, conducting the last evening tour.

Agnes recited her usual tour script, momentarily glancing at a crumpled piece of paper. "While men still aren't allowed past the first floor, they're allowed in one of these parlors. They can meet you all here." She pointed to where we sat in the Greta Garbo and

Marlene Dietrich-themed parlors with gold and white striped wallpaper. "Again, they must check in first. Also, note that many young women today like to use these little parlors to watch movies on their laptops with friends."

Staring at Agnes' hip, Missy shook her head no. "And do they all need to wear those green fanny packs?"

I mimicked a line from The Winifred's 1923 newspaper clipping: "If the beau parlors are as attractive completed as they were when the writer saw them, we may look for a high engagement rate among Winifreds. No man could resist.'"

"Come on, ladies," Agnes said. "We'll go to the ballroom next. While not as famous as The Barbizon, The Winifred's ballroom is similar to the other ballrooms built in hotels for women during the turn of the century." The new Winifreds filed past her in a long line. "And for those asking, The Martha Washington down the street is no longer a hotel for women." She ushered them away, folding up her little piece of paper and tucking it into her fanny pack. "It opened in 1903. Veronica Lake was found there after her heyday in the 1960s, when her fame died, and she was divorced. She was broke and even became a barmaid, although she pretended to be filling in for a friend."

The elevator finally careened open. Missy tugged at my sweater, exhaling an extended sigh of relief. "I'm so tired."

We hobbled over, making it to the elevator before the doors shut.

"I'm sorry." I felt guilty about what a good sport Missy had always been, especially to put up with me for over a year.

Missy fell silent.

"I'm sorry I lost my real job. I'm sorry my hours got cut at Harrison and at my new job that isn't even a real job; I'm sorry that our rent is increasing. I'm sorry that I resent my mother and everyone else who seems to have help through their hardships."

Missy kept silent. The elevator cables echoed as we climbed up.

"How is it fair that my cohorts in undergrad don't have student loan debt now because their parents were divorced, so they qualified for grants? Or that my mother didn't have student loan debt because she irresponsibly had four children too young, and the government was like, 'here are some grants.' Yet, I'm going to be punished with six figures in student loan debt? And she was married. And she at least had my father's financial contributions. And you getting help with rent, and then—"

"And then me and my insurance?" Missy's voice trembled. She focused on the closed elevator door in front of us. We did not press our buttons again. I turned to her while the rickety cables kept dragging us higher, past both our floors—five and six—who knew where we were headed next.

My head fell low in shame from my resentment. But I fessed up to it. "Yes." I turned my head to meet Missy's profile. "I'm sorry I'm always on my worst behavior. I'm sorry that you have to see me on my worst behavior, even though you've been nothing but a best friend." My eyes teared up. "I'm sorry for feeling sorry for myself, and I'm sorry that it feels like I missed some boat—not that it's your fault. But I'm sorry for taking it out on you."

"I will forgive you." Missy turned to me.

"Really?"

She smiled. "I suppose. Beggars can't be choosers, right?"

I smiled back, nudging her shoulder.

Missy continued. "When I land back on my feet, without this bandage, I'll be sure to write once in a while, like you said."

The elevator doors creaked open at its last destination: the rooftop. We scanned left to right as the snow swirled above us. "Huh. Lucky number thirteen," I smiled. "Shall we?"

"Why not?" Missy extended her arm out to keep the door from closing. "Now that I think about it, I don't know if I've ever been on a rooftop in a blizzard.

"Bucket list."

Leaning against the rooftop ledge, we stared across the jagged skyline, watching the snow crown each skyscraper's tip.

"Look." Missy pointed as the snow increased speed and spun around our heads. "The 'New' in the famous New Yorker Hotel sign isn't lit up bright red tonight. I wonder if it's the blizzard."

"Maybe it's going through a never-ending recession too."

Missy laughed. "Maybe it can also put its name on The Winifred's waitlist."

We sighed. We both looked down. Down at the windshield wipers swiftly spitting up snow from yellow cabs and delivery trucks. Then up. "Maybe…" I paused, staring across the blurry sky. "Maybe we're better at this unemployment thing than we think."

"Maybe."

"We certainly are getting better at skating that thin line."

"What do you mean?"

"Anybody can be successful during the good and great times, right? But that's not success to me." I shook my head from left to right. "I think success to me might have something to do with conquering the world even through the hardest of hardships."

"I like that."

"Me too."

Boom! The rooftop door leading to the elevator abruptly slammed shut with the high winds.

"Umm, Jess?" Missy turned back her eyes. "I'm almost positive that door only opens from the inside."

"What the heck are you talking about?"

"Mmm…Mick Jagger's ex broke the handle last week, and The Winifred hasn't gotten to it yet, you know, with the Valentine's Day decorations and all."

A snowflake stung my iris. "Perfect."

"Another obstacle."

"Just when you think the world is through testing me and you."

TWELVE

March again. I'd arrived at Last Chance more tired than usual, broken, defeated, spent. I surveyed my surroundings, noticing that the unusual cleanliness had a weariness and even an eeriness. Sitting at my antique desk, I turned to my right, my eyes assessing the monogrammed Louis Vuitton Speedy and Never Full purses packed neatly atop one another on the shelves. In the adjacent glass cases, classic black lambskin Chanels also appeared too skillfully arranged; they sat a few perfectly measured inches away from each other, the gold chain-link straps tightly tucked away inside. To my left, the coats and clothes hung on the wall even more cleverly coordinated into colors and varying shades of each color. There was elegance to it, but there was also something militaristic about the sudden perfection in the room. It was as if the clothes had stayed up all night organizing themselves into formation reminiscent of the frontlines—every item standing at attention. Everything had its place and its purpose. Everything seemed meant to be where it lay. Everything except for me. Always, except for me. Why did it always have to be me?

"Where is Jess?" I could hear the voice from around the corner. It was Cruella.

Oh no, I thought.

Not now, not today, not that, too. Why couldn't Cruella be at the Soho store today?

"What is wrong with our Twitter, Jessica? Our Twitter?" Cruella came rushing in, throwing a magazine at me like an animal. "Why won't it let me follow anyone? What did you do?"

"So, the way Twitter works is that…" I paused. How do I explain this? "There are 'follow ratios,' a ratio of followers to following—a daily limit. You can't continue to follow more accounts until more accounts follow you back first. And it looks like several other employees have access to the account and have been adding every…" I stopped my sentence, as I didn't want to lay guilt on anybody or incriminate her or her daughters. "Anyway, it takes some time to build up a following, but as long as we continue to participate in the conversation—"

"Some time?" Cruella interrupted, "Fix it. Gabrielle Union, Jessica, Gabrielle Union. She said she was in our store in the latest *People* magazine and that she had bought her Gucci here. But I cannot follow her. Why can I not follow her?!"

Thin hairs on my arms stood above goosebumps while my spine snapped up. I trembled from Cruella's dragon-green eyes and red, fiery breath.

It occurred to me that maybe Last Chance thought their social media and internet presence would make them rich and famous. And then I almost laughed.

"You know what, forget it." Cruella continued, snatching the *People* magazine that had slapped my face before resting in my lap. She walked away, her black leather knee-length boots inconsistently clacking away on the uneven hardwoods like an angry Clydesdale wearing only three horseshoes. She did not turn back as she announced, "my other daughter is coming soon for spring break. She can do it. Grab your coat, Jessica."

"I'm sorry, what?"

"You heard me." She picked up her stride again without turning to look at me. "You no longer have a job here."

The statement was not computing in my brain. "I no longer *what?*"

"Grab your coat. You no longer have a job here. Be sure to clock out. You'll receive your last paycheck in the mail."

My mouth opened, but my body, weighing heavier in the chair, pulled the words back down my throat. Just when I thought things were starting to get better, they appeared to be getting worse. My shallow breath stammered out a few short whispers. "Excuse me, can you please tell me on what grounds I'm being let go?" I didn't even get to say goodbye to Misho. It was the first day he'd managed not to come in before me.

"On the grounds that we've decided to go in a different direction."

A different direction.

She might as well have said, "it wasn't the perfect fit."

***

I made my way down the Last Chance stairwell while throwing on my beanie. To my dismay, I noticed another clump of hair falling to the ground from all the stress. Taking inventory of the past year, I considered all my jobs, which seemed to get worse with time. Luxury travel, scoring for Harrison, house-sitting, pet-sitting, social media coordinator, shoe saleswoman, full-time graduate student; so many things, but nothing in particular. Nothing. I was nothing.

The feeling was overwhelming, and I surprisingly missed the commonplace highways down south, with their predictable views of strip club signs and car dealerships. The blue and silver streamers above rows of shiny new cars. Fast Mexican food. The neon pink Taco Cabana signs or the yellow and green Las Palapas logos of a hut along the Mexican coast. I missed how *taquerias* stood along the exits and drew in the most tireless traffic, forming long lines into drive-thrus for beef fajitas and bean and cheese tacos. I remember when one day, even the gas station, pharmacy, and finally Starbucks surreptitiously surrendered to drive-thrus—it was unanimous. The city had spoken.

Suddenly, I could see that there was comfort in simplicity. Of never leaving your hometown or getting out of your car, but instead safely experiencing the world from behind dark tinted windows and a seatbelt. Of only having to roll the window down just enough to stick your hand out to exchange a bit of money for what you needed without ever having to expose yourself to the world. I missed the hokiness of my hometown, the Girl Scout Centers juxtaposed against the strip clubs. A warning, a cautionary tale to remind women where they would ultimately end up should they ever try to aim higher and then fail.

I walked back to The Winifred that morning because I did not know what else I would do with myself. At some point, too, I'd realized that my walks were meandering more and more, becoming longer stretches of time. Subconsciously, I must have thought that the longer I'd walked, the more likely I'd come to some grand conclusions, some answers by the end of my journey. I traveled west on Seventy-Second Street for a few blocks, finally turning south on Fifth Avenue. I followed the walls surrounding Central Park before I crossed through, circling Naumburg Bandshell and Sheep Meadow. I roamed my way through Central Park West, Central Park South, Columbus Circle, meandering even farther west to Ninth Avenue, and finally winding all the way down, down, down, until I reached Thirty-Fourth Street.

It was a long and arduous walk. First, from the relentless stone-cold weather wearing down my body in snowy Central Park, which was a naked little city in itself without the shelter of old buildings to protect pedestrians from the climate. Once I escaped the silence and solitude of the whiteness, my ears rang with the sound of police sirens, car horns, and buses revving their engines around sharp corners and small hills. Except for a couple of cops removing what looked like yellow caution tape, it appeared they were all leaving The Winifred. Did I miss something when I left this morning?

The Winifred stood in its quiet state, a calm between breakfast and lunch. A staff member in a big bun dragged herself from behind the check-in table to our mailboxes with peek-a-boo windows. She methodically sorted through envelopes and stuffed them into our boxes. I followed, unlocking my own and finding a manila envelope from Texas stuffed inside, next to a letter from The Winifred. I opened the former, which included a short note from my mother:

Jessi,

Your Dad and I are still getting your mail. Here's the latest. Love you! Call us soon. We never hear from you. Praying everything is going well.

Love,

Mom and Dad

I pulled out the mail in the envelope: a past-due notice for a credit card payment, something about student loan deferment, and an old Chicago healthcare bill from an overnight stay for a severe bladder infection. Of course, the universe had perfect timing. The only way that mail could have been worse was if it included my Equifax credit score or bank statement.

A low roar rumbled, housekeeping crisscrossing each section of the carpeted entryway with a vacuum that made its way where the Christmas tree had been disassembled only a couple of months before. Pressing the elevator button, I realized I had no answer. Three-point-five miles later, far away from Last Chance, I still had no answer.

"But what is the question?" I asked myself loud enough for a housekeeper to hear my thoughts over the noise.

She looked up.

I looked down. "But what is the question?" I whispered to myself.

I could no longer contain my thoughts. Like my meandering walks, they seemed to go wherever they wanted. Agnes had said that The Winifred was not as glamorous as The Barbizon on East Sixty-Third Street, where rising stars had lived. But many Winifred women still hoped they could follow in the footsteps of success even if they weren't Grace Kelly, Candice Bergen, Liza Minelli, or Lauren Bacall. But I wondered: When do we accept that we might not be rising like a star? And when do we finally accept that perhaps we are falling stars instead?

If you look real close, falling stars were never stars to begin with. They're simply specks of meteoroids, rocks, and dust, nothing at all. The short burst of shimmering light they trigger in the dark night fools us into believing they could be something.

Stepping onto the elevator, I saw another sign, a memo, a note from The Winifred. I wondered why today the sign was hung on the inside of the elevator instead of the bulletin boards in the hallways of each floor, just like every other sign, just like every other day. I read it. But I wished I hadn't. That was not the day I'd needed to see, to read that sign, that sign of the times:

Dearest Winifreds,

With much sadness, we would like to share our condolences for Gloria Grace Horowitz. She passed away this morning and was The Winifred's longest resident to date, having lived here since 1968. A candlelight vigil will be held in the ballroom at the end of the week. Lastly, please be sure to check your mailboxes for maintenance appointments. In light of the nature of Ms. Horowitz's passing, The Winifred will be adding safety measures to your windows.

Sincerely,

The Winifred Staff

THIRTEEN

I opened my eyes the next morning. A pair of black sweatpants and damp tissues littered the floor below my bed, and when I finally raised my head, the box spring squeaked and spanked against the cardboard mattress. I could feel one of my suitcases below me; maybe it was time to start packing. But where would I go? I threw on my sweatpants and ran to the window, drawing the curtains with their pastel flowers open. I used both hands to tightly pull the blinds' cords so hard the blinds slapped and tossed back and forth as they made their way to the top. How had Gloria Grace died? I'd heard snotty hallway whispers late at night:

"Why do they have to fix our windows? It wasn't our fault. And anyway, hadn't it been a flat smack on the pavement from the rooftop?"

"I know, and I heard she left behind her leather jacket, house slippers, and menthols."

"Oh, and an empty bottle of that Southern Comfort, I bet. Whiskey—that's what she always smelled like."

"Haha, yeah, that and the subway rats."

It *was* our fault, though. We knew Gloria was lonely, but did any of us reach out to her?

The young Winifreds' ruthless words seared into my brain. Life—with its inevitable onslaught of failings, bitterness, resentment, and depression—was coming for them too. But would they have the tools to get through? Did *I* have the tools?

The snow on the ground had started to melt. Sheets of rain fell vertically, picking up speed and eventually joining the remaining piles of snow that clung to the ground.

What if that was my mistake? What if I had been silly to think I belonged somewhere? Did people truly belong anywhere, or did they accept where they had already landed, where life had already blown them? I wished, I prayed, I peered out that window at the skyscrapers disappearing into the murky fog, hoping for some sense of purpose. I looked down, thinking of poor Gloria. Maybe I was selfish to want more, to want a life of meaning, to want all the hours and days and months and years to add up to something special. But work is purpose, I'd thought. Purpose is life.

Or was it?

I thought about Conchita at Christmas, too. About the lies of feminism and the hope of family. About how I felt the most strength when I was both a strong individual and part of a community. Yet I had so much to give and nobody and nothing to give it to. Had Gloria felt the same way?

A steady knocking interrupted my thoughts, and the radiator below my window became hotter. I looked up and higher out the window, beyond the snow and rain, to the buildings hanging over the water, where two men once more climbed along a building in scaffolding. They began hanging a giant ad featuring Apple's latest technology: the iPad. Maybe that is where I would start again—the internet.

***

The season's last snow continued to melt, leaving iced-laden fire hydrants in puddles throughout the city. At Sixth Street and Eleventh Avenue, Kit, Colette, Missy, and I sat at the tiny bistro tables against the French Press windows.

"Hey – sorry, I'm late." Missy peeled off a maroon raincoat and folded it across the back of her chair.

"Don't worry." Kit dipped a napkin in iced water and meticulously scrubbed her scarf while brushing away the dirty blonde bangs from her face. "I was running late, too, and I think I found more baby vomit on my scarf. It never ends." She glanced at Missy. "Oh, you've curled your hair."

"I did." Missy spun around to show off her hair, the ends barely skimming her shoulders. "It's this new beachy wave. I hope it'll help me look a little older and maybe a little more professional. Also, I'm optimistic about spring finally being here."

"I hate to interrupt," Colette jumped in. "But I have to catch a train back to Connecticut today." She aggressively threw off her tweed pageboy hat onto the extra chair between us that lay buried in purses, coats, and scarves.

I couldn't help but tap my foot in anticipation of my mock interview, and did Colette's face seem different? Were her cheekbones higher, her hair shorter? "Colette, have you been working out?"

Colette threw me a skeptical look. "Seriously, Jessica?"

"What? You look so lean. I don't know."

Colette redirected the conversation. "Let's resume, please."

"Right." I threw off my black newsboy hat as if it were a competition, smoothing out my hair and sipping the first hot drops of coffee that morning. Behind us, more yellow cabs accelerated down Sixth Avenue. The sun lazily snuck in and out of the low clouds, brushing our table and warming our spot by the window.

I poured some creamer into my coffee. "Before we start, I must report some of the latest developments. Since when did employers start recording you during an interview? I couldn't concentrate on answering their questions in the last interview because the red light was shining on my face. I was too worried about how I looked. Do I look at the camera? Do I look at the person asking the questions? Do I look at the intern operating the camera? Or do I alternate my gaze between the other employers on the panel?"

Missy and Colette laughed.

"And speaking of the panel," Kit spewed, "why are there panels and panels of employers at every job interview now? Are they judges? Have they spent too much time watching *America's Next Top Model*?"

"I don't know about *Next Top Model*," Colette scribbled on a notepad without making eye contact. "But it would seem that somebody on the panel worked at Google and then told everybody they had to do hiring panels like Google."

"Ugh, I know." Missy sipped her cinnamon cappuccino. "That was how my last interview went. And it was for just a paid internship. That's how all my Tilly interviews for real positions went, too. Now they're doing this 'rounds' thing." Missy put down her cappuccino to make air quotes for emphasis. "You have to make it past the first round and through subsequent rounds, yet they never tell you how many rounds there are." She stopped to wipe the milk mustache off her face. "It's like, when do I get to meet with Tilly again? Why are you hiding, Tilly? I've taken out her trash and laundry as an intern so many times I can tell you exactly when she's ovulating."

"Eww, that's gross." Kit curled up her lips. "I don't want to think about Tilly's soiled panties while we're eating this morning, please."

"Wow," I said. "That makes me feel even worse about myself to know that one of the first self-made female billionaires became a billionaire so young—while she was still ovulating nonetheless—and I can't even get out of The Winifred."

"Ms. Puente." Colette formally interrupted, looking down at her paper and pen. "Let's go ahead and get started, please." The waitress dropped off a couple of plates of scrambled egg whites and muffins to share a la carte. We all picked at the plates, except for Colette, who didn't break face. "You appear to have a wealth of experience creating travel content in this digitized world we now live in."

"So formal, Colette. Jeez, I'm already nervous."

Colette ignored me, choosing instead to make a mark on the paper.

"Wait, sorry, I didn't know we started. Can I take that back?"

Colette's pen quickened.

"What are you writing over there? Is that red? Did you bring a red pen, too?"

Kit pulled out a silver Sony tape recorder.

"Do they even make tape recorders anymore? Okay, sorry. Umm, yes, Ms. Colette. I do have a wealth of experience."

"But you do know, Ms. Puente," Colette's eyes crinkled, and her lips twitched into a sneer, "that post-recession, we have plenty of seasoned candidates lined up, seasoned candidates with Ivy League graduate degrees. What sets you apart? Why should we hire you?"

"That's a good question. I'm glad you asked that question." I stalled, staring at the Campbell's Soup Warhol on the restaurant's wall. My voice pitched higher in confidence as I remembered my answers. "I wore many hats while working in the travel industry, and I'm in a different position than most of your interviewees because I researched and compiled a lot of print content before everything went digital, from brochures to newsletters to marketing copy."

Colette kept scribbling and nodding.

I dangled my head across the table to glimpse at her secret notes. "And I had to re-purpose a lot of that content while also re-packaging it, or re-branding it as we call it today. SEO, social media, and I even learned some HTML and Photoshop in my last job. I'm very hands-on; I do my own research and don't have to rely on tech departments in ways other candidates might."

Colette put her pen to her chin without looking up. "Very well," she smirked. "So, you are two employees for the price of one. You are low overhead."

"Yes, exactly. I can cover many roles by myself. I like to wear many hats. I have many hats in my wardrobe—I mean, repertoire."

Colette made a grand effort to slash out lines on my resume. She added two large circles before passing it across the table. "I'm going to turn it over to my colleagues now, Ms. Puente. Or my panel of employers, as you would say. Would you two like to cut in?"

Kit swallowed the last of her eggs while producing a similar red pen from her bag. "Yes. Today, you appear to be applying for the role of website content manager, but where do you see yourself in five years?"

No more head dangling as I pushed away from the table to sit back in my chair. "Oh no, I hate that question. Are you parachuting me? Are you going to ask what color my parachute is next?"

"It's a fair question," Missy said, buttering her blueberry muffin. "And you'll probably get that question or a similar one about your passion in the interview." She took a bite, then unashamedly spoke with her mouth full. "For example, if money were not an issue, where would you see yourself?"

"That's the thing." I took a deep breath before starting my monologue. "I've always hated those questions. People would ask me, 'No, but what do you *really* want to do? What is your passion? What drives you? What would you do if you could do anything in the world?' But they're bullshit, I'm-a-special-unicorn-young-millennial questions. How about I just want a good job to pay my bills, be independent again, and not live off student loans or unemployment checks?" I momentarily stopped to gather my thoughts among the rowdy restaurant chatter. "Why does there have to be a grand goal? Did our parents have that? No. They aimed to put food on the table, clothe their children, and have insurance."

"Are you saying, Ms. Puente," Colette said calmly and calculatedly while gesturing to Kit, who was scribbling away with more notes on my resume. "That you do not have any goals?"

"No," I scoffed. My voice escalated with my agitation. "That's not what I'm saying, and please put that pen down." I slapped Kit's hand and the pen followed, drawing a line along the page.

"I'd like to remind you," Kit pointed to the recorder while swallowing more water. "That we are still rolling."

"Yeah," Missy copied Colette and Kit. She even pointed her muffin at me for effect. "Let the record show Ms. Puente needs to work on that question. Kit, I hope you can send that recording to her when we're done here."

I was the only one breaking character. "Okay," I breathed to calm my fits and chanted in my head: One Mississippi, two Mississippi, three Mississippi. "In five years, I'd like to see myself settled with a 401(k). I want to start contributing to my Roth IRA again. I'd like to have real health insurance that doesn't have a million-dollar deductible. Maybe live somewhere without roommates again."

Missy nodded at me. "And the job?"

All three of them looked at me, waiting.

Do I not have a goal? I'd been to many interviews at many jobs. Teaching jobs, content managers, scorers, and social media coordinators. I could do any of those jobs, but did I *want* to do any of those jobs? What did I *want* to do? It's like I got desperate in the recession, and I got used to applying for any and all of the gig jobs and, therefore, no longer had a goal. The goal was just a job, any job. God, that sounded so low.

"I. Don't. Know." I clenched my coffee cup and ground my teeth. "I'd always wanted to go to graduate school and to live in New York one day. And before that, my dream and goal were to see the world, so I worked in travel." The waitress stopped at our table to pour more coffee into Kit and Colette's mugs. Kit poured a gallon of milk into hers, then a mountain of sugar. I watched her stir the crystals until they faded away and listened as her spoon dinged the mug. "I never thought I'd make it to thirty. It's like I never even thought to think about thirty. It sounded so old."

Kit finally turned off the recorder. "Yeah, probably don't say that in the interview."

Missy joined in again. "Jess, do you really not know what you want to do? I find that hard to believe since you seem to know everything else."

"Nice." Colette winked at Missy.

My head hurt, and the room began to spin. I could be a good sport regarding jokes at my expense, but jokes about my job? About the one thing at the center of my universe I could no longer control? It felt like they were hitting below the belt. I opened my mouth, waiting to hear the words march off my tongue—waiting to hear the truth of what I really wanted to do with my life. Nothing came out.

"This is depressing, Jessica." Colette drained the last of her coffee. "I cannot believe I took the train in from Connecticut for this. What do you live for? What do you think about when you are *alone* in bed at night?"

"Thank you for reminding me that I often sleep alone," I snapped. "I guess I wanted to be in New York for a while. Maybe I thought I'd figure it out here."

Kit signaled at our waitress as she cross-examined me. "Okay, so maybe it's time for you to start figuring it out."

It was true. As I sat across from Kit, Missy, and Colette, I realized they'd always had something specific in mind. Missy wanted to—well, she used to want to—work for Tilly or to be the next Tilly. Kit wanted to be the next significant playwright. Colette wanted to get her PhD from Oxford and teach on the East Coast. What *did* I want to do? Maybe it was finally time to take responsibility and accept that my lack of success in the job market had as much to do with me as the recession.

"How have you not been asked this question?" Kit signaled to the waitress for the check.

"I, I have. I guess I gloss over it or re-direct it."

Missy flipped her waves. "You are good at re-directing questions, Jess."

"Squirrel—" I pointed to the right.

They all looked up and over, then back to me, not amused. Colette stood up, and Kit followed, handing me my resume covered in red markings. They might as well have added a giant letter F at the top.

"I didn't realize my mock interview would turn into my panel interview would turn into my intervention. I'm guessing I didn't get the job then?"

Colette buttoned up her jacket. "We will be notifying candidates early next week."

"I can stay for a bit." Missy scarfed down the last of her muffin.

"Let me at least pay for all of your eggs for which I do not have money."

Colette and Kit threw a few bucks down for the tip.

Kit nodded. "We're not mad at you."

"Just disappointed," Colette confirmed, making me feel like Missy and her rent subsidy.

"A girl's got to grow up sometime, you know?" Kit said.

"I do know; thank you for that." I mocked Kit as she and Colette disappeared. I hated it when Kit, too, got serious, so I tried to dig in after their departure. "Healthy food *always* needs more seasoning." I rigorously shook the pepper over my plate. "*Mmm*, maybe I'll add a little more salt."

Missy looked down at me again with what looked like pity. I wondered if she thought things would be different for her in her thirties. As longer lines wound through the rows of patrons, restaurant echoes rang louder: the thuds and scratching from several chairs and tables servers moved together; children running through tight rows; grandparents clutching their raincoats brushing along our chairs.

"What is it, Visit-Your-Hipster-Millennial-Grandkid-in-Greenwich-Village-Day?"

Missy kept staring at me. The creases on her forehead seemed to bend into sadness. "Jess, you know Kit and Colette are right, right?"

A lump in my throat made it harder to swallow. Instead of an answer, I chewed the food slower and stared through the window again. A waitress stepped outside to sweep our street view with a wide squeegee. She swept the window up, then down, then diagonally.

"I'm sorry, Missy," I said quietly. "I wish we had met before. Sometimes, I wish you had known me before."

Her eyes lit up with a fissure in the clouds, a bit of sun shining through. "It's never too late." She grabbed her fork and picked at my eggs. "To, you know, get a new dream, job, community, relationship, to be a part of something important again. You can have both roots and wings."

"I have the 'wings' part of the 'roots and wings' down. Forget travel; I'm flying from one thing to the next. How do you build roots when jumping from gig to gig? Isn't that contradictory?"

Missy leaned in so close I could smell the nauseating, unusually potent lavender from her Tilly Worth perfume. "Hey, if anybody can figure it out, you can. Tomorrow's another day. Start planning. Get ready for it. As Oprah says, luck is preparation meeting opportunity."

Missy was smart, but I wasn't used to her being so encouraging and wise—or at least repeating the encouraging and wise she'd heard from somewhere else. Even her smile seemed overly optimistic, her voice transcendent. Something was suspicious. I relaxed, moving farther back in my chair to assess. I could see it now that Colette and Kit had left: More perfume. Big new hair. Matte red lipstick. All very uncharacteristic of her 'less is more' style.

"Is that all you want to tell me? Nothing else? Nothing else that might have to do with the roots part of your roots and wings, perhaps?"

Missy's mouth dropped. She twirled the end of a strand of hair to stall. Then, she verbally vomited. "Listen, I didn't want to say anything until I knew for sure, but who am I kidding? It's already been several weeks, and things are moving forward for us."

I jerked back in puzzlement. "Us? There's an us?"

"He's tall and older, and he's from Connecticut, and like me, he wants three kids and a big white house and a garden, and he manages a hedge fund, and he paid off his student loans, and he has a 401(k) *and* a Roth IRA. We met online literally like the one time The Winifred's internet signal worked. *Ahh*." She took a breath. "That was a lot."

I stared at Missy. Then I picked up my fork and eggs and started chewing, and chewing, and chewing, and chewing—

"Say something, Jess."

I couldn't stop chewing and dividing. Dividing all the phrases Missy stitched together, that didn't add up. "How old is older?"

"He's almost thirty."

"Huh." I stared back down at my plate searching for more eggs, but I'd eaten all of them. Coffee. I needed more coffee. Where was my coffee?

"Hello?" Missy waved her hand in front of me. "Anybody home?"

"He's almost thirty, and he already manages a hedge fund? That can't be righ—"

"I knew it. I knew you were going to do this to me." Missy threw her napkin down on top of her plate and stood up. "This is why I didn't tell you. Life goes on, and there's more to it than, I don't know, applying for jobs you can never get. This is happening, okay? I'm moving on with my life."

Missy grabbed her jacket.

I thought we'd made progress—*I'd* made progress—since my grand apology in the blizzard, but maybe it was only a band-aid. I threw up my hand. "Wait, that's not all I was going to say, that's exciting, I'm happy for yo—"

"You know what, I don't have time for this. I'll see you at The Winifred." She threw on her purse to storm out but stopped to turn back quickly. "Oh, and by the way, I got another job. It's full-time with a salary and benefits."

I gazed across my empty table among the half-eaten plates, crumbs, mugs, and grimy napkins. Then, through the window. The cacophony of traffic was more audible each time the double doors opened. Yellow cabs dashed unforgivingly through slushy puddles, splashing the knees of tourists and pets. A man at his newsstand wiped a rag over his metal counter. He scratched off the stubborn ice chips before smoothing out the surface again, drying off the last of the dripping water. It felt very calming to watch the seasons change. I observed the last of the icicles on rooftops turn to trickles and finally to raindrops. Maybe I couldn't be happy for Missy because things had yet to change for me.

FOURTEEN

By April, I took a break from trekking to my university's renowned library. I repurposed the Hudson Yard McDonald's for my new office since security guards had started asking for an ID at the Starbucks in the Associated Press building. Within walking distance from The Winifred, the two-story McDonald's above a gas station sat across from the Javits Center and included free wi-fi, unlike The Winifred. I often sat along the second-floor window, spending lonely afternoons typing and applying for jobs, or writing about jobs for grad school with pedantic-sounding words; the stench of French fries and hamburgers pervaded my hair long after I'd left, leaving a sense of ambiguity and anonymity, othering me from myself.

For a few weeks, the constant traffic below kept me company. Yellow cabs peeled in and out for passengers and gas—first for breakfast, then breaks, lunch, and finally dinner.

"Excuse me, ma'am," the McDonald's manager said as she made it up the steps. She wore her denim button-down shirt and a dark braid with loose ends around her headset. "I've noticed you've been here for hours without buying anything yet."

When I realized that someone was yet again revoking my free stolen wi-fi privileges, my behavior coincided with the five stages of grief—denial and bargaining, in particular. "Can I please send this last email, pack up all my stuff and buy something?" The manager did not necessarily say "yes" but continued to gather the leftover food and trash along the tables, crumpling up yellow burger wrappers and jingling ice in empty plastic cups. I sent off one last cover letter and resume. But an email hit my inbox as I was about to slap my pink Dell laptop screen shut. The email was titled "Rome Away, My Friend." It was Alessandra, another sister to me. She had been a producer for Telemundo and later an NBC affiliate in my hometown when I met her as an intern. Then I moved to Rome, and she met her husband while visiting me. Ten years later, she was still an ocean away. I clicked on the email while also pretending to stand up and collect my belongings. The McDonald's manager continued to shoot dirty looks at me as if the multi-billion-dollar solvency of the entire McDonald's corporation was now contingent upon my pending five-dollar purchase. I slowly pushed in my chair while wrapping a burnt orange scarf around my neck.

Ciao Jessica,

It has been too long, my friend. I hope this email finds you well and that I may visit you in the big city one day. I am finally doing it. But I need your help. I cannot do it without you, especially since I'm still in the U.N. We filmed Rome and the surrounding areas, and I've already signed contracts with a few agriturismi in the country. Rome Away TV now owns Rome Away Tours. We are a full-fledged tour operator, offering panoramic tours with English-speaking guides, food and wine tastings, cooking, you name it. But we have to sell it. Can you help me write the website? We will need newsletters and blogs, too. I will pay you. It's not full-time but will put more money in your pocket. Let's schedule a Skype."

Tanti baci.

Love from Rome,

Alessandra

The McDonald's manager was called away on her headset and ran down the stairs, allowing me to respond. I sat back down, my hands flying over the keyboard. I logged onto my defunct travel blog for the first time in months. Searching through the three hundred posts, I found one of my favorite photos that I'd taken in Venice. It featured three bald Italian men standing along the extinct *Ponte dei Bareteri* bridge, two in matching black and white horizontal stripes and one in red and white. One sat on the bridge, nonchalantly reading the Italian national newspaper, *Corriere della Sera*. Two stood, holding their signature straw hats with a black ribbon tied in a bow around the brim. I downloaded the photo and attached it to Alessandra's email with the caption: 'Gondoliers Before Work.'

Dear Alessandra,

Here is my first contribution. This photograph calls to mind the smell of an Italian cigarette on a damp Venetian morning. The taste of freshly pressed orange juice—spremuta d'arancia—in a thick but tall Italian glass blown on the neighboring island, Murano. The taste of a cornetto's crispy corners folded in, revealing a sliver of Nutella. Pinoli. I always asked for pine nuts in my crepes, but if only they came in breakfast croissants. What is the word for breakfast again? Oh, I remember—colazione. If I look at this photo long enough, I remember more than just breakfast. The weather, the news, perhaps July—the time of year I wasn't fond of Venice because the marshlands felt more like swamplands, and the tourists felt more like terrorists.

My favorite memory of Venice was also my first. The first time I naively realized everything taken in or out of the island's inlets is done by boat. Instead of garbage trucks, there are garbage boats. Instead of grocery trucks, there are grocery boats. It was just as fascinating for me to witness tomatoes and carrots piled too high, making a tall triangle on a tiny boat as it was to see Michelangelo's ceiling. But why wouldn't it be? Both resemble a Renaissance period that has never departed; even the newer DHL boats—a cross between a gondola and a Vaporetto—reminded me that even people in Italy needed their mail because they get to live there for more than a year or two and carry on their lives like I am carrying on mine in a different part of the world and on the other side of this picture. Working for you will carry me through the last of this lingering winter.

With Love From New York,

Jessica

One gig down, a few more to go, I'd thought as I packed up my belongings. Perhaps putting my roots and wings goals out into the universe, like Missy said, was starting to work. Note to self: I just need a couple more gigs, some community, and to slay grad school.

But as I descended the McDonald's stairs, the list seemed to get longer and overwhelming. An apartment? Who had time for all that? And what was my strategy? I needed a plan. Suddenly, the floor seemed heavy. And sticky. Then, slippery.

"*Awwww…*" Tumbling down and across the last few steps, I landed on my stomach. My eyes stopped right at the yellow wet floor warning cone at the bottom of the landing:

"Caution, *Cuidado*, Wet Floor, *Piso Mojado*."

"You're too late." I barked back at the yellow cone in my numb state; it was staring at me straight in the face.

"Are you okay? Are you okay?" One of the cashiers yelled from behind a register.

Another employee in the opposite direction shot back around and rolled their mop and bucket toward me. "I put the sign, I put the sign, I'm sorry." They hurried to fret over me as I continued to rub my temples and neck.

I raised my hand like a white flag. "It's fine. It's fine." For a moment, I wondered if I could sue for cheeseburgers.

The fall felt paralyzing, and I didn't want to stand up. I could feel the sore spots on my body that would eventually yield to purple bruises, and now I was sticky and smelled like the mop and bucket. My hair maintained its mess across my face, and a fry emerged from who knows where. It slowly slid off my long bangs and rested on my lips.

"Gross," I yelled, but the knee-jerk reaction was literally in poor taste. "Blech."

I could taste the fry. "At least it's still fresh." I accidentally tasted it again, smelling something very familiar, like lavender. "How about that? The McDonald's in Manhattan also scrubs their floors with Fabuloso. My mother will have to hear about this one."

"Ma'am? Ma'am?" the mop and bucket guy began, reminding me I was old enough to be a 'ma'am.' He leaned over me and the Fabuloso french fry, but I pushed him away again with my white flag hand. Face flushed, I grabbed my leg and limped along.

Exiting through the glass doors, the burst of crisp air felt pleasant on my face. The clouds surrounding the skyline receded, shining a late crack of sun as Daylight Saving Time had ended. The year was moving forward, but I was still stuck.

Riing, riing! My phone began to sing. Crossing the parking lot and returning to Tenth Avenue and Thirtieth Street, I saw the caller ID. It was from a 210-area code. San Antonio. At first, I decided not to answer it since there was a high likelihood it was a bill collector from back home.

Riing, riing! But it felt urgent as my phone rang between the car horns and ambulance sirens. It could be Harrison. Maybe Harrison is going to offer me more remote work, I thought. In the middle of this Missy-like positivity of talking to the universe and dolphins and penguins and salvation and optimism, I regretfully, mistakenly, in error, let my guard down and answered the phone.

"Hello, Jessica Puente here. *Ouch.*" I clutched my leg and pressed the crosswalk button.

"Yessica, how are you? I have not heard from you," said the thick Spanglish accent from back home. "Your mother said you would call. But when I didn't hear from you, I reached out instead. Is now a good time? I tried calling a few times earlier. Did your cell phone service get shut off? Yessica, you need to pay your phone bill."

"Hello, Conchita," I said, tempted to drop my phone into the subway grate. "No, my cell service did not get shut off."

"That is good news. Your mother said that you are starting to do so wonderfully in New York that, who knows, perhaps you might even start doing one of those Trump pageants."

"Ha, not quite, Conchita. Believe me, that world is not even on my radar." I marginally crossed the street before delivery trucks and cabs punched the gas against the green light.

"I said to your mother, 'if Yessica needs a pageant coach, I do private coaching sessions with many of the up-and-coming young women down here.' But for you, Yessica, I do for free."

"For free?" I suspected another trick.

"Of course, Yessica, especially since I will stay with you in New York. It is the least I can do for you."

Oh, no. Conchita had called to collect. This was not the community I'd had in mind when I was negotiating with the universe earlier.

"Okay, if I must. I surrender to the cosmos, to the powers that be."

"Esscuse me?"

"Nothing. You are more than welcome to stay with me. Just to let you know, I'm in between apartments at the moment. I'm staying at this hotel. It's only temporary. But I can get an extra roll-out bed."

"A hotel? Yessica? You are living in a hotel like the rich people on TV?"

My first instinct was to say, 'not exactly,' and to confess to Conchita. But if the universe would have some fun with me, why not have fun with the universe right back?

"You know me, Conchita, I do hate to brag. Unfortunately, the Four Seasons was booked, but I pay to ensure that my Manhattan accommodations come with chef-prepared meals."

"Wow."

"That's right. I'm no longer in the penthouse, as I've decided to stay on one of the lower floors and in one of the smallest rooms to save for my fancy upcoming apartment, you see."

Unfortunately, the universe played a little hardball right back. "Look at you, Yessica. It is a good thing we're launching a new city-wide magazine with the slogan: *All Things Fiesta, All Year Round.* I am looking for profile stories for the inaugural edition. How wonderful. You can be my first profile. I can see the headlines now: 'San Antonio's Own Miss Fiesta Finalist Takes Fiesta to the Big Apple.' It will inspire others who do not win the Miss Fiesta pageant. To know that there is still hope. That they might succeed at something else instead."

My lungs grew heavier with my leaps up the hill toward The Winifred, where I could start to see the tip of the American flag. "Oh, you know it. Maybe you can even get a picture of me lying out on the rooftop."

"Huh, you have a rooftop view, too? I have to write all this down."

I heard Conchita's screaming baby in the background.

"I must get back to my family but tell me, when is good for you?"

"When is what good for me?"

"For my flight this summer?"

I wanted to push the trip as far out as possible so Conchita would eventually forget. "August? Maybe the fall?" I suggested. "The fall is a special time to be in New York anyway. Sorry, come to think of it, nobody really cares about the changing seasons and leaves falling from the trees anymore. Late October, nope, November. Yep, definitely November. December is always good."

More baby screams in the background. "August it is, Yessica."

My heart sank.

FIFTEEN

The first day of May. Another birthday. A few graduate students sat in their pantsuits on a bench outside the fishbowl for the last round of panel interviews. To compete for the few teaching assistant positions at the university, we had to dazzle our "judges"—school administrators and professors—with a ten-minute teaching lesson on our chosen topic. While most of us waited on the bench, we kept our eyes on laptop screens to review interview questions.

I couldn't help but peek inside where Air Quote Allie reviewed her PowerPoint lesson. Her ombre hair stood high in a sleek ponytail. She used one of those pretentious laser pointers to click through slides revealing the names of famous authors: Maya Angelou, Alice Walker, and Toni Morrison.

While I could see her lips moving, I couldn't hear Air Quote Allie's lesson.

But I didn't need to.

The emblazoned slides featured the following words: Reconstruction, Sharecropping, Jim Crow, White Supremacy, Patriarchy, Poverty, Marginalization, and Oppression.

A couple of slides illustrated the lower wages of African-American women back then and today.

Air Quote Allie accessed a couple of similar websites and ended with a two-minute YouTube clip of what appeared to be poor, dark-skinned sharecropping women with crying children. Air Quote Allie turned off her technology and packed up her lesson.

I fumbled my belongings while Air Quote Allie exited. She made sure to hold the door open for the next person.

Until she saw the next person.

Me.

She snapped her head back at administrators and professors, who appeared to be jotting rigorous notes. She seemed to swiftly swing the door open so that it would snap shut on me. I tried to catch it in time, but she abruptly withdrew her hand.

The door made a snap, and then there was a *clap, clap, clap* as it swiftly closed, the administrators and professors momentarily looking up, then back down.

While doing her graduate assistant thing inside the fishbowl, Colette looked up from behind a clipboard. She waved a couple of fingers at me and mouthed, "two more minutes."

"Good luck, Jessica." Air Quote Allie sneered a Mr. Grinch smirk.

As if I needed a reminder that people like her were always stealing my Christmas. I envisioned her curled by a fire at night, satisfyingly twirling the ends of a Grinch mustache.

"Why thank you," I responded in an equally patronizing tone as she turned away. "Oh, and by the way, Allie?"

"Yes?" She circled her body back toward me.

"At a later date, I'd love to hear more of your intersectional feminist manifesto." I poked my head back to the fishbowl, ensuring the panel of judges was still scribbling and whispering away. Then, back to Air Quote Allie. "How is it that your demographic manages to make sixty-five whole cents to the dollar while mine still manages to make only fifty-five cents to the dollar?"

As soon as the words slipped out of my mouth, I felt a sudden pang of regret and humiliation. To make matters worse, some students sitting closest to us on the bench lifted their heads at us as if to hold me accountable. I was supposed to be the adult in the room.

"Let me rephrase that," I tried again. "When was the last time you read something by a minority that wasn't about being an abjectly impoverished minority? I know that the institutions, publishers, the state, the fourth estate—whatever you want to call it—are encouraging and incentivizing such nonsense, but isn't that even more racist since it assumes that we're not only abjectly impoverished minorities but that we have no other contribution to society than being an abjectly impoverished minority?"

"Jessica?" Colette checked off my name from the clipboard against her chest. "You are next."

"Thank you." I turned away from Air Quote Allie and clenched a wide grin. "It's a pleasure to be here today."

As I made my way in, the professors behind their tables slowly scrambled to their feet to shake my hand. Sitting back down, a couple of them jotted final notes.

Colette avoided my eyes as she spoke. "Remember that the four people you see today on the panel will be your students. Please be sure to direct your lesson to them. You are more than welcome to have them participate."

"Thank you." I opened my bag to remove a folder. The nerves, the tickle against my skin, started faintly in my legs and burst to my head. My feelings were about everything all at once. My interactions and meetings with Colette since my mock panel interview at French Press became shorter, like she was still irritated with me. And despite my choice of words for Air Quote Allie, I worried whether I should have found a way to incorporate race relations into everything. I suspected the younger generations' recent, renewed interest in race was related to The Great Recession and the lack of resources. My lesson about planning and research for writing job letters, resumes, and thank you letters with Google Analytics and SEO suddenly seemed so prosaic. I passed out packets of student examples and worksheets to the panel of professors. Then to Colette. She smiled at me with her eyes, but I couldn't tell if that was a wink or a twitch. My heart, heavier than when I entered, leaped so fast I thought it would fly out of my chest. Who cared what the professors thought now that I had to contend with Colette?

***

My hands shook as I wrapped up my lesson. It was as if I were saying goodbye to the Queen, stealthily walking in reverse until my back was no longer visible when I turned. I ran to the restroom, taking my time inside to splash rounds and rounds of cold water across my red face. After that, I checked my emails in the computer lab—still, no job offers—before exiting the building.

I stepped off the elevator and went through the empty lobby, revolving through the doors. "Colette?" I saw her a few steps in front of me. "You're already done? Wait up, will you?"

Colette dangled her head back as she waited for me, shuffling her leather messenger bag to the other shoulder. "Yes. You were one of the last students of the day."

"Oh." I stopped below the hackberry tree that had started to bloom. The tree's arms drooped down, pointing to its smothered fruit on the pavement, the purple berries staining the sidewalk where black American crows continued to pick. A few birds flew away with our passage through them. "You going back to your place?"

"Yes." Colette hesitated, scratching her nose and not welcoming me.

"Can I walk with you up to Twentieth Street?"

"Sure. I suppose I could use some company." She smirked. "But do not expect me to tell you anything I heard in there. That would be against the rules." We resumed our walk past an organic coffee shop, then Sixth Avenue, where taxi cabs and bike messengers stood at the red light waiting for us to pass. She looked up at me genuinely. Then, mischievously smiled. "How did you enjoy your 'panel' interview, as you would say?"

"Ha, panel, yes, it was. I know the position is for fall since it's almost June. But I hope they get back to us soon. What about you? Can you apply if you're already a Graduate Assistant in the office?"

"I did not apply." Colette took a moment to pull a rubber band out of her pocket. She only tied up her dreads when she was stressed.

"No? But Colette, I thought you wanted to teach before the PhD program?"

"I did, and I am."

"You are?" My steps stalled. Why hadn't she been telling me things?

"Yes."

"Where?"

Colette coughed into her fist before she finally spoke. "I will be at a CUNY campus."

We passed the pharmacy, and I stopped to shove Colette's shoulder playfully. "What? That's fantastic! Why didn't you say anything? That's such great news."

Colette brushed my hand away before resuming her gait. "I did not want to make it a big deal, with, you know…" She contrived a fishy sideway glance, avoiding direct eye contact. "You losing your job again."

It stung a little, no matter how much I didn't want it to.

"Are you kidding me?" I picked up my pace. Now, *I* was the one avoiding eye contact. "Come on. We're adults. And seeing my friends recovering from the recession gives me hope and motivation."

"Does it?"

"It does," I insisted. Sort of.

"That is great to hear." Colette sped up and then slowed to a shuffle as we continued to the next avenue, navigating around the steep steps of a couple of brownstones on Twelfth Street.

I waited, gazing at Colette, who seemed to search for her words begrudgingly. She came to a complete stop at a scaffolded building with green tarps. "I may need motivation myself," she admitted.

"You?" I jerked my head to the side in bewilderment. "Why?"

"They would like me to create content for my class to host on their website." Colette resumed her steps. "I was trying to map out my plan of attack before work in the computer lab this morning. I must write a bio and syllabus for the internet, and there is this discussion board for which I have to create engaging questions. I am told my students will be quite tech-savvy, and I do not do internet."

"Are you kidding me? Colette, hello." I politely pushed her shoulder again. "I do internet."

"Excuse me?" She stopped with a bit of a shock. Turning her head up at me, she wrangled with one of her ponytail's loose dreads.

The afternoon sun faintly drifted in and out of the patchy sky. The sun cleared a few round clouds and brightened the tall, watered bushes and freshly sprinkled pavement. Colette's dark eyes appeared momentarily vacant, her pupils disappearing, then suddenly emerging. She resumed her pace with the approaching train vibrating below us toward the Fourteenth Street Station.

"Seriously. That's all I did before I left my travel job at A&K. We had to move most of our content online. I'm also creating a lot of digital content for Rome Away. And let's not forget the progress I made with the fancy pawn shop—Last Chance—although we won't tell anybody about that."

Colette dug her hands into her pockets. "Are you saying you would like to be helpful, Jessica?"

"Absolutely. Send me what you have, and I'll take care of it. We can do a few rounds of edits this summer until you see fit."

"How much would you like for this?"

"Please." I turned to my side. "You don't have to pay me. It's the least I can do for you."

"That would be most helpful, thank you." Colette added a few more words beneath her breath. "What a surprise."

"Surprise?" I could see the skepticism in Colette's eyes, the snarl lines around her lips. This was more than about the job. I tucked my hair behind my ears and told myself to relax. "What is that supposed to mean? Is that an insult? And why have you been short with me since my mock interview at French Press?" I stared down at the tops of her hands peeking out from her slacks. Were they still purple even in the warmer weather?

Colette pulled her hands out of her pockets and hurled them in front of my face. A damp air and the smell of a curry supper from a garden apartment pervaded as her voice ascended. "Because you are still not hearing me, Jessica, which means you are unable to or unwilling to. Instead of gracefully answering the most standard, innocuous of interview questions, such as, 'where do you see yourself in five years,' you were still ranting about special, millennial unicorns and how pursuing passions and dreams is a new American thing as if you were not doing the same with your travel anyway. Who the hell cares?" She made a fist and then aggressively pointed to the left of my chest, landing at my heart. "Your answers to life should be answered with gratitude. Yet you still lead with attitude. With resentment. Why would I want to offer that person the job?"

"Oh." I expelled all the air I had left inside me, deflated, dejected, defeated. A pounding rushed inside me. I stared down at Colette's finger, still pointing to the left of my chest. Why did the truth always come in waves? "You're right. And maybe it is my heart. I'm trying, but I still don't know how to do the trite things where you live and love unconditionally, as if the world hadn't just handed you the opposite. I guess I'm your rotten apple or your wrought apple looking for love or sun, or I don't know." I sighed, staring up into the sky. "Poetry was my worst genre."

Colette turned away and walked ahead in rhythm with the traffic driving past us. Her hands flew up here and there as she continued to gesture. "But what if it is nobody's fault? I am not saying to forego accountability. What if you stop fretting about the past?

What if the things that happened happened because that's life? And we learn and move on? Control what we can and let go of the rest?"

I sidestepped two huskies and a pug as a dogwalker pulled back their leashes. "I know that's what we're supposed to do. Acquiesce, in a sense. Obviously."

"Yes." She careened her head back. "It is obvious. It is hard but obvious. So do it. We are supposed to do the things before we are ready so that when our moment comes, we are already there." Colette lowered her voice with the last wave of her hand. "Be the person we were born to be and all that."

My knees felt weak. "I'm sorry."

She completely stopped again to turn to me with a smile, a relief. While her face extended into a fuller shape, it seemed gaunt and pale, and I wondered if she felt depleted like me. "Do not say sorry. Just do. How are your interviews? How is your chick lit or your thesis writing? Your self-help travel book on jobs? I have not seen your recent pages."

I lowered my head, feeling a sudden hunch in my back. "Oh, yeah, about that. What if Air Quote Allie got it right? Am I at a disadvantage because I'm not doing the 'special topics' of a minority to get ahead?"

Colette paused. Her words seemed to struggle through labored breaths as she ambled. "The system encourages people to do that, but that is selling out. I do not recommend qualifying your responsibilities and accomplishments on your resume by including your ancestors' struggles. But I predict that will soon become a requirement."

"Great. 'Maternal Grandmother Ventura: Escaped the Mexican Revolution at age four.' She did literally *crawl* across that border."

"No. Speak truth to power. It would seem that you are getting closer. Keep going."

As we continued, the wind seemed to pick up with the late sun, creating a pressurized vacuum between each passing street along Seventh and Eighth Avenue. Turning north, we strolled through each street, reaching Colette's building at Twenty-Second Street. She said goodbye, but I couldn't leave. I watched her back until she disappeared through the glass doors. I sat on the front steps for a second to catch my breath. To digest. In one sense, Colette's support was priceless. Uplifting. Inspiring. But in another sense, it shined a light on what she and I did not have: What my mother, Conchita, Kit, and now even Missy all had. Life was never meant to do alone, and sometimes it felt like here we were, doing just that.

SIXTEEN

Miniature American flags bordered The Winifred's Memorial Day bulletin, highlighting the upcoming rooftop fireworks and hot dog stand. I stepped onto the elevator at eight a.m., fastening my pencil skirt and pearl earrings as I awkwardly pushed in among the other Winifred women.

"Hey, how are you? I didn't expect to see you," I said to Missy. "It's been a while. I guess you haven't been here much the last couple of months? I just wanted to say—"

"I'm over it." Missy signaled 'stop' with her lip gloss before smearing it on her mouth and straightening her high-rise denim. She went through the motions as if pretending everything was okay even though, like Colette, I hadn't seen her much since my mock panel interview. "You look great," Missy said, her voice steady but unconvincing. "Did you get the teaching job?"

"Thank you. I'm still waiting to hear back about that, but I have a couple of jobs lined up for the summer. One is at Rome Away, and hopefully, one is at the Viacom Headquarters in Times Square."

"O-M-G, Times Square? That's only a mile from The Winifred. You could walk there every day. Umm, what is Viacom? It sounds like a spaceship."

"I know, or like a Vulcan on Star Trek."

"You're not going to be a Times Square street performer, are you?"

I laughed. "That's not a bad idea. I'll put that on the list. But no. Basically, Viacom is the corporation that owns Comedy Central, MTV, and Nickelodeon, among many television stations that nobody watches much anymore because of the internet. But Viacom has websites where I might be able to manage content."

"Look at you. And did you figure out your 'where do you see yourself in five years question?'"

"Absolutely," I answered, probably a little too quickly. "Obviously, I have to say something different for every job. For Viacom, it's leading the content strategy for their up-and-coming websites."

Missy raised an eyebrow at me as if to say, that wasn't what I meant, and you know it. But it would have to do for now. The *real* answer to that question was more complicated.

The elevator door dinged open on the first floor.

Missy checked her watch. "I'm going south. You headed north?"

"Yes," I waved.

"Hey—" Missy finished as she headed for the other side of the street. "Should we order Chinese takeout tonight and catch up?"

"I would love that."

***

A once gritty part of the city, Hell's Kitchen grew popular due to its convenient Midtown location and proximity to Broadway's theater district and television stations. I thought about this during my safe, gentrified walk through Hell's Kitchen up to Times Square. Making a few detours, I side-stepped street sweepers and white trucks making morning deliveries. Drivers yelled about their deliveries to men in green aprons at back doors. Tourists from nearby hotels ordered coffee and roamed the streets slowly as they began their morning. A few owners hosed down the concrete surrounding their entrances at Restaurant Row. One watered a few new bouquets in baskets of ivy and blooming azaleas, some a sharper pink than the rest. Another worker whistled up a ladder to fix a broken light bulb and a collapsed sign hanging by a cable. I smiled at freshly planted pansies, their hues of purples and blues surrounding bright yellow centers—the last of the hanging pots overflowing with ivy and moss.

Midtown buildings climbed a little higher with each crossing street until they soared into the clouds that hung very low; a morning fog faded along the ads of people parading fake white smiles amid the Times Square lights. The Gap. Broadway. Lion King. Coke. Bulova. Sbarro. Sony. Apple. T-Mobile. Ducati. McDonald's. Toys "R" Us. Buzz Lightyear. Sheriff Woody. Ads twinkled, everything blending in unity. By the time I reached Forty-Fourth Street and Broadway, I couldn't tell if the fog had lifted to make way for the sun or if Times Square had brought the sun to New York.

A Minnie Mouse in her red dress and white polka dots waved at me, pointing to my attire and then pointing two thumbs up. I gestured my finest fake pearls at her, which sat above my beige silk blouse and scarf from the most expensive rack at Forever 21. I tucked the blouse into a black pencil skirt that—fingers crossed—did not state 'college student.' Spinning through the revolving doors, I quickly made it through Viacom security, grabbing my ID and a badge in exchange for some signed paperwork. At the top of the escalator, other personnel escorted me through another marbled lobby, an elevator to the thirty-second floor, and then through a long hallway until we reached a conference room with not one but two walls of sweeping floor-to-ceiling Hudson River views. I was excited to be back on top of the world where I belonged. I wanted to pinch myself but thought it best to pretend my life was business as usual. How wonderful it would be to walk up Ninth Avenue daily for work.

I left Last Chance off my resume because—as my mother pointed out—I didn't want anybody to think I'd worked at a pawn shop, even in my most desperate times. Luckily, full-time grad school was a good cover-up for gaps in work history.

Finally, a beautiful black woman wearing an expensive navy pantsuit walked in. "Hi, Patricia Samuels. Great to meet you." She grabbed my hand and walked around the conference table, sitting with her back against the Hudson River.

"Hi." I straightened my posture. "Lovely to meet you. Thank you for this opportunity."

"Of course. Shall we get started?" She put on a pair of tortoise-shell reading glasses and began to scan a copy of my resume.

Where was my panel? "Oh, right now? Do we, uh, are we awaiting your remaining team members?"

"Oh no, unfortunately, everybody is far too busy today, and I'm usually the one who makes this hire."

"I understand. Well, I'm excited to be here today."

We went through a round of standard interview questions about my past education and experience before Patricia seemed to lose a bit of interest.

"It looks like you've also applied for a few positions with Viacom." She continued to question while shuffling papers on her lap.

"I have. I aspire to be a writer and reporter, to present my work in a way like I've done in the travel industry. I have a lot of experience creating topical digital content—"

"Wonderful. And it looks like you're getting a graduate degree at New School. Wow, that's impressive. I looked into them, but Columbia is, well, Columbia."

This was awkward. I smiled and kept nodding in agreement.

"I see that you also have a lot of experience writing—my goodness—entire websites. About travel for Rome Away and A&K?"

"I wrote the whole website for Rome Away. For A&K, I researched and wrote a significant chunk. Still, I also managed a print-to-web migration, moving pre-existing content from our brochures and itineraries to our website and blog. I continue to do occasional freelance work for Rome Away. But I can do it in the evenings and on the weekends to avoid interfering with my job here."

"I understand. We encourage ambition here at Viacom, and I tell all my employees to remember to take a lunch break every day. You will get one full hour, so please use it. We have a wonderful dining hall, and of course, you can head down to Times Square for falafel, Sbarro, or anything else."

"Wonderful." She was talking as though the job was already mine. So why was I sweating profusely under my cheap silk blouse? Should I talk about my five-year plan?

Patricia smiled awkwardly again, so I continued. "It's been so rewarding watching the digital revolution unfold. I graduated from college when the medium was still print, so it's been wild to experience it evolve. I was published in print first, and I still incorporate my formal training in print journalism from undergrad. Working for the travel industry was my education and entrance into the digital medium."

"Fantastic!" Patricia jotted notes on my resume. She kept scribbling while nodding her head. Then, she quickly put the pen down to adjust her glasses and check her BlackBerry. Her over-grown French manicure clicked against the plastic keys, so I did the awkward thing I always do—answer my own rehearsed interview questions that had yet to be posed.

"I have a five-year plan. I'm excited to be a part of Viacom's digitization, and I'm excited about how my travel experience can contribute to its globalization."

Patricia kept nodding. Adjusting her glasses again, she looked up, down, then back up. "I'm sorry. Marissa didn't tell you, did she? My apologies. We are busy this time of year with summer starting, and we're trying to plan for the end of the summer and the start of fall." She rolled her chair closer to the table, removed her glasses, and crossed her hands over my resume. "Are you a Rhythm and Blues TV fan, by any chance?"

I hadn't watched R&B TV in years. It seemed a bit tacky, and did they even play music anymore, or did they play pandering reality shows that supposedly appealed to the 'more diverse and urban community,' as their old slogan sold it? Luckily, I'd seen the trailers for some of those shows while buying animal crackers from the vending machine on the second-floor lounge at The Winifred. But of course, I didn't say any of that.

"I love R&B TV, especially *Love, Hate, and Rhythm*. But my favorite shows are *Mafia Wives* and *Mafia Daughters*, since I lived in Chicago. My last apartment wasn't too far from Al Capone's joint, The Green Mill."

"My goodness, I lived in Chicago, too."

"Really?" We were hitting it off already, except I hadn't expected her to be in love with my last words. Please do not ask me to answer any pointed questions on either show.

"I guess it's meant to be. We both lived in Chicago and now live in New York City. Chicago was always too small for me. I grew up there. What led you to leave?"

Uh-oh. Do not share the dirty details of your ugly break-up with A&K. "Oh, you know, the same. The Windy City was too small for this tropical storm. I had my sights set on Times Square. New York City has always been my dream."

"Agreed. We hope to have you three days a week starting in late August. Can you commit to us from ten a.m. to six p.m.?"

"Oh yes." My heart sank. "To clarify, this is a part-time job?"

"Yes, you'll work twenty-four hours a week. That's all we have in our budget right now, but I'm sure that can change. We can review your progress and our budget at the end of your semester. The position starts in August."

Not great, but not terrible either. "Excellent." I smiled brightly. "I'd love to join your team."

"I'll be doing more writing websites, perhaps social media?"

"Duh, sorry. Where is my head?" Patricia removed her glasses and slapped them against the table. "How rude of me. The internship is paid. Viacom no longer does unpaid internships. You'll receive ten dollars an hour. I'll send you the paperwork to fill out. Does that sound good?"

The faux silk scarf knotted around my neck felt tight, strangling, suffocating. I could feel the heat rush through my body from humiliation. An internship. At thirty-one years old? The position I applied for was an internet and television writing fellowship. I guess those were just fancy synonyms for "internship." Great. I wore my fake pearls and finest Forever 21 blouse for an internship. Maybe that's why there wasn't a panel interview this time.

That was precisely what happened to Missy with Tilly—the ol' switcheroo. But I hadn't heard back about the teaching job. Rome Away would die down in the shoulder season, too, and Harrison was unreliable, so I'd needed just about anything. I quickly did the math in my head. The three days a week at R&B TV meant making almost an extra thousand a month. Did I have a choice at that point? Hurry up and decide, I thought. Better answer quickly. Her smile is shrinking.

"Of course. Sorry, I was coordinating my schedule in my head. My classes aren't until evening, so everything sounds absolutely perfect."

"Excellent." She let out a sigh of relief. "We'll see you in your new school year. Please do email me if you have any questions. I'll be doing most of the training, but you will have a couple of tub buddies in your cubicle to whom you can reference for guidance." Patricia proceeded to get up, grabbing her badge from her wallet. Her driver's license slipped out onto the carpet and landed face-up. And then I saw it—the date on her license.

***

We met up in one of The Winifred's Marlene Dietrich-themed "beau parlors," the rooms with suitably shaded lighting historically dedicated to wooing prospective gentleman callers. But more recently, for wine and Chinese to-go boxed dinners.

"Her ID said 1986, Missy!" I was leaning back against one of the dramatic, shabby sofas. "I have more experience than the woman who interviewed me."

"But how amazing," Missy said in her upbeat, eye-on-the-prize voice. You get to go to Viacom and Times Square. Your internship is not only paid, but it has a beginning and an end time. My work schedule with Tilly was all the time. For free. And anyway, someone wise once told me, at least you've got your foot in the door."

"And someone wise once told me, 'a pinky toe. No, more like a pinky toenail.'"

Missy slurped her Chianti. "So, more blogging? They have three verticals on their website, right?"

"Yes. Music, shows, and celebrities. Anyway, I don't really have a choice." I grabbed my chopsticks. "Tell me something good about you. I need to think about something other than my depressing life."

"I did get that job *and* an apartment."

"What?" I coughed up my chow mein.

"I'm moving to the East Village in the fall, kind of like Alphabet City. Everything is lining up, you know? The new job, the apartment, and in a year, Jon says he thinks we'll be ready for the next step," Missy's eyes wandered up to the ceiling as she calculated. "Then I'd be engaged by twenty-four, married by twenty-five, then…" Missy stopped midsentence. Her eyes went askew, and she shifted from me.

The air left my lungs, and my mouth ran dry. Had I heard that right? First, her job, and now Missy was leaving me? And for the East Village, of all places? And she was already planning her wedding and babies? Kit, now her? My diaphragm tightened as I tried to breathe and finally speak. "I always knew that all along you were just waiting for the mothership to call you home to Planet Hipster."

"Very funny. But yes, one of my roommates is this fiercely independent woman. She's a DJ. My other roommate is this cool, gay Asian guy. He's a fashion buyer. And speaking of fashion..." She seemed to wiggle in her seat as though she'd been sitting on this news all night, and it was finally about to squirm its way out. "The job I found is in Fashion PR and Marketing!"

Hiding behind my glass of wine, swishing it from side to side, I tried to will away my envy. Not that I wanted a job in fashion, but why were all the stars lining up for Missy and not me? It made me feel like a toddler. I wanted to throw a temper tantrum, stomp my foot on the ground, and tell a grown-up how unfair life was. "Congratulations!" My voice sounded artificially high in my ears. "Please tell me it's not at Tilly."

"It's for Uniqlo's corporate office, which is kind of like H&M. The company is from Japan but big in Europe. They're starting to open stores in the U.S. You've probably passed by a couple of them. It's that place with the red sign and four Japanese letters."

"It's like an H&M?"

"Yes, unless you're my mom. I thought she'd be happy for me. She'd seen the store while she was visiting over Christmas. But she says it's Ikea for clothes."

"Of course she did." I poked at Missy's fried rice with my chopsticks. "My mom thought I worked at a pawn shop. Does it pay well? Salary and benefits?"

"Not exactly."

I waited.

She scrunched up her face. "It's another internship."

It felt like a ten-pound weight had been lifted off my shoulders. Missy was just as messed up as me. Hallelujah! "Noooooooo!" I said, trying to look more bummed. I raised my arms and gestured toward the ceiling. "We are officially little dumb monkeys swinging from one internship branch to the next internship branch. At some point, will we graduate and move on to this place called the Real World? How can you possibly afford to move into a new place?"

"Umm, hello?" Missy bobbed her head. "I've already graduated and moved on. This job is legit. It's a paid internship with a mandatory review period. I'll get paid fourteen dollars an hour, and they'll extend my full-time salary and benefits position within ninety days. Things are lining up. I finally have it all figured out." She flipped her hair and laughed. "And you will, too. Hey, what happened to that teaching assistant position? Are you going to start teaching in the fall?"

I tapped the chopsticks against my chin. "That's been another case of the ol' switcheroo. I heard from them after my R&B interview."

"Did you get another automated rejection letter?"

"It was a semi-rejection letter this time, which was certainly a thoughtful break from all the standard automated rejection letters hitting my inbox daily."

"A semi-rejection letter?"

"There aren't enough teaching assistant positions at the university. Instead, I was offered a part-time, twenty-hour-a-week, weekend workshop coordinator position. I don't even want to know if Air Quote Allie stole my job."

"That's awesome. I'm happy for you! Maybe that'll turn into a teaching position. Umm, what's a workshop coordinator?"

"Writers and actors do these workshops to ameliorate their work and to make themselves feel special and important. I'll open and close the School of Writing department office and classrooms on the weekends, during which we'll host extra special and famous instructors to teach workshops to students. I'll send reminder emails, print out signs, and hang them around the building."

"Look at us with all our work, Jess."

"Yep. Here's to the future. Luckily, Rome Away will get me through the summer. We are moving on up in the world." I chin-chinned my wine glass at Marlene Dietrich's face.

SEVENTEEN

We all stood around in a circle with pens and pads in our hands.

"Good morning to those of you who managed to make it in today," a handsome black man in hip-hop clothing began. "Thank you for making it to another editorial meeting. I see some are still struggling from the Labor Day weekend." He was one of the executive producers overseeing our entire department on the thirtieth floor at R&B TV. His name was Tallahassee, like the city. I'd never met anyone named Tallahassee. "Call me Mr. T," he'd said my first day when I dropped my hiring paperwork at his desk.

We all met behind a set of cubicles in the corner, and he sat against the long radiator lining the bottom of the floor-to-ceiling windows. Behind him, the Hudson River peeked through the skyscrapers. I could see two small defunct jets sitting above the aircraft carrier at the Intrepid Sea, Air, and Space Museum. I wished I, too, were back out on the water, but then I realized perhaps I already was, in a sense, as I had a paid internship. Still, I couldn't help but worry that I was like those two defunct jets that would never fly again.

"Please remember that we meet every Tuesday at eleven a.m. That's for your benefit, folks, in case some of you are returning from vacation, sick days, and whatnot. Please do not take advantage of this. Okay, announcements. Patricia, go."

Patricia straightened the oversized black frames on her tiny face as she spoke. "Firstly, please say hello to our new intern."

Everyone collectively responded. "Hello, new intern."

I chimed back. "Hello, new team."

"Jessica is her name. She arrived here two weeks ago, but I was training her. Jessica is a graduate student with a lot of experience. We're lucky to have her twenty-four hours a week. She's eager to assist every one of you. Oh, and she has some mad Photoshop skills. Please run your projects by me first for approval. I want to make sure we're using her time wisely."

Mr. T. interrupted. "You from New York, Jessica?"

"Oh, uh, no, I'm actually from Texas, but I've lived—"

"Texas in da' house! You watch football? You keeping up right now?"

I hated football. That's one of the many reasons I wanted to leave Texas when I turned eighteen. Once you headed to college, it was all about the big state schools, tailgating, and beer drinking. To me, football culture reflected the absence of any culture at all. Would they be attending my Chopin flautist concerto on Sunday? No? So why would I be attending their grunting and tackling? "Oh my God, Go Cowboys! Football is the essence of Texas!" I didn't even know who played for the Cowboys anymore. Was it still Emmitt Smith? All I knew was that I got an autographed picture with the Dallas Cowboys cheerleaders at the mall when I was a little girl. They had those sexy white patent leather go-go boots. Back then, I thought that was what women aspired to be when they grew up.

"*A'ight, a'ight,* you can be a Dallas fan. Maybe we'll see you in the playoffs. It's all about the Jets this year, you see."

"Oh, I definitely see." So long as he didn't ask me anything specific.

"Who's your favorite player? Who gets you in the game?"

I suddenly straightened out the boring beige button-down sweater I had specifically chosen that morning to blend into the background, which clearly did not work.

"*Umm*, the quarterback?" I didn't know football terminology. The only two things I knew were quarterback and interception because I had to play flag football in my middle school P.E. class.

Thankfully, a guy wearing an intentionally torn grungy Kurt Cobain T-shirt with suspenders and a light brown corduroy blazer interrupted. "Sorry to cut in, Boss, but I must finish this story on Ringo. I was lucky to get the interview."

"*A'ight, a'ight*, let's keep this going. One at a time and hurry; let's start from this corner."

Everyone went around the room one by one, stating what they were working on, while Mr. T occasionally cut in with suggestions, although I got the sense that his comments were more like commandments.

Someone talked about this breakout singer I'd never heard of. Her name was Lana Del Rey. She would be on TRL the following week, during which we'd also cover her on R&B TV.

Finally, Patricia chimed in. "And I will have Jessica do celebrity birthday blogging for the next few months. I'm thinking she'll be doing a variation of 'Ten Best Moments,' or 'Top Ten Reasons We Love Our Favorite Celebrities on Their Birthdays.'"

"Good idea," Mr. T said. "Yo, Jessica, we're all about catchy titles here that draw in subscribers. We're at one million unique monthly visits, but we'd like four million visits by Christmas."

"Right," I began, pretending to scribble something meaningful in my notebook. "Of course. I'll get right on that."

The meeting ended, and I returned to the cubicle I shared with a twenty-two-year-old white woman from Northeastern University named Kim, who'd been in the working world for two years. She had fine waist-length dirty blonde hair and two dimples on the exact opposite ends of her smile. Behind her sat an intelligent, skinny black woman named Ramona, who had graduated from Georgetown University a few years back. I met Ramona during training. She wished she could return to writing about politics at *The Washington Post*. But alas, it seemed life had come for her too, as she came out on the other side of the recession working for

R&B TV. Ramona often wore her hair in a ponytail and sat in the corner, her head covered in headphones, which I learned could easily be removed when detecting any office gossip. Like Patricia, they, too, were embarrassingly younger than me. I realized that despite what feminism would have us believe, women dropped out of the workforce like flies before the clock struck midnight on their thirtieth birthday.

***

Each week was more difficult than I thought it would be, transitioning from full-time graduate student to R&B TV and then back to grad school for my job as a workshop coordinator. One evening, when the school hallways were quiet and most of the offices in the building were already closed, I heard a low voice.

"Ugh, not again," someone said. "What am I going to do?" The familiar voice seemed to be pleading from the other side of the wall. "I can't go back home. To those racists. To those Jesus freaks and gender-phobes."

I clicked 'save' on my computer. I got up and walked through my door to the other side of the department office, where only a few lights were left on. Near the faculty offices, I saw Air Quote Allie with even shorter, chin-length ombre hair tucked behind her ears. She sat on a bench below a free-floating bookshelf, twiddling the small silver loops and diamond studs along her lobes.

"Oh, I—I'm sorry." Allie sniffled and wiped her brown eyes with a torn tissue. "I thought everyone was gone for the day." She glanced down at her tissue. "Or that everybody was at that reading in the Aula Magna."

I tread lightly near her since she kept crying. "Hi, Allie. Allie," I said again. "That's a pretty name. I've always wondered if it was short for—"

"I hate it." She kept sniffling, her eyes downcast as she crumbled her tissue. "It's short for Alyson. Alyson with a 'Y.'"

"Alyson is a pretty name," I continued as she stared at the floor and the wadded-up tissue in her hands. "But I get it. My mother once told me she almost named me Anastacia. Can you imagine that? What a disturbing name. It means resurrection or something. Yet, all I can think of when I hear it is the most famous Anastacia, a haunting dead little girl from those old black and white photos, because, you know, she was a famous daughter of Tsar Nicholas II from Russia and her whole family was murdered by the Bolshevi—"

"Then, you could've been called Stacey." Allie's sniffles slowed. She smirked, followed by a small laugh escaping through her tears. "But Stacey would've been way worse."

"Oh, I know. Can you imagine? I'd be a Valley Girl from one of those Sweet Sixteen novels."

"And…" She paused, lifting her head and wiping a couple of slow tears. "Instead of lecturing us about jobs in workshops, you'd be telling us to recycle."

I couldn't help but grin. Did I really talk about jobs that much? "Oh no, that's optimistic. I'd probably be lecturing you all on how to dye your gray hair back to its perfect golden blonde color because, you know, ageism exists in the workforce."

Allie laughed so hard she snorted, then covered her mouth with embarrassment. We locked eyes as she waited for me to react. Then we laughed harder together.

"Wow, I haven't heard anybody snort from laughing since I was a little girl. But don't worry. I had the biggest Dumbo ears on this tiny head growing up." I pulled my hair back to show her. "See?"

"O-M-G!" Allie's eyes intensified. "They're still big!"

"Thanks. Although, I'd like to think they're smaller now that my head has grown." I tilted my head from side to side, showing them off. "But now that I'm getting older, I've been wondering, will I also grow hair out of my ears too, or is that just men?"

Allie kept laughing. "If you start growing hair out of your ears, you can shave it, like most men. Your nose keeps growing, too, as you get older. So maybe the rest of your features will eventually catch up to your ears when you're fifty."

"Gee, thanks. I guess that's something to look forward to." I let my hair down and went to sit beside her on the bench. "Oh, that's life," I shrugged. "Just when one thing seems to resolve itself, when one thing seems to be getting better, another thing pops up."

"I know, right?" Allie looked up at me again. "Doesn't it seem that way?"

"It does. One big game of whack-a-mole."

She bobbed her head up and down. "I wish someone had told me that."

"Oh, well, I seem to know that, but it still doesn't always make things easier."

"It doesn't?"

"I think getting older helps us to have the tools at our disposal to combat those little suckers that keep popping up."

"Yeah, I guess that makes sense." Allie kept rolling the tissue over in her hands. "I need some of those tools . . . need to start making some of those tools."

I nudged her shoulder. "I've got a whole toolbox you can choose from if you ever need to. Thirty-one, almost thirty-two years of tools to choose from."

"Why—why didn't we ever talk like this before?"

"Before? Before when?"

"Like, you never said anything positive about my work, about my race, about me being non-binary, and, and . . ."

I filled in the blanks. "And about that story you wrote? Your experience with that guy in your dorm room and that creepy old uncle?"

Allie laughed again, but this time, a nervous laugh as her voice grew louder. "He was pretty creepy, wasn't he?"

"That's all you had to say in your story, but you were so eloquent with your words for a man who was not so eloquent. The entire time, I kept thinking, 'creepy old man, creepy old man, creepy old man coming.' And then finally, at the end of your story, 'creepy old man that preys on beautiful young women.'"

"You think I'm beautiful? Well, not sure I'm a woman anymore, but—"

Squinting at Allie, I wondered why it had taken this long to have a meaningful conversation. Why did it have to feel like we were always in competition? In some sense, we were and always would be for graduate spots, teaching positions, and even apartment waitlists. But I knew that wasn't our fault. And I learned another thing or two: that the world could take so much from you, and then it could discard you. "Absolutely. You're beautiful and young." I nudged her shoulder again. "Unfortunately, the world has a history of taking advantage of youth and beauty."

Allie exhaled a short snicker. "Why didn't you say much in your notes or speak up in class when we workshopped my story?"

"Good question." I tried to think. "Can you take it if I tell you?"

"Yes, I'm a big girl—you know what I mean. Even though I happen to be crying like a big baby right now."

"Honestly, I know I'm not much older than you in the grand scheme of things. But we didn't talk about those things like that, in those ways."

"Why didn't you all talk about those things like that?"

"I mean, we hid in our dorms, cried to ourselves, and endured the pain without ever talking about it. *The Real World* and *90210* were groundbreaking for us, you know? Before that, I think the world only had Madonna."

Allie winced. "Really? You would let yourselves be silenced like that?"

"See, that's what I'm talking about. Not everybody had or has the knowledge, education, or vocabulary to articulate that we were 'being silenced' or that we were the 'other' in society. What we couldn't articulate affected how we dealt with life. Our relationships with our family, friends, lovers, coworkers, but, but—"

"But what?"

I searched the office as if those tools were lying in a tangible box. I glanced from left to right.

"Yes?" She brushed mascara off her cheek.

"Do you think a mouse in a maze says to itself, 'I'm just a mouse in a maze. And all these scientists and people and the world are doing things to me, and I don't even know if I want them to be doing these things to me, so I better find a hole, and then when I get out of this maze, I think I'll have the surf and turf at Morton's. And my steak had better be rare this time, and the lobster tail had better not be overcooked this time. I'm going to ask for extra garnishes. Maybe lemons and that buttery garlic dip.'"

"Oh. Well, I guess when you put it that way. So, you all just waited around in dark rooms?" Allie incredulously wrinkled her forehead at me. "Crying to yourselves, crying aloud for help when no one would help you?

Catastrophe, catastrophe. Everything was a big catastrophe, Allie's words said to me. I knew she was partially right. I was only beginning to share the shame of unemployment, and even then, I hadn't yet told anyone how I'd really lost my job. And the job stuff was so public. The private stuff was so private. How could I share anything else if I couldn't even share the full story about my job?

"Initially, yes," I said. "But then one mouse said, 'hey, what's that over there? Is that a hole?' And the mouse started to explore it and sneak through it, and then the mouse got out and realized that another mouse had already gotten out before them, but didn't tell the other mice—how cruel! So, that mouse decided they would be the mouse that returned for all the other mice. And that mouse returned to the maze." I teared up. I didn't know why my simple analogy struck me. I thought of Colette. Of what she would say. But also, I thought of her dark purple hands.

Allie rifled through her backpack, sitting on the floor below. She found a tissue and handed it to me. "And then what did the mouse do? What did the mouse say?"

"The mouse said, 'guys, there's this great big hole I've made for us, and now we can all squeeze through it, and when we get to the other side, there's plenty more room to explore, and there's food and air.' But by then, there were so many mice. So, it would take a lot of time for all the mice to escape and access the world outside the maze."

"And to the surf and turf at Morton's?"

I laughed while wiping my tears. "The surf and turf at Morton's sounds so good right now."

"And then?" Allie slid forward on the bench.

"And then, when more mice got out, they noticed that so many mice had already gotten out ahead of them, and those preceding mice had already set up their little mazes in the exact nice way they wanted. So the newer mice got their feelings hurt, wondering why the older mice hadn't told them sooner, so the newer mice started fighting with the older mice, while the older mice were like, 'we didn't know either. We're just trying to have our own comfy and happy maze, too. We're too busy being preoccupied with that. And taking care of our own little mice kids and mice elderly.'" I laughed.

Allie scratched her chin and gasped. "Wow. I guess I'm lucky, huh? I never would have thought about it like that."

"Exactly. Many of us never would have thought about it either without the Susan B. Anthonys, the Elizabeth Cady Stantons, the Simone de Beavouirs or Betty Friedans of the world. I guess so many of us got used to our mazes and to wearing our scarlet letters on the inside. Because we had to for survival."

"O-M-G, that's awful."

"Yep," I leaned in, thinking of her private personal essay. "And did you know that until the 70s, the little women mice still couldn't refuse to have sex with their husbands?"

"What? That cannot be true!"

"Yep. True fact."

"Wow."

"And it's only recently that we've been able to talk about it all so much. Maybe that's why some of us don't know how to discuss it yet. I mean, when I read your story in workshop, I kept thinking, does she have to see this man every time she returns to New Jersey for the holidays?"

Allie tucked a loose strand of hair behind her ear. "The answer is yes."

"Wow. You are the strongest person I know because all my creepers live in different states and countries."

Allie smirked. "Why wouldn't you want to talk about it, though? Why wouldn't you want to discuss that?"

I was starting to think that because that was how things had always been for Allie, she thought that was how things had always been. As if asking for help provided all this support, compassion, and empathy instead of rabid ridicule and more infliction of pain. Even with all her forward-thinking presentations on race, she still couldn't grasp a time when sharing such private stories could publicly ruin reputations and, in earlier times, destroy them for life and even have economic repercussions spanning generations. "For a variety of reasons. I do agree that there's healing in discussing the pain, but there can be consequences."

"Consequences?" Allie's tone rose in irritation. "How could there be consequences? The truth is supposed to set you free, right?"

I slid away to give myself some space. "Yes, in a way, but it can also shackle you if you aren't careful."

"What's that supposed to mean? We're supposed to lie to ourselves and everyone else?"

"No, I didn't mean it like that. I meant, look, don't let it or others define who you are now that you've announced that. Don't let it define who you're going to be or who you want to be. Also, your generation grew up on the internet, so you all think you are responsible for providing these press conferences to your constituents over every uncomfortable and intimate life event. But you're allowed the right to privacy and the time to process things. You don't owe anybody anything. My life ain't nobody's damn business. I also don't have to justify my actions to the world. Does that make sense?"

She smiled. "It does."

"Good."

"Allie, what's the real reason why you're crying?"

She looked down.

"You can tell me. Whatever it is. It can't be that bad." I pulled up my hair again. "Remember, I'm an old lady with big hairy ears."

"And a big nose." She looked up.

"There ya go," I dramatically sniffed. "I'm so old that I've heard it all and smelled it all before. And like Colette said in class—"

"Everything we are feeling in our hearts has already been addressed by those that came before. I think about that sometimes. But now I'll also be thinking about the mice in the maze. Anyway, it's my job. I don't have one anymore."

"Oooh," welcome to the club." Allie's news tugged at my heart. And here I'd been resenting her again because I'd thought she landed the teaching assistantship.

"It was only part-time anyway. And I thought I'd get hired full-time after six months. But it was time for my review, and at first, I thought it was because they would tell me they were extending me a full-time job offer. I was looking forward to it. It would be my first real job besides the bar, but that didn't count. Then I got called into one of my boss's offices, and there were three of them. It was weird that three of them wanted to meet with me. I don't know, they like—"

"Ganged up on you?"

"Yeah!" Allie yelled. "But I'd thought I'd done everything. They didn't even have a website before me or know HTML or Photoshop or what a handle or a hashtag was. They acted like I was playing video games behind the computer or something. Like they were paying me to have fun. They kept saying how I was producing some good work at the outset but then blamed it on the fact that I'm in school, and maybe that's taking priority over their—"

"Over their job that pays you seven dollars an hour for three days a week?"

"Yeah, except it was ten dollars an hour for two days a week, and eventually four days, but I still had to do much of the coding at home without pay."

"Yep, that's about right. I'd think you were lying to me if you hadn't just said all that. I had a similar experience at this pawn shop for high-end clothes."

"My parents said they wouldn't keep helping me with rent after this year."

"I can't believe you didn't get one of the teaching assistant positions."

Allie smiled. "I did get the teaching assistant position. But it didn't pay well, and I thought this job would lead to a real salary and benefits. I guess I made the wrong decision."

My stomach dropped. Of course, Allie got your job. But stay focused, I willed myself. You can do this. "I'm graduating, so you could probably take my job. I could recommend you to my boss."

"You would do that for me? I do have an extra year for the dual bachelor's and master's program."

"Yes. You made it to every class early. You also worked hard and produced great work. Now that I think about it, your peers also relied on you. If you get it, the position doesn't pay much. Maybe enough to cover the rent. But the hours are flexible."

"But I'm a bad interviewer."

I returned to the office, opened a file from my USB drive, and printed some interview questions. "It's usually quiet on weekends since everybody's in a workshop. If you ever want to come in, we can practice. Here, take one. If you want to rehearse, I'm pretty much a pro at them."

Allie quietly studied the document while I reviewed the questions. My stature climbed with confidence as I blazed through them in my head. Of course, I'd perfected and memorized all my answers. But then came the last question, which haunted me all over again: "Where do you see yourself in five years?"

EIGHTEEN

Surprisingly, I couldn't wait for Conchita to come to New York for Halloween. Over the last few months of phone calls, she had manipulatively played to my strengths, flattering me with what a great tour guide I would be with all my worldly travel experience. She had even recounted how she'd been reading my R&B TV posts, Rome Away, and my old Gal Around the World blog from my A&K Travel days. But I was sure there were other tricks up her sleeve.

"Delayed, delayed, delayed," read most of the overhead monitors at JFK.

I'd waited for two hours before Conchita finally made her way out of the gate. It was easy to see the top of her high head of hair emerging from behind crowds dragging carry-ons. Missy helped me create a giant neon orange poster board with purple glitter, bows, and black Halloween letters. All meant to embarrass her. I waved the sign high above my head. It read, "Miss Fiestas Forever."

"Yessicaaa!" Conchita waved at me. Then stopped, "*ouch...*" She rubbed her collarbone as she remained faceless in the crowd, being pushed along with everybody else.

"Conchita!" I yelled. "Don't they know who you are? Tell them who you are! My friend is a three-time Miss Fiesta Winner!"

Although, the first two times she was a runner-up, I wanted to say. But that was the old me.

Like a pendulum, her skeptical eyes shifted, swinging side to side. First slow, then fast, as shoulder-to-shoulder crowds of tall men, women, and children speaking myriad languages collapsed together. Many were tired and quiet. Some were angry and yelling at each other, at their cell phones, and even crying. As Conchita approached, the crowds eventually fanned out, expanding like an accordion around their respective carousels.

When she reached me, Conchita stopped, breathless, and suddenly bent over her luggage. She tore off a black raincoat, revealing a white T-shirt that read, "I Heart New York."

I was kind of pleased to see Conchita so harried, stressed, and out of her element. "What, no hug? I thought you'd be proud of my sign. It's like the Jennifer Lopez movie you were an extra in. Instead of 'Selenas Forever,' I put, 'Miss Fiestas Forever.'"

"Yessica, I love the sign, thank you." Conchita took a couple of deep breaths and panted in and out, trying to stand up against her carry-on handle. She almost fell as the handle retreated into the top of her suitcase. "I wanted to be here in August, but back-to-school responsibilities kept me home. And this is my first Halloween away from my kids, so my husband and all the kids kept calling after I landed. Then, there was a long hallway. I had to go through a few long hallways and was told I had to take a train."

"Oh, you were in a different terminal than you were assigned? That sounds about right. Storms are coming, so there were a lot of delays. I'm sure flights got shuffled around quite a bit. You're probably lucky you made it here. I heard something about closing down the airports."

Conchita kept going. "I was sitting between two crying babies the whole flight."

"Oh, the irony to finally leave your crying babies only to end up between somebody else's crying babies."

"And to make it worse, you will understand when you have children one day, Yessica. But everybody prefers their own crying babies over other people's crying babies. And my seat would not recline, Yessica. It would not recline." Conchita extended her arms down to reach her feet. Then she stretched her arms high, crossing her elbows behind her head and tugging them toward her shoulder. "Are the planes getting smaller? I thought they were getting bigger with all the technologies. But maybe I am getting bigger."

"The planes are getting bigger for the first class and business passengers. For everybody else, they are definitely getting smaller." I rolled up the Miss Fiestas Forever posterboard and grabbed the stuffed carry-on from her. "Okay, Conchita, I got this." I began to stroll away, but Conchita stopped me.

"Yessica, where are you going?"

"Umm, Manhattan."

"I need to get my luggage."

"There's more luggage? You're only here for a few days."

"Oh, Yessica, that's very funny."

I rolled the carry-on right back around. "Okay, let's get your luggage." We headed toward the overhead monitors. "Let's see. San Antonio, ah, there it is. Carousel five."

Crowds closed in on their respective carousels as a loud buzzer went off at the top of the conveyor belt slide: *MEEP!*

Conchita jumped, flinching in search of the source of the noise. "What was that?"

"Uh, carousel five? You see that light blinking at the top? Your flight's luggage is about to come out next. Conchita, you helped with the spiffy San Antonio 'International Airport' sign. Don't you know this stuff?"

"Yessica, I have not slept. Please do not get me started."

"Okay, fair enough." I decided to continue my upbeat attitude. And anyway, it was fun to see Conchita a fish out of water, a fiesta out of water. Some of the luggage slid down the conveyor belt slide and out onto the carousel. "Be sure to book La Guardia next time so that you won't be running marathons through terminals."

"Yessica, the new Delta flight from our airport goes to JFK And it was the cheapest flight. Even though I went to bed at midnight and woke up at three o'clock to be at the airport before six."

JFK was the farthest airport from Manhattan and The Winifred, so we would be taking a train, a bus, subways, and lots of 'hallways,' as Conchita put it. Plus, that long final trek up the hill from Seventh Avenue to The Winifred between Ninth and Tenth.

And then the rain.

That's when it dawned on me. As I considered Conchita's 'hallway' terminology to describe terminals, I wondered. Had Conchita ever been on a subway before? I wanted to connect with Conchita and make up for my bad behavior at her baby shower. But this was going to be such a real treat for me. 'Try,' I told myself, 'not to enjoy this so much.'

"There it is!" Conchita yelled, jumping up and down and clapping her hands like her home team had scored a touchdown.

Unfortunately, her suitcase would not make it to the end zone. Conchita's giant neon pink suitcase stopped and remained stuck at the top. Some gaudy clothes were also coming out of the sides and zippers of her suitcase.

"Is that sequin? And a dress made out of pink ballet tutu? What the—."

"*Sí*, Yessica. For our Halloween tonight."

"Did you bring your roller skates, too? You do know that we roller skate everywhere in New York, right? How else would we get anywhere on time?"

"Roller skates?" Conchita looked alarmed.

"I'm kidding. The 90s are back in New York, so it's all about the Rollerblades."

But Conchita didn't even seem to hear my joke. She was too busy straining her neck to see what was happening with her suitcase. The carousel buzzed again, except it produced a different cacophonous sound instead as if communicating in Morse code: *MEEP! MEEP! MEEP!*

"Umm, Conchita?"

MEEP! MEEP! MEEP!

"*Sí*, Yessica? What's happening right now? And what is that noise again? It is a different noise, no?"

MEEP! MEEP! MEEP! A man wearing a black JFK jacket over a red and white Spiderman Halloween costume hopped up the carousel to the top of the slide with a metal stick.

MEEP! MEEP! MEEP!

I raised an eyebrow at Conchita. "I think your 'baggage' has completely stalled the machine. But look at that. Spiderman is saving the city from your baggage already. He only scales skyscrapers for special occasions; it's good to know his leaps and bounds include airport carousels. What a good Samaritan."

MEEP! MEEP! MEEP! Airport staff finally pressed a button to halt the sound. Several passengers beside us shot disapproving sideways glances and then checked their watches.

"Maybe next time don't jump up and down clapping at the suitcase that is delaying everybody else's suitcase to give away our location. We don't want to blow our cover."

Conchita kept her hands together like she was praying, staring at the JFK Spiderman working and praying. I was waiting for the Catholic sign of the cross next.

"Now, Conchita, I did want to wait until we left the airport, but it seems that the big city lessons must commence immediately."

"Huh, lessons, Yessica?" Conchita tinged with excitement and quickly turned to me with her praying fists against her lips. "I thought you would just show me the Big Apple tour sites?"

"You're gonna get two for the price of one." I watched Spiderman, who kept jiggling Conchita's baggage. "You know how in San Antonio everything is sunny, everybody wears bright colors, and acts happy, even when they are not?"

"Go Spurs!"

"We're more low-key here, which means darker weather and darker colors. So, lesson number one: Maybe don't wear your heart on your sleeve so much."

"Why, Yessica?" Conchita clapped her hands at me for a second, then returned to her baggage and praying position.

"New York is the complete opposite of Texas. You are coming from a place with the most resources to one with the fewest resources. And we must compete for those few resources." I leaned my head down to the left. "But, if it helps to think of it this way, we're in the Wild West again."

"The Wild West?" Conchita perked up in excitement. "I like it."

The pink baggage at the top of the slide slipped loose with the last of Spiderman's prodding. "Huh," Conchita said. "I think they got it." The final jiggles of Conchita's suitcase revealed other stuffed suitcases vying to plunge out of the conveyor belt slide. One of the suitcases was reminiscent of a yellow polka-dot bikini, while another was reminiscent of a Betsey Johnson dress covered in black and white stripes with pink roses.

"See what I mean about competing for resources, Conchita? It wasn't just your baggage. It seems that the Miss Fiestas of all the other small towns are also competing to march their whole past life down the conveyor belt slide. If only we had little Spidermen to fix everything for us once we left this building."

Suddenly, Miss Fiesta's baggage began backflipping slowly down the carousel slide, pushing Spiderman to the side and paving the way for the other suitcases. He scrambled to balance himself with the metal stick. The loud buzzer triggered again to signal business as usual, and crowds of passengers around the carousel immediately dispersed, making way for Conchita's baggage. "There it goes." I rolled the carry-on away from the carousel. "Conchita, what are you doing?"

Conchita was the only person who did not disperse. She squatted down like an umpire, her arms extending straight out as if she were going to catch her baggage mid-air.

DOO, DOO, DA, DUNK, CRASH, KERPLUNK!

Conchita hit the floor, right side up, with her baggage atop her.

I dropped her carry-on and stared down at her. She surprisingly had a big smile on her face. "I caught it, Yessica." The crowd clapped at Conchita. I bent down to help her up.

"I suppose that brings me to lesson two of living in New York, Conchita."

"Oh, I am already at lesson number two?" Conchita clapped and bent down to straighten out her cowgirl pants.

"There will be a test, so keep up. New York comes with a lot of high highs and a lot of low lows. But it is futile to give up. We must never give up. Failure is not an option."

"Oh, I like this."

"I thought it would appeal to your Miss Fiesta-winning sensibilities."

Putting ourselves back together, we made our way toward the exit.

"Oh no," Conchita grinned. "That's the taxi line?"

Miserable people dragged their suitcases through several wet rows of stanchions. Rain began to pour down harder, gushing out from the edges of the terminal rooftop, run-off spraying diagonally as the sky dimmed darker.

"Ah, yes. But don't worry. That's not for us."

"Oh, good. Phew." Conchita shot an approving look at me. "You called one of those black town cars? With the private driver? Like on my novellas?"

"*M*mm, not exactly. First stop, Queens." I led Conchita toward the sky train that would take us to the bus stop.

"Queens?"

***

By the time we made it to the subway, Conchita's high head of hair had fallen over with the rain, and her eyes swelled red, highlighting the lines and sagging bags running down her face. On any other day, I would have felt strangely proud to show off the hard work and grind it takes to live in New York City—not everybody can do it. But the inclement weather increased, corralling every last straggler onto the bus. Exhausted, we ran from one ride to the next, competing with the crowds, winds, and rain and wet. There was no place to sit on our shoulder-to-shoulder two-hour commute of trains, busses, and subways, so we often stood in the middle of our transportation.

"Conchita, grab the rail already." She awkwardly tried to jimmy her luggage against the center pole to maintain her balance on the moving subway car.

"I cannot, Yessica. My kids' hand sanitizer is in my luggage. I thought you would be picking me up in a car."

"Don't be ridiculous. You're telling me if you had access to your kids' hand sanitizer you would use it to sanitize the pole?"

"Absolutely." The doors opened, dropping off more passengers and picking up new ones. Then the doors closed. Conchita squatted down even lower as the train accelerated to the next stop.

"Conchita!" I yelled again at her over the train's screeching noise against the rail tracks and turns. She held her low squat position. "You seriously look like you're constipated and about to take a dump right now." Passengers standing above Conchita snickered. But she kept her focus ahead. "Not that using the cars as toilets would be a first for this city's subway system." Finally, I pulled out a handkerchief from my cross-body bag. "Here."

"Thank you, Yessica." Conchita gripped the pole with my handkerchief. Straightening herself into a standing position, she announced, "I think I understand your lessons one through one hundred right now. And my thighs are killing me."

"Wow. And we haven't even made it to Manhattan yet." The doors opened again. "I take that back. We are officially in Manhattan now. Hello, Grand Central Station. Quick, grab your luggage. We have to get to the shuttle to Times Square, where we can grab the 1, 2, or 3."

"There's still more?" Conchita's eyes kindled with terror as she stood frozen.

I wheeled her carry-on toward the platform.

"Oh, yes. Remember that in New York, there is always more. More levels of exhaustion. You're a mommy, right?"

"I thought this was supposed to be a vacation." Conchita struggled to drag her heavy suitcase out. During the journey from JFK, two wheels on the opposite ends of her suitcase broke, leaving only two wheels functioning. But not the two wheels on the same side of her luggage. That would've been helpful. Two wheels from opposite sides of her luggage appeared to have broken off, making the suitcase even more challenging to maneuver.

"Conchita, hurry." The subway doors closed on Conchita's luggage. I waited on the platform, staring at the fear in Conchita's eyes as she realized I might not go with her to the next stop. "Push, push!" I yelled. "Like you're having another baby."

Conchita kept pushing, but the fruitless results produced swelling in her eyes. While she pushed out, she fought to keep the tears in. And I wondered if there was something else.

"Okay, okay." Maybe my baby joke took things too far. I finally relented, pressing the button outside the subway car. The doors jerked open.

"There was a button the whole time?" Conchita barked at me while struggling to push out the last of her suitcase.

I pointed below her feet. "Mind the gap."

"Why didn't you press the button, Yessica?"

I'd be lying if I didn't say a part of me took pleasure in exercising a slight superiority over my old rival. But I paused with pity. Conchita's gaze may have been fleeting, but the fear and sadness in her eyes were lasting. I couldn't share that then. "You know, Conchita. All I can do is lead the horse to water. But I can't make it drink."

We continued rolling our suitcases through myriad labyrinths of Grand Central. "Sorry, but there are many more 'hallways,' as you would say." My words ricocheted against the wind from accelerating trains, platforms, and vents as our suitcase clacked along the uneven subway tiles. "We can take the 1, 2, or 3, but we have to take the 7 Shuttle to Times Square first." I grabbed Conchita's other suitcase, propping one atop the other so that the bottom one scraped the ground unevenly with its two wheels.

When we reached the 1 train, some orange and yellow seats were open. "Finally." Conchita unfolded my handkerchief into a full square to set it down like a blanket on the seat before throwing herself onto it. Then, she pointed to a stranger a few rows behind us.

I slapped her finger down. "Conchita, what are you doing? You know it's not polite to point."

She leaned in to whisper to me. "Is that what they call a bag lady?"

I tried to lean over Conchita inconspicuously to see the direction she was pointing. A middle-aged woman with long silver hair and a black goose-down coat that ran down to her ankles fixed some items in a small square shopping cart filled with plastic bags. "What? No, that's just a lady with her groceries. You're so ridiculous."

She kept staring wide-eyed at the woman. "How can you tell the difference?"

"Conchita, pretty much everybody in New York looks like a homeless bag lady, especially as winter approaches."

The doors chimed to signal our departure. But the signal seemed to introduce the stage performers stumbling onto the train at the last second. Several young teenagers in red hoodies assembled at the opposite end of the subway car. They spread out, retreating into rehearsed positions above us.

"Ladies and gentlemen, ladies and gentlemen," one said while cupping his hand against his mouth like a megaphone. "Can I please have your attention?" Another performer hit a button on a boombox, screaming the latest Eminem.

Conchita reached over and clutched my arm. "Are we being held up? Is this one of your lessons, Yessica? Did I come to New York to die?"

Two of the men jackknifed up the poles on both ends of the subway car, singing along with the lyrics.

"Huh." Conchita clutched her purse and luggage tighter, eyeing them suspiciously.

"Good thing you broke up with the subway poles, Conchita. No, on second thought, that would have been amazing if you were still squatting down at the pole right now."

One of the young men leaped for his next maneuver, bouncing his feet off the top of Conchita's luggage to flip against the ceiling. He finished by suspending himself upside down, hanging there for a few seconds before landing on his feet.

"They're talented, aren't they?" I ignored the horror on Conchita's face. Another guy jumped off Conchita's suitcases again. "But it can be a nuisance. And hasn't anyone told them they took a left turn at Albuquerque? Broadway and Times Square are literally right there."

Finally exiting, dragging our suitcases up the last subway steps at Thirty-Fourth Street and Seventh Avenue, the rain showered down, washing everything away. "You brought the tropical storm and Texas-sized hail with you, Conchita."

"Except it's getting freezing, Yessica."

Yellow and red umbrellas above hot dog stands and halal carts twirled and swung backward toward the sky, as did the umbrellas above each remaining New Yorker's head. As hard as the rain hit, it seemed funny to see the last of the food, napkins, and plasticware fly off the carts that were staples of most corners in Midtown.

A last stampede of travelers took cover under awnings, inside buildings, cabs, and down the subways. Small, muddy rivers ran down sidewalks and side streets. Passing the mannequins and merchandise in the windows at Macy's, we pushed against the pressure of rising winds and crawled, slipping up the incline leading to The Winifred's entrance. The signature flagpole above The Winifred's awning stood naked, except for a maintenance worker in overalls gathering the drenched American flag and folding a ladder at the bottom of the steps.

An older Winifred staff member ran out, putting her hand above her forehead to shield herself from the wind. The rain blew around, first spraying until it spilled down from the awning above our heads.

"Hurry up, ladies. You shouldn't be outside anymore. We're about to go on lockdown. A hurricane is coming." Realizing she did not recognize Conchita, she yelled over the storm. "Who is this?"

"This is my sister from Texas. She's staying with us."

"The cots sold out, and we're full. Many of the staff had to stay through the hurricane."

I could see Conchita's look of worry, her pupils dilating, and her breathing rate increasing.

"No, I booked her bed weeks ago." Conchita and I rolled the wet suitcases toward the counter.

"Did you pay the sixty-four dollars for the cot?" The Winifred staff member said from behind the desk. "Remember, it's sixty-four dollars a night for additional guests."

"Yes, under Puente, with a 'P.' I'm in room 604. I paid for it a long time ago. They said the cot would be in my room when we arrived."

The staff member turned several pages in an old college-lined notebook, the yellowing paper consumed by tall cursive exceeding the lines across the page. "Oh, I see." She made a checkmark in the margins by my name. "It says reserved. You can go up to your room now. I will make sure they take the cot to you."

Staff members ran around the lobby, issuing flashlights as we rolled our luggage away from the front desk. One of them with a walkie-talkie stopped to look our way. "We've already filled the bathtubs with water and are about to shut off the elevators. Remember, candles still aren't allowed in the guest rooms, but you're welcome to join the ladies in one of the lounges. They're going to try to watch scary Halloween movies. We do have backup generators, but we hope we don't have to use them."

Finally unlocking my guest room, Conchita immediately collapsed atop my bed. Without words, I opened the cot and unfolded the bedspread. We removed our jackets, dried off, threw on pajamas, and slept through the rest of the storm. The pre-war building was strong. If it weren't for a faint whistle worming its way through the tiny crevices of my window below Midtown, we'd have never been reminded of the storm.

***

Our building remained quiet early the following morning.

"Yessica," Conchita whispered as I turned over. Her face pressed against mine with the flashlight between us. She clicked the flashlight on and off, shining the yellow light on her face like a character in a scary movie.

"Conchita, are you trying to frighten me?"

"It's *Día de los Muertos*, Yessica. Boo!" She whispered her scariest boo again, "*Bwah*! Did I scare you?"

I yawned and stretched my arms above my head. But before I could respond, Conchita cut me off, mimicking my voice: "'I mean, there's nothing scarier than that bad breath of yours.' Was that what you were going to say?"

"Oh, stop, Conchita. That was the old me."

Conchita fell to her back while continuing to click the flashlight along the closed window in front of us. "Also, where were these two meals we were to have? We fell asleep too early."

"Seriously? After all that? I barely got you to and from the airport alive. Please don't pick the farthest airport from civilization next time."

"Oh, okay. I am sorry about this. But I wanted to say thank you."

Conchita's sincere gratitude surprised me, and I felt a drop in my stomach. She could put my sarcasm aside to tell me I finally did something right. "Thank you? For what?"

"For booking me and for paying my accommodations so far in advance. Can you believe it? What if you had not done that? I was standing there when the lady was grilling with her questions. And I thought, if I know Yessica well enough, she did not do that."

"It's good to hear how much confidence you have in me, Conchita."

"How much do I owe you?"

"Nothing."

"Nothing? What do you mean, nothing?"

"It's fine. I got it. My treat. Which brings us to lesson number—whatever—of fight club: The city will never accommodate you. Life will never accommodate you. It will never ask you how you would like to be accommodated. You must pursue what you want and show how you would like to be accommodated. Also, the last trick is that you must demand the accommodations in a particular, disguised way. Nobody can know you are demanding anything from them. You must be so convincing that by the end of your demands, they feel you are doing them a favor instead."

Conchita flickered her flashlight at me on and off again.

I pushed it away from my face. I gradually rolled out of bed and read my electronic clock on the desk. "It's eight-thirty a.m. I guess the power didn't go out up here."

Crossing the last two feet of the guest room, I pushed the pastel-flowered curtains open. Grabbing the strings to the blinds, I peered back at Conchita in anticipation of my next trick. "Are you ready for it?"

"Ready for what, Yessica?"

I pulled hard and fast until the fat wooden blinds reached the top of the windowsill.

"Huh!" Conchita struggled to inch out of bed. She moved forward in slow motion like a zombie in a trance. Then, she clasped her hands together again to make a prayer across her lips.

"Oh, come on, Conchita, it's not that—" I swung my head back. "Ma—je—s—t—i—c." But it was. It was majestic. It was magic. It was magnificent.

"Yessica," she whispered. "It's the high highs and the low lows. Last night, the hurricane, and now—" Conchita kept her praying hands together and turned her head back and forth in disbelief.

The harsh wind and rains of the hurricane had ceased. But not without ushering in the first quiet snow of the season, the complete opposite of the storm's chaos and destruction. Like confetti, the snow sprinkled and scattered along the water towers, rooftops, and skyscrapers above us. The sun had not risen, but we didn't need it. Instead, the snow cast a white light, a blanket, a canvas across the city. It took its time flying and spreading across the sky. Like the still-dark windows of the city's tall buildings, the snow postponed the morning and its eventual landing; a million little specks crossed our window, spinning in circles and coalescing together in a cloud of peace above us before finally landing below like a fluffy pillow.

"Another performance." More flurries pirouetted in front of us, painting our Midtown postcard white. A few rested on the windowsill. "It's rare. To get snow after a hurricane, you know. The likelihood of that happening is…" I turned to Conchita and laughed. "I guess that's about as likely as you and me ending up together in New York."

"I get it now. You have to be here to see it. And to understand it. To see is to believe." A small tear moseyed down her face. "Oh, Yessica, how can I—how can *anyone*—ever go back home after all this?"

"Another note to add to that book?" I was concerned for Conchita, but it wasn't time to say anything, so I put my arm around her shoulder. She lowered her head against my neck. "Welcome to New York."

Conchita unlocked the window and pried at the bottom to open it.

I thought of Gloria Grace but tried to hide my sad face. "It only opens a quarter of the way now. You know, so you can be bad and smoke a smooth Dunhill every once in a while."

Conchita's stunned eyes jumped to mine. "What?"

"Not that I would know or anything."

I went to wash my face over the sink. Wiping off my forehead and cheeks with a hand towel, I grabbed a crumpled envelope under the door. "It seems the power, water, and subways below Thirtieth Street are down. How about that?"

I thought it remarkable that residing four blocks north meant that we had every necessity and even the excesses of Forty-Second Street. Work and school were canceled since power below Thirty-Fourth Street was out. But since the hurricane postponed Halloween the night before, many of us marched north toward the lights in our costumes and coats. Conchita had been quiet since the snow at my window, so I put my arms inside hers like a chain as we walked east and north toward Fifth Avenue and Forty-Second Street.

I began first with small talk. "Thank you for your pink ballerina costume. I do love all the sequins and frills. But are you sure you're allowed to wear your Miss Fiesta dress and crown during non-official Fiesta events?"

Conchita kept silent. Then, she finally responded in a low monotone. "It is to take pictures in front of the sites for the Fiesta Commission."

"You mean to tell me you're like one of those army guys who wear their uniform on the plane?" I slowed. "Oh, you should wear it on the plane. Cause you also serve the community." I made a big salute. "Thank you for your service, Miss Fiesta."

Conchita laughed softly, then quickly reeled in her smile as a snowplow scratched against the street.

"Out of my way," a young voice yelled. Dressed as a mummy, a teenage skateboarder crashed through us, briefly breaking up our chain.

"Say excuse me, next time," I yelled, looping my arm through Conchita's again, as I noticed the skater had yet to phase her.

"And skateboarders." Conchita finally spoke in the low monotone of a muffle.

"Skateboarders?" I questioned.

"You said that roller-skates, no, rollerblades, are making a comeback in the city. But you forgot to mention the skateboarders."

I played along. "Oh, sorry about that. We can add that to our lessons. Be on the lookout for the sixteen-year-old mummy skateboarders that just arose from the dead. They are making a comeback."

"Yes." She dragged me forward, periodically slowing down to stare up at the skyscrapers.

I looked at her. "The buildings climb higher the farther you make it into Midtown. Supposedly, a skyscraper is anything above forty stories."

Conchita stopped to finally get a full view of the Empire State Building behind us. She scanned the icon, up, down, then back up again.

"Forty stories for a skyscraper doesn't seem that high of a standard." We spun our heads back north. "But it does feel good to know that..." I trailed off, considering she wasn't listening.

Except that she was. "It feels good to know that what, Yessica?"

"That even though there are skyscrapers in the world as tall as mountains, that doesn't mean the rest of us still can't touch the clouds—."

"At just forty stories."

"That's right."

"Huh."

"How's home, Conchita? How have things been with you since I saw you last? My goodness. Can you believe it has been almost a year? Mortimer must be so big and independent now. I bet you're finding more time for yourself."

"Yes. And the fire meant we got to add an extra bedroom and loft anyway. It was time for renovations for my big family." Conchita kept updating me. "The mayor announced a couple of city-wide initiatives. After campaigning for a fitter city—you know San Antonio won the Michelle Obama grant? —we now have a Fitness Council that is creating more walking and biking paths and educating the children on nutrition. There's also talk of a new initiative called a 'Decade of Downtown' and 'SA2020.' It's a ten-year plan to revitalize downtown San Antonio and possibly turn it into a global city by 2020. And we have that internet company joining the initiative, MoreSpace. I bet you didn't know they were only one of a few companies besides Google that made real money during the dot-com bust."

"Conchita, that's great. I love that San Antonio is moving on up in the world. So many exciting things that you get to be a part of."

Conchita took a deep breath and sighed. "I don't know, Yessica. I guess one always thinks that..."

I slowed my steps. The snow crunched louder beneath my feet. I wanted to be there for Conchita, but whatever it was, I worried I wouldn't be able to help her.

"That one day you will be an adult, and life will be organized and fall into place."

"Yep, when we're young, we always think that. I know you love organization, Conchita, but the longer I live, the more I realize that life is not one big closet we can organize."

Another gang of teenagers in all six Power Ranger costumes and skateboards surrounded us. They were slushing through the snow, finally giving up and picking up their boards.

Conchita lowered her voice and slouched her back in guilt as she confessed. "I love my husband. I love my children. I'm good at the Fiesta Commission work. But sometimes, I feel as though something is missing. I feel as though I'm worth more. I'm doing so much, and my work is not compensated. Sometimes I don't even get paid. And I think, if I were to get paid enough, I could give back much more."

Huh. Conchita and I were more alike than I'd thought. Why did all roads lead to jobs? Maybe because they had become synonymous with purpose. "Oh, how I understand."

"You do?"

"I do."

"What do you do about it?"

"Me? What do I do about it? Good question. Well, I'm embracing that gig economy for one thing. It's a balancing act that doesn't pay the best, but I'm trying not to focus on the short term. Once I finish the graduate program, I can devote more time to something more ideal and negotiate better pay."

"Good for you, but that doesn't really help me."

"Okay, is this a brainstorming session? Conchita, you're the best cheerleader for the city, and you're so good at all the Fiesta stuff, and you know so many people. If I were you, I would just find a way to leverage that network to build my own thing."

Conchita's eyes magnified. "There was this magazine. Do you know how the city only has one big newspaper? The *San Antonio Light* shut down when we were kids, and now there's only the *Express-News* and the alt-weekly *San Antonio Current*. Sometimes, people try to create a magazine. But the magazines come and go. If I could do anything, I would have a magazine."

I nodded. "A magazine that would not come and go."

"Yes," Conchita nodded back. "Preferably a magazine that would not come and go."

"What would it be about?"

Conchita absent-mindedly unlocked our arms to adjust her crown.

That's when I knew. "Oh, I know exactly what it will be about."

She winked at me. "I don't have a title yet, but I thought the subtitle or slogan could be, *All Things Fiesta, All Year Round.*

"How sneaky. You told me you were working for a new Fiesta Commission magazine."

"I know, I know," Conchita's head bopped up and down and around in guilt. "But it's my turn to have something of my own. If I'm not properly compensated after all these years, I might as well bootstrap my own company."

"I like where this is going."

"Really?" Conchita jumped up and clapped.

"Are you kidding me?" I clapped back for funsies. "You were born for this."

Conchita put her hands up to make an air banner. "I was thinking "¡Olé! *Viva Fiesta!* Or just, ¡*Viva Fiesta!*"

"With all your contacts, you can find advertising and sponsors easily to get the magazine up and running. You're like a local celebrity. People would jump all over that to be associated with you. And you could make it easy. Start with a monthly publication, and I can help you with a free website, domain, and socials. I'm helping Colette with that, too, so I've gotten better at it. You might even be able to hire the same printing press from the other few publications in town and negotiate a lower rate beca—"

"How do you know these things?"

"Umm, hello, because I've done travel writing for both print and web and I'm perpetually contracting my services out."

A grin spread across Conchita's face. "You would really help me then?"

"I would really help you then."

Conchita got giddy. "Oh, Yessica, I've been thinking about this for years!"

I found myself smiling, too. "Hey, if anybody could do it, you can."

"If you help me, Yessica, I can pay you a little in the beginning and then more as we grow—"

"I'm sure we can work something out," I said, surprising myself by agreeing to be Conchita's first employee.

"And I will write your profile story for the inaugural edition. It will inspire others who do not win the Miss Fiesta pageant. Like I said, to know that there is still hope. That they might succeed at something else instead."

I shot her a skeptical look.

As we approached Times Square, I threw my coat on a bench and ran into the middle of the square, wearing nothing but my leotard, pantyhose, and a tutu. I stuck my tongue out to catch the dropping snow amongst the Disney characters, slutty costumes, and the Naked Cowboy. "*Ahh.*" I waited a moment for a few flakes to settle on my tongue. Then, I twirled around on my tiptoes, slow, then fast, until finally, I collapsed.

"Gross, Yessica!"

I lied on the soft blanket of whiteness, briefly lifting my head. "Oh, come on. You aren't going to hand sanitize the snow now too, are you?"

Conchita gave in, dragging her feet over and laying down beside me. "Make room."

I scooted farther from her. "We can't leave without making a snow angel."

Conchita and I swooshed the snow up and down, back and forth into angels. My hands froze numb, so I curled them closed. Open. Close. Open again. A little Chinese man with a camera around his neck and two children by his hip hovered above us. I looked up at them. The man took pictures of us and dropped a few dollars into my hand as if I were one of the Times Square street performers.

"No, uh, sir??" I said but then decided against it, thinking of how Missy would get a kick out of it. "Job twelve!" I boasted to Conchita. "I guess I can add the official title of 'Times Square Street Performer' to my list of gigs in the continuously recovering economy. Now I need to find that lucky number thirteen." I smiled at my customers. "Come revisit us, sir, and kids. Happy Halloween!"

"Yessica," Conchita poked her head up to scold me. "Have you forgotten about my magazine already?!"

"Of course not, 'job thirteen!'" I yelled. The lights above flashed at us. The snow turned my back numb. I pulled my head, and finally, my body back up. "Okay, okay. I think that might be it for today. But we should paint your face white next year so you could be Zombie Miss Fiesta."

"Yessica, wait. Stop." Conchita grabbed my elbow. "This. This is what I want to go home with. If we could have something like this. If we could continue revitalizing downtown and have something like this for our kids and maybe even your kids one day, too. The square. The lights. The people. The international tourists. And the jobs." Conchita pointed at all the digital signs. "Look at all the ads from all the global brands." She rolled over, pulled her camera out of her jacket pocket, and snapped pictures of the flashing sky. Then of me.

"The jobs?!" I turned to her. "Now you're speaking my language." I jumped up and pretended to model, waving my arms to introduce the prospects in my ballerina costume. "Imagine one day you're making a living as a street performer." I twirled, pointing to Minnie Mouse and Naked Cowboy, the latter of whom had started to sing Katy Perry's "Teenage Dream" along with his guitar. "Then, you make it on Broadway." I pointed to *The Lion King* sign at Minskoff Theatre. "And one day, you make it on TV." I pointed to the Viacom Building, where CBS and MTV signs blinked as anchors filmed. "And the rest is history."

And then I had an epiphany. They say it takes a village to raise a child. I think it takes a village to raise an adult. We have to lift each other up. And this nonsense about coming of age once? I think we come of age over and over again with every passing decade.

NINETEEN

"Jess? Jess? Jess? Are you sleeping at your desk? Mr. T is going to be in any minute." I was cropping the last Scarlett Johansson photos at R&B TV when I told myself I'd lay my head down for just one second.

Unfortunately, Mr. T's office overlooked our cubicle, so getting away with anything other than working was difficult. Ramona removed her headphones and quietly rolled her chair over to mine. She lowered her shoulders to tap me inconspicuously.

Mr. T rounded the corner. Hungover, I scrambled every ounce of energy, fixing the wavy mane I'd not washed in days. I'd stayed up late helping Colette with her online class, each hour punctuated by another round of drinks.

Ramona and Kim rolled back to their desks in sync, squishing their earbuds in and tactically placing their hands on their corresponding home row keys. *Clack, clack, clickety, clack, space bar, clack, clack, delete, space bar.* I could hear every keystroke and word in my head, recitations from the editorial meetings that seemed to dispense the exact information of catchy titles, top ten lists, and millions and millions of unique website visits. Ramona's blog would mark yet another year that the world remembered Princess Diana's death with a new conspiratorial twist.

"A'ight, a'ight," Mr. T shouted louder as he approached us. "I see you ladies are in the first position."

My screen had gone blank; everything was just blank. "Thank you, Kim." I perked up. "I am almost finished." Wake up, wake up, computer, wake up. I silently thumped my mouse against the desk, covertly pressing the buttons again and again. "Scarlett Johansson's birthday will be the best one we've celebrated yet at R&B TV. Just you wait. I found great Getty images that everyone will be interested in. Man or woman. How does the saying go? Men want her, and women want to be her." Start, start, start, you stupid freaking computer, what, are you like in cahoots with my employer? "My goodness, I must run those updates and restart my computer. This is the second time this morning it has crashed on me—"

"Good morning, ladies."

In unison: "Good morning, Mr. T."

"Nice to see you ladies working well together." Mr. T grabbed a spare office key hidden on the shelf above Kim. "Looking forward to our Thanksgiving potluck today? You ladies will have your newest blogs posted by then, right? You won't be late?"

We chimed in with similar responses:

"We'll be on time," said Kim.

"Of course, we won't be late," said Ramona.

The lady—me—doth protested too much. "Late? We'd never be late. Why would we be late? You'll love this one; it'll be your favorite one yet!"

"Oh, is that so?" Mr. T responded with a bit of a laugh, a smirk I could hear behind my back. "Can we get a little preview?"

Kim and Ramona's eyes darted to me, so I swiveled my whole chair around without any time to think. Naturally, the first thing that sprang to my mind would roll off my tongue.

"Let's just say that it's going to be a very boob-y birthday." Did I just say that to my boss, the executive producer of this entire department? Was it possible I was still drunk, and did that constitute sexual harassment against a man who was married with an infant? I could see my coworker's countenance fall, the looks of despair on Kim and Ramona's faces. They held their breath with mine, waiting for Mr. T to break his silence.

"Wow, okay, wow, that will be some clickbait. That's the holiday spirit! Got to keep them on their toes. Remember, four million visits by Christmas." Mr. T turned around, unlocked his office door, and sat at his desk.

I exhaled.

"That was a close one," Ramona whispered.

"Jess, you are so lucky it's almost the weekend," Kim said. "You need to sleep your life off."

As if my work stops on the weekend, I thought. "Yeah, as soon as I post this blog. And eat some of that Thanksgiving turkey. Somebody sent an email about Puerto Rican rice. Do we still have Puerto Rican rice? And plantains? I need the carbs for my hangover. And, like, ten Cokes."

My computer screen turned on again, and *voila*. Miraculously, Scarlett Johansson's chest remained plastered in front of my face. Within a few minutes, I finished cropping the photos, edited the last paragraph, and posted the celebrity blog, *A Very Boob-y Birthday: Celebrate with Scar Jo's 27 Bustiest Moments*. The blog comprised twenty-seven pictures with my pithy jokes accompanying the actress's outstanding rack. Next to a photo of her surrounded by toddlers at the *SpongeBob SquarePants* premiere: *Milk anyone?* Showcasing her talent on the cover of *W Magazine* to promote *The Other Boleyn Girl*: *Wait, wasn't Natalie Portman supposed to be on this cover too? Oh, there she is.* All dolled up for a Dolce and Gabbana makeup ad: *Oh, there's the microscopic eye shadow icon at the bottom corner, concealed by the actress's "talent."* At her premiere for a Broadway revival: *Cat on a Hot Tin Roof with a Side of Boobs.*

"You ready for lunch?" Kim said to me.

"Are you breathing down my neck right now, Kim?"

Ramona stood up, wrapping her scarf around her neck and adding pink gloss to her lips.

"Sorry," Kim said. "But by the time Ramona and I arrived at the Thanksgiving potluck last year, it had already been picked through. There was a lot of food still, but it looked, I don't know, touched."

"Yeah, Jess, we have to get there early."

On the way to the potluck, we made a pit stop at the restrooms, where we sacrificed a third of our lunch break to long lines. Once we finally arrived on the other side of the floor, more long lines of employees were grazing and waiting.

"There it is. I can smell the rice and plantains." Kim, Ramona, and I were herded into the line, grabbing our plastic plates, forks, and napkins. But by the time we started grabbing spatulas, I felt a tap on my shoulder. It was Producer Patricia. I was surprised since she often worked through events.

"Patricia, hi, are you getting in on this rice? Here, we'll let you cut." I stepped to the side and winked.

"Jessica? Hi. How are you?"

Patricia stood so close I felt her snow boot on the tip of my toe. Please do not let her smell the alcohol on my breath, I thought.

"I'm great." I tried not to breathe in her direction. "How are you?"

She smiled and nodded superficially. "I'm good. Can I talk to you for a second?"

Wide-eyed, Kim and Ramona sympathized, scrolling their eyes to the side, suggesting I better comply.

"Oh, *umm*. Sure." I handed my utensils to Kim. "Save me a spot, okay?"

But Patricia's stance turned more serious. "Maybe in my office?"

Whoa, an office conversation? "Of course." I gave Kim one last helpless glance. "Certainly."

I silently mouthed goodbye to my tub buddies, following Patricia back to her office, first snaking through cubicles and Thanksgiving turkey decorations. "Gobble, gobble, gobble," read a sign lining one of the corridors. I felt the orange and yellow streamers skim my shoulders as I wondered: Can you technically get fired from internships? She isn't going to fire me from an internship, is she? That would be a new low. If only there were an award for hitting so many lows and milestones in a row.

"Please, have a seat." Patricia shifted her pants and straightened her black-framed glasses below the bridge of her nose. Times Square lights and Thanksgiving turkey twinkled from the window behind her.

"You know that you are one of our best interns yet and that your blogs are getting quite a bit of traffic?"

The compliment sandwich. It always arrives before the bad news. "Thank you. Excellent. That's great to hear. It's been an honor to blog for one of the most important and edgy websites online today."

She didn't return my smile. "But you also know that everything you post on the internet must be run by me for preview before you publish it, right?"

"Oh, right." I felt my stomach sink. "You mean this morning?"

"Yes, about this morning—"

"I am so sorry. I wanted to ask you, but you're so busy. I didn't want to bother you. And today's ScarJo's official birthday, so I had to get the blog up right away."

Patricia crossed her other leg.

"We've had quite a bit of reaction to your blog. And as we've discussed things before, your tone, your approach. Sometimes . . . you do know that..." She looked over my head, searching for the words in a popstar poster hanging above us on the adjacent wall. I, too, hoped that she could find the answer, the decency to keep me while staring at this new electronica pop star, Ellie Goulding. I knew what this was about, or perhaps not so suddenly because the theme never really left my consciousness. Seinfeld said it best: "Political correctness is killing comedy."

"We are getting quite a bit of reaction to this morning's blog, and not a good reaction. Mr. T was pleased with all the web traffic. But now the reaction has also turned into hate email directed toward your higher-ups."

"Oh, my goodness." Seriously, in what, thirty minutes? Patricia turned to her computer screen. She opened a window where my blog had been waiting alongside Scarlett Johansson's boobs.

"Her talents? ScarJo's talents?"

"She is a sexy girl, but it's all in good fun. Men want her, and women want to be her." I swung my arms inward as I made my case. "I thought I'd put that in the blog. I thought it was the right mix of controversy while keeping things P.C."

"I'm afraid not." Patricia continued reading my jokes aloud, momentarily glancing back at me for a reaction. I immediately evoked my shameful face, hunching over my shoulders and lowering my head downward as she read the next one. "It was the breast of times, it was the worst of times?"

"Oh, you know, because that was ScarJo's first public appearance since the divorce? Ryan Reynolds?"

She ignored me and kept going, this time pointing to the *W* Magazine cover featuring ScarJo's boobs and Natalie Portman. "Wait, wasn't Natalie Portman supposed to be on this cover too?"

Now, that was a good one and somewhat original, unlike my other jokes. "Oh, you know, because her boobs are like the size of—" I stopped myself. Not the right response. "I mean, they were eclipsing most of the magazine cover, including Natalie Portman, who was in the film too, by the way, but was clearly not getting enough credit, if you know what I mean." Still not the right response. "No press is bad press, right?"

Wrong. Patricia was not amused.

"Sorry. I guess somehow it made sense to me then."

Now, I just wanted to get this over with. Like Last Chance, every company—big or small—seemed to compete for the same ad revenue generated from clickbait titles. However, they seemed to forget a new complication thrown into the mix: Audiences were becoming desensitized from the same old top ten lists. You figure out how to get four million unique visits by freaking Christmas, Mr. Scrooge, without eliciting a little shock and awe. I wasn't going to say that to my boss at a job I didn't really have. I gave up.

"So, am I in trouble then?" I braced myself.

Patricia adjusted her glasses. "Obviously, I'm reading the original version of your blog, as we have since amended it." Patricia clicked on another window, revealing my blog with all the same pictures and my name below it. But the title read: "Happy Birthday to Our Favorite Sagittarius."

I couldn't stop scratching my head. They flattened out all my humor and replaced it with something super boring. "Oh, how about that? I thought she was a Scorpio, but the twenty-second, yeah, that would make sense."

"I'm glad you like the title, Jessica. Now, we've deleted all the photo captions. You'll have to go back to your desk to come up with some different ones. Mr. T thinks you produce good work, and as we've said, despite being an intern, you're already bringing in real traffic."

"I understand."

"But this cannot happen again." Patricia pointed and waved her index finger in the air. My head followed in circles, asking for approval and getting a little too used to people's index fingers waving in the air at me.

"Yes, ma'am, of course."

"You get another chance, but please do not screw it up." Patricia stood, and I followed.

"I'll get right on that," I promised.

I slowly stumbled out of the office, my head hanging low as I made it back to the cubicle of death. I guessed I'd taken longer than I thought as Kim and Ramona returned to their desks, carrying plates piled high with food. Kim couldn't wait to tell me all about it.

"Jess, you missed it. There's a karaoke machine and everything. One of the guys from tech is already so drunk. He jumped on a table, and we still have half the workday left."

I feigned interest. "A tech guy, huh? I wouldn't have thought that."

"It was getting crowded, though. We had to get out of there."

"Is everything okay?" Ramona stuck a fork in her turkey.

I sat down, rolling my chair into my desk and thumping the mouse around to wake up my screen. "Oh, ya know, Patricia had to tell me all about my ScarJo post today."

"That was the best." Kim professed.

"Yeah, not so much." My screen appeared. I pulled up my email only to find an earlier message from Patricia: "You may want to check your Twitter account, not the R&B TV Twitter account, but your private *@jessicapuente* account. Please come see me in my office afterward." Confused, I tried to get clarity from Kim and Ramona. "Hey, how often do you guys use your Twitter? Do you monitor the comments regularly?"

"Oh, yeah, you should. I do." Kim said.

"Me too," Ramona agreed. "Your Twitter account is automatically hyperlinked from your name below the blog, remember? I always click on that and refresh."

I logged onto my account, where all the re-tweets with angry comments appeared: *A woman wrote this? @jessicapuente you should be ashamed of yourself!*; *Let me guess, jealous much? @jessicapuente*; *When are women going to be viewed for their talents and not their tits @jessicapuente?*; *Women holding other women back @jessicapuente.*

The list went on and on. My spine tightened, and I felt as ashamed as my first semester of grad school when Allie called my work casually racist. All the online heads were bobbing back and forth in agreement to pen more hits at me. I started tweeting back to my new fanbase: "I'm more of a second-wave Camille Paglia feminist, although I do believe in inclusivity, the intersectionalism, of third-wave feminism." Too many words. "As a feminist, I believe that women do have the right to use their talents and beauty that God gave them however they wish." But then I stopped, remembering my job and that waging war with the faceless crowds of the internet was the least of my problems. I turned to Kim and Ramona.

"Basically, the theme of my life is that I'm a horrible person who is being lambasted on the internet for my ScarJo boobie blog."

"Oh, honey." Ramona rolled back her chair and paused between chews. "It sounds like you're finally making it."

"Totally," Kim agreed. "I remember when I got my first talking to. My blog wasn't as racy as yours, though. They'll get over it. You'll get over it. Here, I brought you some of that rice."

My eyes lit up.

"And, wait for it, wait for it." Kim opened her boho bag. "Not one, but two Cokes!"

"You guys are the best tub buddies a girl could have in the whole wide world, especially in Times Square."

TWENTY

The first burst of cold December wind cut against my dry skin like sharp ice. The sting did not subside as we left The Winifred and hurried south down Ninth Avenue.

"Thank you for coming with me, Missy," I chattered through my teeth. "I think this might be the one." We zipped up our puffy winter coats and skipped through the crosswalk.

Missy picked up speed. "I've been waiting all week for the surprise. What is it then?"

I grinned. "I found an apartment."

"Oh my God, you did?" Missy playfully hit me on the arm. "That's amazing!"

"It's only a few blocks south of The Winifred. I'm going to live in Chelsea. Like you, I'll have two other roommates, but the apartment has three bedrooms and two bathrooms."

"Two bathrooms for only three people? Like you told me, that's much better than sharing the bathroom with a whole floor."

We crossed another street, passing an electronic store with blazing yellow signs and fluorescent lights. Then, a couple of doors of defunct businesses, boarded-up glass windows, and black tarps. The cold stung less behind each building, but the gush of wind pressed harder with the crossing of each street. Finally, we cleared the exterior of the U.S. General Post Office Building, the original landmark of Pennsylvania Station. From our standpoint, we could not see the Greek and Roman columns, the famous classical architecture revived during the Renaissance. But I thought that maybe I liked that vantage point instead. The sort of blankness. It made me feel as though I was on the fringe of something great, knowing that so many different eras had made their mark on this important place but that there were still many parts of the place that had yet to be touched by time. It was once the only twenty-four-hour post office in the city until The Great Recession.

"Oh wow, hold on, Missy." I stopped at the corner of another crosswalk at Ninth Avenue and Thirty-First Street. A yellow cab turned the corner, and I extended my arm in front of Missy to stop her. "My long case of vertigo is almost gone, but now I'm having more déjà vu." We resumed our walk across the last street, stopping in front of a bodega on the corner of Ninth Avenue and Thirtieth Street. The red letters shining above us read "Café Bravo."

Missy looked higher. "Is this it?" Our eyes examined the sky and another red brick building.

"Yes, and can you believe it?" I skimmed the paper in my hands that listed all the apartment specs. "Chelsea Pointe was built in the year 2000, not 1923 like The Winifred. Maybe that means I'm finally coming on up in the world."

Missy pointed to the door. "And is that a keypad? Do you have one of those keyless entries?"

"Yes, and yes." I pulled another piece of paper from my jacket pocket and pretended to cover the keypad entry with my left hand. "I already have the code."

"Seriously? It's a secret? I can't know the code to get into your building?"

"How do I know you're not a criminal?"

"Very funny."

I put my hands down. The door buzzed open. "I'm kidding. I'll write the code for you so that you can use my rooftop."

We walked across the lobby toward the elevator.

"It doesn't have a doorman, but it's still kind of luxury, Jess. What's up with all these mini palm trees against the wall? And the waterfall pouring down this marble construct?"

"I believe we call that art, Missy, and tasteful décor, as well as ambiance, which is something I once had in my past life, before Winifred bulletin boards with Valentine's Day hearts, cafeteria menus, and rules about not wearing your pajamas in the common areas."

Stepping off the elevator, we reached the thirteenth floor, where we proceeded to the southeast corner of the building. Missy trailed behind me, but I saw her reflection in the hallway window against the building lights radiating in the darkening sky. Her once cheerful eyes seemed worried, hollowed, highlighted with wrinkles creeping from her forehead down to the sides of her lips.

"I'll have roommates," I tried to explain. "But they aren't home right now, so I can give you the grand tour. We can have some time to ourselves." I opened my heavy metal door and immediately noticed the golden parquet floors shone from a recent cleaning, and the black and white granite kitchen had a clear window overlooking a terrace and a barbecue pit.

"This is so pretty." Missy tried to muster enthusiasm. She pointed to a Charlie Brown Christmas tree by the TV. "And you'll have a little flatscreen. How nice it'll be to fight with only two roommates for the remote."

"Oh, I know. And I won't have to go to a front desk to sign up to use the living room."

Missy's eyes scoured the apartment, trailing from the end of the hallway to the kitchen. "So, which room is yours?"

I segued to the other side of the couch. "It's actually through this door behind the living room. As with many of the apartments in Manhattan, half of the living room was illegally converted into a third bedroom."

"There you go again," Missy rallied, but her voice fell flat. "Breaking the rules. It's okay. I don't think they call people to court for that one."

"So the third bedroom was once part of this living room," I started to say. I made my way across the parquet floor. "The new wall and door shaved off a portion. But the best part is that my room took the living room's bay windows with it." I made a grand swoop as I opened the door.

"Huh!" Missy's large eyes jumped from window to window. "Wow."

"I know. I've never felt so poor and rich at the same time."

Missy's eyes remained transfixed on the view, but her voice shook. "Your south-facing window overlooks Chelsea, Meatpacking, Lower Manhattan, and on this side the Hudson River. And a terrace to the west?" Missy dodged my eye contact as she opened the tall glass door, making small talk as she tried not to hit the covered grill. "I wonder if your roommates know how to barbecue for the Fourth. Wow, look at that view of Jersey City."

One by one, more lights in buildings began to flicker, flashing against the Hudson River with the dimming sky. A short horn blast shrieked from a cruise ship. And then Missy just lost it—all of it. Her abrupt exhales had the cadence of hiccups, except with moans and tears. "I'm not over it. And I was wrong. I don't have it all figured out, and I don't know my five-year plan," she griped. "Jon broke up with me. He still has this on-again-off-again girlfriend, and I guess I met him during a long off-again, and you were right. He wasn't a hedge fund manager. He was like the assistant to a hedge fund manager. No, I'm still lying. The assistant to the assistant of a hedge fund manager. He was further behind because he changed careers. And my job—I passed my review period. But it's not what I thought it would be. It's not fulfilling in the way I'd hoped it would be. And the pay is still hourly. Please don't say I told you so."

I hugged Missy. She squeezed me, and I let her sob and sob and sob. I waited until the space between us filled with silence before I spoke. "Are you kidding me?" I lowered my voice to a tranquil hush. "Think about how much progress you've made. We'd never get to the next phase of our lives if we didn't take the steps, as scary as they may be."

Missy wiped the mascara bleeding down her face. "Even the wrong steps?"

"Especially the wrong steps. I truly believe that even the wrong steps lead us to the places we're meant to be. How would we know otherwise?" A weak breeze passed through us. I peeked up at the clear night sky to wish upon a star. I wanted to be for Missy what I wished someone had once been for me, and what I started to feel from Colette. "But we can't let the bad experiences harden our hearts. Life ebbs and flows. Money comes and goes. When we spend too much time obsessing about a perfect future, we fail to build anything in the present. Falling into this trap of waiting for the right job or guy to come along before allowing ourselves to be vulnerable and pursue new things means we lose the best opportunities along the way. Opportunities that could lead to that perfect job one day where we can truly shine like the star we were born to play."

TWENTY-ONE

"We enjoyed having you here over the fall and holiday season, Jessica." Patricia clicked on her mouse cursor and closed out her windows. She opened a file folder to hand me a job description on her desk. "But as you know, we only have a production assistant position open at this time. The position is yours if you'd like, and we can have Kim train you straight away."

"Thank you." I reviewed the bullet points on the job description, my eyes rolling to the bottom of the page where the shocking salary lay: $32,000. Gratitude, gratitude, express gratitude, I told myself. Do not tell her that a wage of $32,000 is only like $15,000 in New York. "I didn't know what to expect on my first day, but I have grown and learned so much from working here. It has been such an honor."

"You're welcome." Patricia straightened out her pants and stood up to shake my hand. "I do wish there were something more."

"Is there any way I may take some time to think about it? I'm finishing up this graduate program, and I, I—"

"Of course. This must be an exciting time for you. Take as much time as you need."

I skirted back over to my cubicle.

Kim slicked her hair back and picked up her mug. "You're back. It's been too long. Happy belated New Year!" Her eyes scrolled at my bag by my side. "Wait, is this it? You're leaving us for good?"

"There is a position opening up." I pointed to her computer screen. "They need me to do what you do."

Kim took a sip and turned to her screen. "Oh, I wouldn't mind training you for it. When do we get started?"

I scratched my nose. I didn't know how to say it. "I'm going to think about it for a little bit."

Ramona removed her headphones to turn to us. "What is there to think about? Why wouldn't you take the job? It's not easy getting a job here, you know."

"No, I know, I know." I needed to be honest, yet I couldn't help but joke about the gig economy. "But now that I have ten part-time jobs, I have to pick just five of them, you know?"

Kim and Ramona both hesitated, but their silence broke into laughter.

"Seriously, now. I'm all about this gig economy but I'm running out of steam here. I can't juggle it all. And the pay—"

"You don't need to tell us how low the pay is for New York." Ramona nodded her head. "But just so you know, it's higher than some of those publishing companies and magazines you used to look up during lunch, including *Conde Nast Traveler*. Yep, I saw that."

"No, I know. Those publishing jobs were never meant to pay anything. Sadly, I learned that many of those small salaries were called 'Dress Money' since it was assumed you were already wealthy. One of the founders of FSG was an heir to the Guggenheim Foundation."

"But no matter what happens," Kim put down her tea, "we'll stay in touch."

"Absolutely!" I gave them both hugs. They hugged back, but as they leaned away from me at the end, I saw the blotchy lipstick stains on Ramona's Georgetown mug and the old Twizzler wrappers from Kim's always messy desk. I couldn't help but pull them back toward me in a sad rush of anxiety. Even with Patricia's offer, I somehow knew this was my last time in the cubicle. No more meetings staring out the window at the Hudson, Pier 86, the Intrepid Sea, Air & Space Museum. No more flashing Times Square signs at my eyeline or Minnie Mouse and Naked Cowboy below.

***

March again. One of my last weekends attending a graduate workshop since we were to spend the rest of our time in the program finishing our theses. I opened the department office, sent out emails and printouts for professors, and then hung up more workshop signs around the building. One sign read: *Sell Your Secrets to Make a Living*. It was the one workshop I didn't want to miss.

The workshop had already started when I arrived. It was taught by Professor Fisher, whose dyed jet-black roots matched her gothic black attire in contrast to her leathery skin. She stood at the front of the class, above students sitting haphazardly around white rectangular desks assembled into a square. Taking a seat above the courtyard, I felt the hot and early morning spring sunshine through our windows, where heaters still warmed our backs. A nearby student jerked open one of the windows, allowing a cool breeze to blow a few loose papers off the pile on Fisher's desk at the front of the class.

"Thank you." Fisher's dark brown eyes gestured to me and then back at the floor laden with papers.

"Oh, of course." I crammed behind the workshop rectangle while shoving chairs to pick up the mess around her desk.

Fisher continued roaming around the classroom with her packets as she recited a mantra for her workshop on selling your secrets: "You know you've made it when you've pissed off your family and friends." She licked her fingers and dog-eared the remaining packets. "I have taken the liberty of printing clips of my students' published essays. We will study the personal essay form and structure."

A couple more students simultaneously rushed in late, tearing off their jackets and fanning themselves with folders and papers. Finally, the last student arrived: Colette.

Of course.

It would make sense that she—the last student to arrive at my very first graduate program class almost two years ago—would now be the last student in this workshop.

Colette settled in, grabbing a seat in the corner of the rectangle. She scratched her head and began sketching in her notebook, eventually slumping low in her chair, her collarbones covered in a turned-up pink Polo collar.

Fisher continued to espouse her beliefs along with her long biography. She'd found purpose with her pen, breaking away from her strict Amish background and aiming to help others do the same. She listed her accomplishments, which accounted for the first third of the class. Snooze. Note to self: Do not talk about yourself so much when in Fisher's shoes one day.

Fisher finally concluded the lecture on herself. "Now, let's go ahead and start with the first personal essay at the top of the packet I handed you. One of my younger star students in the dual-degree program wrote it."

Fisher's famous packets demonstrated her prowess in getting her students' and colleagues' work into print. As some of the sayings around our hallways went: She can get you published even if you've never written before. She can make you famous. She was on TV.

Reading the first published headline at the top of the packet, I no longer felt the tranquil breeze. Instead, my body turned numb. I held my breath. Around me, there was no more fumbling through backpacks or picking up papers and pens. The first headline had sobered and muzzled the usual student shuffling and talking. It was the final draft of one of Allie's personal essays: "I was Raped in My Safe Dorm During My First Week of College."

I felt such a stillness in my heart, yet such a penetrating force squeezed it. As I read on, I could not "read like a writer" and study "form or structure," as Fisher insisted.

Instead, I couldn't help but think of vulnerable cohorts like twenty-two-year-old Allie, who was so young and still processing some of their secrets but had been convinced to sell them instead—in the name of the new digitized personal essay. As I turned the pages of the packet, discerning more private and heart-wrenching headlines, I understood the secret: how Fisher helped to publish her students' work.

And with that, there were a few quick bursts triggered inside me. Disturbing emotions and thoughts warmed my blood until it rose, bubbling, flushing through my face, and begging me to speak. It reminded me that when a young, innocent, aspiring actress moves to Los Angeles, she can easily be duped into porn. When a young, innocent, aspiring writer moves to New York City, she can be duped into selling her rape story online for the right fame and price.

I was disgusted by how Fisher had taken clickbait to a new level.

And then I was disgusted with myself.

Was this what I had been pursuing? Suddenly, an uncontrollable stream of thoughts flooded through my mind:

What about the lives of these vulnerable cohorts later? When they're thirty, forty, fifty, or sixty? How will they feel about the fact that they published stories about their rapes before they even had the time and capacity to process that trauma? And do we publish these private topics because we sincerely don't want to be silenced anymore, and we want to give ourselves and other women a voice? Or is that the lie we tell ourselves because we thought the attention would suddenly equal healing and success? And why do we now live in a world where penning a rape story is incentivized, an expedient way to get published?

Fisher stood up from her desk. "Now that we've all had a moment to read the first essay at the top of the packet and gather our thoughts, let's talk about how this author found their way into the essay. Who would like to go first?"

We were silent. Nobody wanted to speak up.

"Colette?"

We all snapped our heads up at Colette as if we felt fortunate that Fisher had not called on us. I know I was.

Colette scratched her head. I honestly did wonder what the old-school, private, feminist lesbian had to say. As if Colette could read my mind, she agreed, "Miss, you do not want to know what I have to say about this one."

Fisher's lips turned down into a scowl. "We absolutely do."

"I, umm…" Colette twirled another dread, stopping momentarily to grab a pen. "It certainly is a new take on writing what you know."

Huh, I couldn't believe she said that.

Fisher smirked. "Keep going. How did the author find their way into the essay?"

"This is from the 'Modern Love' column at *The New York Times*," Colette hesitated. "Many of the personal essays I have read start with an illustrative, crucial scene from the middle or end of their story to hook you. Then, the authors return to the beginning of their story and work their way back toward the illustrative scene, uh, they end back at that crucial scene with which they started."

"Thank you for explaining the structure of their essays. But that's not enough. You're speaking in general terms. I want you to elaborate more specifically."

There was a lilt in the phrases of Colette's next statements, an assertion met with mocking consternation. "The author opens the essay with a scene of herself and the perpetrator. It was getting late. Some friends left. There was some pot. He was breathing down her neck. She did not ask him to stop. Until she asked him to stop, and he did not."

"Well, that is the gist of it, Colette, thank you," Fisher said in a disappointed tone.

Way to go, Colette, I thought. Don't take the bait. Keep it vague.

Fisher continued her lecture on the rape scene. She sketched out the details on the board and talked about how to build such a powerful scene. The writer had to create tension and write with the senses to put the reader in such a powerful, pin-dropping moment. It was uncomfortable, but perhaps that was the purpose. Peripherally, I noticed a few other students squirming in their chairs. We all wanted to read and write powerful works of art.

But what kind of powerful?

Fisher waved a piece of chalk as she elaborated on writing with the senses. "The sound of the act and the tingling her body felt, as his hot Cheeto breath panted against her cold, virginal neck. The sound of a few drunk partying students coming home outside her dorm door, but not close enough to save her from the loneliness she felt with a stranger, with the person she had just met. The farthest away from home she had ever felt." Fisher wrote the obvious senses on the chalkboard: sight, sound, touch, taste, and smell. Then she continued. "The loud back and forth of his movements as she felt his pelvis, then him penetrating her." And finally, Fisher declared, "the sound of silence. The sound of silence was what?" She flapped her head back at us.

"Jessica?"

Oh no, I thought. "Sorry, the sound of silence, what? Professor Fisher?"

"Tell us, what was the sound of silence like?"

"Oh, uhm." I lowered my eyes back down to the essay. "Well, at first, when the rape was over, there was nothing. The silence was nothing like silence. But then, it was like the act of the rape had created a vacuum. In the absence of such a loud act, a buzzing in the victim's ears grew, which heightened into a loud ringing sound. Especially after he left."

"And?"

She wanted more. Great. Let's make it really uncomfortable for everyone. "It seems that perhaps the silence ringing in her ears was louder than all the noise he had made while assaulting her."

"Excellent, thank you, Jessica. And what does one make of the mother?"

The mother?

I had to pause.

I had to look down again.

I found it sad that the mother was blamed and turned into a villain in the personal essay because she reacted in the way most older people of her generation would respond. She kept it quiet. She asked her daughter to keep it quiet. That was how things were done back in her day when reputations were at stake, and reputations could mean the entirety of your livelihood and your family's livelihood for the rest of their lives and subsequent generations. But today, as this award-winning *New York Times* column demonstrated, your rape could help build your reputation for the rest of your life.

"Well...Professor Fisher...the tone of the essay suggests that the victim's mother asking her daughter to keep quiet is like further silencing her daughter. It suggests the mother is complicit with her daughter's rapist."

I hated saying that, especially since I respected and adored my elders more. They'd lived in a time when these things happened to them, too. Yet, they had so much strength. They got on with their lives. Many of them never mentioned it again. They successfully served their families, spouses, children, and society—and they did it without disrespecting their elders for their ignorance.

Then, as if we hadn't just dissected an essay about rape, Fisher continued. "Now, let's look at this next one. It's about my Israeli student who went to jail for refusing to join the Israeli Army, which, by the way, is mandatory in Israel when you come of age."

***

To my relief, the workshop finally ended. A few of us rushed out in seconds, although I stayed behind to close the department office. Twirling back out through the building's revolving doors, I saw Colette far ahead of me, marching past Sixth Avenue onto Thirteenth Street.

"Hey!" I hurried to catch up with her. "You stay behind at the computer lab again?"

Colette stopped below the Café Soirée entrance, glancing through the windows. A chilly gust blew a bystander's thick menthol cigarette smoke through us. I could smell the mint as we spoke. "Colette?"

She kept her head peeking through the windows. "Poor Allie," she said in a sorrowful tone. Her next words were tinged with fury. "But you should make some headlines. Tell the whole world about your traumatic experience, why it happened, how it happened, and whose fault it was, and while you're at it, throw your own mother, your own mother who nursed you and bred you from her bloody loins, throw her under a bus. Then the celebrities will leave comments about your bravery and blurb about your book." Colette took a breath. She stood quiet, staring at the inaudible people through the window—the inaudible people visibly talking, laughing, crying, eating, and living.

Colette kept her eyes on the inaudible people. She did not turn to me. "I wish my own mother were alive, Jessica."

I swallowed. Then whispered. "I know that you do."

"I have often wished that she were still alive. To tell me important things about the world that only a mother can know. Only a mother knows what her daughter should not show. Only a mother can protect her daughter from a world that would rather her be a vehicle for exploitation."

One of the things I loved the most about Colette was how she could change your perspective of the whole world with a few sentences.

A tear crawled down Colette's eyes, so I gently pressed her right shoulder. "Hey—"

She pulled away and resumed her steps up the street. Sometimes, it felt like she never let me in.

We wandered under a scaffold leading to the subway at Thirteenth Street. Colette's voice quivered. "It is ironic—if I can even say this aloud—that rapes are *en vogue*, *de riguer*, and that we are being taught, trained, groomed, to sell our literal and metaphorical rapes. I am afraid for the future." Colette stopped at her next thought. "Perhaps it is the nature of the beast. Of capitalism. The beast gets bigger and uglier as we figure out how to feed it best. It is part of who we are and who we can be. But we must refrain from becoming beasts while pursuing what we want, as we will ultimately find ourselves pursuing what others want of us instead. Of course..." she paused while stepping forward again, "that is never easy to do."

"But who doesn't want to make it at the young age of nineteen or twenty-two? Maybe it's easier to do what you're told without asking questions."

"It has always been. But Jessica? There is no 'making it.' Because when you acquire something, it will be the next thing, then it will be the next thing." She stopped under a residential awning and patted her chest before pointing to mine. "You must feel you have already made it in your heart to keep going. Otherwise, you will never feel that you are there. But *it* is already here."

I cuffed my hand around her finger, pointing to my heart all over again. "What is *it*?"

Colette's eyes pierced through mine. Her face stiffened as she pulled her fingers from me and insisted. "What you are looking for. You know what *it* is already."

She walked ahead of me and persisted, rattling off her thoughts through strenuous breaths. "Those last essays we discussed today exploited traumatic racial experiences, and you know I am all about decolonizing the world. Why are we still putting ourselves in boxes and answering to the box in which someone else would like to put us?"

Huh, I thought as a shiver grazed my frame. The spring air hung thick, so I crossed my arms against my chest. Colette's remark reminded me of a conversation with Conchita at the Girl Scout Center two years ago. I'd heartlessly told Conchita that she couldn't think outside the box unless she'd actually been outside the box. Yet here we were, outside the box, only to be put back into another one. "Did you hear what she told me when it was time to start working on our first paragraphs?"

"You are a Latina from the border; what a goldmine," Colette said as we passed the glass windows of a dry-cleaning business. A startled lady stopped sorting garments on a conveyor and glanced our way. "Why not write about how that has contributed to your oppression? And you must include, in the first paragraph, that you are 'a *single* Latina from the Texas-Mexico Border.'"

"Goldmine," I repeated Fisher as we arrived near the subway entrance. "Yep, those were her words."

Colette leaned against the stairwell to exhale. "Sharing our stories is important. But we get to choose which stories we tell if and when we are ready to tell them."

Colette pulled an envelope from her satchel. She stuck her other hand in her pocket, leaving the envelope to linger. "This is where we part our ways, my dear friend. I am going to miss you, Jessica Ann Puente."

I mimicked her back sans contractions. "I am going to miss you too. But what is with the formalities?"

"I am not going to be around as much. Going to the country to finish my thesis."

I grabbed the envelope from her. "Don't forget to send me your pages."

"I will."

A young, adoring couple holding hands walked between us on their way down to the train. I held the envelope in my hands.

"I do hope you always have it. To remember me. When I am not here."

Her words felt final. "Can I open it now?"

"Read it another time," she patted me on the back. "Another time, my friend."

"Okay, so, this is it, huh?"

"For now. It would seem."

Colette turned toward the Seventh Avenue traffic as I descended the subway steps.

Then, I heard her repeat my name. "Jessica? Wait."

Turning back, another person side-swiped my shoulder. I dragged myself back up the steps.

"There was something I wanted to put in the letter, but it cannot be read. It must be said."

"So ominous, again, Colette. Come on, I already told you. I don't swing that way. I wish I did. Would save me a lot of trouble."

Colette smirked. "There you go again with the jokes in the moments of truth. Don't change that. Even after I have left."

Brushing off a couple of raindrops, I leaned against the stairway railing. "You're just going to Connecticut. When I visit, you can finally take me to the Mark Twain House."

Colette's gaze wavered from the sky to the ground. "Today, yes. Tomorrow…" She stared at me straight in the face, motionless, frozen, quiet. The wind blew around us as the next train below came to a screeching halt.

I bent my head at her, waiting for a response.

"Jessica," Colette's chest puffed out as she found the words to share. "It is not looking like I will make it to forty. And I wanted you to hear it from me."

Colette's statements didn't make sense. Maybe it was the order in which everything was said. Her words jumbled and collected together, and I could not parse them into a complete sentence. I heard a low plane unevenly buzzing above us. The sounds of its engine faded in and out, and I thought it might crash. I might crash. Later, I would remember that plane and think of the few lone survivors, the victims of various plane crashes, and their normalcy bias. How, because the victims had never experienced a plane crash before, their minds did not have the information from the past to register and act on what was occurring in the present—until it was too late.

"Oh, yeah, no kidding. Me neither," I absently said to Colette in a daze. "I'm staying twenty-nine forever, especially with this new Botox medicine injection thing. I'm waiting for it to come down in price. It's always expensive when it first comes out."

"Jessica, listen to me." Colette placed both her hands on my shoulders and squeezed. "You are not hearing me."

I remained motionless as the sadness in her eyes draped me like a blanket until the light dimmed.

Colette strode to a bench against a building before the subway steps. She sat down. "I have not been very well for a long time. It was stomach cancer in my early thirties. Now it is my heart."

My body felt fuzzy. My stomach was empty. I crawled closer to Colette. "What are you saying to me right now? I don't even know what you're saying to me right now."

My body felt heavy as I attempted to sit down next to her.
Then light.
I thought I could float off.
I wanted to float off.
I did not want to be with Colette at that moment.

She put her hand behind my back. Suddenly, I stopped moving. I hadn't realized I was nervously rocking back and forth, my arms crossed, my chest hunched. A few daffodils mixed with subway trash and spring leaves passed through us with the wind. The fragrance of flowery dryer sheets emanated from the building's vent. Just any other ordinary day. Except it wasn't.

"Everybody dies, Jessica. It turns out that I will do it sooner than others."

"How can you say it like that? How can you be so callous?" Then I selfishly remarked, "you hold all my secrets now. You have to be here. You *always* have to be here."

I paused to catch my breath between the tears bubbling in the corners of my eyes. I tried to choke them back.

"Keep going. Live the life that only you could ever live. The life that you were meant to live. And hey, maybe you can tell a bit of my story. Keep me alive somehow." Colette playfully nudged me, but we weren't there yet. "I liked that description you wrote about me. How I accessorized my preppy look with my thick, short dreads crowned by my salt-and-pepper roots."

I tried to speak above a boulder planted in my throat. "What? I don't know what to say about you, today, your life, and...I don't even know...what I would do."

"These are unprecedented times, yes. When one's ideology is not always popular, but that is why and how leaders are born."

"There you go again." I rubbed the tears from my cheeks. "Talking like you're some sort of oracle sent to save the world."

"Leaders are always the first to step out into the light and speak, no, shout their truth outright. The future is our friend. That is what the future needs—more people to think differently. There will always be a herd, Jessica. But we need those that break away from the herd to lead. Listen to me. This will be the hardest part to hear, Jessica, but you have to hear it. Can you listen to me?"

I kept silently crying while Colette put one of her hands on my shoulder and forced me to look her in the eye again.

"We are no good to anyone on our own. For just as many gifts as you must give to everyone else, there are so many more they can give back to you."

"What was it? The cold, numb hands? Is that why they were purple?" Colette's eyes blinked with disappointment at my unwillingness to accept her revelation. "There must be another way. Tell them to do more, I don't know, more of those panel bloodwork things."

"There are no more tests to conduct, Jessica," she said with a rueful smile.

Colette's words made me angry. I yanked my shoulder from her grasp. "But I thought you were a fighter. I thought you were a Marine. I thought...I thought." I turned away to catch my breath before carelessly saying, "why did we even meet then? What was the point in meeting these last couple of years?"

"Two misfits." She looked into the sky, where another plane passed by. "It wasn't a coincidence. It was never a coincidence that we met."

I followed her eyes and watched the plane descend, its wheels turning down for its landing at La Guardia. Giving in, I said the same thing I often said to Missy. "I wish we had met sooner. I wish you had met the better version of me, the successful Jessica. Not the hot mess, Jessica. Maybe I could've helped you live longer."

"No. Do not ever say that." Colette put her arm around me. "I was destined to meet you at the end of my life. God was like—"

"God?" I turned. "So you *do* believe in God?"

She smiled. Then she pointed to my heart. "I believe in God. That is the *It*. What is in here is already enough. God gave me some extra time to work things out in this life. The funny thing is—"

I jerked away from her tapping fingers. "There's something funny in this?"

Colette inhaled a full breath. "The funny thing is that I've always kind of known I would not die old." She reached forward to wipe a tear from my chin, lightening her tone. "Dying an old, ugly, undignified death was never really for me. Maybe I wanted to die young, during which I was meant to meet you at the end of my life and journey."

I nodded my head and slid back from her.

She opened her satchel again to hand me a tissue. "God was like, you need to help a couple more people out. You need to touch a few more lives. And that Jessica, boy, she really needs your help right now. Throw her a life jacket. No, throw her a whole lifeboat, the Coast Guard, and half the Eastern seaboard. She needs all the support she can get."

I relented, gently nodding my head. I knew it was a joke, but I couldn't help responding in all seriousness. "Thank you."

"I did what I could. But do me a favor. Address your resentments head-on. Serve others. Move forward. Stop looking back. You're always looking back."

I mumbled, yes, but I wondered how I could resolve this. How was this to be resolved?

Colette read my mind. "You move on. You get up, and you breathe every day. In fact, you want to do something for me? Honor my memory. Be a cliché. Go on and live life to the fullest. Do not live today or any other day in vain." She prodded my left shoulder again. "Come on. You can finish that self-help travel job book, or was it a chick-lit self-help travel job book?"

"Oh yeah," I remarked, rolling my eyes. "Just what we need. Another self-help book about coloring your parachute that doesn't work."

"Make it yours. Make it different. Real stories. About real people. Struggling. Speak your truth. Others will listen. There is communion in connecting."

"In the recession."

"In the recession. Because there will be another. And another."

I grabbed Colette hard, pulling her into my shoulders and throwing my arms around her. She had been hiding her thinness under her signature oversized clothes. But I could finally feel her frail body collapsing into mine. How long had she been disintegrating? I immediately remembered the panel interview at French Press. How I had noticed the pounds she'd dropped, how she had put me off when I asked. And here I was, worried about my job as if it were all there was to life. Colette, however, was trying to live the rest of her life.

She relinquished my embrace. I stopped her from pulling back, catching her dark chestnut glance. "I'll be coming to Connecticut, too," I whispered.

***

Standing at the ledge of my rooftop, I stared down at the trains slowly crawling from Penn Station to the island's west end. How nice that there would always be a place for them to go, even if it seemed the destination stayed the same.

Consistency.

I no longer knew what that was like, but I'd begun to think I was ready to find out. Maybe the universe would give me a new kind of consistency. Flicking the black and white ashes off the tip of a last Dunhill cigarette, I watched the wind carry the ashes through a breeze, casting a shudder along my body. Thirty-two. I did not know how I'd arrived at destination thirty-two, but I decided not only would I take inventory of the life I did have, but I would also start taking inventory of the life I needed. I held Colette's envelope. On the card's front cover, an image of a simple feathered quill and ink stood scrolled in gold.

Dear Jessica Ann,

We may go our separate ways after graduation, but I want to let you know that you are a special person. You have made my time here at The New School quite meaningful. You have a lot to give to this world; don't hide it. Speak truth to life, even if they don't like it.

Thank you for being my friend while I was here.

Colette

TWENTY-TWO

I woke early the following morning to a sudden feeling that everything was ending. The darkness lingered, but a soft light rose behind my terrace. I felt it was time to call my mother. It had been several weeks since we last spoke, and I had envisioned her chasing after not one Hazelnut but several grown Hazelnuts and, who knows, maybe another Sancho, too.

"Hello?" my mother said, an hour behind my East Coast schedule. Her voice split through the phone like a bone fracture: hard, disjointed, scrambled. I heard one, then two light woofs.

"The little puppies aren't so little anymore?" I sipped my coffee before placing it back on my terrace ledge.

"No, they are not." I could hear my mother wrestling around with her pillow to sit up. "And Houdie keeps coming back to us," she continued. "Even though the family from the top of the hill has adopted him."

"Hootie? Oh no. Not again. Did you name him after Hootie from Hootie and the Blowfish? Mother, how many times do I have to tell you that's raci—"

"No, no, no. Eleanor's grandkids next door already scolded us at the last neighborhood association meeting..." Her voice got breathy as she whispered the secret into the phone. "From now on, Lenny Kravitz's name is just Lenny."

"Okay, well, that's a start. So, who is Hootie?"

"Not Hootie, as in the singer." My mother snickered. "Houdie with an 'o-u' is his nickname. His full name is Houdini, and when he was little, your father kept filling up all the holes in the backyard so the puppies couldn't escape. But he's a magician. He can escape any fence or trap you try to put him in."

My mother's words resonated, and my eyes unexpectedly filled. "Good for Houdie. I know all about feeling trapped and trying to claw my way out. He sounds like he's certainly a nephew of mine."

"Yes, he is." The intonation of my mother's voice ascended at the end of every sentence, and I could almost see her wagging an assuring finger. "They always come back. You let them go, but they will always come back. Your brother came over yesterday morning before work to drop Dad's tools off. And you know what? Houdie was patiently sitting outside. Staring at our front door. Waiting for it to open."

"Huh, I know the feeling." I gazed below at the increasing traffic heading south down Ninth Avenue. "Always waiting for doors to open."

"Oh, and Lenny has another family now. He has also been adopted."

"Really?" I looked up at the lights turning on one by one in the buildings across me.

"Yes. Lenny is finally on a leash. We have civilized him." My mother continued to recount the details. "I think he likes that he doesn't have to hunt for his food. That's not a good life, you know, to always be hunting for your food."

I almost snorted. "Tell me about it."

I thought of my own life. It made me happy to think of my mother, father, and brothers returning tools, the puppies, and even of Lenny growing up and moving on.

The traffic spread farther down Ninth Avenue and across the West Side Highway. I gazed over the water and stared at the docked cruise ships and tall buildings peeking out from the fog on the other side of the river in Jersey.

"It was my fault," I said but stopped myself.

I heard my voice on the verge of a crack and tried to conceal my tears from my mother through all the distance. I'd only told Colette, but now I was ready to tell everybody else.

Taking a deep breath and looking up into the sky, I imagined the country spread out in front of us.

Me standing at the top.

Her at the bottom.

"*Mijita?* Are you crying? Why are you crying?"

"I was going on my last year with the company. Only I didn't know it yet. My coworkers had been laid off, then, finally, Kit. And I got to stay because I had seniority. My last two performance reviews were great, but the company didn't have money for my raises."

My mother didn't say anything.

"And who could live in Chicago on that small salary? I couldn't pay rent, my unsubsidized student loans, and the interest. So, I had to get more credit cards, but I couldn't afford those payments with the high interest rates either. My health insurance premiums also increased twice in six months. Twice they had to deduct more from my paycheck in just one year. They promised me profit sharing. But there was no profit sharing. I asked in my last review, 'but what about the profit sharing?' And my bitchy hot yoga lunch boss said, 'you only get profit sharing if there's a profit.'"

"Everybody was hurting," my mother reassured.

"That's why these tour operators hire the twenty-two-year-olds, you know?" I raised my voice over the crescendoing traffic below, speeding up, slowing down, speeding up, and a few horns crying out. "They keep the young kids happy with the sponsored trips. Meanwhile, I was drowning as my student loan and credit card debt were compounded annually, and my rent and insurance kept increasing. But there was no solution. What would be the solution? Stop living? You are not allowed to live on Planet Earth anymore? I wondered if there was a colony I could have signed up for to start somewhere else, on some other planet in the universe."

I stopped myself mid-rant, or maybe at the end of the rant, or maybe at the end of a novel of a rant. It didn't make any sense—too much coffee on an empty stomach, always too much coffee between all the jobs. It was getting to my head.

"What are you saying?" my mother asked. "It was not your fault. Everybody in the business was struggling. Everybody in every business was struggling."

"It was my fault!" I burst out. "I took my suitcase to work. I was supposed to catch my flight to Rendez-Vous Paris afterward. I finished making my list of the ten top luxury boutique hotels I'd inspect once the tradeshow ended. I said goodbye. I got in a cab I could not pay for because my boss had made it clear that we had to start taking the bus to the airport. The company would not reimburse for business trips anymore. But when the cab driver said, 'where to?' I did not say 'O'Hare Airport, please.' I said, 'Four-hundred West Belmont, between North Broadway and Sheridan, please.'"

"You went home?! You didn't even go to Rendez-Vous Paris after all? I thought you loved Rendez-Vous?"

"It wasn't like it was me making the decision." I got quieter as I heard my neighbor open their terrace door on the other side of the wall. "The words automatically came out of my mouth. I didn't know what was happening. I didn't even know I had decided that. I was having a panic attack, and I had never had a panic attack, so I couldn't place it or diagnose myself, or assign professional terminology. I thought that was a joke, an excuse people made. I don't remember the whole way home, but I do remember telling myself: I cannot get on that flight. I cannot get on that flight. Please do not make me get on that flight. Like I was bargaining with myself or someone else, or as if there was even someone to bargain with. And the flights to Europe always departed in the evening, just as the darkness began. I envisioned myself trapped and alone on the Airbus for eight hours, staring down at an ocean that was a never-ending abyss that could swallow me, the plane, and the whole wide world in one gulp. I imagined that darkness only breaking with the sky's hues of purple and blue thunder and lightning, long enough to illustrate my horrific end."

"You needed to get out of your head. It is unthinkable what we can imagine when we are in our own heads for too long," my mother said sensibly. "And anyway, what would you have continued to do in Chicago? You were ready to move on."

I knew that long before I'd left A&K. Yet, being ready to move on didn't mean that you miraculously knew where to go next. An eastern wind clipped my phrases and blew through my brittle fingers clinging to the phone. "Lately, I don't know. Lately, I keep thinking about what happens when a dream stops giving. Or when a dream brings more costs than rewards year after year. We always think that, I don't know—"

"When a dream stops giving," my mother said, "it might mean that it's time for a new dream."

I felt like crying again. "Is it?"

"It is. My daughter has found a new dream. She is pursuing her new dream, but she doesn't even know it yet."

I nodded my head up and down as if my mother were near me and could see me agreeing. Staring up and off into the sky, into the low-roving clouds, I thought about my first recession:

"When the oil fields went bust," my father would often say when I became a young adult scouring the job market.

And my mother would intervene like they were ping-ponging. "We already had four kids."

"I had a full-time job as a sales engineer for Dow Chemical," my father would continue.

"And we'd just built our first house," my mother would say.

"It was small," my father would add.

"But it was ours."

"And then we lost it," my father would end with.

"Jessica?" My mother said over the phone in a hushed tone as if she could see my memories. "We were only nineteen when we started our family of six and spent a great deal of our lives—your lives—playing catch up. We failed you and your brothers in many ways because we couldn't always provide, to say the least."

Tears poured down my face. "Mom, you don't have to—"

"We lost a few homes. We were on food stamps at one point. You always needed what we couldn't give you. It didn't help to see the money on your dad's side of the family. So, you left to do it on your own. I think you were always frustrated and thought you couldn't always rely on the people closest to you, so you didn't."

"I'm sorry. I'm sorry I needed more. I'm sorry I always wanted more."

"Give yourself grace. Remember, no matter what happens tomorrow, you've already accomplished so much today."

I nodded again as if to say yes.

"I do have good news for you, though." My mother's tone lightened. "Go to Conchita's Fiesta site. Her new magazine arrived at our house yesterday. And guess who is the first profile to be featured?"

"Conchita?"

"No. You."

My stomach did a quick flip. "Me? Mom, what are you even talking about?"

"Conchita's profile story. Of you. You can read it on the website."

"Is the website I worked on already live? I thought that was still a few weeks off. Wait. What name did she go with? What is the title of the magazine??"

"¡*Olé*!"

"As in, '¡*Olé*! *Viva Fiesta*?'"

"But short and sweet. And there is a beautiful picture of you in Times Square with a tutu. Silly girl. What were you thinking wearing nothing in all that snow? Prancing around so you could get sick."

"Hey, I got paid."

***

An article? Me in the tutu? Conchita, I thought you were kidding about me being the first feature. You mean the whole time you were here? You were really taking notes?

I pulled up the website. It was true. Me in the tutu. Times Square ten times as bright, shining, refracting from the snowy white. My smile after the hurricane.

Miss Fiesta Finalist Wins Big in New York

Jessica Ann Ventura Puente, now, where do we even begin? I call her Yessica. I first met Yessica in the new year and the new Millennium. It was January 2,000, and we practiced very early every Saturday morning to compete in the Miss Fiesta Pageant. Yessica was one of the youngest to compete. While she did not have the same resume, experience, or skills as the rest of us ladies, she was enthusiastic about playing the game – as evidenced by her performance at the Majestic Theatre many moons ago. If there is anything you should know about Yessica, she has such a passion and fire inside of her, and that passion is exhibited best when she is playing the game of life.

Because Yessica has such a passion for playing the game of life, she is often more devoted to playing the game than worrying about whether she is winning. And I think she now knows this; her passion for life is her strength and weakness. But to know her is to love her, flaws and all, because she knows better than anybody else that the only way to win big is to think big and risk big. So, she has become successful. She has learned that you have to fall again and again and that no matter how many times you fall, you have to get up and do it all over again. That is why she flies; that is why she has soared to great heights. But before we get to her travel work, or as her best friend Missy says, "her fabulous jet-setting life," let's talk about her childhood.

Yessica has always had a rebellious spirit, possibly due to being the youngest of four siblings and the only girl. Or possibly from being a Hispanic in a strict Catholic family from South Texas, which we can all relate to. Back then, San Antonio was a good ol' white boys club. Only they got to run the show, although the Fiesta Commission was trying to change that. But while the rest of us were staying safe in our place and dreaming of what our Miss Fiesta reign would bring to San Antonio, Yessica was calculating how she could pawn the fiesta winnings to fund her dream of seeing the world. We did not understand it then. We did not understand why she would ever want to leave *la familia*, especially when many of us started getting married and having babies. Yet, I will never forget what she said before moving to Rome. Yessica said, "I cannot imagine loving anybody more than my love for seeing the world. And anyway, how am I supposed to have babies and teach them about the world if I've never even seen it for myself?"

I thought this was selfish, but the funny thing is that top *economistas* say that the best way to make a city better and more global is to have more of us locals with the roots and wings. To leave and to bring the rest of the world back with us.

Since Yessica left us, she has lived in a few countries and several global cities to study and work. She learned some Italian (although Yessica, you must practice your Spanish more, do not forget us and your Spanish language). With Yessica's worldly travel work and her graduate degree from the impressive News Schools (I am told they do not just report the news, that you can study other things if you would like), she is finally bringing the world to everybody else. She writes about the world for Rome Away, Gal Around the World, and R&B TV (this is the one with the shows where the wives fight over their basketball husbands; Yessica says they also play music sometimes).

But perhaps most fortunate is that Yessica has promised to help with our SA2020 initiative to make San Antonio global by 2020! She has also accepted an offer to be my first staff writer for this magazine! And the website, as Yessica says, the internet has gobbled up all the jobs. I visited her, and we discussed this recently, especially when she dropped me off at the JFK Airport (by the way, Yessica says flying to La Guardia or Newark is okay, too).

When I asked Yessica about our SA2020 initiative, Yessica's exact words were, "Conchita, please. I'm a futurist. You're on SA2020; I'm already on SA2050."

I said, "okay, Yessica. Show me." She has worked on the website and advertising, and for our next issue, we will have an article from Ms. Yessica Puente herself. She is winning big in New York and worldwide, so we hope to split the winnings with her here as *economistas* say to do. She will also have a column. It is up to her what she decides to share. But I have a feeling it will be about jobs. Yessica also says that if she could do anything, she would love to "inspire people and help them to find their purpose and meaning in life. To help people get paid for their purpose and to help them share that purpose and good with others. To make other lives more meaningful too." She said, "when one has opportunities, reasons, goals, purpose, and a future that excite them enough to get out of bed every morning and do good, the less likely they are to settle. The less likely they are to get into trouble, violence, to get pregnant, to get into a bad marriage."

Yessica likes to play the game of life with passion, so everything will be an adventure when you are in Yessica's company. Lunch or dinner will never be the same. You will laugh, cry, get into shenanigans, get into trouble, and even get very angry at her, but you will sleep it off and realize that you will do it all over again. Also, you might not make friends with her the first or second time but let us hope by the third time. Because when you become her friend, you realize she has tried to do things on her own and in her way for so long that she does not let people close. But that is changing. And if you are one of the lucky ones she lets in, she will save you from the hurricane. Of course, she will save you from the hurricane after she has burnt your Christmas tree down, but that is another story. I would not have it any other way.

TWENTY-THREE

Like on my initial nights at The Winifred, one of the first things I did upon my arrival at Chelsea Pointe was head up to the rooftop for panoramic views facing north, south, east, and west. On days when I needed to breathe and see life from a different perspective, I loved the different view of the west, where my building overlooked Ninth Avenue, the Hudson River, Jersey City, and finally, beneath me, a railyard where train after train met before and after departure to Penn Station. I loved how the trains chugged on slower and slower as they made their way to and from the end of the island. Their distance below often put the island and my whole life into perspective. The trains looked so miniature that they reminded me of toys on a track that I could reach out and grab. Things from that height seemed like they could be fixed. However, within a few years, those little toy trains and tracks would be paved to feature the most significant development since Rockefeller Center, Hudson Yards. It would be a new commercial center of Manhattan with even more innovative, futuristic skyscrapers and restaurants, retail, condos, parks, and another train station. But for the time being, I could stare across a flat demolished lot of rocks and rubble from the project, the railyard, and through pieces of the unobstructed skyline where another view of the cruise ships passed through. Everything made sense when I was on that rooftop looking down at the world; I, too, could be built anew.

"Missy, you made it!" I yelled over all the construction noise—short spurts of jackhammers in concrete.

"Of course, I made it. I wasn't going to miss our first warm sun of the spring. Wow, that's loud."

"They're working by that new public park under construction called The Highline. It'll run through all the abandoned elevated train track buildings."

We rearranged a couple of lounge chairs left for sunbathing. The rooftop door opened behind us.

"Kit!" Missy yelled, rushing over to Kit's side. "You made it. And you brought your baby. Why didn't you tell us you were coming after all? We could have come down to help you."

"Ladies, please gather around now to join in all my frumpiness." Responsible Kit folded up her stroller and grabbed her diaper bag.

I caught a bottle falling out. "Kit, you are the prettiest frumpy mommy I have ever met."

"Here, have a seat." Missy shuffled the chairs around.

"Guess what?" Kit carefully sat down between us and adjusted the baby in her lap. "Today is Baby's very first day on a rooftop. Her very first New York City rooftop."

Missy clapped. "That is so exciting."

I clapped along. "Now Sofia can add that to her resume."

"Now we can add her to The Winifred waitlist." Missy loved that joke. It would be the one that kept on giving for her.

"High five!" I bent down to see Baby Girl coddled tightly inside her yellow blanket. I reached my hand out to her hand, no longer the size of my pinky. Then, I jumped up. "Baby's first rooftop." I chanted and bounced up and down in a circle. Missy followed as we sang together around her. "Baby's first rooftop, Baby's first rooftop, Baby's first rooftop, yeah!" I motioned with my jazz hands.

"Alright, alright!" Kit yelled. "That's enough!"

"Yeesh, Mom. Calm down."

"Yeah, we're just celebrating."

"Ladies," Kit quickly signaled stop with one hand before returning to Baby. "You will understand when you are mothers someday. I can't have all this commotion around the baby. It makes me nervous."

I put on my Mary Poppins accent. "And so proper, too."

Missy threw her hands on her hips. "Calling us ladies."

"Never." I sat down beside Kit to tickle the baby's belly. "Always gonna be young and have fun in the spring sun."

"Here." Kit lifted the squirming bundle and handed it to me. "It's your turn."

I stared down at the thing as though it might attack me. "My turn to what?"

"To carry the baby? I let you get away without touching her when she was born, but not this time. She's almost seven months old. You aren't going to break her now. Soon, she'll be walking."

I struggled at first, but then I hugged her tightly. "Why hello, Little Sofia. I don't know if you remember me, but we've met before." The baby looked back at me, smiling. "I wouldn't expect you to remember me or anything, but there's something I've been wanting to tell you."

Missy stood to the west above us, blocking the sun as she looked down.

I took a deep breath. "You are Mommy's little torch now. One day, it will be your turn to carry through the world after us, long after we've gone."

"Hey," Kit scowled. "You're going to be there too, Godmother."

"Huh?" I pressed the baby to my chest. "But I thought you were a WASP this whole time with paternal Jewish ancestry?"

"I am. But, you can be her honorary Fairy Godmother."

"I'll take it." The tears filled my eyes.

Missy bent down to face me. "Oh no, Jess. You're so mushy."

"I'm sorry, Missy and Kit. You will understand when you are honorary Fairy Godmothers someday. I can't have all this commotion around the baby. It makes me nervous." Drops of tears began to fall on Sofia's face.

Kit grabbed a small rag to wipe Sofia's cheeks. "Now she's officially been baptized."

Kit removed a camera from her diaper bag.

I took a deep breath to give my first blessing. "Dear Little Sofia: May the world always come to you instead. May you never have to fly around looking for jobs where they do not exist."

"Unless," Missy paused and put a finger to her lips, "she wants to work for the great Tilly or Missy someday?"

"My daughter is not going to get you coffee," Kit cringed.

Missy's voice shrilled. "But I promise to teach her real life skills."

Another jackhammer beat down into the concrete.

"Whaaaa!" Sofia jumped and yelped.

"There, there, Sofia," I coddled. "That is your first lesson in competing for resources on Planet Earth. I cannot promise you it gets any better, but I can promise you that building a community along the way helps."

"And marrying wealthy." Kit brushed her bangs back very matter-of-fact. Seeing my stunned face, she continued. "What? You'll get it when you have a kid one day. Other people's kids can be artists. I want mine to be secure and realistic."

Missy's chair scratched like nails on a chalkboard as she scooted closer. "Since we're celebrating and discussing jobs, congratulations are in order. I know the position at R&B TV is not executive or even mid-level management where you were before the recession, Jess. But think about how quickly you'll be able to move up with all your experience. Aren't you excited?"

"I'm so excited, woohoo," I feigned, gently bouncing the baby. I still hadn't figured out how to tell them I accepted a position at Conchita's startup instead. "I wouldn't want executive anyway, and even mid-level feels so far away."

"You took the job, right?" Kit put her arms between us to steady the baby down to a slower bounce. "Right? Jess?"

I was finally starting to understand this whole gig economy thing. Harrison, house-sitting, pet-sitting, social media, Rome Away websites, R&B TV, grad school, Last Chance, ¡Olé!, and random jobs nobody has heard of, like workshop coordinator. I joked to Kit and Missy. "The gig economy does have its perks, you know? Flexible hours and no permanent commitment being at the top of the list."

"What are you saying?" Missy shrieked.

"Are you kidding me? Okay, you're cut off. Give me back my Sofia now." Kit put her arms out toward her daughter.

I pretended to keep Sofia from her cruelly. "Committing to only one moment and enjoying one moment at a time fully, without dwelling much on the next. Maybe I spent the last couple of years fixating on who I thought I was supposed to be as if my happiness could be tied to my status, right, Baby?" I looked down at Sofia again. "I wouldn't be a very good honorary Fairy Godmother if I didn't teach you this wise knowledge." I tickled her with one finger. "I can't take full credit for this omniscience, though. You are already inspiring me to be a better person and Fairy Godmother."

"Wait." Missy sounded like the old me. "What is happening right now? I don't understand what is happening right now. Where is my friend Jess and the fight she puts up with the rest of the world?"

"Nothing. It's just," I paused, thinking of Colette. Of my own family back home. Of the time work flexibility would buy me. Of how I'd already done the corporate thing and wanted to do something so much more. "But what if I could support women-led businesses like Rome Away and ¡Olé¡ instead?"

Kit brushed Sofia's head and smiled. "Well, Missy, it took Jess long enough, but I think she answered our question: Where do you see yourself in five years?"

I kissed Sofia's head and inhaled her sweet baby scent. It smelled of hope. It smelled of new. "I want to spend the next thirty-some years of my life differently. I want to spend them happy. I want to spend them me. I don't want to spend the rest of my life chasing something I thought I was supposed to be."

Missy threw her hands up. "Look what's making its way over to us in the sky. It's the Goodyear blimp."

"And it's slowing down over The Winifred's rooftop," Kit laughed.

"Jess, would you change anything? If you could? Do you ever think—Sometimes I still think, what if I had never left Tilly in Texas? I could be running the store. Not that I'm not happy right now. But I think about where it could have led if I'd stayed where it was safe."

"I used to. And I still dream about flying, about being in the sky."

"Yeah?"

"But then I wake up and realize I don't want to stagnate in one moment, in one job forever, just because I'm afraid I'll fail should I try to reach for something greater. I want to live and feel every moment, good or bad. I want to come back down to dry land. I don't want a whole life lost in the clouds."

"So, it sounds like you changed your mind?" Missy nonchalantly questioned as she produced a bottle of prosecco. "About the Girl Scout cookies?"

I turned to smile at Missy. The past felt both so far and still so near. "How could I forget? I can't believe how much has happened since the Girl Scout Center." I'd always thought life was linear, like a ladder, one step leading to the next. Who would've thought that life could still be so rich even through all the chaos?

"What were your last words as the planes flew up at San Antonio International Airport and we drove away?"

"Is the best part of our lives seasonal and short-lived? I think I wondered if anything good lasts."

Kit took Sofia from my hands and placed her in the stroller, collapsing the canopy above her. "Here, it's time for your bottle while you lie out with us for the first time, Baby."

"Yes, the sun." I laid down beside her. "Let my Goddaughter have the sun." I gestured my hands over Sofia's head like I'd sprinkled fairy dust on her. "Poof. Sofia shall have her first rooftop sun now. It shall be the very first of many rooftop suns."

We lay down on our lounge chairs together, the baby drinking a bottle in her stroller. The Goodyear blimp drifted over us with the last shine of the sun before it set behind the river.

***

ACKNOWLEDGEMENTS

I am so grateful for beating my head against the wall for a couple of decades to publish this one book. With rejection comes time, practice, and experience, during which I met so many incredible, lovely human beings and cities that inspired this book.

So much love and thanks to my New School thesis group, in particular two beautiful souls, Simone Tyrell and Timothy Ryan, who are sadly no longer with us. I often deferred to your wisdom and guidance as if we were still having a drink and discussing our thesis at Bar Six or Café Loup in The Village. Thank you to Sean Pompea, who also read early drafts of this. On day one of Helen Schulman's fiction workshop, you roasted me, but years later, you read another draft and told me that even though this started as light chick lit, I'd gone beyond and written something more. Thank you to other New School beta readers who have given me valuable, thoughtful manuscript and essay critiques over the years, Payal Doshi Moradian and Ross Schneiderman. Thank you to my professor and thesis advisor, Susan Cheever, for asking me, "so, what is this really about?"

Thank you to my brilliant professors at Texas A&M University-San Antonio, Dr. Ann Bliss, and Dr. Rebecca Brown. You two gave me community and hope when, like Jess, I was "in between" things.

Thank you to my peers and other beta readers I met at the Writers' League of Texas conference, especially Michelle Cruz and Tobie Carter. I needed your criticism and tough love as I often complained about the publishing world.

Thank you to my dear friend and beta reader, Gabrielle Sinclair Compton, for reading many drafts of this, starting in our twenties when we were a couple of dreamers at a European travel company in Chicago, later in New York City, and digitally when we continued to live apart.

Thank you to my other fabulous beta reader, Araceli Cardenas, in Rome. You have been a big, loving sister with sage advice and mentorship. Thank you to Monica Garcia, Jaquennette Harris, Kathleen Smith, and Fiona Wright. You four came in at the eleventh hour, uplifting my spirit and helping me crawl across the finish line. Thanks to my other wonderful beta readers for your valuable and honest criticism: Robin Patchen, Julie Cook, Deb Collins, Sarah Loeffler, Aimee LaCour, and Leslie Doeseckle. Thank you to my savvy essay editor, Heather Creekmore, and my awesome editor at Yellow Bird, Sara Kocek. Thank you to Kimberly Spencer, Chelsea Dischinger, and Susan Moffitt for your endless book launch support.

Thank you to my beta reader, bestie, cheerleader, and mentor, Luz-Cristal Glangchai, for supporting me over the years, employing me, and giving me a role in your own book, *VentureGirls*.

Thank you to my Maid of Honor, bestie, and muse, Macy Jett, for all the tears of joy and sadness in making our professional and personal dreams come true during and after The Webster.

Thank you to my family, especially my parents, José Luis and Maria Adriana Prieto, for always supporting me, loving me unconditionally, and believing in this book many moons ago before I'd even put pen to paper. Thank you to my brother and tech department Rick Prieto, for being a whiz with the technical stuffs so I could upload my manuscript for the millionth time.

Thank you to my love, my husband Tyler, for often challenging my worldview and encouraging me to question everything and to begrudgingly channel the great Thomas Sowell or Milton Friedman in matters of economics—even while writing a fun book about the lingering effects of The Great Recession (The Federal Reserve noted that The Great Recession began in December 2007 and ended in June 2009, but the economic effects would continue for almost a decade as the unemployment rate didn't hit pre-recession levels until 2014 and the median household income didn't hit pre-recession levels until 2016).

And lastly, thank you to our beautiful daughter Ava. You are the best thing that has ever happened to us. Your birth inspired me to finish this last dream. I love you more than there are stars in the sky. May you never fly around in search of opportunities that do not exist. May the world always come to you instead. Also, Mommy finished formatting this book while you were napping so sweetly in your swing.

ABOUT THE AUTHOR

DESIREE PRIETO GROFT has written for the Emmy award-winning *NBC Chicago Street Team*, *Newsweek*, *Huffington Post*, *Rome Today*, and more. She also had a print column and blog at the San Antonio *Current*. She currently teaches literature and writing at Arizona State University's New College.

Desiree has an M.A. in English Literature from Texas A&M University-San Antonio and an M.F.A. in Creative Writing-Nonfiction from The New School. Born in Laredo, Texas and raised in San Antonio, she has also lived in Rome, London, Chicago, New York City, and Austin. Desiree also calls Arizona and California homes, thanks to family and work.

She lives in the Texas Hill Country with her husband and daughter.